# ZEITGEIST

# ZEITGEIST

a novel by

## Todd Wiggins

VICTOR GOLLANCZ

LONDON

First published simultaneously in hardback and paperback
in Great Britain 1996
by Victor Gollancz
An imprint of the Cassell Group
Wellington House, 125 Strand, London WC2R 0BB

© Todd Wiggins 1996

The right of Todd Wiggins to be identified as author of
this work has been asserted by him in accordance with
the Copyright, Designs and Patents Act, 1988.

A catalogue record for this book is
available from the British Library.

ISBN 0 575 06234 7 hb
ISBN 0 575 06316 5 pb

Typeset by Rowland Phototypesetting Ltd,
Bury St Edmunds, Suffolk
Printed in Great Britain by
St Edmundsbury Press Ltd, Bury St Edmunds, Suffolk

96  97  98  99     5  4  3  2  1

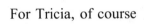

For Tricia, of course

# ACKNOWLEDGEMENTS

No university student with a compulsion toward chain-reading and benevolent anarchy could have hoped for a better teacher than Professor Ben Boretz, one of the great thinkers of the late twentieth century, whose radical Music Program Zero curriculum at Bard College provided the framework for much interdisciplinary work in music, film, art, literature, education, philosophy, psychology, history, and anthropology; a man whose intellect is eclipsed only by his modesty and compassion. I would also like to thank the brilliant Professor Charles Stein, a Bodhisattva if ever I saw one.

No writer of literary fiction could ask for a better editor than Ray Roberts, a man of quintessential taste and elegance whose ongoing conspiracy with my wife keeps me alert at all times. Similarly, no such writer could ask for a better publisher than Dr. Michael Naumann. In an age when many of the finer aspects of publishing are in decline, I consider it a great privilege to count these men as friends and colleagues.

Thanks are also due Mike Petty for running the show in London, and very special thanks to Lisa Rogers; plus a fond hello to Gerard Byrne and Sisco the cat.

Mic Cheetham is no mere literary agent, but rather a force of nature. They just don't come any better. Further thanks are due Paul Marsh for keeping astride the world.

To Jeff Kloske at Little, Brown in New York: Thanks. I owe you one.

To Mark Rudolph, M.D.: The consignment of scalpels you requested has now arrived.

Finally, a warm acknowledgement of the love and support of my parents and everyone in the Wiggins, Ramey, and Sullivan families.

It's a mutual, joint-stock world, in all meridians. We cannibals must help these Christians.

—Herman Melville, *Moby-Dick*

# PROLOGUE

## *Here at the Millennium . . .*

I am meeting him tonight—his final night—only hours before the new year, the new decade, the new century, the new millennium. In recognition of their advent, he will be executed at 12:01. I've been permitted to interview him between ten and ten-thirty, after which he'll be put in a holding cell to await the firing squad. When he is gone I will have only these pages to remember him by, but as a eulogy they are more than his alone. With my usual presumption and arrogance, I am billing them as a requiem for us all: a requiem for the twentieth century.

Darkness has come; it is now six-thirty. I sit at the living room window, pen and paper in hand, lights off. Manhattan lies still and silent without, gripped by the brilliant supernatural chill. These have been the coldest holidays on record: as I write, the temperature is forty below zero. Oddly, there has been no snow—only a thin, impenetrable layer of ice that glazes the fabric of New York like an infection. The mercury is forecast to drop yet another ten degrees this evening, and residents have been advised to remain indoors. No ball will drop tonight in Times Square. How then will New York—and by proxy, the rest of the country—herald the new millennium?

To put it another way: Where's the party?

Of course we've got it all wrong. As usual.

Today is December 31, 1999. Chronologically, the next millennium won't begin until 2001. We have been deceived by appearances yet again. Goaded by the precipitous shift on our calendars (and the symbolism of those zeroes is rich, if simplistic), we are celebrating the new millennium a year early—the new century and decade as well. Not that I could persuade my countrymen of their error: Americans rarely study the past, and still less do they understand it. The omphalos lies somewhere between the present and the near future. We are disciples of the phenomenal; the noumenal hold no sway. Why should the fine print of History preclude us from doing what we do best?

Again: Where's the party?

*

11

Tonight, at long last, the party is nowhere, and History will have Her revenge. Tonight—*gentlemen*— it is too fucking cold to go outside. Like the pariah who delights in rainy days, who savors the limitations of others—who indeed relishes failure in all its aspects (for does failure not vindicate passivity?)—I am shivering with malicious glee. There will be no leering revelers for the cameras tonight, no drunken vows of New Year's Resolution. There are few things I despise worse than people who think they are having fun. Homicidal impulses are evoked; I want to kill every one of them. I nurture similar velleities during food commercials—the close-ups of grinning idiots masticating, the smug swoons of endorsement, the culprits invariably fat-faced Caucasians who should have no reason to exist—

I digress. Forgive me.

Have I mentioned that the furnace is broken?

Returning to our prisoner: Only eight months ago he was still a free man, as anonymous as you or I. During the course of a sultry May evening, he and three imperfect strangers, newly met, became America's Most Wanted—a sterling accolade, especially in light of everything *else* that was happening at the time. (The last of the soldiers departed New York only in November; had they stayed, the celebration tonight in Times Square would have been canceled twice over, again to History's approval.) In the most authentic true-crime fashion, their capture was broadcast on live television. As the law and media closed in like forceps, a rapt nation, barricaded in their homes, marveled at the nonfiction thriller evolving upon their screens. Of the four fugitives, he alone was brought to trial; but he will not be the first among them to die.

After his sentencing last October I began corresponding with him in prison. Like everyone else, I wanted to know his story—the whole story. I also wanted to write it down and sell it to the world, which is precisely what I am about to do.

A good thing, too. He might have died without anyone knowing the truth.

But wait. There's more to it than that. How can I explain . . .

Let's put it this way: my own life is at stake here as well.

For I am not merely a connoisseur of failure: I am an exquisite failure myself, and this achievement fills me with Dostoyevskian pride. *(I am a sick woman, a spiteful woman . . .)* I have failed in life and

12

love, but most importantly I have failed in letters. I have always defined myself by stories: the fabric of my identity is woven head to toe with Fiction, since Fact alone has proved inadequate. I grew up in a library, and those books, rather than any great deeds, accumulated into the foundation of my character. As a result my life is literary theater, created moment by moment like a novel or play unraveling in real time. Any distinction between truth and lie is immaterial; all that matters is telling a good story.

Since words are my lifeblood, it seemed natural that I should try my hand as a novelist. The upshot: I have yet to sell my first sentence. I sell my body instead: I am a whore. Words have failed me, or perhaps vice versa. I take up my pen, I defy the empty page . . . and I am beaten. Time has betrayed me, having brought not perspective but rather a lingering anoesis that leaves me gravid with apocalypse and yet unable even to miscarry. Once merely inarticulate, I am now, at age twenty-four, confined to a silence that feeds on the last of my tabescent youth. Which is probably just as well; for in the end, I'll be the first to admit that my writings have been nothing more than inchoate, epigonic gestures, hapless fragments of abandoned whimsy that reveal no truths except my own verbal bankruptcy. Have a glance through my oeuvre; you'll find the same three sentences recurring on every page:

*I do not want to grow old.*

*I do not want to die.*

*I hate everyone.*

Beyond that, I have nothing of importance to say.

Hence this story of crime and punishment. Having accepted that fiction is currently impossible for me, I am climbing into bed with my old nemesis: nonfiction. And why not? My true-crime thriller will provide the classic staples of public consumption, indeed everything I need for a bestseller—love, betrayal, and of course murder. Years ago I had ambitions toward cultivating a unique artistic vision. These have brought me nothing, and now languish forsaken. I am a whore in affairs of the pen as well as of the flesh. I doubt there's an original bone in my body—or yours, for that matter.

As for my subject, understand this: despite his predicament, I envy him beyond distraction. I envy his infamy. I envy his *consequence* upon a world in which I've been faceless and marginalized for years. On impulse I wrote to him in prison, trying to explain some of this. Imagine my surprise, four days later, when I received his letter of reply.

In the past two months we have corresponded many times, and become the strangest of friends. I alone am his confidante; indeed, I have become his biographer, and ex officio a commentator on the end of this desperate century. Not that my motives are pure: I am not an historian, nor am I an altruist. I welcome his generosity, but make no mistake—I'm writing this for entirely selfish reasons. America at the millennium is a cathartine society, and who am I to buck the tide? I've always had my own advancement in mind, my own hidden agenda. I want to write a bestseller; as luck would have it, his story fits the bill perfectly. I've needed to suck him, leech him, and much of what follows is the fruit of that labor. Not until much later—not until today, in fact—did I realize how personal this story has become, and how alone I will be when that bullet enters his heart. I even have reason to love him, but never mind that for now.

The truth is, I owe him my life. I've been sequestered these past months in a different sort of prison, that of my own conscience. Justice is indeed blind, for his crimes are nothing compared to mine. I know him to be innocent, whereas I am guilty of murder and still roam free. It is I, if anyone, who should meet the firing squad tomorrow. I spoke of consequence, and therein lies the irony: he is famous for crimes he didn't commit, whereas I am anonymous concerning my own. You'd think that crime might have changed my circumstances, might have truncated my isolation, might at least have provided me with incontrovertible proof that I was alive and had effected change upon the world, however fleeting; yet there again I failed. Taking credit for one's crimes, even pseudonymously, is half the bargain; otherwise it's like fucking without the orgasm. But try as I might, I can't find the courage. I remain as I was before: beautiful, insignificant, and very, very alone. My crimes—so long as I remain silent—can offer no remedy.

But maybe his story can.

Maybe it'll even give me the strength to confess—or to bury my guilt forever.

Because god knows it's all I've got left. Silence equals death, or so went the slogan; if true, this story is my last attempt to lift myself from the grave. It is my umbilical cord, my conduit to life, and he is my mother.

More than that: he is also my Christ. He is the means of my deliverance. He will die, and give me redemption.

# CHAPTER ONE

## *Discount Euthanasia . . .*

The priest, a flushed young Caucasian, was running down Broadway when they saw him, carrying a briefcase in one hand and a Kalashnikov in the other. Dorian had stopped for a red light at 125th, beneath the girders of the 1/9 el. The priest, fifty feet distant, vestments billowing, veered suddenly toward the car—a black '65 Mustang, top down in the oppressive May heat. He bounded through the intersection, dodging traffic, and vaulted into the back seat in a tangle of polyester with the admonition *"Drive, drive, drive!"*

Growing up in the sanctum of a Gwynedd valley had not prepared Dorian for New York's preternatural humidity, let alone armed clergymen at Harlem's edge. A creeping midday funk embalmed his pallid face, an intimate sheen virtually fused with the skin, impossible to brush or wish away. Nor was he dressed for the occasion: in conformity with his perception of Left Bank chic, Dorian's wardrobe was a uniform parade of decrepit black suits and matching turtlenecks, thanks to which he now perspired copiously. His weak blue eyes appealed to his black companion for support.

Prophet, resplendent in white boubou, fez, and wire-rimmed glasses, did not deign to look at the gunman/priest. Instead he gave a bored sigh and said, "Get the fuck out of the car."

The priest, having arranged his skirts as primly as a debutante, leaned forward in disbelief. He appeared not much older than they— twenty-five at most—and his features were dark and beautiful, possibly Italian. "Excuse me?" he said.

A green light supplanted the red. Dorian gripped the wheel, his foot wavering on the accelerator. Prophet gazed into the middle distance, unperturbed. Other motorists were scattering from this small corner of the City toward any avenue of escape. The Mustang remained inert, with not a horn raised in protest.

Prophet sighed again. "I said get the fuck out of here."

The priest sank back, clearly at a loss; then, belatedly, he jabbed the rifle into Prophet's neck. "I think you should reconsider."

Prophet snorted. "You got ten seconds," he said, "then I kick your ass. One."

". . . Wait a second."

"Two."

"I *will* use this gun, asshole."

"Three."

"Goddamn it I said *move*—"

"*Four.*"

"Prophet," said Dorian.

"Five."

"I said—"

"Six."

"*Prophet.*"

"Seven, *what?*" He followed Dorian's gesture toward a company of uniformed policemen, all heaving ever closer. Pedestrians crouched behind cars and telephone poles, watching with detached expectancy. *(This again . . . )*

"Jesus Christ," said the priest.

The policemen were thirty yards away, guns drawn. "*Police!!!*" they screamed, as if to dispel any lingering skepticism.

"Prophet for god sake what—"

"Move. Now."

"Toward there . . . ?"

"*Move!*"

With an indignant shriek the car lurched into motion, shuddering west along 125th Street, where the promise of New Jersey sprang to life upon the horizon.

"Which—"

"Take a right up here," said Prophet.

Beneath the imposing trestles of Riverside Drive they passed among grim warehouses and car cemeteries, and then "Left!" toward the river and finally "Right! Go right!" ("All *right*, Christ!") pursuing an entrance ramp until it merged with its fellows into a three-lane conspiracy heading north, under the steady vigilance of high-rises and billboards, one of which proclaimed the opening of a discount euthanasia clinic in Times Square.

"Faster," said Prophet.

"Christ I'm already going eighty!"

"Faster; what?" He turned as the priest leaned forward. The

priest's eyes looked brown from a distance, but up close Prophet could see they were gold as the burnish of a wedding ring.

"I didn't mean to go this way," said the priest.

"You wanna get out, be my guest. Faster Dorian."

"Well fuck at least stop the car!"

"Can't stop now Pater, less you want a thousand cops on your ass OK here Dorian, take a right here."

"The bridge? Do I take the bridge or Cross Bronx—"

"The bridge, you idiot."

"Upper or lower le—"

"Doesn't matter *there*, take the upper level *watch it!*—" as a van fled bleating off their left flank "—now good, just follow this around and you'll be fine."

"Goddamn it," said the priest.

"What's your problem?"

"I meant to go to SoHo, that's what!"

"Risk you run, leading a life of crime," said Prophet cheerfully. "Way I see it, we're doing you a favor. And hey, quit waving that shit around and put it under the seat."

"Why the hell did we drive away?" snapped Dorian. "We should have left him for the police. Come to think of it, *I* should never have left Abergynolwyn."

"Pining for the Celtic hinterlands," said Prophet, adopting a credible Welsh accent. "Taliesin, Taliesin, wherefore art thou—man what the fuck you want now?" as the priest tapped his shoulder.

"Listen I *really* need to—"

"Look shut up, right? Soon as we stop I'm gonna get out and kick your fat papist butt."

"Prophet," said Dorian, as the bridge yielded to the welcome of Fort Lee, the City vanishing behind them in a sickly haze, "where should I—"

"Just follow 95 south, and stay in the express lane. The traffic, Jesus."

"I think I should warn you," said the priest.

"Warn me what, Aquinas?"

"Well first, I'm not really a priest."

"I never would have guessed," said Prophet.

"No I mean I was until yesterday afternoon, but then I sort of got excommunicated."

"S'too bad. After I kicked your ass I was gonna confess my sins, ease the burden of my poor black soul. Now I'll just have to kick your ass and feel guilty."

The ex-priest stared at him. "Yeah? Yeah well *fuck you*, you little—"

"Shut up, both of you," said Dorian. "Prophet, where the hell are we going?"

"Going to California, I thought."

"Yes but I mean *now*, where are we—"

"California?" said the ex-priest.

"Get onto 80 west up ahead and stay there," said Prophet. And, turning: "That's right Augustine, you wanna get out you better do it quick."

"Goddamn it I wanted to go to SoHo! Jesus *shit*—"

"What's in SoHo?" asked Dorian.

"My squat. My *medication* . . ."

"You got allergies?" said Prophet.

"No I don't have allergies I'm schizo*phrenic* you little—"

"Ai! Yo!"

"Fuck off Prophet," said Dorian. "How long before the medication wears off? Maybe we could stop and pick some up."

"No no no it's *Stelazine* it's a *prescription* drug you don't just *waltz* in—"

"Maybe we should take him back, Prophet."

"Fuck that, the man holds a gun to my head he'll go wherever the hell I say. He flips out, we'll lock him in the trunk." He glanced back at the ex-priest. "The fuck's your name, anyway?"

"Fish."

"*Fish?*"

"Well it's no worse than *Prophet* now is it?"

Prophet sank nearly to the floor, cackling. "*Fish!!*"

"What exactly were you doing back there, before you jumped in the car?" asked Dorian.

"Armed robbery."

"You mean a bank?"

"Crack house."

"God damn are you stupid," said Prophet, recovering himself. "You make a habit of it?"

"Armed robbery? Let's get something straight: I've got the *worst* fucking disease in the world and it's *barely* under control and I was *kicked* out of the Church and *no* parish'll hire me and *everything*

18

*sucks*, OK? I've got fifty dollars to my name, so don't blame me for armed robbery. Blame the goddamn century."

"The what?"

"The twentieth century. It's not just an era: it's a disease, a pathology. It's the scene of the crime."

"Well you'll like us then," said Dorian, as they entered a landscape of factories and motels, some offering hourly rates, not to mention a billboard from which a scowling female octogenarian wielding a small pistol assured passersby that the Lady Zygote® was so compact even *she* could use it . . . "We're philosophers, just like yourself."

"Shut up Dorian I am not a philosopher," said Prophet. "I'm a propagandist, got it? Have to kick your ass too."

"Aw quit with the black attitude," sneered Fish. "You look like you're barely five feet tall, I mean I've known *hedgehogs* that could kick your ass—"

Prophet lunged toward the back seat, jostling Dorian's hand on the wheel. The car swerved across two lanes to the startled outrage of a neighboring semi and the detriment of a red Porsche gone spinning onto the berm.

"*Jesus!*" Dorian slowed the car to forty as the semi rumbled past accusingly and barreled into the distance, while the chastened Porsche lingered a wary fifty yards to the rear. Fish, meanwhile, had imposed a wrist-lock on Prophet, who howled like a voice in the wilderness.

"*Quit it both of you!*"

Fish relinquished his hold, glowering.

"Now," said Dorian. "Let's get everything nice and sparkling clear, before we proceed any further. Fish, I'm driving to California. If you'd like to come along—"

"Yeah but what about my Stelazine?"

"Well Fish, there's nothing I can do about that. I'd be happy to let you off here, where are we, Willowbrook?" as they passed a broad expanse of parking lots, all full, the cars like drones attending a queen, in this case a shopping mall. "You could probably catch a bus into the City, although I suppose you'd have to leave that rifle in the car."

"Fuck!"

"Indeed yes: 'Fuck.' In fact," said Dorian, always glad for the chance to expound, "I'd say that word has become the fulcrum of Western civilization. If one could recapitulate your beloved twentieth

19

century in a single word—well, I certainly can't think of a better one. Anyway, what's the verdict? I mean obviously if you have a family or something one doesn't just rush off to California."

"I was a priest, remember? Besides, my parents disowned me. They're Jewish."

". . . Ah. All right then, fair enough. Now I should mention that I'm bisexual, in case you're sensitive about that sort of thing."

"Please, it's 1999. Why should I care?"

Dorian glanced at Fish. "Well, I've always been a sucker for men in black, not to mention Mediterraneans. Do you intend to keep wearing that?"

"Ain't like he brought something else," Prophet pointed out. And to Fish: "How much money you get, anyway?"

"I haven't counted it yet," Fish replied, snapping open the brief-case and riffling through stacks of bills from which the knowing countenance of Benjamin Franklin stared back at him. "Jesus— maybe fifty grand?"

"*What!*" said Dorian.

"Look I had no idea it would be so much, I mean petty theft was all I ever—"

"Oh *Christ* are we fucked."

"Don't think I'll be paying you gas money Dorian, know what I'm sayin?"

"Well at least the serial numbers are discontinuous," said Fish, scrutinizing the fine print. "What, are we stopping . . . ?"

The car was slowing along the berm. "We're getting rid of that money," said Dorian. "I don't even live in this country. The last thing I need is—"

"Is your pretty ass in jail, right?" sniggered Prophet. "Ah Dorian, you're so clean and white and, and *sacrosanct*. Some big-ass brother comes along in the shower, how bisexual you gonna be then?"

"Prophet—"

"Bet you never had it that rough, eh Glendower? Can just see it, back in Oxford, pretty blond men just like you, everybody in cricket whites, that shared moment in some quiet backwater punting the Cherwell, eh old boy? You and some viscount in a blue-eyed clinch—"

"Prophet for god sake!"

"Long way from Attica, thass for sure. I mean think about it, s'ard imagining Oxford and Attica on the same *planet*, eh old boy?"

20

"Prophet you're scaring him!" said Fish.

"If you ever say anything like that to me again," Dorian grated, "I'll—I'll—"

"Yeah, sure you will," said Prophet. "Welsh *ubermenschen*, they haunt my dreams. All hail the Plaid Cymru."

"Look I don't want to get anyone in trouble," said Fish. "Drop me off in the next town, I'll figure out what to do then."

"No no no, you stay right there. We'll drive to California, have ourselves a good old time."

"Well what the fuck," said Dorian, goading the car into motion. "At the end of the summer I'll be back in Gwynedd, and who the hell could track me *there*?"

"That's *right*!" said Prophet, slapping the dashboard.

"And it's not as if *I* committed the robbery."

"I'll say you were my hostages," said Fish.

"We won't press charges," Prophet assured him.

"I mean what the hell do I care?" queried Dorian, as much to the sky as to his companions. "My book has been declined by every publisher in New York. I failed all my classes at Columbia. I've been expelled from the foreign exchange program. I'm down to my last five hundred dollars and all my friends back at Oxford are HIV-positive. My future lies in farming, assuming I don't have AIDS. What have I got to lose?"

"Precisely," said Prophet. "I couldn't have put it better myself. You with us Fish?"

"Well," Fish replied, "there'll be a warrant for my arrest, once they do a little research. My neurochemistry is the laughingstock of God's creation. I've been excommunicated for sins of the flesh. I know *I* don't have anything to lose." He sighed. "I guess there's nothing special about SoHo after all."

# CHAPTER TWO

## *Post-Hexaemeronic Stress . . .*

Not a bad beginning, is it.

I think this story just might work.

Did you notice the snappiness of the writing, the paciness that nicely counterbalances the rich, mandarin sentences of my own commentary? Perfect for shorter attention spans.

And just so we're clear on everything: one of those three men—Prophet, Dorian, or Fish—is my correspondent on Death Row. The preceding chapter marked the beginning of his journey there.

It gets even better.

I have a narrative of my own which runs parallel to that of my friends, and to which I will repair from time to time throughout these pages. The diversion will not be unprofitable—trust me on that. I can promise you considerable entertainment at my expense, in part because murder has been the least of my accomplishments. For example, I was almost murdered myself. I even died for a short time, and my report on the afterlife will be included for your review. Was Lazarus so forthcoming?

At any rate, I cannot explain my involvement in his story without telling you some of mine, and you'll see that they dovetail rather nicely in the end. The more I think about it, the more I'm convinced that my recent life makes for not uncompelling reading; and perhaps, as I intimated earlier, I might persuade myself to reveal why murder is sometimes best for all concerned.

\*　　\*　　\*

On a wet and steamy night in Manhattan, September 1998, I, Venus Wicked, existentialist call girl and self-styled autodidact, presented myself at 923 Fifth Avenue at eight o'clock, inquiring after Mr. Yoram Bickel. "He's expecting me," I added haughtily to the concierge, who appraised me with flaring nostrils and curling upper lip. It must be the perfume, I thought. I'd received a free sample only that afternoon. It was called *Narcissa*, and aptly so: after a generous application I'd begun to salivate, filled with a self-esteem I hadn't known in years. Perhaps the concierge was merely subverting his lust, but that would have been par for the course, with or without the perfume. I tend to have that effect on men, and on many women as well.

Not that I was dressed like a whore. Per the client's request, I wore a black skirt and matching jacket, with starched white shirt and black stockings. I might have been going to a job interview. In fact, given the price of the outfit (paid for by my agency, which had a wholesale deal with some mob family in the garment district), I might have been buying the goddamn company.

This was my first assignment. I'd changed careers only that morning, after realizing I had forty dollars in the bank and bills mounting toward a thousand. I had come to New York to write novels, but in the end I wrote very little. I was too busy *thinking* about writing. There are a thousand and one distractions to which unpublished writers succumb, like spending long hours in the bookstore or library perusing the new releases and glibly assuring ourselves that we can do much, much better. Envy is the mother of invention, and conceit the father; necessity paints on a much narrower canvas. The intent of every serious novelist, at heart, is to surpass, discredit, and ultimately negate the work of her peers and mentors (at least it's sure as hell mine). But though I stockpiled envy and conceit ad nauseam, the prophylactic called Laziness rendered me sterile. I filled my days by assiduously denigrating the work of others, which left precious little time for my own. In spare moments I considered the many uses of my impending fortune, while slowly I went broke.

On impulse I'd turned to theater, which seemed the next-best outlet for my fictionalist proclivities. I'd pursued the lead in a psychosexual lesbian thriller called *Here's the Rub*, by one Kell Sumner. The audition had been a disaster, largely because I'd come down with food poisoning and vomited on (or in) the playwright's girlfriend scant milliseconds before a French kiss.

On the brink of fiscal collapse, I'd filed a résumé, wholly mendacious, with a Midtown headhunter called Ploy, which proved another useless maneuver. (I should have added a second Ph.D to my CV; one just didn't suffice any more.) My final conversation with Mindi, my "account executive," had gone as follows:

23

"That janitorial position in the Port Authority," I said. "Has it been filled?"

"I didn't tell you?" Mindi's voice was both chirpy and husky, like that of a songbird with throat cancer.

"I don't think you did."

"They hired someone else."

"Figures. Was I overqualified?"

"No," replied Mindi, "it's just the other guy had a Ph.D in *engineering*, and they thought it might come in handy when he flushed the toilets."

"That's bullshit, Mindi. I've got a doctorate from Yale."

"Yeah but like his was from Harvard. What can you do."

"Well do you have anything else?"

"There's a street sweeper position in Midtown."

"Which blocks?"

"57th between Fifth and Lex. Interested?"

I thought it over, running a hand through my hair. "Why not. But do me a favor, Mindi: change my résumé. I want my Ph.D in physics. Tell them I've calculated the best angle to push the broom, and I can supply the proofs in triplicate."

"That's lying, sweetie."

"No it's not, babydoll. My Ph.D in chemistry was a lie. It's really in physics. I only wanted to convince the Port Authority that I knew about detergents."

She still hasn't called me back.

Einstein once wrote that a man could flourish only by losing himself in a community, a sanctuary "in which he felt himself a fully privileged member, which asked nothing of him that was contrary to his natural habits of thought." Which provides another reason for my failures: I was an outcast among the mainstream and an outcast among the outcasts, i.e., the "counterculture" that runs parallel to the Establishment in weary symbiosis, trapped in its own rigid mores. The "avant-garde" have the same agenda as the Establishment; they simply favor different means to fulfill it. Whereas I liked to think of myself as a genuine Independent. How else could I feel so alone?

Before New York I had wandered the breadth of America, living a parenthetical existence. I slept on the open plains, or in the hollows of trees, or in abandoned barns. I was a migrant, observing much and participating little. I traveled on a vintage Harley that I'd won

24

from a Sioux drunkard in Nebraska. A janitor at the orphanage had taught me how to play chess, and I used this skill whenever I needed money. Still, not many people play chess, and I found myself wishing I'd learned poker or straight-pool or something more market-friendly in the bowels of rural America.

The jackpot I treasured most was a chimpanzee named Gerard, who became my only friend and confidant. I won Gerard from an old Hell's Angel, who'd inherited the animal from a slain colleague. I've always preferred fauna to humans, and it was I who'd suggested Gerard as a bounty—especially since he could ride tandem on a motorcycle. We were quite a sight along the open road, blood cousins only a few million years removed.

The orphanage where I grew up was a converted gothic manor house in upstate New York whose original furnishings had been carefully preserved. The library contained a fairly good mixture of Romantic, Victorian, and Modernist literature, through which I systematically labored. When I'd finished every book on the shelves I began walking to the public library in Rhinebeck, half a mile away.

There is a word for my kind: *artifacts*. We do not belong to the eras that produced us: we are throwbacks to the past. I kept the company of writers long dead, and I strained back through time to receive them. Eliot, Wollstonecraft, Dickinson, Woolf—these were my mothers and friends, succoring me in the vast landscapes of Imagination: Eliot for her learning; Wollstonecraft for her politics; Dickinson for her sensibility; and Woolf for giving herself to the waves. But as I grew older, I began to realize that such ancestors could not help me negotiate modern society with the same level of sophistication as normal girls my age. For that I would have needed a syllabus more representative of our mass-market culture, something like—what? (help me out here)—*Sweet Valley High*? Something from the bestseller lists? Or (even worse) something akin to those "literary" autobiographical novels produced in graduate writing workshops, full of childhood abuse and drug addiction and godawful similes?

Better: forget books altogether. Stick with TV. Stick with snuff films, for christ sake. Anything but literature.

I left the orphanage at eighteen and vagranted for five years, learning all the street smarts I'd missed; learning how to be *cool*. When I finally arrived in Manhattan, I set about finding an apartment where Gerard would be welcome, which ruled out virtually every place available. Among landlords Gerard evoked only dismay, and not the childlike wonder I'd expected. (The trouble with landlords— the trouble with adults in general—is their singular lack of curiosity.) I thought about keeping him secret, but Gerard is far too vocal: he likes to shriek and cackle. Since New York is not famous for its tolerance, or its restraint, and since I've never owned a gun, I decided I'd better not provoke my neighbors.

I eventually took rooms on the Upper West Side, near Columbia University. I share the apartment with an English professor named Lank, who owns the brownstone in which we live and rents out the other floors. Lank is tall and decrepit, and spends most of his life in a black velvet suit that hasn't been cleaned in years. His face is narrow and gaunt, his jowls flaccid, and his blue eyes so watery and bloodshot that upon regarding them one's own begin to smart reflexively. Matted grey wisps of hair encircle his reflective pate, which is covered with liver spots. His lips are thin and his tongue slightly protrusive, as though forever poised to lick a stamp. Yet by far his most prominent attribute is the colostomy. He is obliged to defecate through his left hip into a leather bag, which is his constant appendage. He is prone to voiding his bowel without warning, whereupon he'll glance down and proclaim, "How's that for a burnt offering, old girl?" The olfactory repercussions, always conspicuous, are at their worst when he contracts a stomach virus. Lank, his litany and bowels spent, will stand up muttering and shamble off to the bathroom, his excreta sloshing noisily as he walks.

Another thing about Lank, which explained his welcoming of Gerard: his apartment is a fucking *zoo*. Like God and Adam reviewing the teeming life, Lank guided me through the rooms, naming his companions: Anne Boleyn, a spiteful macaw; Lovelace, a glaring tabby; nine piranhas, each named after a Bacchante; a tank of anonymous goldfish with which to feed them; a fleet of cockatiels, each named after a subatomic particle; three polecat ferrets called Licker and Sticker and Pricker; a hutch of fat, leering bunnies; a lugubrious armadillo, Ponce; a spooked collie, Boudicca; and a snarling dachshund, Muzzlehatch.

Lastly I was led down a dusty, unfrequented corridor. I could hear rats scurrying through the eaves, and I noticed that the ceiling was rotting. (Hantavirus Unlimited, I thought.) At the end of the hall was a closed door.

"Please keep this shut at all times," said Lank, his hand on the knob. "Otherwise Gerard will become lunch." He unlocked and opened the door and I peered inside. Two burly rats were loitering nearby, but it was the snake that caught my attention.

"Anaconda," whispered Lank, as the thing raised its head to stare at us. "Thirty feet long. Foot in diameter. Goes by the name of Killjoy."

I met its gaze and felt my blood freeze. Sprawled over most of the floor, ponderously coiled, Killjoy was a monster: no other noun sufficed. His scales were emerald green and elegantly patterned in zigzag shapes. Gerard, after a brief glance, fled screaming down the hall.

"My god," I whispered. "What the hell do you feed him?"

"Well, he eats plenty of rats," said Lank, "but of course they aren't enough. He could theoretically swallow a crocodile, but rabbits are the best I can manage. I've raised him practically from birth, don't you know." Lank shut the door and turned the key. "As I said: Just keep it locked. We could become lunch too."

I was only too glad to have a roof over my head, snakes and shit notwithstanding. In fact there was little to complain about. Like me, Lank is antediluvian, obsolete, a relic of an age long banished. His library includes most of the literary canon, plus various history, philosophy, and science texts. Instead of writing my Great Unamerican Novel, I spent many an evening breathing the air of antiquity and the fumes of Lank's shit. Often he would discourse on his favorite literature, Cavalier poetry. He had memorized the oeuvre of Sir John Suckling and was apt to cite that man's verse during the ordinary progression of daily life. "Why the long face, young sinner?" he would inquire, standing at the window, watching a drug bust on the street below. "Prithee, why?"

As the months passed, my refrigerator grew empty and my stomach emptier. I watched the money dwindle away with dismissive nonchalance, planning whole sections of my novel and never writing a word. (Come to think of it, I really *hate* writing . . .) When the threat of starvation became less abstract and more corporeal, and when Ploy failed to deliver the American Dream, I gravely contemplated my options—busking, panhandling, aggravated robbery. Prostitution didn't suggest itself until my bra spontaneously burst open, and I was reminded of my biggest gifts.

I'll admit it: I'm a dish, a knockout, a stunner, a *babe*—but don't take my word for it. Come on, have a look at me. Rate me, appraise me, take stock of my defects. That's what women are for, isn't it. To see how much use we'll be. To see whether we'll *do*. And fools that we are, we play right along—like I'm doing right now.

For starters, consider this unique distinction: I have been presumed to represent virtually every race in the world. Even more curiously, I am unable to confirm which impression is closest to the truth. I have never known my parents, and this is why fiction is so important to me. I have no blood ancestors, no culture in which to ground myself, and my appearance only compounds the problem. On the one hand, I can borrow any ethnicity, each proposition as valid as the next. On the other hand, I often feel weightless and disenfranchised, bereft of any genealogical anchor. I have no history, no roots to mark a particular section of the Earth as my own. I am everything and nothing, all at the same time.

The particulars:

I am basically olive-skinned, and my hair is straight and black and thick. Already the canvas is broad, though one's first thought is Mediterranean.

My eyes are dark—another universal feature—but their corners are delicately, almost imperceptibly tapered, giving a faint suggestion of oriental blood.

My nose is small, straight, and relatively neutral. There is a flare to the nostrils, however, that seems rather Negroid.

My lips have won praise from many men, and it's easy to see why: they're soft and full and they revert, when not in use, into a frankly invitational pout. Often, when putting on lipstick, I used to kiss myself in the mirror—usually the high point of the evening. Anyway they're thin enough to be Caucasoid but thick enough to be African.

Depending upon the length and style of my hair, the quality of ambient light, and the time of year (I'm pale in winter, sienna in summer), I have been variously perceived as Native American, Mexican, Cuban, Puerto Rican, Brazilian, Peruvian, Spanish, Portugese, "Hispanic," Israeli, "Jewish," Lebanese, Turkish, Iranian, Egyptian, Moroccan, Arab, "Black," French, Dark Irish, Italian, Greek, Bulgarian, Romanian, Russian, Indian, Pakistani, Bangladeshi, Burmese, Malaysian, Indonesian, Filipino, "Asian," Hawaiian . . . (whew!) . . . and numerous combinations thereof. If I bleach my hair—a viable option from January until mid-spring, when

28

my skin is at its lightest—the possibilities expand even further.

I assume and discard these mantles like fashion, according to whim. Each has equal (in)validity and appeal, and I'm unable to wear the same one for long. Other people are more presumptuous. First comes the label, often after considerable wrangling ("What *are* you, anyway?"). Next comes the matching stereotype, as if they know me better than I know myself. Since every perception seems to need a context, I've known many people who, until I've been adequately classified, see everything I do with a certain ambiguity, as if my actions and opinions must be interpreted according to my geographic origin. For example, I once attended an editorial seminar at a major New York publishing house. Afterward I'd wandered through the halls, perusing the upcoming titles, and I was frequently mistaken for a new employee. As an experiment, I went along with the supposition, but gave a different pseudonym to each person who asked my name. The ethnicity of each pseudonym was deliberately unmistakable—Lakeesha Washington, Myra Katzenblum, Sook-Hee Kim. Now blacks are rare in New York publishing, whereas Jews are ubiquitous. Thus Myra was regarded with solicitous familiarity ("Where did you go to school?") and Lakeesha with delicate unease ("You're from what department . . . ?"—a polite way of asking whether she was the new receptionist, or whether she actually *read*).

What people don't understand—and what I don't try to explain—is that I am making myself up as I go along. I am apatetic, adapting to each new environment so that my true self, if indeed one exists, remains safely invisible. When words are a religion, literature a pantheon, and Fiction a supreme deity, Hell is constituted by permanence, constancy, immutability. I resented those who would get a handle on me, because I've never had a handle on myself—and because I like to change my mind. Knowledge confers both grace and damnation, both enlightenment and despair, both hope and disillusionment; and this was the paradox I carried through my world of make-believe.

To put it more simply: I wanted all the power I could get.

Back to my physique. There's one more thing you'll be wondering about.

I am a 36D, and have been since the age of thirteen.

It's nice, at the end of the day, to have excellent curves and minimal fat, all thanks to genetic whimsy. The net effect is devastating, or so it seems as I navigate the mean streets, especially in warm weather. Once upon a time, cat-calling was the province of loiterers and construction workers. Nowadays it's a free-for-all, with pinstriped salarymen giving voice beside their lumpen brethren. You'd think that ten thousand years of civilization might have yielded an evolution in mating rituals, but I've concluded differently. Men today are little changed from their ancestors who roamed the savannas, scratching their asses. I have no use for such heresies as freewill, monogamy, and fidelity. Every man, regardless of race or class, is subservient to what I call the One Commandment. Acculturate yourselves to the gills, my boys, but you will never disobey the One Commandment. Why else am I so successful a whore?

It seems strangely appropriate that, lacking a past or heritage, my primary link with humanity is the oldest profession of all.

I speak of being a whore in the present tense, which is somewhat inaccurate: I took early retirement last spring. But like a career military officer who keeps his title to the grave, I will always consider myself a whore. Whoring came to define my character as much as literature: outside of reading, I never felt more alive than during a session. It is the only true profession I've ever had, and though my tenure was brief, it remains in my blood. Besides, who knows? I may resume active duty in time, so it's premature to speak of retirement. Call it indefinite medical leave, without pay, for being killed in the line of duty.

My specialty was very rough (and very expensive) sex. Word of mouth spreads fast in Manhattan, and within a few months of my debut I'd accumulated a loyal and needy clientele. I was paid to beat and be beaten; I was paid to bind and be bound. I was paid to scratch, bite, flog, pummel, strangle, fustigate, lapidate, videotape. In sum, I was paid to do what rich men crave at the end of the twentieth century, and what their wives cannot give them. My price was two thousand dollars. Not bad, you're thinking, but wait: three-quarters went to my agency. Moreover, I usually had to rest a few days between these pancratial duels. The wounds needed time to heal, you see, and some clients were leery of fucking a girl with open sores.

Still, I feel no shame whatsoever about my vocation, nor do I romanticize it. The decision to rent out my body was made on purely rational, utilitarian grounds. Yet in time I realized that whoring—

30

especially considering my artistic failures—endowed me with a strength I'd never experienced. Indeed, there is no other profession that so empowers women. Impotent as a writer, I articulated myself as a whore instead. Now the fictionalist, as DeLillo suggests, is close cousin to the terrorist; and even in this illiterate age I sometimes allow myself to believe that words, if properly used, can be as influential as bullets. Nevertheless, neither writer nor terrorist wields the power of a single whore. The cunt is mightier than pen and sword combined. The writer's demands upon her audience, or the terrorist's demands upon her government—these can be resisted, even ignored. Yet by simple virtue of being female, the whore—like any other woman—will always be invincible. She may be abused; she may even be killed; but she may never be dominated. The act of sexual intercourse, for every man, is one of submission. As a whore, feminist, and would-be novelist, I fed on that submission. I lived to wring it from them.

Hence I do not endorse any of the politically correct euphemisms for "whore"—copulation agent, hormone therapist, semenologist. I am a whore. Given the primacy of my function, and given the dearth of my heritage, I think of myself as more elemental than human. I am like water, timeless and unchanging. I am drunk; and though I will be pissed out in the end, and leave no trace of my passing, I will be thirsted for again soon enough.

So I'd leafed through the Yellow Pages, discovering that Escort Services comprised the largest section after Lawyers. There was even a regional guide, a neighborhood-by-neighborhood directory of all the corresponding local suppliers. The mainline organizations were co-ed and had names like Sophisitique and Panache. There were also specialty shops (Butch Country, for lesbians) and even sub-specialty shops (Fat 'n' Sassy, for overweight lesbians). I skimmed past the all-male services (Moustache Love, Symposium (rich, that)) and settled finally upon a unisex outfit on Broadway and 53rd called Providence. I spoke with the director, one Cornell Bodleian, and was told to show up immediately.

The lounge of Providence was done up in Bauhaus leather and chrome, with halogen lighting and gunmetal ashtrays. The receptionist was a svelte, hairless black woman who spoke with a non-specific, non-American accent that was obviously feigned. ("Could you please fill this out?" became "Cudyew plees full zees oot?"—

Sudanese via Zagreb, one supposed. Clearly my kind of girl.)

The room was cluttered with applicants, male and female, each in his or her Saturday best. Scent lay heavy in the air; one applicant suffered an allergic reaction and was overcome with hives. The receptionist dialled 911 and promptly lost her accent ("Yeah I need someone here like fucking yesterday Jack"). The victim—a blonde in a black nano-skirt—was laid on the floor, sneezing copiously. We all huddled over her, checking her pulse and murmuring anxious support—never mind that our close proximity only made things worse, with my *Narcissa* making its own ironic contribution. When the paramedics arrived, half an hour later, her face was the color of licorice and bathed in snot. She was given a shot of epinephrine and, quaking and gasping, wheeled away to face the Midtown traffic.

At length I was summoned for my interview. Bodleian was a former Mr. Olympia in his mid-thirties, blond and scrubbed and immaculately polished, his countenance fresh as whipped butter. His pink golf shirt and white chinos fit like shackles, unable to restrain his teeming bulk. The muscles rippled like tectonic shifts, an ever-changing pattern of fault-lines and geological rethink.

"Dr. Wicked!" he exclaimed, offering a hand, which felt like a damp sock. "How'd you get that name, anyway?"

Venus Wicked is of course a sobriquet, and you know about my doctorate already. Well—what of it? Telling the truth has lost its charm, and in the stock exchange of modern life it's worthless currency.

"Venus was a Siberian folk heroine," I replied. "She was crucial at Yalta."

"Siberian?"

". . . It's in New Jersey."

"Yeah?" said Bodleian. "Well, you can just call me Corn. Now before we sit down, let's see what you got."

"You don't waste time," I said, unbuttoning my shirt.

"Call it pre-screening. Saves everybody a lot of hassle in the long run."

At length I was duly ungirded. "Wow!" said Bodleian, leaning over for a closer look. His face wore the expression of a scientist whose petri dish has spawned an unexpected bounty. "What beauties! And they're *real*!" Transfixed, he considered his subjects from various angles and finally (without looking away) groped across his desk for a tape measure.

"Look, could we not quantify them," I said, like a protective parent.

Bodleian looked up, grinning. "You available tonight?"

Let us return, then, to 923 Fifth Avenue. I emerged from the elevator into an elegant oak-paneled foyer, whose battery of mirrors cast my image into infinity. I reined in a few locks of hair and then stood smart and poised as a man entered the room.

He was short and paunchy and wore a navy suit and yellow tie. His hair was the color and texture of steel wool. His face was pocked and fleshy and his blue eyes tightly set, lending him an inquisitive yet retarded expression. He looked at least sixty, and his appearance indicated quite plainly why I'd been hired.

"You must be Dr. Wicked," he said, offering his hand.

"Mr. Bickel?" I replied, using the interrogative out of courtesy. His hand was warm and soft, like a fresh bun.

"Yoram," he said, smiling confidentially. "Follow me."

He led me into a living room of epic dimensions, a museum-like space where the furniture was meant to be decorative and not functional. A life among books allows me to know a little about everything, and I inspected the furnishings with a critical eye. The Madras gilt sofa appeared genuine, placing its origin in Barcelona circa 1805. The Charles I chairs belonged to a set once owned by the Duke of Gloucester, and sold at auction to help refurbish his crumbling ancestral pile. The Jvorak chandelier that presided overhead with regal serenity had once blessed the dining room of a Vatican powerbroker. The paintings included two Vaublins and one of three Pol Pot nudes in creation. All of which placed Yoram's net worth comfortably into eight figures, perhaps nine.

We passed into the next room, a greenhouse whispering with foliage. An oblong swimming pool lay in the center. A nearby door led outside to the terrace, which overlooked the park. He motioned me into a Neruda wicker chair, whose high back loomed behind me as though poised for attack. He seated himself opposite.

"Tell me a little about yourself before we begin," he said. "I—I mean I've never done this before, and I feel like maybe we should break the ice first, get to know each other and so forth."

"Of course." I smiled. "I was born in Venezuela, the child of Baptist missionaries. We lived among an Indian tribe called the Waorani. I spent my formative years in the rain forest and didn't

33

come to America until I was seventeen. My parents were massacred by a renegade native faction that an American oil company was in the process of evicting, but I managed to escape with another family."

"My god," he whispered.

"Following that," I continued briskly, "I matriculated at the University of Chicago and took a Ph.D in Comparative Religion. I'm in law school now at NYU. My ambition is to defend creationists from secular persecution."

"So this, this *job*," he said, gesturing vaguely, unwilling to name my vocation, "it's just to pay the bills?" He seemed concerned that I would make a career of it, poor fool, as if whoring only part-time somehow exonerated me. And him.

"I'm a consummate professional, Mr. Bickel," I replied, changing tack. "Why not leave it at that."

"Well, let me tell you about myself," he said, warming to his subject. "I'm sixty-one and my wife is thirty-two. She's had a double mastectomy and her chest looks like a highway construction site. I been playing Mr. Sensitive for two years and it's getting real old, you know? I'm still young. I got needs. You understand?"

"Of course," I said, thinking: You asinine little shit.

"I mean my life can't stop just cause she ain't got tits, right?"

Brooklyn Jew, nouveau riche. Couldn't shake that accent if he tried; the Protestants can all sleep safely. "Really," I said.

"I mean look at this." He indicated the general vicinity. "I got everything money can buy, but what's money after awhile?"

"*Also sprach Sisyphus.*"

". . . Excuse me? Did you say syphilis?"

"Don't worry, it's hardly Nietzschean."

"Good." He seemed to relax slightly. "Now. How bout a drink?"

We bullshat for half an hour over a bottle of '64 Sarrault. He had no children. He was a real estate developer. He was negotiating to build army barracks and a truck mall on a Long Island bird sanctuary. He was balding, but the first transplant looked promising, didn't it? He pulled a few strands to demonstrate its resilience.

"So. Yoram," I said at length, thinking I'd better push things along. "What would you like?"

He lowered his eyes. "Yeah, well, um," he commenced, "I think maybe what I want is something along the lines of . . . See I thought maybe to start off you could uh, you could like suck me, and, and

I dunno maybe we could have sex in the pool, and, and you know maybe at some point if you don't mind you could uh, uh, maybe kinda like hit me a little bit . . ."

Well, that didn't sound too difficult.

Improvising, I stood, languidly pulling off one shoe and then another (he perked up, giving me his full attention); strolled casually among the plants as though admiring their beauty (his gaze fast upon my ass); pensively doffed my jacket, and draped it across his lap (he swallowed as if in great pain, gasping on the rebound); distractedly fingered the buttons of my shirt, working my way down until, without hurry, I peeled it away (his eyes doubled in circumference); absently unzipped my skirt, coaxing it to the floor (he took in the black, translucent underwear, and licked dry lips); painstakingly unrolled one stocking and then another, and deposited them on my vacated chair, adding the garter belt (he drew an asthmatic breath) . . . and there I stopped, for the moment, allowing Yoram to stoke his furnace and suffer for the sake of suffering. I knelt before him, sliding a hand along his thigh, circling lackadaisically until at last, as if by chance, I closed on his apparatus—his doughy, diminutive apparatus. Nonplussed, I yanked off his trousers, realizing (with some outrage) that my performance had been wasted on him. I dispensed with his briefs (red, racing cut) and confronted my nemesis—a stubby little implement skulking in Yoram's pubic shrub. (Was there not a querulous aspect to the way it peeped out? or perhaps something downright furtive? I had the urge to tweak and prod, as if to agitate a slothful pet.)

Christ.

I didn't dare meet Yoram's gaze.

Instead I began a series of fellative ministrations, but no amount of tonguing or sucking could rouse that little fucker, nor indeed a course of perineal acupressure. Finally, when lockjaw threatened, I pulled away and sank back on my haunches. The recalcitrant penis slumped on Yoram's belly, pointing toward his chin like a rubbery finger, as if flipping me the bird. This was going to be a long night.

"I don't know what's wrong with it," Yoram said plaintively. He was silent for a moment; then: "I got an idea. Maybe if you hit me some it might work a little better."

". . . If you say so. Yoram."

He stood and stripped fully naked, revealing a bandy-legged, stoop-shouldered physique and a swaggeringly expansive gut. He

35

then bade me come round behind and start spanking. Shrugging, I whacked him a few times.

"*There* it is," he purred.

It was quite extraordinary. Each time I hit him, his penis shot out a little further. It reminded me of a ketchup bottle whose bottom one clobbers to expel the reluctant contents. By degrees Yoram's cock forged its way into the wide world, accruing into a three-inch husk that bobbed perpendicular to the floor. This appeared to be its limit.

Gratefully I unfastened my bra and tossed it aside. I removed my panties. I then reached for my purse, extracted a female condom (which is more durable than its male counterpart, and affords less sensation) and sealed myself up like a time capsule.

At last I faced Yoram, otherwise naked.

"Jesus Christ," he whispered, cupping my breasts hesitantly.

"My father, my father, why have you abandoned me," I replied, pleased with my quick thinking.

"I wanna fuck you," he said. "This fucking minute."

"Shall we do it in the pool?" I suggested.

We settled on the steps of the shallow end. Once hilted, Yoram crowed appreciatively, as if marveling at the beauty of human design. As if so much *thought* had gone into it.

I gripped him firmly, and the water created additional friction. Even so—and even with two ripe tits in his face—Yoram was unable to fulfill his biological mandate. Twenty minutes passed, but no amount of inner film footage and frantic suckling could propel him across that tender threshold—at least, not until we heard footsteps approaching from the living room.

"Oh my god," he whispered as the newcomer entered.

She appeared to be in her early thirties, with a canopy of luxuriant blonde hair and half-lidded, china-blue eyes. She wore a white evening gown that did nothing to conceal the blighted canvas of her chest and its mosaic of surgical scars. Far from being repelled, I found myself admiring her courage. She was not afraid of who she was, and damn anybody who blenched.

Yoram's jaw dropped; his sperm crusaded forth. By the third contraction I'd succeeded in pushing him out, and he expelled the remainder of his seed into a chlorine Gehenna.

"What is fuck?" queried the woman in a thick, vaguely eastern European accent.

"Hera!" Yoram gasped, backing away to the pool's opposite wall. The water barely reached his hips; his penis dangled at quarter-mast, exhausted, like a fallen weather-vane. "I thought the opera . . ."

She turned to appraise me, and was obviously not impressed. "What in fuck are you? You are new girlfriend?"

"This is Dr. Wicked," said Yoram, paddling over to stand beside me. He slid a proprietary arm around my waist, which I shook off.

"Hello Hera," I said quietly.

"*Doctor?* What is fuck, you are giving him feezical?"

"Um . . . Doctor of Theology, actually," I replied meekly. "Specialist in the Targumic approach to the gospels. Wycliffe scholar. *You* know."

"You sock his penis, yes?" she demanded, moving a step closer. "Ees plow chob, yes?"

I glanced at Yoram. "Well, not exactly. He—"

"I tell you something," she said, raising a finger. "Always he want plow chob, always I tell him no, yes?"

". . . *Really?*"

"I once svallowed an onion, you see, and the memory haunts me."

"Oh," I said, inching toward the ladder. "That's—*terrible?*"

"No," she snapped. "You understand *nossing.*" She circumambulated the pool, heading for the chairs. "I hope you give pig plow chob, for now I make you sorry." She knelt, retrieved my clothes. "Ees yours, no?"

I did not reply. Hera left the room and returned a moment later with a garbage bag. "Watch us," she advised in passing, as she bundled my clothes within. She opened the door to the terrace and stepped outside. Then, with a running start, she flung the bag high over Fifth Avenue and stood at the railing, following its course. Upon re-entering the greenhouse, she sneered, "You see about finding *sat* in dark."

I skimmed the surface of the water with my palm, dousing her. She stepped back, gaping at her stained gown. I followed with another volley, and another. I wasn't angry with her, nor had I the right to be: I was angry that Yoram had used me at her expense. Yet the loss of my clothes caused me to misdirect my response. By the time I had finished she was thoroughly soaked.

Hera shrieked and disappeared once more. When she came back

37

she was carrying a small black revolver. "Out of pool," she ordered, waving the gun at me. "Right now."

"Hera—" pleaded Yoram.

"Ees quiet, fat husband. I show her. Moving, please."

I clambered out of the pool and stood there naked, my pulse like a jackhammer. I did not fancy dying, not just then.

"Out, out," urged Hera, prodding me toward the living room. Shivering, and dripping generously on the Persian rug, I hurried into the foyer, where Hera pressed the elevator button. As we waited, she said, "I not see you again, yes, I shoot you viss gun."

The elevator door opened, revealing a wizened, startled attendant. "In, in," said Hera, giving me a shove. "You make her go away, Seamus. She not come back, yes?"

"Yes ma'am."

Seamus stared at me the entire way down, or at any rate stared at my breasts. Irritated, I asked if I could borrow his clothes. Without averting his gaze, Seamus reached distractedly for his bellhop's cap and placed it on my head. I jerked it away and used it to brush water off my arms and legs. When the elevator stopped I slapped it back on his head.

Lobby. Untrusting of my speedy exodus, though plainly saddened by its advent, Seamus escorted me to the front door, readjusting his cap. I searched for a newspaper or fig leaf with which to cover myself, but found nothing. Outside, under the awning, the doorman gawked and offered me his umbrella.

I pulled out the condom and handed it to him. "Fuck you," I said, stepping into the downpour.

Pedestrian traffic was mercifully light, but I had a good mile's walk to my Upper West Side apartment—not an appealing prospect. Rain or no rain, I was sure to be unceremoniously raped. A few dozen cabs queued up to offer me a ride, and I was lavished with endearments in a hundred different accents. Throwing an arm across my breasts, and laying a palm over my cunt, I slipped among the cars until I reached the park.

Approximating the trajectory of Hera's toss, I hopped over the wall and began searching among the trees. The ground was slippery with mud, and I was half-expecting to encounter rat poison, if not rats. I paced back and forth, scrutinizing the messy earth. Half an hour later, cut and filthy, I stumbled upon the bag. Part of it had torn on impact, disgorging the contents. The clothes were soaked;

I felt a clammy chill as I put them on. Still, in the immortal words of Beckett, via Estragon, there was nothing to be done. At least Hera had included my purse.

Carrying my shoes, I plodded back to Fifth Avenue and (what else?) hailed a cab. The driver, a grinning Italian named Rudolfo, took one look at me and, seeing the warning in my eyes, raised his hands in placation. "Don't worry," he said. "I ain't even gonna ask."

# CHAPTER THREE

## *A Portrait of Dorian Bray, with Incidental Music . . .*

His most distinguishing feature is a video clip that plays continually in his head, over and over, with only slight variations. **Fade In** reveals a coastal mansion, a flagstone patio, a sweeping view of the Pacific. He reclines on a deck chair, martini close at hand, waiting patiently for the middle-aged blonde—who wears enough makeup to frost a cake—to clip a microphone onto her white Coutieurine blazer. A gentle breeze settles in, and he squints in such a way— knowing, empathic, yet somehow pointed—as to lend himself an air of wisdom. Anonymous flunkies lurk in the background, tending to lights and cameras and sound levels.

**Are we rolling?** says the interviewer.

**You're on.**

The world where he grew up is unlike any other: the Dysinni Valley, Gwynedd, Wales, home to a ruined castle and ten thousand sheep. The rain does not cease, and the fields are a hundred shades of green. From his bedroom window he could see the towering spire of Cader Idris, Seat of the Giants. In Welsh legend, the ascent of this mountain confers immortality. He'd assayed the climb on four occasions, and each time the weather had driven him back. On his last attempt, just before leaving for university, he came within a hundred yards of the summit when a sudden wind almost flung him to his death down a nearby gully. The experience would become a metaphor for his adult life.

**I'm sitting with one of the most influential and photographed men in the world . . .**

Legends defined his youth. His valley was a dreamscape, a land as mythic as any in fiction. Though Christianity had bled into the furthest corners of Wales, Gwynedd's character was irrevocably pagan. Spectres of the old gods still lingered in the forests, in the dark pools beneath waterfalls, testament to the forces in this world we can never comprehend. For to walk in the Dysinni Valley is to find oneself a trespasser in heaven's unearthly sanctuary, a land claimed by ghosts and leased unkindly to the living.

**In just three short years since emigrating to the United States from Great Britain, philosopher and self-described Minister of Culture Dorian Bray has risen to prominence as the foremost spokesman of his generation. He first caught the Public Eye in 1999 with his book *The Theory of Everything*, which has sold fourteen million copies worldwide and is generally regarded as the bible of pop-culture philosophy. Since the book's publication he has become a syndicated columnist, a founding editor and critic-at-large for the award-winning magazine *Askew*, host of his own TV show on the Vixen Network, consultant on national affairs to the White House, broker of corporate mergers, Archibald Fairfax Huntington Professor of Social Science at Harvard University, and of course head of the Dorian Bray Foundation, which sponsors famine relief, medical research, and educational funding all over the world. Mr. Bray, welcome to *The Power and the Glory*.**

In many ways the twentieth century had never encroached upon the valley, and the Bray family adapted only gradually to the modern world. Electricity was installed in 1948, a telephone in 1964. The main farmhouse still had no central heating, and in winter (or in summer, for that matter) Dorian could see the vapor of his breath indoors as well as out.

**Now as you were growing up, did you have any idea that— that all this would *happen* to you?**
**A very interesting question. Originally I had expected to become a farmer like my father, but when I was twelve years old we bought our first TV, and suddenly everything changed.**

Indeed it did . . . He would sit before that television, hour after hour, witness to a thousand new worlds that beckoned like religion, urging flight from the heathen outback, whispering sweet betrayal. He had never been outside Wales. He was an only child, the last of his line, and the farm had passed from father to son for ten generations. But having now glimpsed the wide world, if only second-hand, there was no question of remaining in Gwynedd. His father, surprisingly, had few objections. The Brays owned a thousand acres, an equal number of ewes, a hundred cattle, and employed four distaff cousins as laborers. By local standards they were rich. Euan Bray demanded, however, that his son's departure bear some stamp of legitimacy; and so Dorian, previously a mediocre student, now bent all his energy toward earning top marks.

Fast forward to Oxford University, 1997. The naif from Gwynedd entered Magdalen College like a hatchling fresh from the egg. Physically a late developer, his nascent sexuality took a number of strange turns. He fell in with a group of young anarchists, all English, who were vaguely heterosexual but happy to service one another as the need arose. Though each man sought True Love in the arms of a woman, he could always fall back on his chums. More often than not, Dorian would be there waiting for him.

Tall, thin, and delicately featured, Dorian had never found the courage to approach women. Despite his foppish good looks, he was shy and uneasy in their presence. This awkwardness had little to do with self-esteem, or fear of embarrassment: to him the Female was an enigma, something of divine yet fell beauty that could never be understood, indeed could scarcely be considered *human*. Girls were like talismans, full of spontaneous magic: one needed arcane lore to invoke them safely. Possessing no such learning himself, Dorian settled into the role of voyeur. He was *attracted* to women, or so he told himself. At any rate he spent more time studying them than doing anything else. He watched them in the library, bent over their texts, spellbound by the furrows in their brows, the tentative set of their lips. (Whenever they wrote anything down, he nursed the curious hope that, having noticed him nearby, they had promptly fallen in love and were penning missives to that effect, and not simply taking notes.) He watched as they congregated in pubs, wine glistening on their lips. And in the bustle of Oxford's town center, they distracted him regardless of shape or size. (In one instance, while borrowing a friend's car, he nearly drove off Magdalen Bridge after spotting the vague blur of an Afghan hound in a passing convertible, mistaking it for windblown hair.) At some point in the unspecified future, though assuredly soon, he would embark upon one of those normal young-adult relationships that everyone else took for granted, and finally get laid. In the meantime, he hardly lacked for pleasure. Fucking men was the easiest thing in the world; and despite his fixation with and theoretical preference for women—despite his persistent, if untested hypothesis that heterosexual love was symbolically, aesthetically, and essentially superior—he was neither hesitant nor ashamed about chatting up the lads. There was no mystery to them, nothing undiscovered. They sated him physically, if not quite spiritually. And when they too were unavailable, Dorian masturbated until his skin had nearly peeled away, and only the faintest trickle of semen remained in his exhausted testes.

**Now I understand that you attended Oxford University for a year and then finished your degree at Columbia. When did you begin work on *The Theory of Everything*?**

**I suppose the initial conception took place at Magdalen. Basically I had this idea about fame—how one obtains it, maintains it, et cetera. Fame is based on consumption, and consumption upon commodity. For politics the commodity is rhetoric, for journalism it's scandal, for actors it's themselves—you get my drift. Now fame crests and dwindles in direct proportion to appetite. Some commodities are fast foods, some are five-course dinners, some manage to keep fresh indefinitely. Some are allergenic, whereby the celebrity or fan commits suicide. Anyway, I began to wonder how one might achieve fame that never diminished over time. Is there, for example, a fame at the epicenter of all other fame—*metafame*, if you will—to which all other fame refers? A fame which is for all intentions permanent, beyond the vagaries of public taste?**

For six years his only conduit to pop culture had been the television; now he sought first-hand exposure. He wanted to navigate the extremes of experience, to walk the high-wire of Youth in giddy defiance of the gulf beneath—a gulf called Reality, patient to the last. He pursued the biggest, the brightest, the fastest, the mostest. He wanted sophistication; he wanted *cool*. London was pleasingly decadent, with its chemical dependencies and unique androgynous lustre. But let's face it: England hasn't mattered for fifteen years, and Dorian sensed that the real action lay in America. He arranged to spend a year at Columbia College and thus experience the true vanguard of popular culture.

Manhattan, 1998 . . . As always, a nexus where modernity continually redefined itself with dizzying, infinite speed. His suspicion was confirmed: London had proved a revelation, but New York was in a different league entirely. He absorbed the worst the City had to offer like a desert traveler come suddenly upon water—greedily, deeply, impatiently. He tried every drug once, most of them twice, and cultivated a particular fondness for Antimatter, an hallucinogen that gave birth to new myths, vivid as those of childhood. The sheer speed and violence of New York beguiled him, and he viewed its relentless chaos as a liberation, championing the ragged yet sumptuous anarchy. Anything could happen in America, where escapism had been elevated into a fine art (all you need is velocity, babe). Self-indulgence was considered a virtue; indeed, it was the very bedrock of the culture, the cornerstone of a vast and otherwise meaningless economy.

Watch Dorian map this new world, the mists of Dysinni now forgotten. Watch, in his tireless pursuit of the *cutting edge*, as he penetrates the brothels of his generation—the clubs.

He enters a club, and is reminded of Hades: the air is thick with smoke and despair, and after a time one abandons all hope. Everything is comprised of shadows, vague shifting tides of movement. It is a festival, a commingling of asserted presences, of vying auras. The air is ripe with proposal. We offer ourselves to each other, and the frenetic motion and pulsing rhythms assure us that we're young and immortal and yes, truly living. We are resolutely escaping life, surrendering to a thousand potentials—the benediction of a stranger's kiss, or the swoon of an even greater release. Here, where life assumes infinite personalities, there is beauty amid the darkness, however subtle—the way a lock of hair falls across a woman's face, the braceleted thinness of her wrist, the fleeting accidence of a shared glance where possibilities are suggested and never consummated; where strangers briefly met will continue as strangers forever after . . .

Dorian charts this Stygian deep, fascinated and repelled. He craves membership into this culture, but applications are nowhere to be found. Instead there are passwords, hand-signals, myriad rites to which he has no access. How might he take his place here, and reach a position of eminence? The penultimate bane is exclusion; anonymity is worst of all. Yet to ignore this world is impossible. There is something vital here, some quintessence of Youth as holy as the Grail and just as elusive. So many people who would drink from Lethe . . . So many people following, following . . . how is it that they are led?

Dorian leans against the bar, Scotch in hand, wondering how he might not merely enter but indeed dominate this culture, and subvert it according to his own design. Domination requires either brute force or exceptional cunning. Dorian is unsuited for the role of Attila, but what about that of Witch Doctor? Control through *revelation*, through the husbandry of some hidden ultimate truth (or at least the appearance thereof)—this was as old as religion itself. Was there some truth that America might be persuaded it lacked? And if so, what?

**You've made philosophy quite fashionable these days.**
**Well there *has* been ample precedent. The great philosophers have endured for centuries, even millennia. My genius has been to create a philosophy rooted in mass culture—what you might call a philosophy for the new millennium—and to package it as a commodity like everything else. It's enormously gratifying that the appetite has been so bottomless.**

At Columbia he was failing every class by Halloween. Worse, he learned that one of his friends at Magdalen had been diagnosed with HIV. One by one the others were tested, all with the same result. A whole troupe of young men had received their death sentences, quick as you like.

The news devastated him. Though safe sex had generally been the rule among his friends, he could remember four or five orgies where everyone, himself included, had been dangerously lax. He was afraid to get tested himself: chemical surfeit was ravaging his body already, never mind disease. He looked and felt like shit.

He already knew that Columbia would not invite him back the following year, and he suspected Magdalen would follow suit. But he also felt that to return to Britain—to return to the wilderness of Gwynedd—would be an acknowledgement of defeat. In Dorian television had inculcated the desire for fame—never mind how, never mind why. Youth is as Darwinian as adulthood, and competition pervades among friends and enemies alike. To Dorian's mind, only fame could place him at the top of the food chain. Only fame could elevate him above the common denominator, above the masses who surely had the same ambitions as he—to be noticed.

He had looked upon his first months in New York as research; now the fulfillment of his quest became his immediate priority. He withdrew from society as surely as he had plunged in, devoting every waking moment to the text of his Revelation. He registered for five courses in the second semester and did not attend a single class; indeed, he scarcely left his room. He worked through the nights, fueled by liquor, until his hand became cramped and arthritic. He'd collapse at dawn and wake at four in the afternoon, usually with a hangover, to a breakfast of whisky and dark chocolate. He weaned himself from drugs but grew increasingly dependent on Scotch, particularly Glenlivet. He neglected to wash or shave, and came to abhor even the slightest exertion. He resented *standing*, never mind locomotion. All that mattered was the Revelation, though it now took a slightly different form than the nonfiction treatise which, in the privacy of his own mind, had sold fourteen million copies.

For a novel had come to him. He was not interested in fiction per se, nor indeed art for its own sake. Instead the novel was a vehicle for his philosophical platforms, his Revelation. Its title remained *The Theory of Everything*, and like most first novels resorted to autobiography. It was a coming-of-age story of a Welsh bumpkin who fell in love with a rich American beauty, an amalgam of the hundred-odd classmates whom Dorian had craved from a distance. The protagonist was given to lengthy soliloquies on the meaning of life, and rather an excess of introspection; in the end, his love remained unconsummated. The climactic scene depicted the hero committing suicide in the presence of his beloved, which he accomplished by ingesting an explosive, striding to the middle of the dining hall, summoning her attention, and fulminating all over her. By this deed she would always remember him, as she gaped at their one flesh and blood and then succumbed to clinical shock . . .

When the novel was finished Dorian's hair was shoulder-length. His beard was matted and crusty. His room was a killing field of plastic and mildew, a rotting exile to which a battalion of insects had relocated. But he felt overcome with contumelious fulfillment, with a sense of gloating over carefully prepared vengeance. He gathered the pages together—tattered, stained, taped—and hired a neighbor to type the manuscript.

As to the substance of his Revelation: Dorian was, it must be admitted, an intellectual charlatan. He'd read enough of the Greats

46

to win a place at Magdalen, but their wisdom had quickly evaporated from his memory, like tenants newly departed after the termination of a summer lease. Instead he'd bought a used encyclopedia set and perused the paragraph-length biographies of all the famous artists and thinkers he could find. Though the appearance of erudition went over well in pop-culture circles, erudition itself did not—so why bother? Society lacked Freud's Incitement Premium for real discourse; he must strive to articulate himself with sound-bite economy. Thus when summarizing his philosophy, which he'd taken to calling the New Hedonism, Dorian would start with the "ideological foundation" upon which it was based. Briefly: America purported to be based upon a Kantian style of ethics. Early New England culture was famously puritanical, rife with *thou shalt not*s, and a sense of duty prevailed. But America had swiftly transformed into an *Aristotelian* culture of self-improvement and the pursuit of individual accomplishment, utilitarianism be damned. (As Dorian would also point out, Nietzsche took Aristotle a step further and so developed his famous will to power.) Dorian used this principle as the basis for his New Hedonism, which ridiculed the notion that *everyone* could be happy. Society, he proclaimed, was forever damned to wars of attrition among its constituents. Accordingly, the New Hedonism was forged upon two ideals: the Bullet and the Hard Sell. Its manifesto, quite simply, was *Go For It*.

Such, then, was Dorian's hidden lore, the bible whose wisdom only he possessed, and which America would pay to receive. One has to give him credit: beyond his need for fame and fortune, beyond the earnest fraudulence of his posturing, he genuinely believed that he was on to something profound. Then again, all delusions are sincere.

**But isn't it true that some have called this the philosophy of decadence?**

**Yes, but apparently they miss their own irony in using that word pejoratively.**

**What do you mean?**

**Simply that I agree with them. I mean look, people have been whining for years—decades, in fact—that American pop culture is promoting some sort of decline in society. They should remember that pop culture is only one outgrowth of the tree of free-market economics, and blaming the artists themselves is beside**

the point. You're attacking the branches, not the roots. The first principle of capitalism is profit, and the first principle of profit is acquisition. In a capitalist economy, an Aristotelian or Nietzschean framework is the natural—is indeed the only *tenable*—modus operandi. The New Hedonism acknowledges this and sees no reason but to endorse it. You can't have capitalism without decadence, and therefore the pursuit of fame and wealth becomes the highest possible virtue. Everyone should practice it.

But can this sort of culture sustain itself indefinitely?

I remember Ayn Rand writing that even pollution was a sign of progress. I think that says it all.

With the manuscript typed, Dorian marched to Kinko's at Broadway and 114th and ordered twenty copies. When they were finished he hauled them in two trips to the post office, where he spent three hours stuffing envelopes and writing address labels. Then, with a prayer and a kiss, he released them into the wide world.

The semester was drawing to a close, and the spectre of final exams had settled upon the campus. His academic standing irrevocably destroyed, Dorian spent half his savings on a battered vintage Mustang, which he restored during the long spring afternoons while everyone else was studying. Having experienced New York, he was ready to pursue another American myth: driving to California.

Exempt from Finals Hell, he nevertheless felt a keen longing as he witnessed the spectacle—the all-night sessions in the library, the group therapy meetings and stress reduction clinics, the optimal-study seminars. This was a campus with purpose, fulfilling a time-honored ritual from which he was now excluded. His own failure seemed implicit in every book, every backpack that was hauled through the quad—especially because his own reading material consisted of *Gentleman's HindQuarterly*, *Vanity Snare*, *Daily Sobriety*, and similar fame-fucking indispensables. His head became a database of annual celebrity earnings, Q-ratings, high-priced divorces. He couldn't care less about the celebrities' actual *work*: all that mattered was joining their ranks as soon as possible.

The novel, he told himself, would provide salvation. He envisioned delirious editors, hurried board meetings, bidding wars. Flush with a record advance, he would return from California, install himself in a Manhattan penthouse, and settle in as the foremost advocate of a world gone mad. The novel would become a bestseller. There would be a promotional tour, foreign editions, televised interviews. Critics would be unanimously hagiographic. (He imagined himself, under gentle duress, admitting that it was quite the finest novel ever written.) At night, as other students read until they pissed ink, he polished acceptance speeches for the National Book Award, Pulitzer Prize, and of course the Booker—the first author to win all three. (The Americans, he reasoned, would be only too glad to grant him citizenship.) Most gratifyingly, he wasn't a real *novelist*: he was a brilliant and iconoclastic thinker who had deigned, rather triflingly but with requisite good humor, to make use (if only this once) of that quaint and archaic art form. He might as easily have used film or the stage for his unique gifts. Such was the prerogative of visionaries, of the *metafamous* . . .

**(*Aerial shot of sprawling residential compound; female voice-over continues:*) Revenues from his book, television show, lecture fees, brokering commissions, *Askew* magazine, and stock portfolio have given Dorian Bray an estimated net worth of $250 million. In addition to this 16,000 square-foot mansion in Malibu, Bray maintains a triplex on Fifth Avenue in Manhattan, a town-house in London's exclusive Knightsbridge district . . .**

The date of departure drew near, and self-addressed envelopes began arriving one by one. Too haughty to provide for the return of his manuscript—and convinced there would be no need to do so—he had furnished only a letter-sized SASE with the submission, and this merely to assuage the fear that someone might simply discard the manuscript without informing him of a verdict. He'd done enough research to know that editors, when seduced by a story, head for the telephone: the postal service is the medium of failure. He did not open the letters yet: no, he intended to laugh at them after a healthy six- (or seven-) figure deal had been arranged and he had the leisure and eminence to vilify those who wouldn't know genius if it raped them. In the meantime, their more enlightened counterparts at other houses were sure to be seeking management approval for the commitment of very large funds . . .

**. . . an 80,000-acre estate in the Scottish Highlands, a private island in the Aegean . . .**

\*

Aside from all this, there remained the problem of getting laid. Once he left Columbia—once he was on the open road—he would no longer have a ready pool of candidates. Then an idea hit him: he would post an advertisement for a traveling companion, one who might be willing to share more than the driving. But to specifically request a woman—let alone a beautiful woman—would only bring on the Thought Police. In the end he opted for restraint—**Driving to Frisco. Any takers?**—and hoped for the best.

**. . . a controlling interest in Harrod's, a seat on the New York Stock Exchange . . .**

By the morning of the journey, Dorian had already received envelopes from nineteen of the twenty publishers. He shuffled to the post office to close his mailbox, still entertaining hope that the one remaining house—Kaput, Man & Sons—would honor its duty to Western civilization and commission a million-copy first printing. As he approached his mailbox he saw, through the window, a sliver of white paper. Grimly he opened the door and withdrew a single envelope, which bore his own neurotic scrawl and thus the impossibility of his redemption.

**. . . also owns half of North America, most of Europe, and one hundred percent of . . . of . . . ? . . .**

He walked bug-eyed to the service window, clenched against the onset of lachrymose hell. He could not afford a nervous breakdown in the post office; otherwise he would have to be carried out, probably to an emergency room. So he blinked, he leered hideously, he feigned allergies. He pushed his mailbox key across the counter at the woman in attendance, a young Latina who in other circumstances would have aroused ithyphallic sympathies.

"Coming back next year?" she asked.

**. . . is considered by many to be nothing less than a deity, God's chosen messenger to the—to the—**

Fuck it. *Fuck everything.*

After a crying jag in his car, he drove to the designated meeting place—the west gates, on Broadway—to see if anyone had responded to his advertisement. Awaiting him stood a small black man of perhaps nineteen years, handsome and dignified in Senegalese chic. Dorian sighed as he contemplated his newfound passenger, who was not precisely the woman of his dreams. Or the man of his dreams, for that matter.

"I'm bisexual," said Dorian for no apparent reason, as they loaded the trunk. "Not that I'm attracted to you—which is of course to say that you're not unattractive—but I thought you might like to know."

"I'm a racist," answered Prophet cheerfully. "I hate all white people, which is of course to say yourself included. I thought you'd like to know."

"Fair enough," said Dorian. "But you'll still pay for gas?"

With the car loaded and the top down, Dorian headed toward 125th Street and the West, waiting for an epiphany.

# CHAPTER FOUR

## *Saved by Technology; or,*
## *Another Satisfied Customer . . .*

"Pornography," breathed Dorian, ogling the brochure on the television set. "Three whole channels of *pornography.*"

Prophet, sprawled on the couch nearby, was attempting to order room service. "I don't see a wine list on this menu," he said to the telephone.

Fish stood on the balcony at the far end of the suite, watching the dusk. The wooded hills were bathed in a gentle crimson, and a chorus of cicadas had taken up voice. There was not a house or building in sight, here in the bowels of the countryside, at the end of the first day's journey. He studied the ground forty feet below and wondered if he could survive the jump. If he were to land in just such a way . . .

"Don't wanna house white baby wanna see a list, last thing I need's a chardonnay or zinfindel or that other cheap shit, I'm talking '32 Pauillac and '34 St Julien, know what I'm saying? Or a '58 Artaud, *lovely* little vineyard just outside of Nice—"

"How the hell am I going to *choose*," mused Dorian.

"Fuck that shit now listen up. I wanna plate of capellini, lightly sauced. I wanna side of brown rice. I wannan order of sliced tomatoes, plain. I want . . . I want some *broccoli*, and I wannit steamed, not boiled. Yeah. Yeah good now wait a second . . . Fish? Come order."

"Anyone heard of Debbi Deutschemark?" said Dorian.

"Are these vegetables cooked in butter?" Fish asked the telephone. "No I'm not worried about cholesterol I'm allergic to dairy . . . OK but can you *guarantee* that the pot was scoured after any previous exposure to butter?"

"Fuck, there's only one bed," said Prophet from the bedroom.

"All right give me the New York sirloin well done, and when I say well done I mean I want the thing *extinct*, OK? If there's any red—if there's any *brown* I'm sending it back. And bring some rolls, like maybe ten or twelve of them. No, that's just for me. Right. Dorian?"

"There really should be more than one television," he said, taking the phone. "Yes is that room service? Yes I'd like a bottle of your best Scotch; better yet make it two . . . Yes and I'll need a tall glass, all right? the tallest you have. No we'll pay cash, thank you."

Fish had wandered over to the desk, where Prophet was sitting with a laptop computer. "What are you doing?"

"Oh, I'm up to all kinds of no good, you old Pisces you."

"No seriously, what is that?"

"Remote cellular fax/modem. See I keep a list of passwords and PIN numbers and what I can do is break into systems and download or upload files without anyone knowing. I call it riding a false passport, it's almost untraceable unless there's someone real smart on the other end now see that? That's the fax number for the editorial department of *Time* magazine, so watch what I do . . ." And with a few keystrokes a document filled the screen, Fish scanning its contents:

### FOR IMMEDIATE RELEASE

**A spokesman for the black nationalist group African Fist! warned that a bomb will detonate on May 16 at one or more of the following locations: the Metropolitan Opera, Lincoln Center; the Metropolitan Museum of Art; or at the Pierre Hotel. The spokesman warned all African-Americans to avoid these locations on the night in question, and then advised all whites to watch their backs.**

"Jesus Prophet!"

"Shit's wide, ain't it."

"Have you done this before?"

"Done some shit you wouldn't believe—network disturbances, database crashing, stuff like that. Now watch, I press this and the fax is on its way. Next I'll set it up so all the newspapers in the City receive it, plus the NYPD."

"But Jesus you could go to jail for this!"

"You could go to jail for armed robbery. And listen up man, you need to keep quiet about this. It's only a joke but I'm not supposed to be showing it to anybody."

Fish pulled up a chair. "I thought I was crazy."

53

"Oh you're bad in your own little way," said Prophet, "but you ain't black my man, and that says it all."

"Well I *am* schizophrenic. I'm a victim too."

"Seems your beef lies with God and not the government, but hey—you wanna try this sometime, be my guest."

"Have you seen this Dorian?"

"M'mm? No but I think it's brilliant," he said as the evening news came to life on the television screen, revealing a group of young black men gleefully frisking three dozen bloody white corpses on what appeared to be a major urban boulevard, followed by a worried Caucasian reporter and footage of the National Guard. "The more I think about it, the more I advocate complete anarchy. It's not as if *I* have a stake in the world order any more. Let it all come down."

"What else have you done?" asked Fish as the television acceded to yet another pasty Caucasian male, this one clad in a black three-piece suit, touring what appeared to be the charred ruins of a super-market as a grim-faced black man in similar attire pointed to the wreckage of a cash register.

"Well, speaking of the President, I got his Visa number last week. Sent him a tractor lawn mower at Camp David."

"No!?!"

"Oh yeah, baby. I mean it prolly never got through Customs but it's the thought that counts, right? And the bill."

"Well shit," said Fish. "Could we charge this hotel room to the President?"

"We already paid with stolen cash, remember? Besides, it's good to keep changing tack, not leave a trail. Now, as to a certain senator from Kansas . . ."

"Or Utah . . ."

"Or New York . . ."

"Or either of the Carolinas . . ."

"A certain congressman from Georgia?"

"A Cabinet member?"

"How about," said Prophet dreamily, "how about that certain justice on the Supreme Court?"

"You mean . . . ?"

". . . ?"

". . . !"

"How bout we send him a truckload of leotards?" said Prophet.

"Or spermicidal jelly."

"Fuck it," said Dorian, as the camera tightened upon a gaunt young boy in a wheelchair who, according to a female voice-over, had been flung from a tenth-story window and lived to implicate his father in the deed. "How do we order this . . . ?"

"What?" said Prophet, reaching for the brochure. "Aw forget this lowbrow shit man. You wait a minute, I'll show you the real thing." He rummaged through his suitcase and withdrew a set of patching cables, neatly coiled.

"What are you doing?"

"I'm hooking up my computer to this TV. All right, turn it to channel three."

The image of Prophet's press release filled the screen, followed by a menu offering several telephone numbers. Prophet selected one and the modem began dialling.

"We'll just charge this to someone else's account," he said, as a different menu appeared listing all major credit cards. "How bout the Mayor of New York City? I think I have his Amex number somewhere."

"But what exactly is this?" said Dorian.

"This, my friend, is something called *Wish Theater*. Heard of it?"

"You subscribe to *Wish Theater*?!"

"No, but the Mayor of New York City does, as of now."

"I haven't heard of it," said Fish. "Then again, I've been leading a very sheltered life."

"It's *the* new thing," said Dorian excitedly. "It's completely brilliant. Basically you tap into this national database with gazillions of memory and hard-drive storage and it allows you to program your own short films."

"You mean animation?"

"No, or at least not really. Basically they photograph the bodies of real actors and everyday objects like cars and guns and digitize those images so they can be reproduced in almost any way imaginable. You can have a cast of up to twelve people and you can make them do everything they do in regular movies, only much much worse. You can make them fuck, commit suicide, cannibalize—the possibilities are virtually endless. You can even play with the camera angles—it's 360-degree user-directed, in real time. It's still kind of underground and bloody expensive. I think you can pay a one-time user fee but it's cheaper to subscribe long-term, especially if you use it frequently. I read about it just last week, apparently it's not wholly legal and the government is up in arms. Freedom of speech and all that."

"None of which applies right now," said Prophet as he entered the payment data. "By the way, there's also a One-on-One Mode. Provided there's a vacancy, we can basically rent an actress who'll come to us live through a video downlink. I can plug in my microphone and we can talk to her directly."

"Will she be able to see us?"

"No, cause there's no camera on this end."

"Decisions," muttered Dorian. "God I hate freedom. It's such a burden."

"We've got all night," said Fish. "Why don't we start by making a film?"

"Right." Prophet tapped at the keyboard, and the faces of several young women appeared on the screen. "Now they've got a whole library of people to choose from, male and female. Shit, they've even got animals too. Now watch, we can scroll through the candidates until we find someone we like."

"Christ, it's like being God," said Dorian, scrutinizing the faces and body parts. "Keep going; these women look too lower-class. All right her, and her, and—and *her*, let's get some oriental blood into the mix."

"What are we going to do with them?" asked Prophet.

"Cunnilingus and rimming for a start, and have a couple of them masturbating as well. We can see what we feel like after that."

"Come on man," said Prophet, screwing up his face. "That's total sleaze."

"Well what would you suggest then?"

"Myself," said Prophet, "I say we fuck the idea of sex. The whole point of this is that we can be artists, you know? Why don't we pose them one by one, you know like statues, and—"

"*What?*" snapped Dorian. "Prophet, the whole point of this has nothing to do with art, it's about *sex*, plain and simple. I mean Christ, the sort of thing you're describing one might as well join a life-drawing class."

"So what? I mean why you wanna see women doin that shit? Or men and women, for that matter?"

"Why do you *think*?"

"What *I* think," said Prophet, "is that we should leave something to the imagination. It's . . . I don't know, *funner* that way. Not to mention less degrading."

"Prophet," said Dorian slowly, "I can use my imagination walking down the bloody street. As for the issue of debasement, it's irrelevant. These people don't exist. For god sake stop being so precious."

"Fine," said Prophet. "But I'll tell y'all something: you got *no* aesthetic taste."

By the time dinner arrived they were watching nine young women of various nationalities stimulate themselves in and around a fountain in a public square, accompanied by digitally sampled voices for each character. Prophet, utilizing the mouse, alternately zoomed in for close-ups and pulled back for panoramic surveys.

"That big blonde," said Dorian. "Shrink her teats. And that Egyptian-looking woman, make her shit in the pool. Can you do that?"

"If only the Benedictines could see this," said Fish, hacking at the burnt husk of some poor bovine's loin. "They'd eat this up like you wouldn't believe."

"Can we change the scenario as we go along?" said Dorian, pouring a tall glass of Scotch and drinking deeply.

"No problem. What you want?"

"Well, since these people are essentially facsimiles, I see no reason not to throw in some livestock at this juncture. Better yet, couldn't we *murder* them?"

"God damn it Dorian—"

"Oh come *on* Prophet, surely you've wondered what it must be like to kill somebody. Or is this bad-ass attitude just a facade?"

"All I'm saying is—"

"These people don't exist," Dorian repeated. "We can do anything we want to them, with no guilt or blame. We can carve them up into a thousand pieces and use them as appetizers at a nursing home dinner party. We can do everything that people dream of doing but can't. That's the beauty of it, I mean whoever invented this is a bloody *genius*."

"Stupid shit." Prophet repaired to the menus. "All right, who's gonna murder who?"

"A newcomer," said Dorian. "How about that Cuban woman we bypassed earlier, the one with pubic *fur*."

"All right," said Prophet. "What about the weapon? We got crowbar, ice pick, pistol, rifle, shotgun, machine-gun, kitchen knife, hunting dagger, baseball bat, rope . . . damn, look at that list it's gonna take all night to go through it. Can't we just keep things simple?"

"Rope," Dorian mused. "Well, she can't garrote them all, not unless they sit around like Stephen Hawking. It would be totally unrealistic, and I want these girls to struggle . . . Make it a baseball bat. No wait, make it a baseball bat for the first two, then have her pull out a hunting dagger for the next two, and finally she can use a machine gun for the rest. Make sure we get a tight shot of everything, can you do that?"

"Jesus you are one sick puppy . . . All right, you got it. These pull-down menus have everything, don't they."

"Can she drink all the blood afterward?" said Fish.

"Good idea," said Dorian.

"Come on man, that's going too far."

"I knew you were spineless."

"Man *fuck* you . . . All right, all right, what else?"

"Have her piss on the corpses," said Dorian, "and then have her fistfuck every one of them."

"Dorian—"

"Look, why not let me try." He reached for the mouse.

"Man *get* the fuck away . . . OK look, I've done it but this is it, right? I never realized you could take it this far."

"Fine, fine. You ready Fish?"

"Roll tape."

They watched as a beautiful Latina stepped into the scene with a baseball bat and charged the nearest victim, who was masturbating on the edge of the fountain. As the drama unfolded Dorian leaned forward, his pulse in his throat, marveling at the carnage he had authored. Fish blinked uneasily, recalling the many schizophrenic delusions in which he himself had been murdered. Prophet sat with his arms folded, his eyes running the length of the floor.

As the skit finally ended, a long sigh issued from Dorian's lips. His palms were clammy: he was actually sweating. "God bless technology," he said, heading toward the bathroom. "I don't know about you two, but I could get addicted to this very easily."

Prophet glared at Fish, who had resumed eating.

"What?" said Fish, shrugging. "So the guy's repressed."

"You're saying it didn't bother you at all?"

"What's the big deal? It's just a glorified video game. I'm surprised no one thought of it before now."

"Fish," said Prophet, eyes narrowing, "just what kind of a priest *were* you?"

# CHAPTER FIVE

## *Big Plans for Everybody . . .*

"I look at you," says Gyeppi Natare to the bald, moustachioed stranger standing before him, "and I see a *pale* excuse for a black man."

Columbia University, January 1999. The young man known as Kenley O'Hare Jr. watches the long-awaited confrontation between roommate and father. The walls of the room are covered with black faces—Malcolm, DuBois, Garvey in his Napoleon regalia. Ponderous shelving units contain virtually every Black Studies text in print, neatly alphabetized. And then there is Gyeppi Natare, son of the most prominent black separatist in America. The accusation tendered at Kenley Sr. is all too familiar to his son, who has suffered it for the past four months.

Natare, a first-year student like Kenley, is the leader of a devoted cadre of black intellectuals. His father is one Kweisi Ndugu Natare, president of a neo-socialist collective in upstate New York known as Karibu. Part kibbutz, part utopia, Karibu is a model of self-sufficiency, a refuge where twenty thousand African-Americans live almost exclusively among their own. Kweisi Natare—formerly Jackson Gawain—inherited a fortune originating three generations earlier with the white matriarch who had owned his forebears and left them her estate in a fit of repentance. A century later Kweisi parlayed his share into a much bigger fortune on Wall Street. By age forty he was the richest black man in America, his net worth more than three billion dollars. He founded Karibu—which means Welcome in Swahili—on the site of a defunct liberal arts college in 1994, and disenfranchised blacks have flocked to the colony ever since. Now Karibu is more town than colony, and includes fifteen thousand acres of newly acquired farmland.

Gyeppi took for granted that Kenley would be as militant as himself. He found it inconceivable that any black man, in the waning years of the century, could possibly support integration. To Kenley Jr.—probably the most apolitical beast on campus—black nationalism is an alien religion. To Kenley Sr. the issue is even simpler: radical politics do not lead to good grades. They do not lead to graduate school. They have nothing to do with Kenley's field, which is astrophysics. Above all, they do not lead to *success*.

Kenley Sr. has heard all about Gyeppi Natare during the winter holidays. Now, at the start of the second semester, he has accompanied his son back to school to put the upstart in his place.

"Don't you *dare* speak to me that way, young man," he warns Natare. He is a big man, his voice rich as only a black man's voice can be rich. Most civilians would not want to cross him, but Gyeppi Natare is not intimidated. Though average in stature, his casually folded arms and crooked smile suggest that he has faced down many adversaries in his short life, and never learned the meaning of Retreat.

"Like father, like son," he sneers. "Uncle Tom redux."

"You're quite the gadfly, aren't you," replies Kenley Sr. "Well let me tell you something young man, I am not impressed in the slightest. It's a pity your famous father never taught you any manners."

This is a rather odd statement. It is 1999, after all, and the word "manners" is not often bandied about—certainly not in New York. In the home of Kenley's youth, however, reigned a moral sanctity that was absolute. The canings lasted well into Kenley's adolescence. He was caned for lying. He was caned for coming home late. He was caned once for receiving an A-minus on a trifling pop quiz. The punishment was not brutal—blood was not drawn, the wounds were not permanent—but from age two he learned to tread softly in his father's presence. The subtlest inflections of that basso profundo could—well, could speak volumes. And as a weapon, it was more potent than any cane.

Kenley's father was a math professor, his mother a pediatrician; he had no siblings. Though not religious, the family had a bible of sorts: Emily Post's *Etiquette*, which furnished the guidelines for household conduct. Eating utensils were to be wielded just so; hats were never worn indoors; and until the day he left for college, Kenley addressed his father as Sir.

"That what they teach in *Shaker Heights*?" mocks Natare. "*Manners?*"

Shaker Heights, Ohio, where Kenley was born, is a land of many mansions. Founded by Dutch racists in the early twentieth century as a Protestant enclave, Shaker had transformed over the decades into a roiling polyglot mosaic. Jews and white Catholics, having duly risen from immigrant poverty, were the first to challenge WASP hegemony. Blacks moved in later, colonizing the less fashionable neighborhoods. By 1980, the year of Kenley's birth, they comprised nearly a third of the population; but their income remained, on average, far beneath their white counterparts'.

A short digression concerning the mores of Shaker Heights is worth pursuing. In the spirit of human fellowship, each ethnic group belonged to a separate country club. Protestants dominated the two local clubs, Shaker and Canterbury. Jews were obliged to go further afield, to Oakwood in Cleveland Heights. Blacks laid claim to a decrepit public course, Highland Park, which bordered a cemetery. It was not uncommon for golfers to slice their tee shots among the headstones, with not a starched USGA official in sight to provide a ruling. Shaker and Canterbury hosted national tournaments and were famous for their sculpted fairways and beachy sandtraps. At Highland, fairway and rough were indistinguishable, and its two or three bunkers had the consistency of cement.

In the mid-1990s, as in the previous two decades, the prevailing issue at Shaker Heights High School was race. Blacks formed one subculture, whites another, and rarely the twain would meet. Whites, as was their habit, fell into pernicious little cliques of varying insularity. Blacks formed a single large crowd, where everybody knew everybody else. Whites claimed no territorial rights (among other reasons, they were physically unable to); blacks tended to congregate in one or two particular hallways, and it was a brave white soul who dared venture among those ranks.

It was a brave Kenley O'Hare Jr. who dared the same. He spent most of the school day in honors classes, safely ensconced among the pale elite; but the last period of the day was gym, which has yet to be officially segregated. In the free-for-all trenches, among the numerous blacks, Kenley was an object of perpetual hilarity. Consider: he was five-foot-one and weighed less than a hundred pounds. His best time in the fifty-yard dash was 8.9 seconds. He could manage about five push-ups. His performances on the playing field were a festival of dropped balls, wild throws, whiffed swings. And on the basketball court, that ultimate black stomping ground, Kenley's nickname was Air O'Hare—a reference not to his athleticism but to the trajectory of his free-throws.

61

Truth be told, he hated his black peers. They mocked him for his stature. They mocked him for his grades. And though it wore on him, he never dared protest: he didn't want the shit kicked out of him any more than the next boy. After school he'd retreat to his bedroom and his two constant companions, a computer and a telescope.

Among honors students he was legendary, and the stories were usually true. He knew every constellation in the sky by age six, and acquired a working knowledge of Greek at the same time. He mastered C, PASCAL, and machine language by age nine, and was a nationally ranked chessmaster before reaching middle school. In math class, postgraduate trigonometry and calculus texts were imported to divert him as early as ninth grade. Most impressively to his peers, he was one of the best hackers in the Midwest.

To amuse himself off-hours, Kenley infiltrated corporate databases and rummaged through the financial histories of countless strangers. He never stole a thing; he was just looking around. Had he wanted to, he could have destroyed employment records, credit ratings, medical profiles. He could have transferred vast sums of money between bank accounts at whim. He could have redirected telephone numbers: a funeral home's extension, for example, could be rerouted to a gay sex hotline. He could have altered the grades of thousands of college students across the country. He could have left viruses everywhere in his wake, bringing entire networks to a standstill.

But he hadn't. He trespassed but he never vandalized. The thrill was in the puzzle, not the crime. Besides, he reasoned that if corporations and governments had such intimate knowledge of people's private lives, it was hardly criminal to explore the ramifications of that power. He was merely a self-appointed watchdog, not a sociopath. In temperament he was soft-spoken and mild-mannered, and quite liked by his circle of white friends. Their own nicknames for him were rather more to his liking: Gandalf, Pythagoras, Vulcan, the Dungeon Master.

There was never any question that he would be valedictorian of his class. He didn't bother to visit colleges; instead they beat an Emersonian path to his door. His mailbox was filled with simpering overtures from every Ivy League school, not to mention Stanford, CalTech, Williams, Duke, Swarthmore, Amherst, MIT. Kenley Sr., himself a high school valedictorian, was an alumnus of Columbia

College; and though he never said so explicitly, it was understood that his son would matriculate there as well. As the other Ivy League schools were offering full scholarships and free airfares, enrollment bonuses and stock options, Kenley applied quietly to Columbia, Early Decision. A letter of acceptance—or rather, his compensation package—was Fed-Exed three days later, before he'd even had a chance to arrange an interview. He waded through the contracts, the insurance policies, the securities portfolio. Every expense for the next four years was erased; indeed, the proposal teemed with off-shore bank accounts, payment schedules, tax-exempt stipends. A company car was available after his sophomore year, and would be his to keep upon graduation.

"Things have changed," said Kenley Sr., pulling out a calculator. "In my day I worked three jobs as an undergraduate and four as a doctoral student."

His son shrugged. "As long as I can bring my computer."

"I got a warning for you nigger," says Gyeppi Natare to Kenley Sr. "You think you can hide from us in Shaker Heights well you are *sadly* mistaken. Time'll come when we gonna burn your city down, and don't *think* the color a your skin's gonna save you. No way baby: we got some *very* special treatment planned for y'all, know what I'm sayin?"

For a moment it appears that Kenley Sr. will lose his temper. His lips are compressed into a terrible grimace, and one meaty fist is cocked as he measures the distance to Natare's jaw, savoring the prospect of crushing it. The fist wavers, oscillating back and forth, reminiscent of a bull pawing the ground. "If I ever hear That Word from you again," he grates, "I will see to it that you are expelled from this university. Permanently. Do you understand?"

"And who the fuck are you?" replies Natare, affecting an air of bewilderment, his palms upturned. "My father could *buy* this university. I'm the star attraction on campus, and ain't *nobody* gonna make me unhappy. You go see the President, talk all you want. He'll laugh in your fat albino face."

Trembling, Kenley Sr. lowers his arm, straightens his jacket, and turns on his heel. "Come on Kenley. We're getting you transferred to another dorm."

Natare snorted. "Thass right nigga, you tuck your sorry-ass tail tween your legs. You wanna know somethin man? Your time is

63

*gone.* You ain't nothing but a dinosaur, and you *know* what happened to the dinosaurs."

"Kenley I *said* let's go."

"Gonna listen to him?" Natare jeers at Kenley Jr. "Gonna crawl after your daddy like a good little scarecrow boy?"

During the first semester Kenley spent much of his time away from the room. Natare's disciples tended to appropriate his bed and bullshit until the early hours, forcing him to pitch camp in the laboratory or computer center. He has heard many a Natare diatribe, and none has made an impression. He hadn't asked for a black roommate in the first place, nor indeed to be housed in a largely black dorm. The university made the assignment of its own volition, as though presuming some integrational discomfort on his behalf.

Kenley had not forgotten the derision lavished on him at Shaker High; nor was he surprised, upon arriving at Columbia, at the swiftness of Natare's enmity. Kenley and black people just didn't seem to get along—end of story. Yet the nature of Gyeppi's scorn was different. At Shaker the trouble had been high grades and low jumps; and the ridicule, while pervasive, was essentially superficial, even casual. No one could be bothered to actually *hate* him.

At Columbia everything went deeper. Natare had rigid conceptions of what it meant to be black, and Kenley's failure to conform was seen explicitly as race betrayal. And now, on the first day of the new semester, he at last has an inkling of what this means.

Because of his father.

What is it about his father that begins to repel him? Is it the self-righteous air? that smug certainty of being obeyed, as if Kenley were still a child? a sudden remembrance of those beatings? Is it possibly because Natare, like the finest of rhetoricians, has at last tripped a hidden wire in Kenley's psyche, using his father as the weapon—and now suddenly makes beautiful sense?

As though sensing his ambivalence, Natare presses the point. "I always hoped I could make a black man outta you," he says to Kenley Jr. "I knew your head was fulla shit, but I still thought I could cure you. I don't know—was I wrong?"

*"Kenley! NOW!"*

It is the tone that does it—the tone that once preceded the cane. "No."

The other men stare at him. Neither is accustomed to losing his self-composure, and it is impossible to say who is more surprised.

Then Kenley Sr. speaks quietly, his tone that of a lawyer whose star witness has just deviated from the script. "Would you care to repeat that young man?"

"I said no. I want to stay here."

In all his fathering career, Kenley Sr. has never been disobeyed. He scrambles to adapt to this new territory, probing its dimensions, unsure how to respond. He buys himself some time, his manner unchanged. "You don't really mean that, do you?"

"I'm an adult now. I won't be ordered around."

"Kenley—" the voice is patient, condescending "—let me tell you something. Your grandfather raised me to show unqualified respect toward my elders, and that applies at any age. Your purpose at Columbia is to study. It's not to become a rebel."

*"Don't fucking tell me what my purpose is!"*

In the silence that follows he is already recoiling, his hands rushing to defend his face. He has no idea where those words came from, cannot trace the impetus for their delivery.

But Kenley Sr. does not strike. He regards his son not merely with anger, but also with an expression of almost childlike bereavement. He averts his gaze, as if acknowledging that the landscape of their relationship has irreversibly shifted. His subsequent disavowal of this change—his dogged recourse to habit—is all the more poignant to Kenley Jr., who has finally proven his father mortal. The aching regret that he feels is only compounded by his father's last-ditch attempt to save face.

"You're very lucky, my boy," says Kenley Sr., his voice almost catching—almost *catching!*—as he reaches for the doorknob; "you're very lucky that I'm not paying for you to be here, because I would withdraw that support immediately. You're also very lucky I don't *whup your sorry ass!*" He steps into the hallway and gives a final look back, his eyes damp. "I expect an apology from you. Very. Very. Soon."

The door slams, invoking a tentative silence.

Kenley regards the door, frowning. A dam has burst in the channels of his psyche: suddenly, fresh worlds have made themselves apparent, with startling and disorienting clarity.

He takes a deep breath, looks Natare in the eye. Natare approaches, his own gaze never wavering. There is a long pause during which neither of them blinks, and something passes between them.

Natare smiles, his eyes bright with passion. *"Brother . . ."*

But it wasn't that simple.

Though he sought to transform himself overnight, to imbue himself with racial consciousness—and he duly rechristened himself for the occasion—the man now called Prophet wasn't operating from conviction alone. He had succumbed not merely to black nationalism but to Gyeppi Natare as well, to the charisma of an enemy who would now be his friend—and to the sudden headiness of *inclusion.*

Yet there were difficulties. Four months later, his speech was still an uneasy amalgam of dialects as lifelong habits were undermined with diligent resolve. White English had been the language of his household; but swollen with his newfound blackness, or at least with Natare's idea of such, he felt certain that the long years of conditioning could be overcome. The trick was to keep among black people, where mimesis would come naturally. Since this was impossible in the physics department, or indeed anywhere outside his dorm except the janitor's lounge, he came to spend less time in the lab and more in his room, laboring through a crash course of black history that Natare had drawn up. For the first time in his life he was part of something larger than himself.

Thus politicized, he rediscovered the world from an entirely different perspective. Everything had a new context, and that context was simple: Black people had been the unwilling backbone of the New World since 1619. In a country wrought largely by themselves, they remained an oppressed subculture nearly five hundred years later. The Panthers were ancient history; the King revolution had been forced into retreat. But now, at the millennium's edge, African-Americans were issuing a new Emancipation Proclamation—one that they had drawn up themselves . . .

But there was still another problem.

Kenley's sexual orientation was not merely heterosexual: it was *white* heterosexual, and had been for as long as he could remember. He didn't find black girls unattractive per se; but since they tended to be equally dismissive of him at Shaker High (what with so many exquisites slam-dunking nearby), an inclination toward white girls had been fostered and then reinforced many times over.

In matters of the opposite sex, Kenley was not merely shy: he was a bona fide romantic. His cybergeek friends were always swift to download the latest electronic pornography, but Kenley's tastes were more subtle, more intimate. His masturbatory exertions were soulful, not lusty. His subjects were of cultured, European origin, and he lost himself amid caresses in formal gardens, on riverbank picnics, in lazy rowboat tanglings. The women wore long, elegant dresses. They shaded themselves beneath parasols and had delicate white hands. Their faces were smooth and soft, their eyes bright with Alpine lustre, and they moved to a soundtrack of nocturnes and arabesques. Give him the fleeting glimpse of a milky white calf, beneath a skirt casually disarranged, rather than the movie star who would sit on his face. Speaking of which: he had no patience for modern softcore, with its fool-the-eye montage and faux-noir lighting. He hated the stylish exaggeration, the curiously sleek inelegance. Hardcore was even worse: what could be more tedious than watching other people fucking? (No drama whatsoever: it was always the same, over and over again.) His favorite scenario, when using *Wish Theater* alone, was simply to scroll through dozens of still photographs of nude women in classic poses, often with the relevant areas concealed—not exactly typical of men his age, and consider this too: Prophet secretly hoped that his first lover would become his wife. He believed in *soul-mates*.

He dared not confess his sexual preference to Natare, who discouraged all interracial contact except when necessary. Yet among the women of Natare's circle Prophet found no relief. They liked him, admired him, respected him . . . and left it at that. The dynamics of attraction are impervious to such well-meaning human constructs as racial solidarity. Prophet was basically a dwarf genius, and not perceived in a sexual context.

Thus companionship, and not love, sustained him—plus of course the missionary zeal he was fast assuming. Members of Natare's clique spent long nights in Broadway cafes, where Gyeppi held court as crown prince. With the advent of racial pride came an almost self-conscious intransigence, by which Kenley's amiable demeanor of years past was gradually subsumed. His change of name, then, was all the more fitting: he had become an entirely different person, as had many others under Gyeppi's persuasion. In a culture founded upon white oppression, said Natare, an African man must manifest his blackness at all times. He must be a living symbol of defiance, refusing to be marginalized and mollified. He must remind the white man, at every opportunity, that he is living under active protest. Natare called this the Guerrilla's Uncompromising African Racialist Disposition, which was part of a larger program called Reinvention Immediately (Governmental, Historical, Theological). Its antithesis was the accommodationist mentality, which he called Willful Renouncement Of Nigga Greatness.

"The thing about white people," said Natare one evening, "is that they take everything for granted. They assume that the world's gonna keep going the way it is, that they can go to work every day and get paid and send their kids to college and everything'll be all right, like the whole Race Question'll just take care of itself. They think that black people ain't their problem, like all the old problems are dead and buried. They think the laws'll keep us in our place. They think we ain't got the strength to challenge the system. Well I'm tellin y'all issup to people like us to stand up and shout back at them: *Bullshit, man! B u l l — s h i t.*"

*　　*　　*

During high school, Prophet's worst illegal practice had involved using thousands of dollars' worth of telephone service without paying a cent. But now, feeling the need to impress his new friends—especially given his diminutive physique—he began to wreak havoc over the cellular airwaves. He raided the databases of Fortune 500 companies, sometimes altering data—giving the secretaries million-dollar salaries, for example, while reducing the CEO's pay to minimum wage—and sometimes crashing the systems entirely. He created fictitious bank accounts, especially in poor black neighborhoods, which Natare then "assigned" to an inner-city family in need. ("Fuck Karl Marx, man; we'll do the redistributing ourselves.") He accessed the financial records of celebrities and public officials and, using their credit card numbers, had vast amounts of junk delivered to their doorsteps.

One night in April, only a few weeks before finals, Natare shut the door to their room and asked Prophet, "How much can we trust you?"

Prophet, sitting at his desk, looked up in surprise. "Say what?"

Natare seated himself nearby. Usually he had the habit of propping his feet on his desk; but tonight he leaned forward, hands pressed together, elbows on knees, and regarded Prophet with an intent, almost critical gaze. "You good at keepin secrets?" he said.

Prophet shrugged. "I guess."

"Cause what I'm about to say," said Natare, "is not to leave this room. Understood?"

Aroused by Natare's formality, Prophet sat up in his chair. "What do you mean?"

"I'm sayin you don't repeat any of this. Not to anyone."

Despite the hardness of Gyeppi's tone, and despite the clichéd warning, Prophet's curiosity was piqued. He nodded.

"You haven't seen Karibu yet," Natare began, "but some day you will. Maybe you'll even think about living up there, because we can definitely use you."

"Sounds good to me," said Prophet.

"I been talkin to my father," Natare continued. "Fact I told him all about you. Told him how good you were with that computer, breakin and enterin and all that shit. My father has some ideas about that."

Prophet resettled himself, hoping to mask the delicate tendrils of anxiety suddenly creeping through his gut. "What do you mean?"

"Like I said, this is strickly between you and me." Natare's gaze bore into him. "I've told you before what my father's about. He's dedicated to the creation of a separate black and Native American country within the continental United States. Until that happens he's got Karibu, which is like a state within a state already. Now we're realistic about what the government might do for us and what it ain't never gonna do for us. There ain't no way in hell Uncle Sam's gonna give his colonies away, not without another civil war. So the question becomes, how far is my father prepared to go to realize the dream. Well, I can tell you—and now I'm getting into the shit you can't repeat—I can tell you he's prepared to go all the way. In time."

Prophet tried to ignore his steadily accelerating pulse. "All the way like how?"

"Take something like the IRA," said Natare. "You had these people who wanted to liberate their homeland from its colonial master. You had people who were not only political but into the military side of things too. Which has been our whole problem in this country. We got lots of words over here, but we got no action.

"Now you take something like Oklahoma. Couldn't happen here, they said. Yeah, right—you wanna know what my attitude was? *My* attitude was what the fuck *took* so long! Iss like we got this whole *country*, man, and it could all go off like a fuckin time bomb if only someone knew what they were doing! Half the fuckin population could be mixing explosives in their basements, because I'll tell you somethin man: the police can't watch everybody. America's just too fuckin *big*.

"So with Oklahoma: *Suddenly* you got everyone focused on the militia movement, the white supremacists. *Suddenly* everyone sees some dumb-ass redneck can pull this shit off and fuck the Palestinians. But four years later we *still* ain't got to the point where people think that *black* folks are about to do the same thing. You know why? I bet they think we're too stupid. I bet they think we couldn't even conceive of it."

Prophet swallowed, just managing to hold Natare's gaze. In the past few months there had been a lot of talk in the Black Student Union about revolution—talk and only talk. Natare's disciples would speak dreamily about the 1992 riots, and of how close the black community was to snapping yet again. They were particularly hopeful that the current trial of a white policeman, accused of killing an undercover black policeman by mistake, would spark further unrest if there was an acquittal. The black officer had been mistaken for a mugger; he had also been shot five times in the back.

Beyond the trial, however, the BSU had no concrete plans for the revolution they anticipated. They were not even on the same level, for example, as the Animal Liberation Front. The university administration, and not society at large, was their only immediate punching bag; and having a white professor fired for a slip of the tongue was beginning to lose its novelty.

Now Gyeppi was hinting at something beyond mere rhetoric. Prophet wondered how many others Gyeppi had given this speech to, this seeming rite of initiation. He wondered how many had passed.

"My father figured out the problem," Natare went on. "What keeps White America going is our fragmentation. He knew that black people have motivation enough to bring down a government. What they don't have is organization. They need strong leaders. They need a common purpose. They need a vision, a blueprint of how things *could* be if blacks were runnin the show. With Karibu, we finally have all that. The fun is just beginning."

70

Prophet tried to keep his voice steady. "What do you want me to do? Transfer money? Plant a virus at the Pentagon?"

Natare shook his head. "Nothin like that, least not yet. There's plenty of shit I can't get into right now, things you don't need to know about anyway. Plus I wanna break you in slowly. The point is, my father thinks—and I agree with him—that we can use technology to our advantage. So far he doesn't have too many people who can do the kinda shit you're doing, and he wants to develop more in that area. He's already got a whole PR division, but it's strickly legit. He's got lobbyists in Albany, lobbyists in Washington. But in the coming years we're gonna be takin a big step forward, and you know what the fight'll be about. I'm givin you a chance to be in on everything from the start."

"Yeah but I'm a hacker, Gyeppi," said Prophet, evading that last remark. "What's that got to do with PR?"

"It's got everything to do with it," replied Natare, "especially with what we got in mind. See, we need a better way of spreading information—or misinformation, to be precise. We need ways of flooding the media with propaganda without the source being traceable. I mean yeah, there's a million other things we could use you for, but my father's concerned about covering our ass every step of the way. Like I said, everything he's done up to now's been legit. His tax returns are totally legal, right down to the last cent. But if we keep fuckin around with money and databases we're opening ourselves up without getting what we need in return. What we do need is a link to the media that we can use to stir things up without Karibu being mentioned. We'll make up a name for some phoney black terrorist group instead."

"But what would the purpose be?"

"Same as any terrorism, man! Terror! Be like calling in bomb threats, only we'll use modems, not telephones. The trouble with the mail is the time lag—plus the materials can be traced. The problem with the phone is that you ain't got time to say anything. You gotta be off motherfuckin quick or you're gonna get traced again. With a remote fax-modem, we can keep the propaganda real constant and real detailed, too. We can create *myths,* only there'll be enough truth so we're taken seriously. The goal is to start makin everyday white people nervous. We wanna give em the sense that the Revolution could come any time, know what I'm sayin? The more scared they are, the happier we'll be. And this is just the

71

preliminary shit. This is just to say, Y'all can't sit all comfterble in your suburbs like we don't exist. Ain't no such thing as insulation. The fact is, their whole sense of security is a lie, man! They're wide open! What happened in LA was just *scratchin the surface.* If we get organized—if we think this shit through—how the hell they gonna stop us?"

Prophet sighed. "I'm not gettin something," he said quietly. "This propaganda stuff. I don't mind white people bein afraid, man, but I won't be responsible for them getting hurt. I don't mind feeding em lies, but they gotta stay lies. If I send in a bomb threat, there can't be no bomb."

Natare held up his hands. "What if I tell you there ain't no bomb?"

Prophet finally looked away. He became aware that he was shivering, and could not resist the impulse to hug himself. Jesus, he thought. What the fuck have I gotten myself into?

"Look," said Natare, leaning back in his seat. "I don't want you to feel pressured. You don't wanna do this, I ain't gonna ride you. All I'm sayin's that things are gonna start happenin like you wouldn't believe. I'm givin you a chance to be part of it. I'm givin you a chance to prove yourself. Cause the fact is, change ain't gonna come long as everybody's sittin around on their asses. It ain't gonna come from the boys on Capitol Hill. Everything's polarized now, and you gotta decide which side you're on. You got white conservatives who ain't never gonna help us. You got white liberals who can't even help themselves. You got black people who been co-opted and gotten used to the white man's life, and ain't no way they gonna rock the boat. So the time's come when you either drown or you get the fuck out the water. And I'll tell you something: at Karibu we look after our own. *Twenty thousand black folks* doin it all themselves, plus a few Indians too. That's how it could be, man. You help us now, I *guarantee* you'll have a job waiting for you after graduation."

Still Prophet hesitated, but Natare's tone became seductive.

"Tell you somethin else, man. The new country, it's still years away. I'll admit that. I ain't sayin change is gonna happen overnight. But with people like you helping us, it'll come that much quicker. You gotta do somethin for your people man, fore it's too late."

"Well," said Prophet, with the lightheaded abandon that comes with doing the forbidden, with knowing that one is about to make

72

a choice that will change one's life; "I mean shit, you put it like that how can I refuse?"

When the summer holidays approached he sent a letter to his parents informing them of his new identity, adding that he wouldn't be home for the summer. A black youth camp north of Oakland, loosely affiliated with Karibu, had offered him a position as a computer instructor.

In the meantime a plan was drawn up. At prescribed intervals he would upload his propaganda to various media and law enforcement organizations. Gyeppi would provide the basic facts that were to be transmitted; the wording would be up to him.

"Unity, purpose, and resolve," said Gyeppi, on the morning of Prophet's departure. "This is the real thing, man. The war is officially beginning."

\*     \*     \*

In his study overlooking the back lawn, Kenley Sr. folds the letter and gazes out at the spring rain. His wife sits nearby, watching him.

"Well?" she says at last.

He turns, gestures dismissively. "Don't worry," he says. "It'll pass."

# CHAPTER SIX

## *Of Bikers, Strip Joints, and the Collapse of Logical Positivism . . .*

Neither Prophet nor Fish was so liberated that he cared to sleep in the same bed as Dorian—an arrangement the latter accepted with equanimity. In fact, he could not be happier than spending the night on the couch, in front of the TV. How could he rest easy in the next room knowing that more pornography was his for the asking? He would toss and turn in bed, unable to sleep, imagining all the naked women he was missing, and like a Siren the television would beckon . . .

Once the others had gone to bed, he quietly ordered a movie from the hotel cable system. The decision was not easy: he bypassed the character-driven *Ursula: Heroine, Harlot and Husband* and *A Slut Named Nanscy Nugatory* before settling finally upon *Meow Mixx*, starring Raisa Rubel and Kara Krone, complete with star interviews and "The Making of . . ." appendix.

He'd finished both bottles of Scotch, and his head throbbed. He watched the film glassy-eyed, unable to feel aroused and yet incapable of turning off the television. The parade of silicon breasts, G-stringed bottoms, feigned orgasms, furrowing fingernails—they made not the slighest impression. It must be the Scotch, he thought. It was the only possible explanation, unless . . .

. . . Unless, after all this time, America was finally wearing him down.

To make matters worse, he had his recurring dream. Again.

He is in a hospital room, confined for what seems to be a chemical addiction. The attending woman is named Rachel. She materializes in his room one evening, seeking acid, which is absurd considering the environs. She sits smoking on his bed for a time, and they exchange curricula vitae. She is small and vacuous, spare of frame and sparer of intellect. She refers to herself as "screwy." She has never heard of Adolf Hitler. She is Jewish. After a time she gives him a long stare and meets his lips with hers. There follows a dry, tobacco-ridden kiss, the sort that muddies your saliva for days. She is gently aggressive, unhurriedly direct. When confronted with her breasts he squeezes uncertainly, as though testing fruit at a supermarket. Also, her nipples seem oddly protuberant: he has a momentary urge to hang things from them, like dry cleaning.

Moments later he is puzzling over her cunt. He rubs her pubic bone, expecting orgasm. His hand is promptly repositioned in the damp thicket below, where some quick palpations confirm the veracity of his old biology textbook. He considers the possibilities— probing, pinching, percussing—when Rachel speaks, causing him to jump. "Like this," she whispers, manipulating his hand. "I *know*," he replies, offended. "You think I haven't done this before?" (Off-hours he wondered how it was possible to dream of sensations he'd never experienced. Would they feel the same in real life? Were dreams a conduit to some vast Overmind?)

Time passes. Rachel squirms on the bed, running her hands over her breasts as though to compensate for his inadequacy. In fact he is thinking of a passage from Tennyson, about cruel immortality, when Rachel whispers something in his ear.

". . . What?"

"I want to make love with you," she repeated.

There it is—his passport to oneiric sexual maturity. He looks down at her. Her clothes are askew; her navel protrudes like a shriveled toe. The situation seems suddenly absurd, futile. What the fuck *is* this creature? Why the hell *bother*?

"Forget it," he says.

"Why not?" She feels demoralized, unlovely—he can tell from her pouty intonation.

"I can't," he says, trying to seem penitent. "I should have told you sooner, I know, and I'm sorry I led you on."

She stares at him. "What do you mean?"

In a thick, choking whisper: "I don't have a penis, Rachel. I'm a eunuch. Or maybe it's hermaphrodite, I'm not sure."

She sits up, agape. "You *what?*"

"Birth defect," he replies, crossing his legs to deter further inquiry. "I *really* should have told you earlier . . ."

She is buttoning her pants, smoothing down her shirt. "I don't believe this. You fucking pervert."

"It's just that I really like you, and——"

"Goddamned *freak*," she snaps, donning her jacket. "I'm such a fucking idiot. Fuck you. I mean *really fuck you.*" She exits and slams the door, leaving him to his cherished silence. And the upshot? He reaches between his legs, in contemplative regret. He has told her nothing more than the truth.

Upon waking, he never fails to scream.

\*     \*     \*

They wandered along back roads amid the hills, on this the second day of their journey. The paranormal heat blanketed the countryside with easy vigor, the asphalt shimmering brilliantly, the air rippling like space-time in collapse. Dusk found them heading south through deep woods, the last village miles behind them. Just as the darkness became complete they saw a light in the distance.

Garish neon sprang to life, a beacon that drew them out of the forest and into a dirt parking lot confronting a refurbished barn and a phalanx of Harley-Davidsons protecting its entrance. A blinking sign above the door proclaimed **Dusty's Funhouse**, beneath which lurked the hand-painted addendum **Live Girls Totaly Nude!** Lights glared from every window. A bass drum pulsed through the air.

"America," said Dorian cheerfully, turning off the engine. "Don't you love it."

"Why the fuck are we stopping?" snapped Prophet.

"Can't you *read*?"

"This might be dangerous," said Fish to Dorian.

"Nothing our brown bomber isn't equal to, I'm sure. Coming Prophet?" as he opened his door.

"Dorian," said Prophet, "I think this is goddamned insensitive of you. The last thing I need is—"

"Is a big bad biker with a fetish for black midgets?" He leaned in the car, assuming a poor inflection of Black English. "Ever had it rough, Booker T.? Can just picture it, some big-ass redneck comes along, shimmies outta them Levi's and you thinkin *Damn*, I thought white people's dicks was supposed to be *small*—"

"Man shut the fuck up." Prophet shouldered his door open, stepped out. "Think you can get a rise outta me well forget it. Let's go." He began walking toward the barn.

They ran to catch up. "You're sure about this?" said Fish. "I mean Dorian, we shouldn't make—"

"No no no!" Prophet held up his hands. "Dorian thinks I'm scared, right? Bullshit. I'm gonna exercise my God-given right to go wherever the fuck I want."

"And we do have that gun," mused Fish, as they reached the front door.

They entered a throbbing, smoky egress. Directly ahead of them was the bar, each seat occupied by a bearded, simian hulk who sprawled on his stool as though containing it from escape. Black T-shirts were stretched over rolls of fat which hung loosely under gravity's thumb. To the left stood three pool tables, where further hominids were standing at ease. To the right lay a series of benches, all occupied, beyond which rose a narrow stage with two proscenia. At the end of each stood a tall metal pole, and clutching each pole swayed a human female.

The first was short and white, her face concealed by an umbrageous clot of yellow hair. A lattice of silverine glitter covered her diminutive breasts, obscuring her nipples. She still wore her bikini, which clove her buttocks like dental floss. As if to augment this distinction, she pressed her backside against the pole and began scouring her anus.

The other dancer was a Native American, six feet tall, perhaps three hundred pounds, with breasts that might have nurtured a famished country to health. She wore a crimson bikini with a matching brassiere of industrial utility. Her face was pewterized by glossy makeup; a shawl of dark hair reached nearly to the floor, oscillating in slow-motion like kelp in the tide. She lacked skill—she merely heaved to and fro, grinning stupidly—but she was certainly the crowd favorite. Each movement of her legs initiated a cascade of repercussions as fat roiled in on itself, suggesting the rough-and-tumble frenzy of pigs queueing up at a trough. Her belly spilled over the waistband of her bikini and threatened, once that article was removed, to obscure her pudendum altogether.

"I love it!" cried Dorian, clapping his hands.

Their arrival had attracted a few glances, and it was Fish rather than Prophet who received the most scrutiny; but if anything the bikers seemed amused by his priestly attire. Prophet stared round defiantly, holding every gaze he met, and was somewhat disappointed to find no challenges. The bikers were mellow with drink, and disinclined to stir: the motherlode of attention was devoted to the women onstage, who were now slithering against each other like connubial vipers.

Dorian nudged them toward the bar. As they turned, a young woman entered the room. Apparently she was a greater stimulus than the travelers: all heads pivoted immediately, and forget about mellow.

The newcomer was no indigene: her face betrayed no recognition of her surroundings. She wore a flowered green peasant dress and her bare arms, though thin, were toned and sleek. Her dark hair was pushed back from her forehead, revealing a widow's peak and startling grey eyes. Society would have labeled her merely attractive, and not beautiful—her mouth was rather narrow, her face a bit too round—but there was an immediacy to her presence, a grace and surety of carriage that Dorian found arresting. Both wisdom and naivete were juxtaposed in her features: she might have been fifteen or she might have been thirty. Dorian glanced at Prophet and Fish, and saw that they too were riveted.

The bikers were dumbstruck; the dancers had lost their audience. Even they were now peering out into the haze, swaying only by habit as they sought the reason for the distraction.

Only the briefest uncertainty flickered in the woman's eyes. She pushed toward the bar, wincing from the smoke, her chin held high. The bikers charted her progress with mounting interest. As she reached the bar she wedged herself between two long-haired gorillas and leaned over the counter to speak to the barman.

Greying, bespectacled, but otherwise an enantiomorph of his patrons, the publican appraised her for a long moment, eyes narrowed as though confronting some riddle. He reached unhurriedly beneath the bar and produced a black rotary-style phone, which he set on the counter. Sandwiched and grimacing, the woman picked up the receiver and began rummaging through a small black wallet.

The biker to her left, in smirking collusion with his peers, reached down and grasped her rear end. It was no quick squeeze: his fingers sought and gained leverage and he pressed her further against the bar. She did not respond to the transgression, but grimly withdrew a card from her wallet and cleared the line. Holding the card in front of her, she cradled the phone between cheek and shoulder and dialed.

The biker's hand, meanwhile, remained firmly attached to its prey. His lower lip was smothered behind his teeth as he palpated his bounty and flashed a *how bout this, guys?* look to his comrades, his eyebrows flicking up and down. He seemed to derive encouragement from them, for in the next moment his other hand chanced a slinking advance up her belly.

Immediately the woman twisted in his grasp and brought the receiver hard against his left ear. As he recoiled, she jabbed two fingers into his sunken blue eyes and drove her elbow into his nose. He sagged backward into the lap of a colleague, while the biker originally to her right—now behind her—snaked an arm under her chin. She grabbed his elbow and shoulder and executed a perfect hip-throw. He tumbled to the floor and she stomped on his neck.

She made a run for the door. The travelers, startled into action, moved to cover her retreat. Dorian had never been so afraid in his life, but adrenaline was mitigating his fear and he felt prepared for anything. As two bikers intercepted the woman, she met the first with a thrust-kick to his kneecap (there was a distinct crack, followed by keening) and the second with a punch to the throat, adding a chop to the temple as he fell. Then she was out the door, and the travelers were crowding the exit behind her.

"This way!" yelled Fish, running past her toward the Mustang.

She slowed, staring at him in confusion. Dorian read the look—she had no idea who they were, or if they could be trusted. But then a vanguard of bikers emerged from the barn, some wielding pool cues.

"Come on!" Dorian snapped, pulling her wrist. She allowed herself to be led to the car, where Prophet had leaped into the front seat and Fish was pulling the Kalashnikov from the trunk.

"Start the car," he said as they rushed up. "I'll hold em."

As Dorian gunned the engine and the woman slipped into the back seat, Fish took aim at the gathering swell of men who bristled not twenty feet away.

"Don't move," he advised them, as Dorian backed the car from its space. Without averting his gaze, Fish sidled along the flank of the car until he could swing his leg over and clamber into the back seat.

"Be good, my sons," he called as the car pulled away. "Duty calls . . ."

"Can we put the top up?" said the woman. "I'm a little cold."

When they were safely enclosed, Dorian asked, "What's your name?"

"Lucky," she replied. "And don't ask why, OK? It's kind of personal."

"Of course," said Dorian, modulating his voice poshly. "We're used to that sort of thing anyway." He introduced himself and his two companions. "So what brought you to that cultural mecca?"

"My car was acting up, so I got off the freeway to look for a gas station," she said. "Pretty soon I was lost, and then the car broke down completely. It's about another mile ahead; I walked all the way back." She pushed her hair out of her eyes. "Thanks a lot, all of you. Things got kind of scary back there."

"Barbarians," said Dorian agreeably. "Why, we ourselves only stopped to ask for directions. Anyway, you seemed to acquit yourself rather well. I don't think you needed us at all."

"I'm up," said Prophet. "Was that kung fu or something?"

"Karate, actually—Okinawan *Goju*." She turned to Fish. "So is everyone in the clergy packing these days, or what?"

"Don't ask," Prophet interjected. "It's kind of personal."

"Fair enough." She smiled. "Anyway here it is, coming up on the right."

The men gawked as they passed a silver Bentley skulking at the roadside. Nonplussed, Dorian pulled over and executed a sharp U-turn. He trained the headlights on her car and stopped a few feet away.

The Bentley—a '93 Turbo, Dorian noted—was exquisitely battered, its carapace covered with rust. Something black was dripping underneath. A door handle was missing. He glanced at Lucky, wondering how directly he might question her without seeming rude. He asked, "Are you filthy rich or something?"

Fish snorted in protest, but Lucky was already laughing as she opened the driver's door and climbed in. "It was a gift from my mother, actually. She's the rich one. The reason it looks like shit is cause I drove it as a gypsy cab in New York and parked it on the street to boot. That should tell you how rich I am."

"You were a cab driver," said Prophet wonderingly, "in *this*?"

"'93 to '97. I probably should have sold it and just gone to college or something, but I just couldn't part with it. I was hoping it would last until California." She released the hood. Dorian propped it open and surveyed the innards. The belts were worn, the lines frayed, the battery garnished by coagulating gunk. He felt stirrings of hope.

80

"Try to start it," he called.

The car gave an anemic cough, and sputtered hoarsely without catching.

"Try your lights."

She did, but they were so dim as to be virtually unnoticeable.

Dorian closed the hood. "Your alternator's shot," he said. "I should think it'll be impossible to get it replaced tonight, and to be honest a few other things might give way at any moment. I'm afraid this car's history."

She leaned her forehead against the steering wheel. "I don't believe this," she muttered.

"Don't worry, all's not lost," Dorian continued brightly. "We can drive you anywhere you like tonight, and as for tomorrow—" he shrugged "—we're going to California as well. You're more than welcome to join us."

"Thanks, but I'd rather not," she replied, emerging from the car. She circled it a few times, but her thoughts seemed elsewhere. "You really think there's no hope?"

"I'm certain of it," Dorian lied, undeterred. "This battery's hopeless, and the radiator has seen better years. Why are you going to California, if I might ask?"

"My mother's dying. I'm going home."

"Ah, I *see*. Well in *that* case," said Dorian gravely, "I insist you come with us. It'll be no trouble at all, I assure you."

She glanced at him. "You mean just leave it here?"

"Why not? Eventually someone'll collect it and sell it for scrap. Of course, if the two of you need some time alone . . ."

He watched as she wrestled with herself. Now that the adrenaline had gone—now that she realized she might have to accompany them for longer than expected—she appraised them for the first time as if she'd stepped into somebody else's dream, this incongruous trio every bit as inexplicable as a ruined Bentley. (Because let's face it: you don't usually see a Bentley fit for last rites, at least no more often than you are rescued from a strip joint by a black nationalist, Welsh faux-toff bisexual, and schizophrenic excommunicated Jewish priest with a machine gun.) Indeed, she looked among them— the fop, the friar, the freedom fighter—with such genuine incredulity that Dorian's cheeks began to scald. "We're only students at Columbia," he added, a bit defensively. "I mean there's no need for you to worry."

She measured the silence deliberately, holding his gaze. "Or you," she said. "Yet."

They drove until they reached the next village, stopping finally at a Victorian house with a **Bed & Breakfast** sign posted on the front lawn. The ancient landlady, nostrils flaring at the sight of Prophet, blinked at them for a good half-minute as Dorian offered to double and then treble her price. Only when Lucky asked for a separate bedroom did she finally let them in.

"She feared an orgy, perhaps," said Dorian hopefully as he reached in the car for Lucky's baggage.

"I can manage, Dorian," she answered, shoving him aside. "And no, that wasn't funny."

When Lucky had been installed in her room, the men lost no time in running outside to the backyard, from which they could see her second-floor window. A maple tree grew within twenty feet of the house, its canopy spreading out over the roof. Dorian appraised both house and tree, whose lowest branches were a foot beyond his reach.

"Right," he said. "Give me a boost."

"Wait a minute," said Prophet. "I'm the smallest. I should go first."

"Prophet, I wouldn't miss this for a map to El Dorado Christ *look*!" Another light had declared itself, revealing the tiled walls of a bathroom. "She's taking a shower!" He leaped upward, scrabbling at the trunk in a sciurine fit.

"She might just be brushing her teeth," said Fish.

"Or taking a piss," said Prophet.

"I'd consider it an honor to witness that girl's micturition. Now Fish you just stand right there, up against the trunk." He urged his companion face-first into the tree and lunged upward, eliciting a howl. As he pulled himself astride the branch he experienced a brief recollection of childhood: he hadn't climbed a tree in ten years, and had forgotten how much fun it was.

He moved to the next branch, which passed within five feet of the house. He edged himself forward, intent upon that window, not even a lace curtain to obstruct his view as he drew abreast in time to see the opaque shower curtain close, concealing a pale figure just beyond. He felt his pulse skittering along the length of his penis, and the tingling that warned of approaching climax.

"Well?" called Prophet.

He could not reply: he was struggling furiously to discern the barest of features. But her shape was amorphous, indistinct, with not even an inky blot of pubic hair for a dividend.

"Stay there Fish, I'm going up," said Prophet.

A gradual accrescence of steam on the window began to obscure Dorian's view, provoking muttered obscenities as he leaned outward, fingers extended toward the glass. The condensation was of course on the inside: his fingers rubbed to no reward, and her image was soon lost to him.

"What's up?"

He turned to see Prophet lurking five feet below, robes hanging beneath the branch like sheets out to dry.

"I've got to open this window."

"Not sure that's a good idea hey Fish, the fuck you get up here?"

"Levitation," said Fish, perched just below Prophet, his own robes dangling in nice black counterpoint. "I waited until you weren't looking. Dorian . . . ?"

"This is intolerable," opined the Welshman, swiping at the window.

"I hope the landlady's asleep," said Prophet.

Suddenly Dorian's weight shifted and he fell from the branch. His arms shot out, grabbing the branch by the tiniest of margins. He hung there like a beleaguered gymnast.

"Fuck," said Prophet. "All right, all right, just hold on man, hold on . . ." He pulled himself higher along the branch.

Dorian felt his life slipping through his fingers. The drop, though only fifteen feet, seemed halfway to forever. Instinctively he kicked at the bathroom window; the lower panel disintegrated, and broken glass snickered on the floor inside. He released the branch and grabbed the sill as he fell. Time paused as an ominous swell of repercussion began to suggest itself in the theoretical distance.

Gasping, Dorian pulled himself high enough to rest his elbows on the sill; high enough to peer into the bathroom and behold Lucky perched naked on the toilet, a towel wrapped around her head like a turban, hands rushing to cover her breasts a millisecond before he would have registered their nipples. In another fluid movement she crossed her legs, leaving visible only the glabrous plane of her abdomen with a sweet intimation of the treasure below.

He suffered a cruel moment of recognition (a quick replay hoping for different results, but no—he had seen nothing) as he pondered how close he'd come to glimpsing a naked woman, the weight of his predicament now heavy.

"Er . . . help?" he ventured.

He was answered by a pounding on the door and an elderly female voice. "Hello? Is everything all right?"

"Fine," Lucky called, her eyes meeting Dorian's. "I just broke a glass."

"Do you need any help?"

"No it's all right, everything's fine. Thank you."

"Lucky . . . ?"

"Well Dorian. Just look at you."

"Yes I can explain but please, I can't hold myself up much longer. Will you help me in?"

"Well that could be a problem Dorian. I'm in the middle of a nice plump shit."

"I promise I won't look, I'll keep my eyes closed—"

"I'm afraid I can't trust you Dorian, and anyway it's beside the point."

"Lucky I, I'm bleeding?"

"I know the feeling. Goodbye, Dorian. Just remember to roll when you hit the ground, OK?"

He felt himself slipping and prepared to die.

"Oh, and one more thing," she said, as piecemeal he slipped from view. "If you have any designs on me you should spare yourself the effort. I'm a lesbian, Dorian, and nothing you do can change that." She smiled sweetly, and gave a little wave of her fingers as he fell to earth with a scream.

In the men's room, Dorian lay moaning on his bed while Prophet tapped at his computer, Fish peering over his shoulder:

### FOR IMMEDIATE RELEASE

**African Fist! leaders met today in an undisclosed location in New York City, promising to remove all whites from government by the year 2005.**

**"If you're white, forget about it," suggested one spokeswoman, who goes by the name of Mama Bantu. "We've got other plans for you."**

**The black nationalist movement, almost Masonic in its secrecy,**

84

**is estimated to have 40,000 members in the US. When reached for comment, a senior FBI official, speaking on condition of anonymity, said that the Bureau took the threat quite seriously and did not rule out the possibility of a racial war.**

"Is there cable on that TV?" asked Prophet, as the fax was sent to the usual targets.

Their room featured antique wooden beds and natural pine floors. There was also a fireplace opposite the beds with a series of old hardbound volumes decorating its mantel. A decanter of brandy had been placed on the bedside table. The television was a console unit from the '70s, housed in a large walnut cabinet with sliding doors.

Dorian, after disposing of the brandy, had spent half an hour in the bathroom picking his way through the broken glass (which Lucky, hardly the cause of the accident, had left untouched) and examining his wounds. He was uninjured except for a small cut on the heel of his palm. Rummaging through the medicine cabinet, he came upon a roll of gauze and cut off a three-foot strip.

He surveyed the damage. He hadn't seen any other guests that evening, and he was fairly certain the landlady had her own bathroom. Such being the case, he left the shards as they lay. On the way back to the bedroom he considered visiting Lucky and showing off his wound to gain her sympathy. He paused in the creaky, deserted hallway and knelt at her door, peering through the keyhole. Evidently she'd gone to bed, for the room was in darkness. Then, abruptly, the door shook from a blow delivered to its other side. His forehead smarting from the impact, Dorian fell back on his ass, stunned. "Good *night* Dorian . . ." sang a voice behind the door.

Now he was lying on his bed, suffused with resentment and self-pity. Tonight it was he who wanted to sleep, and the others who were wide awake. Sighing, he considered possible outlets for his misery. "Can I use that computer?" he asked.

"For what?" said Prophet as Fish clicked on the television.

"I want to join that national dating service."

"What about Lucky?" gibed Fish as the image of a uniformed security guard standing next to a Doberman pinscher filled the screen, advising his audience that for $99.95 they too could own a SafeBoy® Trained Assault Hound. **Remember**, he concluded somberly. **Support your local police dog.**

"Turn it to CNN," said Prophet, calling up *The TruLuv Network* on

85

his modem. "Who should we bill this to? The Secretary of Defense?"

"Whoever," said Dorian wearily, as a man in a white coat grinned from the screen, reminding his audience that phalloplasties were now a one-day outpatient procedure and acceptable under most insurance policies.

"That's my father!" Fish breathed, just before the image yielded to a bearded young lumberjack named Dave who confided belligerently that he had once been known as Davina.

"Your father makes artificial *dicks?*" said Prophet.

"Yeah that's his clinic there, Scarsdale Cosmetic Arts. I didn't know he'd gone national."

"What, you ain't talked to him lately?"

"Not for a year."

"Well," Prophet shrugged, "me neither."

Meanwhile, Dorian typed:

*Hindu exile, 45, never toilet-trained, seeks wart-ridden GWF, any age, for joint suicide in Madrid.*

and pressed **SEND**.

"Yo yo check it out there it is!" Prophet exclaimed, pointing to the pug face of New York City Police Commissioner Russell Chunk, who was addressing a press conference, declaring that while neither the police nor the FBI had any data on African Fist!, in light of racial crises in New York and five other cities following yesterday afternoon's acquittal of a white policeman in the shooting of an undercover black colleague, an investigation had been launched into the threats against three Manhattan landmarks.

He was then supplanted by a pallid anchorwoman with a haunted expression, herself a mere prelude to the image of toothy mongrels and teeming rats gnawing busily at several dozen off-white bodies on what appeared to be a major urban boulevard.

"The Revolution's comin y'all!" said Prophet, clapping his hands. "Looks like we got outta New York just in time."

*Celibate male, 29, seeks barren, vengeful widow for scientific research. Reasonable fees.* **[SEND]**

"I'm gonna be famous baby!"

"Unbelievable," said Fish, watching a plump Caucasian man in a dark suit holding a handkerchief over his face while a black man in similar attire pointed to a neat row of corpses in what appeared to be a school gymnasium and impromptu mortuary. "The verdict must have come in like right after we left Manhattan. I should've paid more attention to the news last night, I mean the whole thing didn't even register."

*ME: Kindly, malnourished, 60. YOU: Mulish, tentative, 16.* [SEND]

"Shit's fucked up," said Prophet, "but you can't say them scarecrows didn't have it coming. Still, I'm glad I can do my bit for the cause without anyone getting hurt, know what I'm sayin Goggles?"

**The President met with City Council members later today in a closed-door session, but not before telling reporters that additional National Guard units would be—**

"Can I help with the next one?" asked Fish.
"You got it baby. Know somethin, I think I found my calling," said Prophet, as the camera panned across a courtroom and settled upon a sullen young white man on the witness stand.

*Syphilitic dwarf, 13, playful and recalcitrant, willing to provide stool sample for that Special Someone.* [SEND]

**Are you saying Mr. Oven that you killed Lucy de Kornbluth because she was *ugly*?**
**Yeah.**
**That upon looking her in the eye you experienced flu-like symptoms?**
**Yeah.**
**And did these symptoms also include chest pains?**
**That's right.**
**And is it true that you were certain you were going to die?**
**S'what it felt like to me.**
**That in fact when you attacked Lucy de Kornbluth you were acting in self-defense, trying desperately to prevent a heart attack?**

Yeah.
Mr. Oven, have you ever consulted a psychiatrist?
Yeah, I talked to one.
Did he seemed surprised by your story?
Nope. Said he'd seen a lotta cases like mine.
Did he refer to your condition by name?
What?
Did he have a name for what you were suffering from?
Oh. Yeah. Yeah, he said it was called—it was—uh—
Was it called Aesthetic Malignant Syndrome?
. . . Yeah.

*Arab gentleman, 37, former head of state and jihad veteran, now working as county coroner, seeks four to six SJF, 14–18, for solace between autopsies. Remember: formaldehyde is an aphrodisiac. I want to bathe you in it and lick you clean.* **[SEND]**

"Found your dream woman yet Dorian?"
"What are the chances," said Dorian, looking up, "what are the chances that she'll take another shower before we leave here?"

# CHAPTER SEVEN

## *Trends Among the Heterosexual; or,*
## *The Lawyer's Last Gasp . . .*

I put down my pen and stand. It's time to restore the circulation.

I am wearing long underwear, a tracksuit, a sweatshirt, two sweaters, a down-filled jacket, a ski hat (with pom-pom), and sheepskin utility gloves. I've also wrapped myself in every blanket I own. In this mobile cocoon I shamble back and forth with vague intentions of murdering the furnace repairman. I've left about twenty messages on his machine and heard not one fucking word in reply.

Professor Lank, before leaving for a faculty party next door, was kind enough to order a generous supply of wood and to start a fire in the library. Every cage and hutch has been relocated there; the other animals have put aside their differences and are huddling before the fireplace. I was in there earlier, snuggling with Ponce the armadillo, but found myself too distracted to write. Besides, there's not quite enough room for everybody, and I couldn't bear to see any of them freeze. Only Killjoy is absent. Lank bought a space heater for his room this morning, and it seems to be working well enough. In fact, the rats have been drawn to the heat and Killjoy has had his pick.

The other tenants in our brownstone are all young professionals, among whom the neighborhood has recently become popular. They tend to be entry-level kids just out of college, slogging through their first assistantships and struggling to pay off loans. On weekends they often return to their ancestral homes in Connecticut or Boston, as if still not fully weaned from the roost. Judging by the silence, they certainly haven't stuck around tonight.

I sometimes wish I'd gone into publishing, though in fact there can be no worse profession for a struggling writer. Still, we all compromise ourselves in one way or another, and my presiding over the slow death of literature might have been worth a steady paycheck and decent health insurance. In a few years I'd be a full editor with a list of my own. I'd take agents to lunch and bring manuscripts home to read, my life neatly ordered. (How old I sound. One paid fuck is all it takes; the *Weltanschauung* is never the same.) I might have met someone I could love, and in due course become a *wife and mother*. I might have become an editorial director. I might have had a life.

But such was not my destiny ... I have left the main body of the race and divagated along the dead-end streets of Iconoclasm. Aside from the tedium, there is only one difficulty in achieving success in the mainstream world: kissing ass. If you can kiss ass—something I am congenitally incapable of, thank god—the rest comes easy.

Iconoclasm, on the other hand, is exhausting. Iconoclasm requires vigilance, energy, perseverance. How easy it would be to surrender to the mainstream pull. The occasional rapids are hazardous but navigable. The direction is predetermined; all you have to do is stay the course. *Provided you can kiss that ass.*

How different it is on the banks, in the wilderness that grows at the water's edge. Paths are infrequent, compasses faulty, maps deceptive. Never mind Success: I haven't even found Love, and my profession rubbed salt into the wound. Never mind whether I've been worshiped or abused: carnal attentions, whether servile or combative, are always pathetic in the end, and only love provides redemption. With love, I could forgive a man his weaknesses. With love, I could also forgive my own. But I have never loved, and each session was merely a cruel intimation of what eluded me. The greatest loneliness you can experience, in my opinion, comes in the aftermath of fucking someone you don't love. I hate the man. I hate myself. And I need that hatred like you wouldn't believe, because it's all that sustains me.

Do I contradict myself? Very well then, I contradict myself.

I'm glad I live in this big apartment with its many rooms. I would hate to live in the cubicles known as *studios*, which is a ridiculous misnomer. Is some sort of art practiced in these studios? the art of fucking, perhaps? I think not. Fucking is a science, not an art: it is mechanical and measurable. Love, however—love is an art, and will remain so until the neurobiologists have completed its deconstruction.

*       *       *

Allow me a few observations about the men whom I once called clients—a sociological aside, if you will, to be followed by some hard evidence.

There is no place where a man is more self-divulging than in bed. This openness is not necessarily verbal: the choice of activity, for example, reveals much in itself, as does the choice of position. I find it interesting, if unsurprising, that fucking—like food, art, clothes—is a matter of *taste.* Excepting the odd celibate or moron or Christian, we all agree that fucking is a worthwhile pursuit. Not that we all like it.

I speak of men for whom satiation is impossible, whose coitus is riddled with angst. Climax is no balm, instead triggering haggard outrage, as though the act of fucking, contrary to expectation, had not fulfilled its constitutional promise. As though it were having a laugh at their expense. I in turn became the receptacle for their frustrations, a sponge for their displaced anger. I used to have the urge, as some Hollywood mogul or Wall Street czar was kicking me around the room—I had the urge to ask, What *is* it with you? What the hell is going on? Had I done so, certain patterns might have emerged, and I might have related my findings in some journal of current opinion.

Even before the Incident—the Incident of my near-murder—I'd been growing worried. My sessions were rarely about good clean fun. They were rarely about good dirty fun. My sessions were more like judo, and rarely one passed in which blood wasn't drawn (better his than mine). The limits of bad taste were violated as a matter of course; indeed, the limits of *mortal* taste often seemed in jeopardy, during the headlong nympholeptic rush. Every angle was pursued, literally—upside down, inside out, back-to-front, all of them at once. I like to think that God—if he existed, which he doesn't—never had any of this in mind when he jacked off into the primordial soup and the first amino acids were formed; or when asexual reproduction lost its monopoly, thus creating the whole problem of gender. Procreation is supposed to be a straightforward business—why then all the trimmings? Where along the evolutionary boulevard did we begin to *elaborate?* For decades we have had entire industries devoted to sex, including movies and magazines and books and paraphernalia and eventually one feels compelled to ask, What the fuck? All *this* for the well-tempered orgasm? that fleeting, elusive moment? Is it because the real enemy is not abstinence but *boredom?*

91

The mechanics of reproduction are stale by third grade. Straight-forward, heterosexual intercourse is now a mere hebetic preamble to ever more sophisticated configurations. My theory, for what it's worth, is that we're seeking something *beyond* coitus. As children we run around the connubial baseball diamond, each successive base marking a further advance toward a home run, which of course is fucking. Today the home run no longer satisfies, so what then? Is that what's behind the anguish of these encounters? The quest for the base beyond home plate? the next plateau of thrills? Is sexual desire linear rather than cyclical, and therefore infinitely complex and progressive?

Let me introduce you to Baker Lewis. He was Protestant Good Family, a by-product of the Eastern ruling classes—or what passes for them in 1999, which is thankfully insubstantial. He was a partner in a white-shoe law firm, the sort that still manages to hold aloof from malpractice suits, personal injury claims, hostile takeover deals, criminal defense, and all the other lowbrow clutter that flourishes in our litigious republic. Baker had an attractive wife, a Sutton Place co-op, and a country house in Bedford. In other words, he didn't have much to complain about.

Our encounters usually took place in hotels, often in the middle of the day. Baker was fond of the Carlyle, though occasionally we slummed in the Westbury or Sherry Netherland. He was always tightly wound, and spent most of his time rambling about his problems (frigid wife, frigid secretary, the burden of being white and rich) and hitting me. He had the habit of delivering three or four sentences, which often concluded tragically—say, a female associate filing harassment charges—and then pummeling me to seek relief. There was sex, obviously, but the sex always felt hesitant, complicated, as if Baker wasn't sure of himself or was thinking about something altogether different. Then he'd gather his faculties and hit me again.

All this to say nothing of the varieties in which Baker sought relief. Shortchanged by conventional sexual practices, Baker was always concocting new scenarios in which to enhance his pleasure. On one occasion he bought a pair of sheepdog costumes, and we hopped around on all fours in tribute to animal passion. On another, Baker hired Cornell Bodleian's stud supreme, one Adamo Rogaine, convinced that a bisexual threesome would reward him with bliss. After one glance at Adamo's lunch-box ("My god, he's hung like a *rhino*") Baker decided to initiate himself more gently, and produced a carrot for the purpose. I fed the vegetable into his rectum, seeking his prostate. Not only was Baker unaroused; not only did he look ridiculous with the leafy green top waving insouciantly from his anus; but the carrot broke in half as I was trying to withdraw it. Half an hour's maneuvering with some pliers proved fruitless, obliging Baker to consume a bottle of laxatives and wait grimly for the exodus. On a third occasion, searching for yet another X-factor, Baker insisted upon sex in a public place—i.e., the A train at two in the morning—which resulted in coitus interruptus by a posse of homeboys and the loss of our valuables.

Now for the twist. Actually there are two or three.

We are lying, this spring Tuesday morning, in the master bedroom of Baker's Sutton Place duplex. Conventional wisdom would suggest that Baker's wife is elsewhere, perhaps out of town. On the contrary, she is downstairs in the kitchen, cooking us breakfast.

He lies on his back, glaring at the ceiling. A hand slips beneath the ivory sheet, followed by the noise of sandpaper on wood. Baker is scratching his balls.

"This is getting old, Venus, really fucking old," he says, picking his nose with the other hand. (Baker, incidentally, hates to be perceived as a Wall Street stiff, and spends many a futile cliché attempting to be hip.) "I think it's time we took a long hard look at where this relationship is heading, don't you?"

I've been trying to find a way to escape this breakfast.

"I mean it just can't go on like this," he continues, flicking snot across the room.

"Would you like someone else, Baker?" (After last night, I think it best that I never see this man again. I don't need him—or do I? Why do I put up with this? Why haven't I told Baker to take a flying fuck at a rolling—no, I think a rolling Lifesaver would be more his scale.)

He gives me an odd glance, as if noticing me for the first time. "What? Christ *no*, I mean what I'll have to do is leave my wife."

Ah. Not that.

"Nah, that wouldn't be any good," he says, grimacing, as prayers of gratitude spring to my lips. "Maybe—maybe we'll just have to get rid of her. You remember what I said last night, about murder?"

Oh *that* ... I measure the distance to the door—about twenty feet. I might even be able to retrieve my dress along the way. "What do you mean?"

"Chop chop, dice dice, my wife in the East River, all very nice?" He gives a self-appreciative snort.

"Baker——" I try to sound reassuring but admonitory "——it's been done in the movies."

"Everything's been done in the fucking movies!" he snaps. "There's not an original goddamn thought in the world. Not a single fucking one. Tell me——am I right?"

He has a point. Life rather has been preempted by Hollywood. Simply existing is a cliché; it has all been done before, in every possible combination, and the resale value is not very high.

"I'm taking a shower," he says, clambering out of bed. "You think about it, let me know what you come up with."

As I dress, I consider the events of the previous evening. Baker invited me to Sutton Place "on the spur of the moment," assuring me that his wife was visiting relatives in Newport. When I arrived, about nine o'clock, I discovered that he had lied. Baker's wife——a small, thirtyish brunette——was in fact trussed to a folding chair in the living room, and naked in the bargain. She charted my arrival with wide eyes, which contained a fear I'd never seen in my life.

The room had been decorated with perhaps two dozen white candles, each alight. The furniture had been banished to the perimeter, leaving an open space in the middle where Baker had spray-painted a red pentagram on the white carpeting. Lugubrious brass tones issued from the stereo speakers——Berlioz, I learned later. The curtains had been drawn.

Baker himself was dressed in a black cape and nothing else—— quite chic for a Wall Street lawyer, especially when coupled with his black lipstick. He carried a quarter-staff with a polished brass handle. His blond hair had been slicked back for the occasion, giving full emphasis to his long, narrow face. I think Baker had the smallest mouth of any person I've ever met, male or female. His lips were only fleeting deviations from the rest of his skin, tiny slivers of pink that were invariably dry and stubbly, just like his chin. His teeth were small as well: they reminded me of shoe-peg corn.

Baker had instructed me to wear a black evening gown with nothing underneath. I admit such configurations arouse me——the draughty feeling between my legs, the rustle of silk against my

94

pubis. For Baker it was merely a convenience: he hated impediments, and thus prohibited underwear.

"My dear," he called above the music. "I don't believe you've met Raina."

Seeing her bound like that sent a chill through my body, but I was too dumbstruck to act. Instead I remained frozen, groping for comprehension. The music bleated doomfully in fixed intervals, sounding like a death march.

"I thought we'd do a little role-playing tonight," Baker announced. "I'm going to be the blue-eyed devil. Venus, I want you to stand in the middle of the room. Oh, and take off your shoes."

I did as he asked. Even with candles alone the room was brightly lit, and Baker seemed abruptly displeased by this realization. He strode among them and extinguished more than half, carefully gauging the effect, until the level of illumination conformed with his wishes. The room was now much dimmer, and the paintings flickered hideously on the walls. Baker produced an athame, or ceremonial dagger, with which he severed Raina's bonds. Tentatively she rubbed her chafed wrists, reacclimating to the notion of freedom.

"All right. Now Raina, I want you to join Venus in the center," Baker continued, prodding her in my direction. "Go on, move."

Raina did not look at me as she stepped forward. Her eyes were large and brown, her body thin and bony, her lavish hair all the more pathetic in its disarray. Her face was newly bruised. She must have fought him earlier as he tied her to the chair, and clearly she had nothing left to give. She stopped a few feet away and turned to face him. Baker, meanwhile, had taken her chair to the end of the room, assuming the air of critical observer. He might have been conducting an audition.

"Now," he said, clapping his hands. "Fuck each other."

I glanced at Raina, whose eyes were downcast, and returned my gaze to Baker. He opened his palms expectantly.

"I said, f u c k  e a c h  o t h e r."

"Baker," I said, "I didn't come here to . . ."

He was striding forward, the chair clattering to the floor. Before I could react he swung the quarter-staff, striking my ribs. My knees buckled at the pain, but Baker wasn't appeased. He belted me across the face; I hit the floor. I was partially dazed and unable to move, but he grabbed my hair and yanked me to my feet, supporting me until I regained my balance. Those frigid blue eyes bore into me, incapable of remorse. "You listen to me the first time, got it?" he said, jabbing the staff under my chin so that my eyes met his. "Now. Fuck each other." He retreated to his chair, adding, "And don't look so goddamn hangdog. I want you to look like you're enjoying yourselves, OK? Try to have some *fun*."

A normal woman would have cried at that moment, but I felt strangely exhilarated. There is something powerful about witnessing an act of futility, especially if one is the object in question. I often fed on Baker's rage, absorbed it with a sense of mockery. The more he hit me—the more his anger grew—the stronger I became. I felt as if I contained the key to his salvation, and that his contortions were classic Sisyphus: he'd fuck me and beat me and fuck me again, only to finish right where he'd started.

But tonight there was an innocent bystander to think about ... Raina was trembling as I took her in my arms, her skin cold and smooth. "Don't worry," I whispered. "We'll get through this together, OK? Just go through the motions."

The Berlioz droned on. I kissed her the way a lover might, so much did I want to comfort her. Baker straddled his chair, its back end forward, resting his chin upon his arms and directing us with his quarter-staff. He watched us keenly, judgementally, like a director intent upon catching that perfect take. Of what did it consist?

I had never slept with a woman before, and this wasn't the best inauguration. She followed my lead, kissing half-heartedly, and I found myself wondering who she was and how she had ended up with Baker Lewis. The familiar stuff, I supposed: he wasn't always like this, he was under a lot of stress, their parents had arranged the whole thing. There I was, many years her junior, a hired whore, protecting her from her own husband.

"Shed the dress, Venus," ordered Baker.

As the gown slipped to the floor Raina averted her eyes, shying away from the brush of my nipples against her arm. Baker sprang to his feet, and only the threat of his advance compelled her to face me again, her eyes now luminous with tears. I held her wrist, drew her gently to the floor. The trombones lowed on in their death hymn. "Help me, Raina," I whispered as I began circling her labia. "And let me help you."

Abruptly the music ceased. I glanced at Baker.

"No no no, don't stop," he said, waving me on. "I find this all very fascinating. The fact is, Venus, in our six years of marriage my wife has yet to have a single orgasm. We've gone to every specialist in Manhattan and no one can find a thing wrong with her. Isn't that right old girl?"

I felt Raina trembling again. She was not going to last much longer. I began direct stimulation, hoping somehow to distract her.

"Being the sensitive guy I am," Baker continued, "I got so over-come with guilt that I stopped having sex with my wife. Why should I put her through the trauma if she can't enjoy it? Raina thinks I'm being cruel, but the truth is I'm doing this all for her. Plus, I have this little theory I want to test."

I had established a rhythm now. Surprisingly, she parted her legs a bit wider, making it easier.

"Let me tell you something Venus," Baker went on. "For years all I've been hearing is women's lib this, women's lib that. Sexual harassment. Date rape. It gets to the point where you don't even want to *deal* with women any more, you know? Always bitching and moaning, bitching and moaning. I take one look at a woman on the street and the next thing you know she's taking me to court. Is that justice?"

Something odd was happening with Raina. If I hadn't known any better, I'd have guessed she was becoming *aroused.*

"The fact is, ever since the '80s we've been living a double standard. A woman is allowed to wear whatever the hell she wants, including practically nothing, and a man is supposed to—to refrain from showing the slightest reaction. You wanna know my opinion? *I* think that wearing a mini-skirt is an act of sexual harassment. When I see a woman in a mini-skirt the first thing I want to do is rip it off and fuck her on the spot. There's nothing wrong with that. It's natural. It's biological. It's part of my programming. And that's why women shouldn't be allowed to dress like that, or else someone should change the fucking harassment laws. It's an open risk. It's temptation. At that point I should not be held accountable for my actions."

Raina was slick with vaginal juice, and I found myself dampening as well.

"Now as to this theory. It's still in the hypothetical stage but pretty soon I'm going to write it all down, have it published, the whole nine yards. We're talking major bestseller here. We're talking *60 Minutes, Good Morning America, 20/20.* We're talking *Nightline* deluxe. Anyway, here goes: the basic premise is that the female orgasm is a myth. And not just a myth, mind you—it's a *conspiracy*! It's like this whole goddamn *movement* that goes back thousands of years, with the simple, obvious purpose of controlling men. I've checked all the goddamn biology journals and no one can explain why it exists. It's got no evolutionary function! Oh *sure*, there's plenty of *theories*, but I'm not seeing any real hard evidence. And if women can't *prove* to men that it happens, then how do we know it exists? It's like cold fusion—scam, scam, scam."

Oh but this was feeling good. I pulled her a little closer.

"But the more you think about it, the more you realize that sex is just a scam as well. In the end it's really no big deal; in fact it's a complete let-down. I often think I should just take up celibacy. It would be a hell of a lot easier. Trouble is, once you're exposed there's nothing you can do about it. You're addicted, and it's like every other addiction—you need a little more each time. That's why I've got you, Venus. For what I'm paying you I don't give a shit whether you have orgasms or not."

She was approaching critical mass. I could feel her muscles retracting, her sex opening like a flower.

"But then the day will come when even you're not enough, Venus. I'll be walking up and down 42nd Street, assuming Disney hasn't bought it all up, and jacking off in triple-X movies. I'll hire out fifty prostitutes and fuck half of them and watch the other half fucking themselves and then that won't be enough either. I'm going to need something more, Venus. Sex'll be too boring. The way I see it, the next step is murder. And there's nothing *wrong* with that! Back in the stone ages, you got all that out of your system by chucking spears into the next cave over. Why else do you turn on the evening news and see everybody killing each other? I'm telling you, I can't *wait* to write this all down."

Raina opened wide, and my finger seemed to sink into the very core of her being. I held her close as she shuddered, as indeed she gave astonished voice to a long, primal scream. A moment passed before the tremors subsided.

Baker, meanwhile, wore an expression of utter disbelief. I might have been mistaken, but I could have sworn I saw tears in his eyes. When at last he spoke, he sounded like a child. "She was faking that, right?" he asked, as if it were the most obvious thing in the world.

I was momentarily disarmed, but Raina knew better. By way of reply she kissed me deeply, and I turned rather giddy. In the next moment she stood, however, stalling my own arousal in mid-soak. She moved somewhat unsteadily, and I wondered whether she'd ever had an orgasm before tonight, with or without Baker. As she stalked past her husband, she said, "I'm sleeping in the guest room tonight. And by the way, go fuck yourself."

Baker watched her retreat, clearly at a loss. I too felt disoriented by the sudden silence, the abortion of this bizarre encounter.

"I think I'll be going now," I said presently, gathering my dress.

Baker snapped out of his reverie. "You're not going anywhere," he replied, standing. "I want you to spend the night. Let's go upstairs." He grabbed my arm and pushed me into the hallway.

We had barely reached the master bedroom before he threw me on the bed and issued his usual command: *Spread em . . .*

He pounced, locking a hand on my throat and slapping my face. His eyes shone with exalted purpose, as if he were fulfilling some sort of *geas*. He began to gnaw on my breasts, suckling for perhaps half a minute before, abruptly dissatisfied, he drove a fist into my stomach. He then stared at my cunt for a long moment with a kind of bemused hunger, as if compelled to engage it but unable to imagine why. He lapped tentatively, but once again doubt set in. He pulled me upright, grabbed my head, and shoved his cock into my mouth. When that lost its charm he grabbed me by the ears and debated whether to pull me left or right. Left won out. He then smacked my ass with brutish gusto; as an afterthought, he dug two fingers into my rectum and hesitantly licked his bounty.

He was like a child (or adult, for that matter—these are the '90s) whose attention span can only be measured in milliseconds. At last he thrust inside me, gritting his teeth, his pubic bone jarring against mine, his expression suggesting failed retribution. *(Come on,* I snarled, every nerve receptive to his misguided fury, to his inevitable failure. *Come on, you dumb preppie shit. Give it your best shot.)* He seemed dismayed that I accepted his length like a blow easily absorbed, and thrust even harder. He gripped my breasts as if to wring from them something lost, his eyes expectant, screaming *Come on, dammit!* But again: What was it he wanted? Was Baker Lewis seeking the base beyond home plate?

I looked into that raging face and smiled. *Still here*, I whispered mockingly. *Still here . . .* And I reached down between my legs and pulled myself into the orgasm that had been denied me earlier, howling with relish and contempt. My paroxysms knocked Baker to one side, forcing him to withdraw. I rolled with him, swinging my leg over and mounting him afresh. I looked into those cold eyes and saw fear. I began riding him hard, but his hormones had hit a traffic jam and his dick was shrinking like a stunned soufflé. I held his gaze, driving home his inadequacy.

"You reconsider that theory, old boy," I sneered. "I can do this all fucking night."

Well, I hope Raina learned something about herself last night. Maybe she'll have the courage to leave him. I should leave him too, but of course I won't. I hadn't had so much fun since the last time I saw him. I wouldn't miss this for the fucking world.

Baker wanders into the bedroom and begins to dress. The cat saunters in as well, a cat that Baker Lewis hates. Raina owned her before their marriage, and the cat, like it or not, was part of her dowry. She's a magnificent sight: a black Persian, leonine and imperious, with cold green eyes that appraise her surroundings with shameless contempt. One can imagine how she spends her days, wandering about the place with languid indifference, licking herself and staring at nothing in particular. She is like an expensive household fixture, only animate.

But Baker—yes, even the cat figures into his angst—Baker simply despises this creature. He hates everything about her. He especially hates how she ignores him. She is remote, inaccessible, and no amount of persuasion or coercion can win her attention. Raina named her Sappho, and feeds her chilled caviar and fresh salmon. The cat, of course, accepts these offerings as her just desserts. Personally I find Sappho pretty goddamned *cool* . . .

"Fucking dyke cat," Baker mutters. He is now fully dressed except for his shoes. He inserts his foot into a black loafer and as quickly withdraws same.

"Jesus Christ this fucking cat *goddamn it Raina!*" The soiled foot dangles as Baker hops on the other. "Raina!"

Her voice issues from downstairs. "What?"

"The cat shat in my shoes again!"

". . . Oh."

"Another pair ruined, *goddamn it Raina can't she learn to use her litterbox?*"

"Sorry."

"Yeah you're sorry. That cat's gonna be sorry, is who's gonna be sorry." Baker removes the sock and flings it at his wife's picture, which stands on a bedside table. The sock strikes the photograph, smearing Raina's face with an airbrushed fecal beard, and then rebounds on an ivory pillowcase to leave its mark there.

He is beaten. He won't acknowledge it but I think I have run him into the ground. Maybe there's nothing left for me here after all.

We head downstairs.

There is silence as we enter the kitchen. Raina is bent over the stove.

"I think I should leave," I say. "Let me just get my—"

"I've made you some eggs," she interrupts, reaching for a spatula. "There's juice on the table."

"Raina that's nice of you but—"

"It's OK. Sit down."

She has set a place for me. I sip at the fresh-squeezed orange juice as Baker seats himself across the table.

"Telling you one last time Raina, that cat shits in my shoes again I'm taking revenge."

"I said I was sorry."

"Yeah well stick her face in her litterbox, OK? Next time I'm taking her up to Bedford and hosing her down."

"The hell you will."

"Or watch me put Valium in her food, see if she can get up the stairs then."

"*Baker . . .*"

"Pirandello loafers, hand-crafted in Italy, thousand bucks a pair."

"Can't they be cleaned?" I ask. On the one hand I want to leave immediately; on the other I want to speak with Raina alone, to sort through the events of the previous evening. She's inscrutable at the moment, and has avoided my gaze.

"Yeah with what?" he snaps, glaring at me. "You ever try to get cat shit off hand-made leather?"

"Here's your coffee," Raina says, setting it down before him.

A minute later the three of us are sitting together. I don't have an appetite, but I nibble politely at the scrambled eggs. Her bruises are starkly apparent in the morning light. Jesus, he did a job on her: her face looks like fruit gone bad.

101

"You can clean that shit up in the living room, get rid of those candles," Baker informs her, stabbing an egg. "Ask Williamson to help you with the furniture."

"I'll help you, Raina. Don't worry."

"No, I want you the hell out of here," Baker responds. "The last thing I want—" he frowns, abruptly pensive.

"You feel it?" asks Raina, sitting back, watching him with stony curiosity.

He stares at her. I recognize that expression—the grey pallor, the worried brow, the impotent lips quivering. Something is happening inside his body that shouldn't be.

"I waffled until the very last second," she continues, folding her arms. "Even after last night—even after this past year I still agonized over whether I should do it. You know what clinched it? The cat. What you said about the cat."

"You?" he answers, his eyes growing wide. "You did—*this?*"

"Baker," she says, rather formally, "you will be dead within a minute. Strychnine tends to have that effect on people." She points to his mug. "The coffee, of course. Classic."

Baker is gaping, either at Raina's words—and the sudden, incomprehensible realization of his death—or from the onset of symptoms. Oh, sweet betrayal! His whole body is trembling.

"If you were anything close to being a real man," says Raina, her tone flat, "you might consider apologizing to me before you die."

"Raina," he whispers, clutching his chest. "Raina get the fucking antidote, please . . ." Already his breathing is labored.

"I don't know if there is one," she muses. "In any case I wouldn't begin to know where to look. No, I'm afraid you'll simply have to die, Baker. Now. What about that apology?"

He tries to stand and collapses to the floor. His body convulses violently. Each breath is a desperate victory, and a meaningless one at that. He coughs up blood.

"By the way, I don't expect to go to jail," Raina says. "I haven't made up my mind what to say—heart attack, choking, maybe even self-defense. But don't worry, I'll think of something. Besides: Venus will back me up."

His jaw seems locked open; his swollen tongue protrudes like an offering. He strains to make eye contact with her, gargling blood. She turns away and calmly resumes eating.

All this time I have sat, perfectly still. When he finally expires I have only one thought in my head: I'm not touching the rest of this food.

A minute passes before I find my voice. "Raina, I—I'm sorry."

"It's not your fault."

Thank god. Maybe I've been spared. "Is, um . . . is there anything I can do for you?"

She shrugs, her face expressionless. "No . . . No, I don't think so. I think maybe you'd better just leave?"

"I'm not sure you should be alone."

"Listen—Venus, is it? Really?" She looks faintly amused. There is much between us unsaid, some of which has nothing to do with her ex-husband. "I really wouldn't concern yourself. I have a feeling this is going to be the happiest day of my life."

# CHAPTER EIGHT

## *How to Save the Catholic Church . . .*

"Forgive me father for I have sinned," said the young woman, gazing deeply into his eyes. "And forgive me for what I'm about to do." With that disclaimer she seized the beautiful Jewish priest from Scarsdale and bore him down on the pew, pressing her lips to his and lifting his skirt.

This again, he thought, neither aiding nor prohibiting her advances. Why had he acceded to her request—increasingly common among the women of his flock—to hear her confession in the nave, and not within the anonymous security of the confessional?

Summer had come early in 1999. In this second week of May, the mercury was already pushing toward a hundred degrees, with full humidity in the bargain. There was, of course, no air-conditioning in the West Village church called Our Lady of the Flowers, and priests are always overdressed.

The woman's name was Sonya, and she looked about sixteen. Her hair and eyes were dark, her skin the color of honey. Her thin white dress was virtually diaphanous: the elaborate lace patterns woven into her underwear had the appearance of vague frescoes beneath.

The pew was hard and narrow. After a moment's grappling she sat up and pulled his hand. "Come on," she said. "Let's do it on the altar."

"But Sonya—"

"Oh come *on.*"

"Well—" (she leaned forward, began mining his ear canal) "—all right all right but Jesus, let me at least lock the doors."

She kicked off her shoes. "Hurry up then."

As he walked to the rear of the church he said, "I hope you have a condom."

"I'm on the pill."

"That's not the only issue."

"Oh come on," she said again. "How the hell could a priest have Aids?"

He didn't—he'd been tested only last week—but he was certainly at risk. His recent years in the seminary—a Benedictine outfit on West 27th Street, between Tenth and Eleventh—had been anything but the oasis of contemplation and abstinence he'd been expecting. The location itself was a handicap, given the native populace of whores, thieves, and vagrants that haunted the barren streets like a test flock for the students. He'd shared a room with three acolytes named Hector, McGuigan, and Vesuvius. When he first arrived he found the three of them kneeling tandem on the bed, quite naked. Vesuvius was fucking Hector; Hector was fucking McGuigan; McGuigan was jerking off.

"Ayy, the new roommate," puffed Hector, smiling at Fish. "Don't be shy man. Hop aboard."

Fish stared at them, shocked. "What about celibacy? What about *Hell*?"

Hector scowled, pumping away. "Look," he said, "we're tryin to change all that shit, OK?"

And so it went. By day the Benedictines strode about somberly, hands clasped, miens thoughtful, contemplating the burden of the Fall. They scrutinized the Gospels, they mulled over the Apocrypha, they considered gravely the insights of Augustine, Anselm, and Aquinas. They consecrated everything in sight and Father Beckett gave a memorable course on exorcism. ("They puke green you take it seriously; otherwise it's a total fucking fraud.") They spent lengthy periods in the confessional, scrupulously rinsing their consciences. They fretted about salvation. They practiced chanting that most self-evident of declarations, so childish in its solemnity: *Let us proclaim the mystery of faith . . .*

By night everything changed. Neighborhood whores were leased with Church money. (The acolytes had merely to step outside and beckon some grizzled mistress nearby.) As Fish quickly learned, these Benedictines formed an unofficial splinter sect called the Priests Yearning for a New Christian Heterodoxy (Ecumenical and Dionysian), their views (and habits) wholly secret from the local archdiocese. According to the group's position papers, the Vatican had long outlived its usefulness. In the matter of priestly celibacy, for example, the Protestants were five centuries advanced. Celibacy had been introduced by Pope Gregory Something—no one could remember which one—hundreds of years after the death of Christ. Well—what did *he* know? Was Paul

105

celibate? Was Simon Peter? Were *any* of the Galilean Twelve?

"Tax exemption," gasped Father Beckett one evening, as he was fellated by a hefty streetwalker and Fish waited his turn. "Don't you love it."

Heady days indeed for this child of the Ashkenazim, this young Adonis whose neurochemistry had redrawn the world into dangerous and fantastic shapes.

As he went to bed on June 26, 1994, at 11:43 p.m., Michael Fishbein was merely the son of a famous plastic surgeon (father) and greetings card designer (mother); a recent graduate of Scarsdale High School (G.P.A. 3.52); and a pending first-year student at Vassar. On June 27 at 2:48 a.m., having woken for no reason in particular, he was a babbling wreck suffering a panic attack and the prologue of a major existential crisis.

Oh, but it shouldn't have happened—not in privileged, well-mannered Scarsdale, the clamor of Lodz ever more distant as the elders shuffled off the coil. Even local Zionists have second thoughts about the Holy Land, gazing wistfully at the expansive lawns, the elegant mini-mansions, the triumph of American Jewry, so far from the armed fanatics. Of course we advocate the *concept* of Israel, but meanwhile Scarsdale is so *comfortable* . . .

Such a promising young boy . . . Bright, pampered, and arrogant, young Michael had the gift of beauty. Most teens come to be insecure about their appearances; he never had the chance. On the contrary, girls courted him from the age of twelve, and he yielded to their overtures with courteous and workmanlike aplomb. Ordinarily, high school conjugation depends on both providence and cunning, and the average boy may wait months before making his move. Chance scenarios present themselves, each to be critically evaluated. Some teachers seat their students in alphabetical order, which might afford a potential suitor close proximity to his beloved; then there are the time-honored pretexts of shared homework and exam recapment: "Did you put *Childe Harold's Pilgrimage* on number eleven?", for example, is a useful exploratory maneuver. The key is to avoid rejection, that worst of adolescent fates. In trial-lawyer fashion, one never asks a question unless the answer is known in advance.

None of this applied to Fish. He'd return to his locker after school to find a coterie of admirers loitering nearby, watching his every move. By senior year he had bedded every willing girl his age, and so proceeded to the juniors and sophomores. His friends learned

106

never to double-date with him: as often as not, they'd end the evening in solitary, sulky silence while Fish, cloistered next door, wrestled in a lively ménage à trois. It was not surprising, therefore, when he chose to matriculate at Vassar College. Ugliness is not in the genes at Vassar, where an inclement pulchritude reigns supreme; where the merely Average are Christians among the lions, and devoured accordingly. It would have been perfect for him.

That summer of 1994—which should have been a time of leafy afternoons and languid, self-satisfied reflection—began promisingly enough. He worked part-time at his father's clinic, mostly in the Phalloplasty Department, lazily sorting through photographs of ten-inch penises that were constructed from fatty tissue. A steady procession of women marched through in varying stages of transformation. Some were receiving psychotherapy to probe the certainty of their resolve. Others progressed through a course of hormone injections. Those who went the distance emerged from the operating theater carrying a long plastic rod, which could be inserted into the new urethra to simulate an erection. (Natural erections and liquid ejaculate were still some years away; in the meantime, the vestige of a clitoris remained for the purpose of orgasm.) Fish watched in amusement as pretty young waifs metamorphosed into burly roughnecks; or, in the nearby Phallectomy Department, vice versa.

But to return to that fateful morning of June 27: he was settling back into uneasy sleep when he was struck by a terrible thought. This thought had no precursor: it surfaced without explanation, its pathology impossible to delineate. Whatever its source, the net result was this: Fish realized that he was alive.

One moment he was turning over in bed, half-asleep; the next he was sitting bolt upright, heart pounding, gaping at his anatomy. He wriggled his fingers as if noticing them for the first time—as if the motion itself were alien. What was this husk of flesh, this agglutination of molecules, that he piloted through an uncertain world? Throughout his body a million processes were occurring, all independent of his will. By some happy miracle they seemed to go about their business in good order, thus keeping him alive. And yet ... and yet it all seemed so tenuous, so *fragile*. Something could fail ... how could something *not* fail at any given moment, bringing swift and unceremonious death?

Fish bounded down the hall to his parents' bedroom.

"Dad?" he said hesitantly, knocking on the doorframe.

Jeremy Fishbein was a heavy sleeper, disinclined to perceive even the most violent commotions. His wife was the precise opposite. Indeed, Fish had wondered over the years whether she ever slept at all. She awoke at the slightest compromise of equilibrium—the cat yawning two floors below, an insect scampering through the attic. (Staying out past his curfew was a dicey affair, and he rarely got away with it. He'd creep up the stairs over a period of half an hour, a step every two minutes, hardly daring to breathe. As he reached the threshold of his room the familiar *"Michael..."* would issue from down the hall.) Tonight was no different: she spoke as though she had been waiting for him.

"Michael?"

"Mom?" said Fish urgently, dancing from foot to foot as if to jump out of his skin, to escape his imperfect corpus.

"What is it?" she asked, squinting irritably.

"Mom I—I exist."

". . . What?"

He held up his hands as evidence. "I'm *alive!*"

"Michael are you on something?"

"I have to go to the emergency room!"

She still didn't understand. "You mean you're sick?"

"No but I *could* be dying!"

Her senses now clear, she rose from the bed and padded across the room. She was already going to fat, and had reached the age when scanty nightgowns had given way to shapeless smocks, to designer burlap. She applied a palm to his forehead. "What the hell's going on Michael?"

He pressed a finger to his neck, seeking a pulse. His heart was galloping merrily along, but what did that prove? It might stop at any moment! "I need to go to the emergency room," he repeated.

She withdrew her hand. "You're not feverish. Does your stomach hurt?"

He was growing more agitated, hopping up and down, wringing his hands, overwhelmed by the conviction he was about to die. Death seemed to nip at his very heels ... couldn't he somehow elude it ...? *"Look goddamn it can't we please just fucking GO?"*

She scowled and turned away. "You're on something. I knew it."

"Mom I am *not*—"

108

"No no no, don't worry." She was rummaging in her drawers. "Meet me downstairs, we'll go right away. I'm going to have them do a blood test. If you've been taking drugs I will ground you into the next century."

He provided a pleasant diversion for the bored ER staff, who took one look at this raving exquisite and collapsed in hysterics. Finally a giggling female resident measured his vital stats, drew some blood, and concluded (for even in madness he was oh so gorgeous) with a lengthy quest for hernias. He submitted eagerly: he wanted no stone left unturned.

"Does it hurt when I do this?" she asked, waving his penis about.

He frowned. "No; but do you suspect something?"

She pressed her lips together, shoulders heaving. "Look," she said with difficulty, "maybe you should tell me why you think you're going to die."

"Well it could be anything. I mean leukemia, AIDS, radiation poisoning. Do you think it's prostate cancer?"

Even she was not prepared to examine his prostate. She struggled to formulate a blanket reassurance, but he was already blundering on.

"What if I have some disease they never discovered before? What if I'm the only person in the world who has it?"

"You know something," she answered, looking up, "I think I have just the solution."

He was given a shot of Ativan and sent home in a pleasant daze.

Later, at breakfast, his parents joked with him about the incident. The blood test had revealed no drug consumption, and Jeremy Fishbein declared himself sorry to have missed the show. He gave his son the day off, proffered five hundred dollars, and told Fish— once his wife had left the room—to drive into the City and get laid.

"I can go next door for that," said Fish, handing back the money. "Or across the street, for that matter. Thanks anyway."

His father's voice lowered conspiratorially. "You're bonking *Sarah Tannenbaum*?"

"Well, not in a few weeks. I meant her sister Liza."

Jeremy pocketed the money, shaking his head. "Next thing you'll be telling me you've done their mother too. And no, don't answer that."

After they'd left he sat alone at the kitchen table, convinced of his recovery. He even dozed for about twenty minutes, basking in his drug-induced stupor. When at length he opened his eyes, he discovered that the kitchen was swarming with—

—with *fish*?

There must have been a thousand of them. They glided about the room, all sizes and colors, perfectly silent. There were sharks, turtles, urchins, rays, eels. There was even a sea snake that swam round and round his neck like an animate noose. Ponderous groupers mingled with frisky guppies; an octopus emerged from the refrigerator; a school of piranhas circled his face, leering at him sidelong. Spellbound, he extended a quivering hand among them. They shied away, and he couldn't determine if they were substanstial or not.

Then he noticed a goldfish standing on the kitchen table, perhaps eighteen inches tall and dressed in a black pinstripe suit. He carried a briefcase in one fin; a bowler was perched above the golliwog eyes.

"Who the fuck are you?" said Fish.

"An ambassador," replied the goldfish, "not to mention salesman and attorney. May I sit down?"

Fish didn't reply. The goldfish propped himself on a cereal box and surveyed the other fish. "Have you met them all?" he asked.

"They haven't introduced themselves," said Fish. He had the vague impression that something wasn't quite right, though he was damned if he could say what it was. "What do you want?"

"Let me be frank with you, Michael: I'm something of an ambulance chaser. My employers sent me here after they learned of your little problem this morning. We thought you might need our services."

"I don't understand," said Fish. "You want me to sue the hospital or something?"

"No, nothing like that. It goes much deeper."

"You want me to sue my parents then?"

"If I may—" the goldfish opened his briefcase and consulted a dossier "—ah, here it is, good. 'Patient exhibited symptoms of panic attack disorder, including irrational convictions of impending death.' Interesting." He looked up. "Why were you afraid?"

"Look it was night-time, it was dark. I probably had a bad dream. I'm fine now."

"I wouldn't presume that, Michael. You see, in my experience these things only get worse. How do you know the same thing won't happen again tonight?"

Fish threw out a hand, startling a parade of minnows. "I guess I don't."

"*Precisely*, and that's where we can help. My firm has been managing existential crises for a very long time, Michael. We have an impeccable reputation."

A jellyfish shrugged by. "What exactly do you do?"

"It's very simple," said the goldfish. "Our premise is that life is a kind of minefield, and must be negotiated with the greatest of care. Think of all the ways there are to die, Michael, and how little control you have over them. Strangers might shoot you in the street. Your house might collapse in a tornado. You might get hit by a truck. A lunatic chef might poison your dinner. To say nothing of the many diseases that are still incurable. Any of these can strike at any time, and there's little you can do about it. And consider how things *used* to be! Even with food there was a price to pay. Imagine all the poor fools who, foraging in the primeval forests, came across nightshade and yew berries and hemlock. Similar vegetation had been eaten to no harm; to try it was only natural. Then imagine said fools writhing on the ground, clutching their stomachs. Some nearby colleague, who by chance had been spared, would make a note of the incident and report back to the tribe: *belladonna = death*. The same applied for medicine: trial and error was the rule. Talk about the good old days."

"Fair enough. So what."

"So don't you find it intolerable that your continued existence is by and large predicated by lottery?"

The piranhas were hovering a few inches away, staring him directly in the eye. "I thought there was little I could do about it."

"Ah, but hear me out. You see, Michael, we are specialists in providing our clients with a level of control over their lives that virtually eliminates the sort of problem you experienced this morning. Thanatophobia, if you will."

Fish swatted at the piranhas as if they were mosquitoes. They evaded his attack and resumed their former positions.

"What we do," said the goldfish, "is despatch a team of consultants who will guide you through every decision that arises in life. You can think of them as your own personal advisory board, available twenty-four hours a day."

The piranhas began to nibble at his face. Now there was a tactile relationship between Fish and fish, and the resulting pain was like a revelation. They were gnawing on his lips, his eyeballs, his ears, dozens upon dozens of them; and in that moment, without further ado, he knew that he was insane.

He sprang back from the table, again swatting at his attackers. His hands didn't even pass through them: they seemed to exist on a different material plane, a distinct space-time only slightly conjunctive with his own—which was pretty goddamn unfair. They could attack him but he was unable to return the favor. The goldfish watched gravely.

He lost his balance and fell to the floor, displacing a nurse shark and two stonefish. The shark's body was rougher than sandpaper, so abrasive that the skin on his left forearm was scoured away. His left hip came down upon the sharp dorsal ridge of a third stonefish, the most poisonous creature in the sea. Fire coursed along his leg; the fish lay crushed beneath him, its spine buried in his flesh. The piranhas continued their frenzy all the while. A few seemed to have infiltrated his nostrils and others were devouring his tongue.

"Help!" he screamed at the goldfish, who wore an expression of mournful sympathy. "For god sake get these things off me!"

"Well, I might be able to arrange something," said the goldfish. "You'd have to agree to our terms, of course."

Fish struggled to his knees and grabbed the edge of the table, jerking it toward him. "How much? Tell me goddamn it how much!"

"Oh, that's the best part of all," said the goldfish, his balance undisturbed. "You see our advice, unlike that of so many others, will cost you no money—only your soul."

"Fine, whatever! Just, just *Christ will you get these fucking things off me!*"

The goldfish inserted a pectoral fin into its mouth and gave a shrill whistle.

Startled, the piranhas withdrew, turning to ascertain the source of the interruption.

"We'll be in touch," called the goldfish. "Toodle-oo . . ." He was grinning as the piranhas closed in and devoured him, pinstripes and all.

"Jesus," Fish gasped. The room was suddenly empty; his flesh seemed miraculously restored. Rising, he staggered to the sink and opened the right tap. He shoveled cold water in his face, soaking his T-shirt in the process. Leaving the water on, he limped toward the phone.

The next moment he was lying in the foyer, sprawled like a corpse on the pinewood floor, uncertain of how he'd gotten there, and beset with visions. Vast theaters opened in his psyche housing comedies, tragedies, and even the odd musical. A bestiary of characters entered and exited the stages, the players human and animal and many combinations thereof, a true therianthropic parade; not to mention an assortment of life forms that might have sprung from mythology: basilisks and cockatrices, ogres and elfs, trolls and minotaurs, hippogriffs and medusae. They were quick to develop an interest in his affairs, and each had a blueprint for how he should live during the next five seconds. These, apparently, were the consultants that had been promised. (Conveniently, they all spoke English—even the termites.) They were there to help, they assured him. They had nothing but his best interests at heart.

For the rest of the day they accompanied him everywhere, a company of doppelgängers, berating, wheedling, counseling, or simply offering sage commentary upon every thought in his head— excluding, of course, the thoughts of which they themselves were composed. (But you couldn't tell them that. They harbored the conceit that they were quite independent of him, and who was he to disagree?) They formed an executive committee whose permission was required for all decisions: they had to ratify *everything*, as if his impulses were merely bills to be put through Congress. Unfortunately, they could seldom agree even among themselves: partisan politics was endemic to his madness as well as to Capitol Hill. As they debated and wrangled, bickered and filibustered, Fish, unable to assert his own volition, simply stood by and awaited their verdict. Since he couldn't vote them out of office, he took to calling them the Politburo. They, and only they, could keep Comrade Death at bay.

The hours of that day were lost to him. He tramped through the house, unable to engage in activity, following the Politburo's orders like an automaton. He sat, he stood, he reclined, he paced—it made no difference. He could not conceive of ever being happy again now that he was overwhelmed by the sheer precariousness of life. He marveled that he had lived eighteen years in blissful ignorance, as if the fact of his mortality were a state secret. (How could he not have *known*?) Even the national pastimes, sex and wealth, exerted

113

no appeal. They were meaningless compared to the Void he now faced.

Late that afternoon, as his father pulled into the driveway, Fish was huddled in the kitchen, unable to decide whether to eat and awaiting the Politburo's sanction. He scrutinized an apple for syringe marks—for who knew what psychopaths were lurking in the warehouses, armed with cyanide?—and was about to fetch a magnifying glass when his father walked in the door.

Ten minutes later they were sitting grimly in the waiting room of a psychiatrist friend, one Ira Feldspar. They did not speak. A neurasthenic depressive slumped nearby, half-dead. A gibbering manic stalked the length of the room, arguing with himself. Jeremy, arms folded, stared a hole through the opposite wall, his thoughts nearly screaming: *No Vassar, no grad school, no grandchildren . . .*

When they had been called inside, Dr. Feldspar listened impassively to Fish's description of the Politburo. Scarcely half a minute had passed before he began writing prescriptions, even as Fish rambled on. The doctor quietly informed Jeremy that his son was a paranoid schizophrenic. This was not good news: schizophrenia, if left untreated, is the worst disease in the world, operating at humankind's most fundamental level—consciousness. Perception is distorted in a variety of creative ways; reality becomes amorphous. There were no cures, but the proper pharmaceuticals just *might* keep Fish out of the hospital, and perhaps allow him to live a normal life. Clozapine was the most effective drug but also potentially fatal; instead Fish would try Stelazine. He would experience many side effects—tremors, nausea, dizziness, fatigue—but with any luck he would not suffer brain damage, though of course one couldn't be *sure . . .*

The Stelazine actually worked. Individuals each respond differently to psychiatric drugs, and Fish might well have been condemned to a life of padlocked wards and hallucinatory fury. As it was, the Stelazine dulled his senses and dulled the Politburo as well, restraining them to the sidelines. They still appeared on occasion, promising vengeance for his betrayal (for they were all too aware of the Stelazine's presence), but he found that he could usually ignore them.

In order to have a life, however, he would have to confront the Void. Death was still very much on his mind, and he would never be able to return to his prelapsarian state, where youthful passion and naïve conceit had conspired to make everything seem possible, all of it good. Stelazine could not banish the Void; it could only allow him to face it on his own terms, without the Politburo's intervention.

Delighted with his progress, his parents were hopeful that he could begin at Vassar in January, at the start of the second semester. Fish had other ideas. During the fall of 1994 and the winter of 1995 he billeted himself in the local library, poring over crumbling editions that hadn't been touched in decades. To come to terms with the Void, he turned to the eminent thinkers of the past, who presumably had had some insights on the subject. Unlike with Dorian, this had nothing to do with personal ambition: he was reading to save his life.

In chronological order, he labored through every major philosopher and theologian from the pre-Socratics to Martin Heidegger—and was largely disappointed. Most of the ideas were outdated, and he saw no point in studying philosophy merely in the context of its time. He wanted permanent answers, and science had rendered most of philosophy obsolete. He at once saw through Anselm's (and Descartes's) "proof" of God's existence. Kant was even worse, spending a hundred pages declaring that God's existence could neither be proved nor disproved. Berkeley distinguished himself by the sheer boldness of his ideas—the world is Mind, and perception is the root of reality; not bad for an Occidental in 1710—but ultimately collapsed beneath the weight of logical positivism. Fish plodded gloomily through the existentialists, whose refutation of Cartesian essentialism, ironically, seemed confining rather than liberating. Sartre argued that a man must give his own meaning to his actions—a daunting proposition, since it revealed no clues to the Divine Plan. This above all was what Fish sought: evidence for such a Plan, for a road map to Heaven; evidence that he was more than just a worthless sack of shit in the landfill of a fluctuating impersonal universe.

All of which led to some troubling questions about freewill. If schizophrenia, manic depression, and obsessive-compulsive disorder—the major mental illnesses—were biological in nature, then sanity could not be chosen of one's own volition. Sanity—and by implication, thought itself—arose out of processes beyond conscious control. If Fish could not will himself to be rid of the Politburo, and if a chemical succeeded where he had failed, it followed that he was not free at all. Brain chemistry, and not choice, dictated normalcy.

Neither philosopher nor theologian provided Fish with enough evidence or courage to make the Kierkegaardian Leap, by which humans try so desperately to shirk their accidence. As for Kierkegaard himself, his argument for the absurdity of proving God's existence and his emphasis upon subjective religious experience had the opposite of its intended effect. Fish wasn't interested in creating his own god: he wanted hard proof of the One god. Heidegger was even less comforting: the best advice he could offer was that true freedom arose only from the resolute confrontation with death, and this by itself did nothing to help Fish in that confrontation. Disillusioned, he turned to a new source: Science.

Fish had read the Torah; but like the other theological and philosophical texts he'd been through, the Torah now seemed a colossal waste of time. The displacement of cherished theological notions by good, hard science had been a recurring theme for the past two thousand years; nor was science unlike Laius, immune from its own offspring. Newtonian physics had been supplanted by general relativity, which in turn was usurped by quantum mechanics. For every scientist who dreamed of a final theory, another took the side of Kuhn, declaring the notion ridiculous. Was science itself cumulative and bounded by singularities, or was its struggle infinite and futile?

Fish hoped that science could bring him closer to God, building the necessary foundation from which to make his Leap of Faith. Naturally he was disappointed. Many paleontologists believed that humans arose from circumstances which, though unique and fortuitous, were entirely random in nature. Had a meteor not killed off the dinosaurs, for example, most mammals would never have evolved—the dinosaurs provided too much competition. Further, neurobiologists had long since discovered, in contrast to Descartes's dualism, that the mind does not exist, and is merely a convenient euphemism for describing the collective actions of the brain itself. As Gilbert Ryle had posited in the '40s, there is no mysterious house of the soul, no ghost in the machine: thought is purely physiological in nature. Metaphysics (and metaphysicians) need not apply.

If Sartre had cultivated Fish's sense of isolation, then science only fermented it. He saw himself as a pointless configuration of atoms for which any pretense of *identity* seemed absurd. Freewill could not possibly overcome the biological imperative, which had entirely its own agenda. His consciousness—and thus his identity—was already mediated by a synthetic chemical formula. He briefly considered suicide, Camus's supreme act of freedom, but the biological imperative defeated him even there, in the name of self-preservation.

Slowly he came full circle. Though he knew science to be correct, he resisted the implications of that belief. Harking back to Kierkegaard, he called into play the great ghost of subjectivity, and adopted the position that he could believe whatever the hell he wanted. He decided, for the moment, to believe in a god . . . but how best to worship it?

Christianity, the bane of his ancestors, beckoned like the Devil Himself. Unlike Judaism, Christianity proffered the hope that the Messiah had already come, and that redemption was just around the corner. It was tragic, Fish thought, that the worship of a Jew, propagated by Jews to non-Jews, had come back to haunt Jews—a distinctly Jewish irony. But the sins of history were beside the point. That Christianity had been malpracticed for centuries did not mean it was *inherently* evil (did it?); and in questions of theological doctrine, the Christians might in fact be *right*.

Next choice: Orthodox, Catholic, or Protestant. Orthodoxy seemed too alien culturally; and Protestantism, though intellectually sound as these things go, placed too much emphasis on blind faith. Fish could not simply recline in his bed and feel close to God: he needed ritual, and the Catholics do Ritual better than anyone else, except of course the Druids. Ah, Ritual . . . such indispensible rigging for the suspension of disbelief.

Armed with his newfound piety, Fish applied to various seminaries with the intention of becoming a priest and cementing his faith. His parents threatened to disown him; he betrayed them anyway. Marshaling his assets—a savings account, a few bonds, a small portfolio of stock—he liquidated the holdings into hard cash, which amounted to about ten thousand dollars. He then sought a priest who could be bribed.

Baptized, communicated, and confirmed, Fish took up his place at the Benedictine monastery on 27th Street, certain that he had made the correct choice. Kneeling before Christ, suffused with the power of God, he marveled at the holiness he now felt. Suddenly the world was rich with meaning again. Suddenly the mere fact of *life* was not a crisis. Suddenly he had an *agenda* . . .

His parents were true to their word: Jeremy forbade him to return until he could recite the Talmud from memory—in Hebrew, of course. The Fishbeins were not religious, but they were Jewish enough psychologically to resent his defection to the goyim. As Jeremy put it, "Maybe God can forgive them, but that's his job, not mine." Meanwhile, they cursed whatever god there might be for the advent of schizophrenia. Every other illness seemed confined within distinct parameters. Blacks got sickle-cell anemia, excepting the odd Italian or Greek. Women got breast and ovarian cancer. Alzheimer's was a disease of the elderly. Muscular dystrophy was inherited. AIDS was easily prevented. Why then had their son been chosen by schizophrenia?

"I have no doubt," said Jeremy a few days later, "that this monastery thing is a fad. He'll be back. You watch."

Well, it was May of 1999, and he hadn't returned once. Now a junior priest at Our Lady of the Flowers, he was hearing yet another woman's confession and getting laid in the bargain. The Stelazine somewhat muted his sexual impulses, but this did not preclude others from advancing on *him*. Moreover, he was too polite to refuse. He hated to disappoint women.

"How do I know," he said, returning along the nave, "that you don't have any diseases yourself?"

"Trust me, baby." She was waiting for him at the altar, barefoot and flushed, with half-lidded eyes and parted wet lips. She stood in a radiance of sunlight that issued from the clerestory, her body enticingly visible beneath the cotton dress. He drew her closer, trying to plant a kiss, but she flung him to the ground and perched herself astride. She lifted his frock, attacked his belt, and at length he was duly exposed. She extracted her panties, threw them aside (they landed on a candle nearby, like a flag of surrender), and grafted her pelvis to his.

During most of these encounters he remained passive, largely because of the Stelazine's interdict. Often his partner would seize his hands and affix them to her breasts, or even slap him around to make sure he wasn't falling asleep. But today, for perhaps the first time in years, he squirmed with concupiscence of his own. His jaunts at the seminary had arisen largely from peer pressure—social fucking, along the lines of social drinking—and were hardly apotheotic. (On occasion he had paid the price, which was not addiction but rather disease. He had awoken one morning to find his entire groin sheathed in what appeared to be puce lichen. Not soap nor

118

water nor prayer could exorcise that growth, which teemed with spores and took a month to recede.)

But with this particular woman, this beautiful brunette ... well, goddamn it if he wasn't *enjoying* himself. He drew his hands along her chest, felt his penis enlarge a notch. "Why don't we take off *all* our clothes?" he suggested.

He struggled out of his vestments. She lifted the dress over her head and disposed of her bra. Her breasts were large and narrowly set: they seemed to crowd each other for space and their nipples slanted inward, lending them a cross-eyed expression. Her pubic hair was severely if immaculately trimmed, growing just within the thrifty confines of her bikini line. He was rather disappointed: his tastes inclined toward the hirsute, toward pubic *copses.*

But not to complain—not with a full erection to attend to. They met in a headlong clash near the tabernacle, against which they soon crashed. Fish reached inside and withdrew a chalice intended for the next Mass. He poured the wine over her breasts; it spilled down their abdomens and soaked their genitals. She was dangerously aroused by this, and when he began to lick the wine from her nipples she launched into a shricking oratory and smashed a nearby madonna figurine.

They fucked on the dais that held the Bible, itself heaved aside and sent tumbling to the floor with an ignominious crash. They put holy wafers on their tongues and French-kissed, allowing the putative body of Christ to dissolve in their communal saliva. As for the Man himself, he gazed down from his gilt prison with great sorrow—or was it perhaps longing, or even jealousy?

Sweat puddled between them, augmenting his desire. Her neck tasted of salt. Wasn't there something eminently divine about their naked, lubricious bodies, galvanizcd in this febrile clasp? Wasn't this what Catholicism *should* be? A theology where purity arose from orgasm, and not abstinence? PYNCHED had been right all along: there was no surer way to save the ailing Catholic Church than to elevate fucking to sacramental status. *The holy estate of fucking* ... All that was needed was an inversion of the party line, and the faithful would return in droves. Confession would assume a whole new significance. *(Forgive me father for I have sinned; it has been two days since last I fucked ...)*

She was bending over the railing in front of the altar. He stood immediately behind, thrusting away, his hands cupping hcr breasts,

119

while she in turn reached beneath the railing and stroked herself. He hadn't felt this good in ages.

The doors rattled.

He looked up, alarmed, and ceased his motion.

"Come on!" she snapped, gyrating her hips. "They're locked!"

The proximity of a third party began to arouse him even further. The doors shuddered, as if in the grip of some poltergeist, and he felt himself turning along that last avenue, the mall that leads to the palace, and everything was sweat and flesh and cunt and cum and a key turned in the lock and the door opened.

Silhouetted in the doorway, framed starkly against the daylight outside, stood the unmistakable ursine form of Bishop Abdul, the surly Lebanese prelate from the local archdiocese.

The lovers did not part, did not rush to conceal their nakedness as Adam and Eve were said to have done. They remained exhaustedly conjoined, sagging in tandem against the railing. Abdul advanced slowly up the nave, his face expressionless, his black beard seeming like the vanguard of some forthcoming assault from those grim lips.

"May I ask," he queried, cocking his head slightly, "may I ask what it is you're doing?" The question was not rhetorical: he seemed genuinely curious.

Fish, still panting, licked wine-stained lips. "I was hearing this woman's confession," he said querulously, as if his current disposition were the most natural consequence of that duty. "And this—well, this is her penance."

"Very interesting," said Abdul, advancing still further. "I thought perhaps you were purging her of demons."

"Well," said Fish, trembling now, "that too."

Abdul smiled. He was now only a few feet away, a bear closing upon prey that had no escape. He scrutinized them carefully, his eyes running the length of Sonya's body with keen interest and perhaps the faintest hint of perplexity, as if unable to verify some long-held suspicion.

"I think," he said at last, turning his back, "I think you both had better get dressed."

Six hours later, in the Cimmerian depths of the Bowery, Fish was standing in a deserted parking lot with yet another Lebanese, this one an arms dealer, and spending the last of his money on a Kalashnikov. Bishop Abdul's words still rang in his inner ear: *I think it is safe*

120

*to assume, young man, that you will be excommunicated.* Unable to face the judgement of his brethren, and unable to return to Scardsdale, he had fled with nothing but the (reapplied) clothes on his back. He had roughly a thousand dollars in a nearby bank account, all of which he withdrew.

He was buying the AK-47 because it was the most powerful rifle of the bunch. Already he anticipated a grim life of crime to keep body and fallen soul together. He'd found a squat in a SoHo warehouse only a few blocks away, which would serve him for a day or two, but he also had the future to think about. He was unemployed, and he had no marketable skills. He had a high school education, a degree in theology, and twenty-one tablets of Stelazine. For what did this qualify him?

It did not occur to him that he should buy a handgun, which would have been less expensive and easier to conceal. No, he reasoned that the Kalashnikov, being the crown jewel of the dealer's collection, would therefore provide the best value—especially because he was patently incapable of using it. The dealer, sensing something amiss in this young priest, retrieved an equipment bag lying in the back of the van. He offered this to Fish free of charge, with the proviso that Fish conceal the gun in public.

The next morning, following the local grapevine, he was casing a crack den in Morningside Heights. Some locals were selling out of a townhouse near Amsterdam, and it seemed a relatively small operation. A fellow squatter had advised Fish that cash couriers made excellent targets, and also never to operate in his own backyard. So there he stood in his sacerdotal attire, equipment bag in hand, the only white person in sight. He had no idea what he would do; he knew only that he was hungry and that he needed more Stelazine.

Toward noon an Audi pulled up to the townhouse and a sharply dressed Latino emerged, leaving the engine running. Aha, thought Fish, perking up. He pulled out his gun and hid behind a car. Sure enough, the courier emerged five minutes later with a briefcase. (Unknown to Fish, the townhouse was an outpost for a large, city-wide ring. He could never have guessed the amount of money he was about to earn.)

Heart pounding, trying to assume the mantle of grim assassin, he stole from hiding and was upon the courier in seconds, jabbing the gun into his kidneys. "Drop the briefcase," he said. "Now."

The courier didn't know whether to smirk or frown, to threaten or plead: he wasn't sure who this assailant was, or for whom he worked. He craned his head around as he released the briefcase, taking in collar and frock and rifle. "*Ahnn?*" he inquired, startled.

Once he'd snatched the briefcase, Fish ordered the man to lie face down on the pavement. Baffled—evidently he'd never been accosted by a priest—the courier complied. "God bless you," said Fish in parting, and sprinted toward Broadway. He was halfway there, and slowing to put away the gun, when he saw the policemen. And they saw him.

The previous twenty-four hours had marked a profound change in his personality, thanks largely to his night in the rough. In a deserted warehouse, sitting among homeless drunks (the rifle lending him due eminence), Fish had absorbed the guidelines for a whole different existence. With his survival in jeopardy, he had surprised even himself by how quickly he adopted a hard, street-smart carapace. He was no longer the self-absorbed rich kid of his adolescence. He was no longer the frail acolyte seeking God and grace, inches from the cusp of oblivion. He suddenly felt shorn of a past, as if he were creating a new identity from scratch and all that mattered was the present. After years of passivity, he felt intoxicated by the sheer *physicality* of his new milieu, by the quickness at which life moved. His senses had never seemed so finely tuned.

But now, as he began to run, faster than he'd ever run in his life, he realized that he was no master criminal, no would-be *capo:* he was merely the stupidest ex-priest in America. Barring divine intervention, he would soon be trading pulpit for prison, and no one on earth would give a shit.

He had even forgotten his Stelazine.

# CHAPTER NINE

## *The Fate of the American Novel; or,*
## *Rednecks on the Make . . .*

The interstate wound through endless grey hills. Heat descended once again, the sky like milkweed; layers of pollen settled gently on the windshield. The top was down; Prophet was at the wheel, Fish in the passenger seat. Dorian and Lucky sat together in the back, in that fresh and wary intimacy to which only youth is privileged. She was inclined to forgive him for his escapade, if only because he'd come off worst and had looked a complete idiot. More to the point, she had lost her wallet at the strip joint and had little choice but to accompany them. The possibility of her rich mother wiring money was never raised.

"You're so pathetic, Dorian," she said, indicating the gauze on his right hand.

"Yes well you happen to be the first attractive lesbian I've met."

"Oh *really*? And how many lesbians have you known personally?"

"Oh quite a few, quite a few. They tend to be big and sturdy and they dress like hell."

She sighed. "You're so predictable. It's not the idea of women fucking that galls you, it's the idea that you're excluded. You expect lesbians to look like supermodels. You expect them to get it on with each other while you watch from the sidelines until you're good and ready to jump in yourself and you can all get down to the real thing. Pretty strange coming from an alleged bisexual."

"Yes well that's the point. I'm open to everything, to all possibilities."

"You're horny is the point, and because of that you're my slave. You want nothing more than to get me into bed and you've already spilled blood in the process."

"You cruel little bitch."

"Thank you. Now I want you to tell me something Dorian: What do you think you could possibly offer me that I need? A dick?"

". . . Yes well that would be a start."

"Dildos work much better, in my opinion. Not to mention vibrators."

"It's not the same."

"No, not to *you* it isn't. Let me ask you this: Has any woman ever jacked you off as well as you can do it yourself?"

". . . Truth be told, Lucky, I really wouldn't know."

She studied him, the wind rustling her hair. "You're a virgin?"

"Heterosexually speaking, yes. There. Now you've got real power over me."

She pursed her lips sadly. "Well Dorian I do sympathize. A woman's touch is very erotic. The feel of her naked body is *gorgeous*. If you only knew what you've been missing . . ."

"Fucking hell you *are* a cruel little bitch. This conversation is terminated." He reached into his backpack and withdrew a handful of envelopes.

"What are those?"

"These, Lucky, are all the rejection slips I've been afraid to open."

"Rejection slips?"

"Yes you see I'm a philosopher, or at least I pretend to be, and what we have here represents a year's work on a novel of ideas. Since we're agreed that I'm at rock bottom, now is as good a time as any to have a look." He riffled through them, Stymied & Shyster, Sprocket, Wanton, Doubleplay, Smell, Drown, Tandem Louse, LarkerFollies, Thicket Pissific, Alfred Canuck, Kaput Man, Big Black, Quilliam Sorrow, Norse Cormorant, New American Lumpen/ Mutton-Piglet, Scribbler, ROT, Hysterion, St. Marvin's Dress, Henry Dolt . . . "Yes they're all here, and look—I can't even get published by ROT. I should've tried Wildebeest, they're even worse."

"What's the book about?"

"Life and love and sex and death and just about everything else you can think of." He skewered an envelope. "Right, let's see: **Dear Mr. Bray, Thank you for your submission of *The Theory of Everything* but it's not quite right for our list** yes well that figures, have you seen the *shit* they publish?" He flung the paper aside and attacked the next envelope. "**Dear Author, We are not considering unsolicited material at this time** ah yes, of course, one has to be a celebrity in advance these days, doesn't one, so don't bother sending us the next *Ulysses*." The paper was given to the mercy of the wind. "Next. **Dear *Dorian*** well that's a start, presumptuous little twat **Thanks so much for allowing me the opportunity to consider *The Theory of Everything*** yes well it was a mighty fucking privilege wasn't it, **Although there is much to like here, I'm afraid the characters were just not sympathetic enough for me to take this any further here** now take note, Lucky, you must never offend the sensibilities of the feel-good crowd, d'you hear? Everybody needs a hero these days, good conquers evil all's well with the world I mean Jesus Christ these stupid little fucks, next: **Dear Mr. Bray, Many thanks for your submission but we are only looking for material with breakout bestseller potential that can also be adapted for movies** well couldn't be much plainer, and you know something? Let's see what the good Mr. Friskemdown means." He rummaged through the backpack and extracted a tabloid newspaper. "Here we are, the *New York Times Book Review.* Let's just see what's what, shall we? Let's take the pulse of our vast American reading public, and have a gander at the bibliophile barometer." He fought against the wind, folding back the paper. "Right, hardcover bestsellers . . . Bubba Gristle's at number one with *Habeas Cadaverous.* **An unshaven lawyer battles the forces of evil in a mortuary sex scandal.** Now I might just buy that if the corpses all sang 'Jingle Bells' in unison. Number two: *Limousine Queen*, by Dawn Querulous. **A supermodel's quest for identity in post-glasnost Moscow.** H'mm . . . Why not **A supermodel's entrails are scrutinized for the meaning of life?** Call it *Haruspicating Heather.* Three: *Bozeman Beguine*, by Lionel Bay Dollar. **A campus cleaning lady is seduced by a visiting lecturer, then dies from an allegic reaction to their wedding cake.** The question is whether she sauteés his balls in the bargain." He sighed. "Weighing in at four is *Grave Plight*, by Bryce Kellogg. **A CIA operative must prevent the Albanians from introducing a homosexuality gene into the Pentagon's water supply.** Right from today's headlines, eh? Next time it'll be those feckless Burmese. One more, at number five: *The Milky Way Afflatus*, by Skippy MacScurvy. **The secrets of the universe are discovered in a treasure chest off Bora Bora** you see what I mean?" He flung the paper into the wind, where it was summarily dismembered and came to a rest pulverized on the berm. "I can't compete, Lucky. Lawyers, doctors, machinists, strippers, whores— they all think they can write. They're all would-be laureates, and there's a whole conspiracy of expensively educated and intellectually

125

deficient New York editors who agree with them. Meanwhile I'm reduced to a vanity press, provided I don't kill myself first. But as Swift said, 'When a true genius appears in this world, you may know him by this sign, that the dunces are all in confederacy against him.'"

"Well I have to say I'm impressed Dorian, that you've written a book and everything. Will you let me read it?"

He was silent, and she thought she glimpsed a tear, as quickly brushed away. "I burned it."

". . . You *burned* it?"

"Two days ago. Just before we left New York."

"But how did you know they were all going to be rejections?"

He explained.

". . . So there aren't any copies left?"

"Only handwritten."

"Well I wish I could read it."

He glanced at her. "I thought you despised me."

"I don't despise you Dorian; I just don't have any use for you, at least not in the way you'd like. For what it's worth, I think you're a pretty decent-looking guy, at least in that limp-wristed English kind of way."

"I'm Welsh actually. Totally different concept."

"Yeah well I'm a lesbian," she answered. "You could be from, from *Cameroon* and I still wouldn't need your dick, OK? End of story."


The afternoon brought thunderstorms and premature dusk. Rain pummeled the car spitefully, as though in retribution, and the interstate quickly flooded. Visibility was reduced to thirty feet; the blurred streaks of tail-lights appeared from nowhere and vanished the same way, ghostly and fleeting. Dorian had taken over the wheel; Lucky was in the passenger seat. The top had been raised, but the rain seemed powerful enough to drill through it.

As Nature cowed them into silence, Dorian slowed the Mustang to a crawl. The car moved as if within a timeless grey lacuna, a tenebrous self-contained world. Lightning jabbed at them, thunder heckling in its wake. Only Fish was at ease, watching the torrent with childlike absorption. "Look at it!" he whispered.

Even Prophet seemed nervous. "Maybe we should pull over, Dorian."

"If you like."

"Keep going," said Fish.

"Hey! What was that?" said Lucky, as they passed a white shape at the side of the road.

Dorian glanced in the rear-view mirror. "Looks like a girl."

"Well stop! Back up!"

"Lucky I can't back up, there might be a car right behind us."

"Fine but at least stop, OK? Just pull over here, I want to see if she needs help."

Dorian eased the car onto the shoulder, gliding to a halt.

"Do we have an umbrella?" asked Lucky.

"I don't," said Dorian. "I know Fish doesn't. Prophet?"

"Didn't think to pack one."

"Never mind." She pulled off her shoes and opened her door, admitting a scatter of rain. She climbed out of the car, slammed the door shut, and began wading through the puddles, hitching up her dress. The raindrops soaked her immediately, prodding her like a thousand fingers and forming a curtain so thick that she felt the impulse to part it like underbrush, as if she were warding off thorns.

The girl appeared suddenly, standing perfectly still. She looked to be about fifteen and her skin was unevenly toned, somehow ashen and bronze at once, as if mottled by disease. She turned to Lucky, frail and unresistant to the rain, her thin blue dress clinging to the fragile contours of her body, her blonde hair straggling to her shoulders. Her face was exquisitely sad, the eyes hollow, the lips quivering.

"Do you need a ride?" Lucky called.

The girl's expression did not change; she gave no indication that she understood the question. Lucky moved closer, blinking away rain. "Do you need help?"

The girl smiled and looked away shyly, as if she'd been asked whether she liked a particular boy and the answer was affirmative. She might be autistic, Lucky thought. When Lucky touched her arm she did not react. Lucky bent slightly, placing herself at eye level.

"Are you alone?" She sought the girl's dark blue eyes, held them briefly. "Do you need help?"

The girl began to tremble; and despite the rain, Lucky saw the tear escape and course down her cheek. Lucky rested a palm on her forehead, and found it simmering with fever.

"My god," she whispered. She looked around, confirming the

127

absence of cars in the vicinity, and said, "Come with me. I promise I won't hurt you, OK? Just come with me?"

The girl was docile enough, allowing herself to be led by the hand through water that was now calf-deep, approaching the hem-lines of their dresses. When they reached the car Lucky opened the door and eased the girl into the front seat, gently guiding her to the middle. Dorian recoiled from her wet form, but then paused to take closer notice. The girl was arrestingly lovely, her features small and delicately formed. Her dress was made of cotton, and opportunely he registered the outlines of her breasts, the faint impressions of her nipples. She was certainly a viable alternative to Lucky, who was proving difficult with her insistence upon lesbianism. The girl hugged herself, shivering, and then Lucky had clambered in and slammed the door.

"Turn on the heat," she said.

"Lucky the humidity—"

"Turn on the fucking heat!" Lucky felt herself quivering, less from the damp than from the strangeness of the encounter. When Dorian still hesitated she leaned over and jerked the switch, and they were buffeted by a blast of dry air.

Prophet stared at the girl with an eerie flush of recognition, his body responding with almost visceral sympathy. Even soaked through, she was startlingly evocative of the women who'd been haunting his imagination for so many years, witness to the little death. The perfect symmetry of her features, the slender slope of her neck, the naked innocence behind her eyes—these inspired a passion so disorienting in its acuity that for a moment he nearly swooned . . .

"What's her name?" he asked, his GUARD lowering by reflex.

"I don't know yet, all right? Just let her dry off. Dorian maybe we should stop at the next motel and figure out who she is. Besides, there's no point in traveling in this weather."

"What, are we taking her in?"

"Just move, damn it!"

"She's very pretty," said Prophet softly.

"She could be a murderer," said Fish. "Aren't we in Kentucky or something?"

"She could be a princess," Prophet whispered. "She could be *anything*."

Dorian coaxed the Mustang onto the road, stirring plumes of

128

water. The rain continued with no hint of reprieve as he navigated among dead and dying cars. The Mustang's engine sputtered but clung to life. Each yard seemed a victory.

"There," said Lucky, as a blue sign presented itself on the side of the road. "Gas food lodging excellent, just keep going we're almost there."

The motel was called Pleasant Acres, its units packaged one after another in rowhouse fashion, each with a sheltered porch. A scattering of senior citizens reclined on folding chairs, staring at the rain. On the other side of the parking lot stood a detached shanty, which bore the sign **OFFICE**. Dorian stopped the car and they made a dash.

A fat middle-aged woman sat behind the desk, reading a paperback book with the left side folded back, like a tabloid. A vending machine stood nearby, its promise of soda negated by the handwritten notice **BROKEN**. The travelers dripped expectantly. She looked up, peering at them in frank disgust.

"Two rooms," said Lucky.

The woman's face did not change, though words issued from her mouth. "Not sure there's any vacancies."

"Bullshit," Lucky replied evenly. "Two rooms."

The woman stared a moment longer, then stirred her great bulk by degrees. After two false starts she rose ponderously, the chair creaking in relief. She waddled toward the counter, her lime-green pants hissing abrasively at each stride, as if the friction of her thighs was an attempt to create fire. She groped beneath the counter; a pudgy hand emerged with two cards.

"Fill these out," she said.

"A writing utensil might help," said Dorian, smiling.

The woman's eyes lingered on his, and her thoughts spoke for themselves: *a Catholic, a nigger, a foreigner, and two little sluts* . . . She pushed an old coffee mug across the counter. It contained half-pencils with no erasers, the sort used by golfers.

Dorian took up a pencil and scribbled **Lionel Bay Dollar, 14 Wankum Lane, Cedar Bend, SD 12345.** The receptionist held up the card and appraised it with sunken eyes. She frowned. She bent down and again foraged behind the counter, producing a slim hardcover volume: *Bozeman Beguine*, by Lionel Bay Dollar. Deliberately she opened the back cover and peered at the flap, where a small black-and-white photograph depicted an old man with ranine features pensively fingering an acoustic guitar. The woman peered from the photograph to Dorian's face and back again; he could sense the sluggish machinery of her brain churning along.

"Well," he said, flashing his most disarming smile. "What a hideous coincidence."

Out in the rain, under the collective scrutiny of their elders, whose faces were blank as Buddha's (one had the urge to train firehoses on them, to unleash the lions, to goad life from such stubborn inanimacy), the young people hauled their luggage into two adjacent rooms at the end of a row.

Someone had thoughtfully placed the complimentary Bibles on the nightstand instead of concealing them in the drawers, where they might have been missed. Fish immediately settled down to read, puzzling over that meddlesome inconsistency in Genesis in which God creates the universe twice and under different circumstances each time. Prophet set his computer on a table near the window while Dorian hovered next door with the women.

"What are you doing?" asked Lucky.

"I thought I'd make myself useful." He gestured grandly. "How can I help?"

"Leave?" she replied, inspecting the bathroom.

He followed her in. "I thought you might need me."

She pulled the tap in the bathtub, placed her hand under the ensuing cascade. "No Dorian, I think we can manage just fine."

Dorian turned toward the new girl, who was standing in the doorway, watching the rain. Yes, she was quite a viable alternative. So young, and probably as virginal as he . . .

Lucky closed the drain and stood. "I know exactly what's on your mind, Dorian," she said, breezing past, "and I suggest you leave before I have to embarrass you."

Dorian glanced at the bathtub, then allowed his eyes to rove upward along the wall. Without another word he fled.

Back in the men's room—Prophet tapping away at his computer, Fish snorting over Leviticus—he moved directly into their own bathroom, which was flush against the one next door. He ran his gaze over the wall, searching for holes or fissures or any anomaly that might provide a visual conduit next door. He glanced at the fan duct in the ceiling, and considered the possibility of removing it and looking for a crawlspace above. He could hear the other bath running,

130

and felt his penis stir. In a few moments, naked women would be just on the other side of the wall—but inaccessible, as always.

*As always ...*

He leaned his forehead against the cold tile wall, his only solace the drone of the television in the bedroom, to which he didn't precisely listen but heard nonetheless:

Isn't it true, Ms. Pilgrim, that until his murder your husband had been a loving and devoted spouse?

Well—yeah.

Isn't it also true that he was a caring father to your baby daughter?

Yeah but—

And isn't it true, Ms. Pilgrim, that in the four years you were married your husband never acted violently toward you in any way?

Look that's—

*Yes* or *no*, Ms. Pilgrim.

...Yeah.

Then why is it, Ms. Pilgrim, that you expect this jury to acquit you of his murder?

I already told—

Do you *honestly* expect us to believe that you should be excused for this heinous crime because a *fortune-teller* claimed your life was in danger?

Look she *told* me she saw a man with a knife in my future.

And why did you have cause to believe her? Did she even *name* your husband as this mysterious assailant?

No but—

Did she even *describe* him?

No but she said it was someone I knew.

How many men do you know, Ms. Pilgrim?

...*I* don't know.

Hundreds, probably?

I—I *guess* so.

Had this fortune-teller—er, this Madame Finkelsteen—had she *ever* successfully predicted the future for you?

Well like I never visited her before, like it was my first time you know?

And isn't it true, Ms. Pilgrim, that you hope us to excuse

131

**your actions because of something called Misapplied Divination Syndrome?**

**Well yeah like I mean that's what my lawyer told me.**

Dorian shambled into the bedroom in time to learn that testimony from the State of Wisconsin vs. Pilgrim would resume after a fifteen-minute recess, during which special guests Kevin Bonus and Leigh Yalie would respond with their interpretation of **[click]**

"Find the news," said Prophet, still typing, but the screen revealed only a slow pan across a suburban adolescent bedroom whose walls boasted the airbrushed likenesses of various Caucasian males as a voiceover announced the sale of a new series of true-crime wallpaper for only **[click]**

"You don't think dinosaurs could have fit on the ark, do you?" asked Fish.

"Looks like CNN," said Dorian, as the screen settled upon a tracking shot of an upscale suburban neighborhood, Georgian and Tudor and Colonial mansions gliding past, all of which had been set ablaze. At a street corner the camera chanced upon a young black man staggering under the weight of a television set.

"The brothers been toppin," said Prophet, gazing absently at the screen.

"Which city is that?"

"Can't tell, I'm not sure how far they've spread. Looks like they're still going strong in any case. We should keep clear."

"This is all very interesting," said Dorian, settling back on one of the beds and opening a bottle of Jack Daniel's he'd stowed in his luggage. "It's like the storming of the Bastille. White people are the monarchy, and blacks are making Bourbons of them all. Bottoms up."

\*     \*     \*

Lucky shut off the tap and drew a finger through the water. She then stood and went into the bedroom. The girl was huddled on the edge of the bed, still trembling. Her tears seemed frozen in place like rivers half-formed, ceramically fixed, but at least she had stopped crying.

"I've drawn a bath," said Lucky, liking the formal expression,

132

which one might say to a lover. "The last thing we need is you catching pneumonia. Come with me."

The girl neither helped nor resisted as Lucky escorted her into the bathroom. Lucky paused, studying their reflections in the mirror. Each of them looked ghostly in the fluorescent light—an inhuman light, she thought—yet there was a fetching vulnerability to them: their straggling hair, their etiolated faces, their soaked and clinging dresses. Lucky felt maternal, filial, and conjugal all at once. The girl caught her eye, and she thought she perceived recognition.

She was unsure what to do next. She had assumed that the girl would take in the bathtub and then proceed of her own volition; but the girl simply stood there, regarding herself blankly. To buy time, Lucky bent down to test the water again, which was fast cooling.

"Do you have a name?" she asked. She did not expect a reply but she felt the need to ask, if only out of courtesy. When the girl said nothing, she continued, "Mine's Lucky. It's a silly name, I know, but it was given to me by someone I once loved." She paused, startled by the way she'd framed the sentence in the past tense. She felt a shiver of guilt: her mother didn't deserve *that* much pain. Or did she?

Slowly, as though unsure of her movements, the girl reached up to her neck and pulled free a necklace that had been concealed beneath her dress. The imitation gold lettering read **ARIEL**.

"Ariel," said Lucky, holding it close. "It's a beautiful name. And I know that you can hear me at least." She released the necklace. "Something bad must have happened to you, but don't worry. I would never hurt you, do you understand?" She was relieved when Ariel managed a small nod in reply.

"Let's get you in this bath now," said Lucky.

Ariel merely stood there, quivering.

Lucky took a deep breath. "OK, listen . . . I'm going to help you, all right? Tell me if you want me to stop." Her own hands were trembling as she unbuttoned Ariel's dress down the front. Ariel remained motionless. When Lucky had finished she pushed the dress from Ariel's shoulders and coaxed it to the floor. The girl wore nothing else, and Lucky gasped.

A lattice of scars and welts covered her stomach and breasts and thighs, some livid and red, others white and cruel. They formed a horrific network of anguish, violating even the tenderest of areas— the large nipples on Ariel's breasts, the soft skin of her sex.

"My god," Lucky whispered. "Who did this to you?" Ariel hugged herself again, and the way her breasts swelled up (what men would consider voluptuous) could only be called plaintive. Her eyes were hooded as Lucky stepped behind her, appraising the full extent of the trauma. There was further corruption on Ariel's back, and a hideous confluence on her buttocks. Her arms were not as severely wounded, but Lucky now realized why her skin appeared mottled. The girl had been beaten to within inches of her life.

"Do they still hurt?" Lucky asked. Tentatively she extended her hand to Ariel's shoulder. The girl did not flinch, so Lucky gently drew her fingers down Ariel's back. The welts passed beneath her touch in the manner that road markings are unaffected by footstep, tire, or rain—permanent, invincible.

"Well," said Lucky, "we're going to have to find out a few things."

The bathwater was now lukewarm. Lucky released the drain and ran the shower until the temperature was almost hot. She removed her own clothes and then encouraged Ariel into the tub. The water blanketed them like forgiveness. She guided Ariel into the stream and saw the girl's features convulse in a spasm of relief. Lucky held her under the spray until she was no longer shivering. Ariel became more responsive, closing her eyes and inclining her head back to receive the water on her face. The necklace hung forlornly, as though containing answers it could never divulge.

Lucky poured shampoo on her palm and worked it through Ariel's hair, trying to sort out her own feelings. Foremost rose a protective, nurturing instinct, something she had never experienced but which struck her quite powerfully. Behind this stirred a frank sexual longing, for Ariel was beautiful. She fought to still this impulse, and hated herself for feeling it at all.

As she rinsed Ariel's hair she sensed the girl was sobbing again. Immediately Lucky drew her close. She was startled when Ariel reciprocated, holding her fast as a life-raft. Lucky pressed her lips to Ariel's ear, gently kissing, and murmuring, "Don't worry, everything will be all right. Everything will be just fine. I promise."

Later, after Lucky had given her a clean dress, Ariel fell into an exhausted sleep. Propped up by pillows, Lucky cradled the girl's head on her chest, idly stroking her hair.

There was a knock at the door, and Dorian called her name.

Sighing, Lucky bade him enter. She watched his face as he took in the scene, his desire impossible to conceal.

"Is she all right?" he said at last.

"Too soon to tell. She won't discuss it, at least not yet."

He was about to say something but his voice caught. Lucky read his emotions, and softened. There was more to him than simple lust. She knew he recognized the love that she was giving to Ariel at that moment. He wanted love like that from her, and a greater love besides.

"We thought you might like to eat soon," he said.

"I'd love to," she replied, "but I don't want to wake her. Suffice to say this, Dorian: she's been through pure hell, and I don't know how we can help her. Anyway, would you be a dear and bring some food back to us?"

She saw the endearment take effect. She knew those four letters would remain with him for a long time, to be seized upon in the idle moments when men think about women and disacknowledge what can never be.

"Of course," he said. "I'm not sure what they've got around here, but we'll bring you a decent variety. Oh—vegetarian?"

"Doesn't matter," she answered.

As he was about to leave she called his name. He turned.

"Thank you," she said.

# CHAPTER TEN

## *Broadening One's Mind; or,*
## *How To Get Away With Murder . . .*

Eight o'clock. Christ is it freezing in here. I need some coffee. "Gerard?" I call.

There is scampering in the hall, and a moment later he appears in the doorway. Ah, Gerard . . . I find it impossible to convey how much I love him. He's about four feet tall and he has the wisest, most compassionate face I've ever seen. I must emphasize that he is not my pet. He is a friend, pure and simple, who understands me as well as anyone on the planet. It's not merely that he is strikingly intelligent: he also has an infinite capacity for forgiving. No matter how much I fuck up in this world, Gerard never presumes to judge me. He accepts me as I am. And lest you think I succumb to the Pathetic Fallacy, understand this: I don't give a good goddamned fuck about the empiricist/reductionist party line concerning primate intelligence.

"Hey you," I say. "Why don't you make the two of us some coffee? I'm too cold and lazy to do it myself."

The word "coffee" is one of Gerard's buzzwords, not least because he loves it himself. He bounds down the hall and soon there's clattering in the kitchen.

Take that, you fucking positivists. Take that and fuck *off*.

\* \* \*

This past April, scarcely a month before the Incident, I was rented by a man named J.S. Bane, who'd come to require my talents on a regular basis. He was president of a media consultancy called ! (known verbally as Point), which functioned as both an advertising and PR firm. A chinless, fat-faced Caucasoid, Bane claimed to be forty but looked twenty years older. He had lost much of his hair: only a grey-white floccus snarled the fringes of his scalp, giving him the appearance of an old circus clown.

Bane had no wife, which was a blessing—I'd ruined enough women's lives already. But I had yet to ruin a man's life, unless you counted Baker Lewis. With J.S. Bane, I began to redress the balance.

We're in his corner office overlooking 60th and Fifth. The furnishings include a Khan-Wittgenstein desk, a multimedia terminal (replete with virtuality interface), and a gamut of posters depicting various products and celebrities that ! has represented. (My favorite is one from the Lady Zygote handgun series, in which a glaring mini-skirted vixen—the NRA's answer to the women's movement—is pointing a sleek little pistol at the viewer. Beneath lies the caption **STOP The Violence.** The runner-up, judged too controversial, was **You're going a long way down, baby . . .**)

The postmodern desk is a mere slab of black marble with no drawers. J.S. lies naked on this desk; I'm straddling his thighs. I am also choking him with a black silk scarf, so that he may achieve (in his words) maximal orgasmic intensity.

It is nine-thirty in the morning. Whenever we fuck in his office, J.S. likes to maintain a running conversation with his speaker-phone. Sure enough, I have barely climbed astride when the intercom squawks. The effeminate purr of Sloane Lisp, Bane's efficient gay secretary, issues from the speaker.

"I have Liz Unger from *Fortune* on line one."

"Put her *oof!* through . . . J.S. Bane."

"Mr. Bane, I was wondering if I could just have a moment of your time . . . ?"

"Maybe Liz. Depends on what you want."

"These rumors that the IRS is going to bring up charges—"

"No *hwuh!* no comment, Liz, except that Point categorically denies any wrongdoing . . . next Sloane?"

His face is turning a little too blue for comfort. I ease the pressure.

"Dov Weissfeld from *Time* on three."

"I'll take it . . . Dov, what's happening."

"J.S.? Listen, I understand you're being interviewed by presidential candidates this week."

"Next two weeks, actually."

"Can I ask who?"

"Birdsong, Lumumba, Pine, a few others."

"How about our erstwhile VP?"

"Yeah, his people are making overtures. Nothing *ah!*—nothing firm yet."

"You think you can handle it?"

"Look at it this way. We got Goldblatt, Hinds, and Picardi into the House in ninety-eight, and Junkins and Malibu in the Senate. Our current mayor and governor were made by Point. Every candidate we've represented has won."

"What's your retainer fee?"

"More *puh!*—more than you'll ever make, Dov. Anyway, gotta go, talk to you later . . . next?"

His cock is hardening, his eyes glazing over. I'm really rather good at this.

"Madelein on one."

"Put her through . . . *hi.*"

"I've been thinking about you, J.S."

"Likewise."

I slow my rhythm, listening.

"Have you made up your mind yet?" she asks.

"You really are shameless, you know that?"

"Life is short, J.S. I want something, I go after it. Anyway, I hear your mistress is there even as we speak."

I frown. He averts his gaze, and there is a long pause.

"You want me too, don't you?" she says.

I smirk at him. He scowls back, as if to say *None of your fucking business.*

". . . Yes, I *hee!*—of course I do."

"I've seen her. She's beautiful."

Why *thank* you, Madelein.

"This is true."

"It's kinda funny though, I can't figure out what she is. Is she Italian or Hispanic?"

Here we go again.

"I never asked, Madelein."

"I mean she looks like she could even be Jewish, or maybe Black Irish. Then again, with those eyes maybe it's more like . . . Indonesian or something? In any case, I'd like to fuck her myself, you know."

I burst out laughing. He reaches up to smother my face. I accelerate the tempo, strangling with one hand and tickling his scrotum with the other. *(This little testis went to market . . .)*

138

"... Really?"

"Really. You don't think she'd be up—"

"No, Madelein, she—*kah! kah!*—wouldn't. She's a bit more ... *orthodox* than what you're used to."

That's what you think, pricko.

"More's the pity," she said. "But anyway, even if you love her I'm not going to get upset. Love or no love, human beings aren't meant to be monogamous. It's not in the genes."

"*Guh*—really."

"We're meant to fuck, nothing more. Everything else is ... I don't know, a construction."

"I'm sure you're right Madelein. Now, don't you think we should get ready for Birdsong? He's *uhn!*—he's due in ten minutes."

Ah ha. Madelein is an *employee* ...

"Whatever you say, J.S."

"I'll see you there."

"Oh, and J.S.? One more thing."

"... Yes, Madelein?"

"When you see me this morning, keep one thing in mind."

"*Umph* ... What."

"I'm not wearing any underwear."

His penis swells an extra half-inch. "Ahhh ... Oh Jesus *wait*, Madelein, you're not wearing that white dress, are you?"

"Bye, J.S."

Approaching climax ... I grip his neck harder.

"Christ I mean ... Madelein? Madelein ...? *Whooooo* ..." His eyes roll back in his head. The idiot.

"J.S.?" titters the speaker.

His head lolls to one side. "... Fuck. What is it, Sloane?"

"Hy Slatkin from Farenheit Studios on six."

"Take a message. Next?"

"Biff Audrey from St. Marvin's Dress on four."

"I'll call him back this afternoon. Next?"

Climbing off, I start to mop up.

"Just a message from Chadwick Elder at Messiah Condoms. Apparently the Christian Brigade is threatening a protest over that last commercial."

"What, that bit about Mary Magdalene? Tell Chad to cool off. Completely harmless, I mean Christ it's not like people didn't fuck

139

back then." His gaze lingers on my breasts. "Where's that interne by the way? Tell her I want a dish of green M&M's in five minutes, before the Birdsong meeting."

"Right."

"Tell her to clean out the men's toilets too, in case Birdsong has to take a shit."

"Right."

"And tell her to call Wolfgang and see if my Ferrari is ready."

"You got it."

"And know what? Tell her to get down to the public library. We've got the Honeyman Banquet coming up next week, and I need her to do some research."

"Righty-o. On what, by the way?"

"Art. Tell her to read everything she can about art, especially philosophy. I mean Plato, Aristotle—anyone who said anything about art, I want to know about it."

". . . All right." Through the speaker, I can hear Sloane scribbling to keep pace. I reach for a shoe.

"And when she's read everything tell her to write a summary. I want her to highlight the really good quotes so I can use em in my speech."

"Will do, J.S."

"Good. Now pull up Birdsong's folder so I don't look like an idiot at the meeting."

I am now fully dressed and running a comb through my hair. He remains on the table, his slick little penis sagging toward his left hip. He looks as if he's waiting to be autopsied. I have really done a job on him. I blow him a kiss goodbye.

And who should I encounter in the reception lounge but the former Vice President himself. He is staring at a poster for Messiah Condoms **(Fit For More Than a King . . . )** with an expression of scandalized appreciation. Six minders lurk in the background. His ridiculous wife scowls nearby, her equine features more hideous than ever. She barks a reprimand; he sheepishly turns away.

This is the man who would run our country.

As I'm standing in the elevator, waiting for the doors to close, I have a sudden inspiration. Quickly I remove my panties. "Mrs. Birdsong?" I inquire sweetly.

Wife and husband turn, frowning. My eyes locked on hers, I

140

slowly lift my skirt. "Did anyone ever tell you," I say, tossing her my panties, "that you're the sexiest woman alive?"

*       *       *

The very next week, I was asked by J.S. to escort him to the aforementioned Honeyman Banquet at the St. Phlebus. Roughly a hundred advertising and PR executives would be assembling to congratulate themselves, and Bane had been appointed keynote speaker.

One can't help but like the high life. Bane chaperoned me to the hotel in a stretch limousine, and at the banquet I was plied with caviar and champagne. As we moved among the glitterati I thought wryly of Professor Lank and our fur-ridden apartment. The problem with whoring, at my level, was the illusion that the client's milieu was my own.

We were seated at a table for six with two other ! executives and their companions. One of the former was VP McStoat Bourbenal, a Bronxville WASP with the rigid larynx, glued teeth, and clenched hair of his ilk. His wife Flookie was a boobless saffron waif whose page-boy haircut and stovepipe physique gave her the appearance of a toddler playing dress-up.

Also present was the inexplicable Madelein, Bane's interoffice paramour. She was a slender six-foot blonde, elaborately constructed for the evening in a translucent rayon jumpsuit through which nipple and pubic hair vied murkily for one's attention. Merely standing still afforded her an ungainly air, as though "poised" could have no meaning in her lexicon. Her date was a squirmingly-contoured Latina in a blood-red mini-dress and matching lipstick, the sort of woman who makes every non-gay male in sight act half his age, and every non-gay female rethink her preferences.

The collective social chemistry of a room must reconfigure upon the entrance of beauty, and the tripartite splendor of myself, Madelein, and the Latina challenged the circuitry to its limit. Each man in the room sought to include us in his field of view, contriving to appear as if his roving gaze had simply chanced upon us in brief contemplation before sliding evasively to a different subject, only to return at the first opportunity.

I imagine that the only thing worse than sitting through an evening with spin doctors is sitting through an evening with lawyers. My

141

tablemates whiled away the time in a furious debate of rival campaign analyses, market demographics, and flash-poll mechanics. McStoat claimed to have developed a new philosophy of damage control in which, "Aikido-style," the energy of interrogators was used against themselves. J.S. consumed a fair amount of red wine, and by the time he was called to give his speech he was quite drunk.

He stood and aimed for the podium, coddled by envious applause. He stumbled on the first step and plummeted face-first into the stage, evoking an anxious murmur. But he recovered quickly, declining offers of assistance, and—grinning all the while—staggered on to the lectern.

"Evening, boys and girls," he said, with a brief wave to his audience. He began slapping at his torso, and his smile contracted into a frown. In fact, a look of almost childlike perplexity overcame his features as he frisked himself with growing urgency and ransacked his pockets. When he realized he would not find his note cards, he glanced to his colleagues for support. McStoat shrugged, but Madelein waved him on, meaning he should improvise. He smiled and confronted his listeners.

"I can't tell you how thrilled I am to be up here addressing you all," he said, gesturing expansively. "Thought maybe the bunch of us could shoot the breeze for awhile on the subject of art. Now just what the hell *is* art, anyway? Great philosophers have been wrestling with that question for a long, long time. Some people say one thing, some people say another. Who are you supposed to believe? It can definitely be a confusing issue. I mean it's a *hell* of a complex issue." He paused to overturn his brain, perhaps intending to quote Plato and Tolstoy and Lord Shaftesbury there, from passages the interne had exhumed after her day's sabbatical at the public library. But no pearls of wisdom made themselves available to J.S., and the silence began to cloy.

"So this big question arises," he resumed, forging ahead. "Namely: What Is Art? I mean think about it: *What The Fuck Is Art?* It's funny, because art can mean so many different things to so many different people. You can think about that question for a long time and not come to many conclusions, you know what I'm saying?" He paused as though to let this sink in.

"So one day," continued J.S., raising a finger for no apparent reason, "yours truly decided to bend his mind to that most grandiose

142

of questions, i.e., What Is Art? And after some *really deep thought* I came up with, shall we say, some truly unexpected answers.

"I thought to myself: *Why is it* that certain art from a long time ago is still around today—like opera, for example. You and I all go to the Met, and we see the same old stuff—you know, Beethoven, and Brahms, and of course the great Italian composers, e.g., er . . . what's his face . . . *Vivaldi.* Now I don't know about you guys, but I figure there's gotta be people sitting around today trying to write operas. How come they aren't getting performed? I mean, it's not like you go to Lincoln Center and hear the latest work of—of *Reggie Pinto* from Des Moines, right?

"It does add up, though. You can't escape the fact that opera is dead. I mean yeah we revive all that ancient stuff and it's a cultural event and everything, but the point is if we're still doing the same old shit it's prolly cause those old guys thought of all the best possible good music and now it's time to do something new, right? I mean look around. You see any new paintings in the Metropolitan Museum? You see a new collection of—of *Hank Flanagan originals*?"

Bane had jammed his hands into his pockets and was standing slightly to the side of the podium, gazing toward some point in the back of the room. "I could go on. There's millions of examples. But you know sometimes it pays to think about these things." He nodded sagaciously, as if a *koan* had just been deconstructed. "Now where was I? Right, I was talking about What Is Art. So I ask myself: If books are dead—cause let's face it, no one reads any more—and opera is dead, it's like: *What are* the *avant-garde, cutting-edge* art forms of today? Music? Forget it: it's all recycled. Film? All right, I'll buy that. But is film all that there is?

"And then it hits me! *Advertising; public relations: these* are the new arts! Isn't art a question—" here he thought for a good half-minute, doubtless trying to recall the interne's notes "—isn't art's *function* to *shape society*? To *reflect* and *change society*? And if so aren't *we* the ones who are doing just that? Think of it people— it's all about *perception.* We not only gauge markets, we *create* them. Our slogans, our terminology pass into the *language.* We have the power to *design culture.* Isn't what we're doing *exactly the same thing*—" he pounded the lectern for emphasis "—as what the great artists were doing thousands of years ago? I'm telling you, *our* work is what's going to be studied in the universties in a hundred years.

143

People will remember the best campaigns of today and reflect on how a small company went Fortune 500 and changed society with a product. They'll remember those celebrities whose press agents can keep them in the public conscience permanently. Never mind the art per se; it's whether the agent makes people *think* it's good art that matters. The product is subordinate to the pitch! And with so much out there you need someone to be your—your *culture broker,* so you don't miss out on being hip, and that's what advertising and PR people do. And *that,* ladies and gentlemen, is why we are the architects of the future."

*   *   *

"You know something? Let's go to *your* place," said J.S. Bane.

We were in the limousine, heading down the sparkling glass concourse of Park Avenue, itself a city of light. His tie loosened, his shirt unbuttoned, he was sprawled on the seat with one hand down his pants and the other up my dress. A half-empty vodka bottle had spilled nearby.

In fact he wasn't paying much attention to me. Cold sober, I stared out the window while he shuffled through his thoughts. He seemed preoccupied, but perhaps I was overestimating his capacities. There might have been nothing on his mind. He might have found the poor man's road to Nirvana.

"Yeah," he continued, parting my labia absently. "Let's definitely go to your place."

I was strict about not bringing clients to the apartment. Usually they never asked, so there wasn't a problem. My apartment was the one place where I could retreat from my job and this desperate City in general; and besides, I didn't want these johns to know where I lived. They could not contact me except through Providence, and Bodleian was zealous in his refusal to divulge our phone numbers, lest he fall out of the loop.

"I don't think so," I said.

"Come *on,*" he said, in that petulant glissando that means Don't be such a wimp/tight-ass/nay-sayer.

"Why can't we use your house?"

"Renovations."

"J.S. . . ."

"I'll pay you double. Hell, I'll pay you five grand." He rummaged in his jacket, producing a checkbook. "Five grand. Whaddaya say?"

I looked at the checkbook. To me that was a hell of a lot of money, and Cornell Bodleian need never know.

"All right," I said, "but make it out to cash."

He grinned. "So your name isn't Dr. Wicked after all?"

Lank knew all about my vocation, and even referred to it as "a noble endeavor, eminently dignified." (?!) To his great credit he never asked for my services. When I arrived with Bane he had already gone to bed, which made everything a lot less awkward.

Bane tramped through the rooms, ogling the fauna. He whistled at the dogs, hissed at the cat. He rapped on the goldfish tank, squinting inside. He chased the armadillo under the couch. He chirped at the macaw; the macaw told him to fuck off. He shadow-boxed with Gerard; Gerard gave me a reproving look and fled into the kitchen. Bane was especially fascinated by the piranhas, and wanted to feed them right away.

"I don't think my roommate would like that," I said, taking his arm. "Let those goldfish live another day. Come on."

He wandered through my bedroom, poking at mementos and scrutinizing photographs. He was like a college student visiting his girlfriend's dormitory for the first time. I began to undress. I wanted to fuck him, evict him, and then go to sleep.

"Are these your parents?" He was pointing to the Hell's Angel who had given me Gerard. I had saved a picture of him and his teen-age girlfriend.

"Yes."

"Where do they live?"

"They don't."

"Ah . . . What happened to them?"

"Freak accident."

"Car? Plane?"

"Tiger."

He glanced at me, not sure whether to laugh. "*Tiger?*"

"At the zoo."

He decided that I was serious, and shook his head. "You must hate cats. How can you live with the one here?"

I was naked, sitting on the edge of the bed. "You can't blame the

145

tiger," I said, shrugging. "He was trapped, out of his element. He was hungry."

"Jesus."

"It's incredible how people delude themselves about some things. Anyway, come here while I'm still awake."

He wanted the usual that evening. I used one of my own scarves, riding his cock and watching impassively as his features tumesced in joy. It was hard to extract the same satisfaction that I'd done with Baker Lewis, because there was nothing futile about Bane's exertions. He derived genuine pleasure from our encounters; even worse, he paid little attention to me. He tended to retreat into his own mind's eye, letting me set the tempo. But though I controlled him physically, I had no psychological grip on J.S. Bane. He was too self-satisfied, too easy to please. To him I was little more than fresh pussy, and if need be I could be replaced. He was not dependent upon *me*, and on that night I began to resent it.

How was it, I wondered, that he should gain so much from this experience and I so little? What gave him the right to such self-indulgence at my expense? Five thousand dollars? Fine. But let it not be said that money can't buy happiness.

Thinking about *that* pissed me off even further.

Perhaps that was why, as he hurtled toward climax, I grew careless about the pressure being applied to his neck. He was thrusting with great relish, with great *zeal*, as if he wholly *believed* in what he was doing, his hands gripping my breasts, head thrown back, as if God were personally teasing him along. The little shit. I rode him still harder. How glorious it was to pull that scarf tight, to expend all my energy with such terrible, animalian purpose. And fool that he was, he grew all the happier, as if he were approaching the most dick-splitting orgasm of his life.

I opened my eyes and sighed, utterly spent. Looking down, I saw the half-lidded, adukarescent eyes staring back at me, and the fat smile on the glaucous face.

The moments that followed were oddly exhilarating. The realization that I had murdered J.S. Bane overcame me very gradually, like horsemen in the distant hills whose first, faint tremors ripple through the village, a delicate anomaly in the fabric of space-time, until the hoofbeats accrue into a wall of sound, cascading upon itself, and the peasants look up to see the riders descending from the moors, a seeming flood-tide of moving earth, a roiling mass, the first swords already drawn and catching the sunlight in cruel portent . . .

I laughed, and then I laughed a lot more. I laughed because, as with a glass of milk that has been inadvertently knocked to the floor, the situation was suddenly very immediate and yet should have been so avoidable. What had been the *point* of killing him? Had I really meant to? (Probably not, I thought conveniently.) Absurdity rose like bile in my throat until I was choking on it, gasping hysterically for breath as I sat astride the withered phallus of J.S. Bane and giggled in manic disbelief. That I could have killed a man seemed as unlikely as the storyline of a pop novel . . . but of course people buy them in the millions, and J.S. Bane was plainly quite dead . . .

Ah, what to do, what to do . . . I started by dismounting Bane's corpse, and out of curiosity checked to see if he'd come. Well, he had: already a thin trail of semen was coagulating on his balls. If nothing else, he had died at the very zenith of male experience.

I pulled out my condom, tied a knot in the end, and padded myself dry. I donned a sweatshirt and sweatpants, considering my options all the while. The problem with corpses, I realized with timely insight, is that they're so much *trouble.* A corpse means phone calls, visits, measurements, arrangements, *questions.*

Another thing: even in a city littered with corpses, this was sure to make the news. Bane was famous, at least within his profession and New York society in general. That he had died while fucking a hired mistress would be carrion for the tabloid vultures—that and my naughty nickname. The spotlight would be trained on me as America flushed out every client I'd ever serviced and ransacked the annals of my insignificant life. I'd be put on mock trial on some TV show **(Wicked or not?** *You* **decide).** I would be transformed into a character I did not recognize. I would lose every sense of privacy, both past and present, until two or three weeks elapsed; then I'd be cast aside for the next scandal, a sad footnote in pop-culture history.

Then again, there might be movie offers, book offers (wouldn't *that* be an irony?) . . . I could give up whoring, become famous for a day, retire in some other country, keep a few bees, think great thoughts . . .

147

I laughed again. The whole notion was ridiculous. There would be no inquest, no instant books. I knew exactly what I would do.

In death J.S. Bane was not beautiful. The chest was hirsute and flaccid, the breasts pseudocyetic; the nipples appeared to be squinting. A profligate abdomen splayed onto the bed as though anxious to flee its corpus. The phallus was limp and irrelevant, the legs incongruously spindly. This, then, was the sum total of J.S. Bane— a sum that now equalled zero.

I gathered his clothes into a bag. I then grasped his ankles and dragged him into the hall. Gerard appeared in the kitchen doorway to watch. His solemn countenance seemed to indicate that he understood all too well what had happened.

At the end of the hallway I released an ankle and turned the key in the door. I pushed the door open a few inches and turned on the light. Killjoy raised his head, staring.

"Had dinner yet, friend?" I asked, hauling Bane inside. Killjoy regarded the corpse for a moment, his head questing forward; then he glanced at me. I waved and backed discreetly out of the room. I had a brief glimpse of those hingeless jaws opening wide and was reminded of that chapter from *Le Petit Prince*, about the hat that wasn't a hat. I closed the door and turned the key.

I had hardly reached my bedroom when I began to tremble and my laughter yielded to tears. My knees gave out and I collapsed. I lay huddled on the floor, unable to think about what I'd done but feeling its import nonetheless. Gerard loped into the room and sat nearby, stroking my head. Dear Gerard, my only friend in the world . . . what would *you* do under these circumstances?

I resolved not to feel guilty. Bane had no family, no one to care if he lived or died. He belonged to a carcinogenic profession. Maybe I *had* murdered him . . . well, what of it? No one ever had to know. Meanwhile, I had the best of both worlds: I had killed a man, thus proving that I was alive *(I kill therefore I am),* but I hadn't really *meant* to, not in my proverbial heart of hearts. It was like cheating God.

My conscience suddenly clean—hadn't I done a great service to my country, if it meant Jay Birdsong would never become President?—I determined to worry about it no more. I'd throw his clothes

148

into (where else?) the East River and that would be the end of it. It was really that simple.

Or almost. There was still the chance of getting caught.

A few hours later I crept down the hallway to check on Killjoy. The anaconda lay asleep, but halfway down his length was a cylindrical bulge, six feet long—Killjoy's digestive fluids converting the spin doctor into ATP. So far so good, but what about evidence?

I scrutinized the living room and bedroom for signs of Bane's passage. I hauled out the vacuum cleaner and sucked the apartment of stray particles or filaments, hoping Lank wouldn't awaken. I scrubbed every surface to erase fingerprints. I was not up on the latest crime fiction, but I had vague intuitions that the police, using infrared scanning and ultraviolet sensors and electron microscopes and ruthless sniffer dogs could somehow reconstruct this crime scene down to the finest of details unless I was very, very careful.

It was dawn by the time I finished. The only remaining problem was the limo driver, who'd dropped us both at the apartment last night. Ah well—fuck him. I would say that Bane had left at sunrise and that I hadn't seen him since. They couldn't prove a bloody thing.

Besides: Gerard would back me up.

# CHAPTER ELEVEN

## *On the Future of Y-Chromosomes . . .*

She lay on the water's surface, gently floating, amid a verdant array of flower petals that spread toward the pool's edge in myriad whites, yellows, and burgundies, gently swirling. The pool was oblong and rimmed with stones, and fed by a small waterfall that descended a rock formation at the deep end. Beyond the pool, the glass walls of the room rose some forty feet to a domed ceiling, through which the stars and waxing moon glimmered in a country-black sky. Soft light emanated from the ten or twelve candles that stood nearby, and the air was colored with jasmine.

The room was circular in shape, with a diameter of perhaps a hundred feet. It was constructed directly behind the mansion, almost like a separate wing. One door led into the interior of the house; a second led outside to the gardens, now invisible in the darkness. There were gardens inside the room as well, and for that reason it was called the Arboretum. The pool lay opposite the first door, some thirty yards distant, between which the plants spread in a lush mosaic—rhododendrons, bluebells, violets, azaleas. Their presence could be felt as well as seen, like an audience in the shadows; and their scent, coupled with the jasmine, gave the room a soft, narcotic ambience.

A woman entered the room and started along the path of cedar chips that led toward the pool. A second followed two paces behind; both were naked. The first was tall and blonde and moved with the easy, upright gait of a royal at leisure, each stride one of subconscious composition. There was an uncanny symmetry and proportion to her body, an almost pre-conceived aesthetic suggesting the handiwork of an exacting sculptor. Her waist was narrow, her hips wide, her breasts neither small nor large. Her skin was pale and almost preternaturally smooth, and her hair fell richly onto her shoulders as if fresh from a loom. She seemed about thirty.

The second woman looked a few years older. Her body was thin and unremarkable, and Age seemed to be having Its way without a struggle. The breasts appeared functional but worn, the face was uncompromisingly lined, and the hair—short and dark and curly— seemed like coarse surplus when juxtaposed with the flaxen silk of her companion. She carried a towel in one hand and a stone jar in the other.

A wide strip of grass lay at the fringe of the pool. Here the first newcomer stood and gazed down upon the swimmer, who was still floating, eyes closed, so beautifully framed by the floral tapestry, her sex pouting beneath its thin, dark fleece. "Mary?" the swimmer murmured, without opening her eyes.

The tall woman nodded to her companion, who knelt and placed the jar and towel near the pool's edge. She then bowed slightly and retreated along the path. Mary waited until the footsteps were inaudible before speaking.

"Darling Lucky," she said, smiling. "I've got you all to myself, haven't I." Ignoring the steps at the shallow end, she dived into the pool and surfaced near the center, lilac blooms caught in her hair. The smile had vanished; her wet lips were slightly parted, her eyes quietly imploring. Righting herself, treading water, Lucky felt a tremor of both desire and apprehension. Tentatively, she drew her hand along Mary's cheek, across the lips, her forefinger sucked in by the gently abrasive tongue. A thrill coursed along her hand and arm and reached fruition in her loins. She shuddered, pulling the other woman closer, arm sliding around her waist. "You want to make love," she said.

Mary released the finger, brushed her lips against Lucky's ear. "Later," she whispered, taking the lobe in her lips. "Right now I want to fuck you."

Lucky's breath caught, her fingers closing on Mary's hip.

"Come on," Mary said, pulling her toward the stairs.

On the grass at the edge of the pool, she lay on her back as Mary, reaching into the stone jar, began to spread sugar glaze over Lucky's body, her fingers just grazing the skin, attenuating each nerve so that every receptor came alive. When Mary had finished, Lucky felt impossibly stoked. Squirming with impatience, she watched as Mary stood and applied the icing to herself, without hurry, hand lingering between her legs. When she had finished she knelt and extended that hand to Lucky's mouth, and Lucky reciprocated Mary's earlier gesture in the pool.

"Do you want me?" asked Mary—a bit oddly, given that nothing could be plainer. But the question was not rhetorical.

Lucky met her eyes. "Yes," she whispered.

For long moments they kissed upon the grass, Mary atop Lucky, their bodies pointing lengthwise in opposite directions. As Mary inched forward, descending toward Lucky's breasts, Lucky progressed in similar fashion until she was able to take Mary's glazed nipple in her mouth, feeling it swell against her tongue, exquisitely sweet. As Mary proceded further, Lucky arched her hips in anticipation, only half-conscious of her own actions. But Mary was in no rush: once in the vicinity of Lucky's pubis she strayed wide of her mark, a digression that in itself elicited the first orgasm.

Abruptly Mary stopped. Swinging her legs round, she pulled Lucky forward until they were face to face, Lucky on top. Mary positioned her hips to allow their clitorises to rub together, her hand firm on Lucky's rear. The other hand she drew along Lucky's forehead, pushing the hair from her eyes.

"You love me, don't you," she said, her hips gyrating.

Another orgasm was approaching. Lucky resisted the pressure, struggling to articulate a cogent reply.

"Well?" Mary smiled, her eyes both serene and terrible.

"Of—course I do," Lucky gasped, and then screamed as the orgasm tore through her.

Mary held her in place, did not relinquish her gaze. There was something hard in her placid expression, and also something needy; something . . . anaclitic?

"And you know I love you," she said, grinding her pelvis until Lucky screamed again.

"You're my best—friend," said Lucky hoarsely.

"And you won't ever leave me?"

Slowly Lucky pushed away and sat up. Her body felt wrung out, and for a moment she thought she would faint. "Mary—Mary please. Not now."

Mary pulled her back, and Lucky was unable to resist. She sagged against Mary's breast, where the sugar now lay melting, forgotten.

"Because I'd never forgive you," Mary said gently, stroking her head.

Lucky watched the icing drip along Mary's abdomen, considering the narrowness of context in which sexual activity was tolerable, and how absurd it seemed otherwise. "Who was she."

"Who was who?"

"Your valet. When you came in."

"She's new."

"Isn't she a little old for you?"

"She's thirty-four."

"She looks forty."

"I didn't think you'd noticed her. She's English, a writer, here to do some research. A Lothario in her native country, or so she claims, though personally I can't imagine why."

"You sure can pick them, can't you. Are you fucking her?"

"I am," Mary replied evenly.

Once more Lucky pushed away, this time climbing to her feet. "You hypocrite."

Mary stood as well, hand reaching out, but Lucky avoided her touch and jumped into the pool. She surfaced, brushing off any sugar that remained.

"Lucky."

"I have to hand it to you, Mary. I don't know how you get away with it but I have to say I'm—no, damn it, I don't want you in here with me."

Mary had descended two of the steps. She paused, calf-deep, and spoke wearily. "Lucky, we've been through this before. You'll always be first. You know that."

Lucky hugged herself, rubbing arms now broken out in gooseflesh. "You don't have the right," she said, "to talk about forgiveness. You don't have the—oh Mary, please don't."

Mary had eased into the water, smiling, and glided over to where Lucky stood. With unexpected force she pulled Lucky against her. "If you ever leave me," she said, her hand sliding toward Lucky's vulva, "I will never forgive you. Understood?"

Lucky struggled for a moment, but Mary would not relinquish her hold. Her fingers found their reward and Lucky went limp, a tear coursing down her cheek. "Yes," she whispered, looking up into those kindly, condescending, pale blue eyes.

Mary's face had gone soft and beneficent. "You're so simple, in the end, aren't you," she murmured, shaking her head in mock exasperation, watching the orgasm gather itself in Lucky's glistening eyes. "So easy to please."

A moment later, without warning, she sneezed in Lucky's face.

153

The room is square-shaped, the floor hardwood; a mirror covers one of the walls. A heavy-bag dangles like a pendulum in one corner, gently swaying. A large wooden post, or *makiwara*, is nailed to the floor nearby.

She is the only woman among twelve men of varying age and race. She stands in the center of the room, her back to the mirror. With one exception, the men form a line along the opposite wall. Their loose-fitting white uniforms are somewhat like pajamas, though each is made of canvas and immaculately pressed. All are tightly cinched at the waist by a long black belt, a few of which are marked with gold stripes.

One man stands apart from the rest—a bald, thickset Caucasian whose gnarled forearms, convex pectorals, and sloping trapezoids suggest a body hard as granite. His black belt is severely frayed, and a series of gold *kanji* characters has been stitched upon one end, marking him as the *sensei*.

She too wears a uniform, or *gi*, but her own belt is brown. She stands with her bare feet shoulder-width, her knees slightly bent, her toes gripping the floor. The heel of her right foot is even with the big toe of her left, and turned slightly outward. Her back is perfectly straight, her gaze directly forward. Her arms are held out before her, bent ninety degrees at the elbow and angled forty degrees to the floor, palms up, fists clenched, elbows almost touching her ribs. Nearly every muscle in her body is at full tension. Even her throat is constricted: each breath is a slow, rasping wheeze, like a death-rattle.

She emerged naked and dripping from the Arboretum and entered the mansion proper, Mary keeping pace. Their steps fell in perfect unison down the long rosewood hallway, as if they were performing a military exercise.

"I won't be seen arguing with you," Mary said through clenched teeth.

"Then leave me the fuck alone," answered Lucky, wiping the last of the snot from her face.

The *makiwara* is six feet tall, four inches wide and an inch thick, with a thinly padded striking surface at shoulder height. It is either driven into the ground or nailed to the floor; when struck, it yields only slightly and springs back to its original position. The *makiwara* is most often hit with a closed fist, specifically with the large knuckles of the index and middle fingers. You punch softly at first, ten times a day with each hand, allowing calcium deposits to build gradually on the knuckles.

The *sensei* is holding a short wooden plank, half an inch thick and six inches wide. He steps forward and swings it at her left forearm. Upon impact the board splits in half, the loose end clattering to the floor. Her gaze does not waver; her posture is uncompromised.

Discarding the board, the *sensei* tries to push her arms together and then to pull them apart. He fails on both accounts. He drives the outer edge of his palm into her stomach. She exhales at the moment of impact and remains in position.

Grunting, he strides behind her. He kicks behind each of her knees, but her balance is unaffected. He claps her shoulders and biceps and the flesh does not yield. He then swings his foot between her legs. Were she male, and her stance imperfect, his instep would strike a crippling blow to the scrotum. Never mind gender: her stance is perfect. Her thighs are mercilessly clenched. His progress is halted midway between her knees and groin, and the blow is neutralized.

The anteroom of the house now served as the administrative office for the colony. Two secretaries were seated at mahogany desks just inside the front door amid a network of computer terminals, fax machines, and photocopiers. An oak-paneled door near the stairway led to Mary's private office, once the butler's quarters. The secretaries—one young and one middle-aged, each dressed in a forest-green kimono—looked up, startled, as the lovers strode through the anteroom without a word and swept up the stairs, leaving a trail of water behind.

A month later, you hit the *makiwara* a little harder, twenty times a day with each fist.

"*Kumite*," the *sensei* orders—free-fighting.
She bows to the men in line, and they to her.
The *sensei* barks a command. The man farthest to her left detaches himself from the line and trots forward. She slides into a forward combat stance, her arms poised to block or strike, eyes trained upon the center of his chest.

Few restrictions apply to the combat that follows. Full contact is permitted anywhere below the neck; medium contact is allowed to the head. Only biting, gouging, and blows to the neck are prohibited.

In the bedroom that they shared, Lucky filled her suitcase while Mary looked on with a smirk.

"You have no power outside of this place," said Mary. "You realize that, don't you."

"That would make two of us now wouldn't it," sneered Lucky. "You might be a goddess to these women but out there nobody gives a shit. And neither do I, not anymore."

When the edge of your hand, or the large knuckles of your fist, pass for the first time through even a single wooden board, your reaction is one of elation and disbelief. Surely there was some fault with the board that made it so easy. You have to break a few more to convince yourself that it's not a fluke—and it isn't. By now you're hitting the *makiwara* thirty times a day with each fist, medium-hard.

The first man is named Witherspoon, a taurine slab in his mid-thirties. She counters his jabs with kicks to the legs, twice nearly sweeping his feet from under him. Though far stronger than she, Witherspoon is probably no faster: her reflexes have been trained to the same hair-trigger standards. Her body has been equally conditioned to absorb all but the severest punishment. She responds to each of his attacks by pure instinct, never once pausing to think. At her level, self-defense is merely second nature.

Witherspoon launches a side-kick. She slips under the attack and traps his leg, dumping him to the floor. Still gripping his leg, she stomps on his crotch. Witherspoon has remembered his groin protector today, but practically speaking the fight is over. She applies an ankle-lock for the sake of formality, and Witherspoon taps the floor three times—surrender.

"I would like to know," said Mary, "precisely what you're qualified to do in the so-called Real World."

She bit her lip. She had hoped to leave without losing her composure, and she hadn't even finished packing. "I can thank *you* for that, can't I," she replied, closing the suitcase, "seeing as I've never been more than ten miles from this place in my life."

There is no reason to believe that a human fist can penetrate a cinder block, even when your teacher makes it look easy. But the worst thing you can do here is hold back: even the slightest lack of commitment will result in your hand getting broken, and not the block. It's not a matter of all or nothing: it's a matter of all or minus-all. You stand over it, measuring the distance, summoning your concentration, tightening your fist, taking a few deep breaths . . . and when you watch the block split in half and fall to the floor you think, It hurts, yes, but it's worth it.

On the *makiwara:* fifty times a day with each fist, striking with full power. The large knuckles of your first two fingers look and feel like stones, grotesquely misshapen and not particularly *feminine.* As you stand there, pounding the wood relentlessly, you remember the *sensei*'s observation that any fist which can break a cinder block can also break human bones all the more easily.

The second man, Ramirez. Makes the mistake of going easy on her, of being a bit too squeamish about hitting a woman. The martial arts don't allow for these delicacies, and it's only right that Ramirez should pay. His few tentative kicks are contemptuously knocked aside, and finally she takes the fight to him: a roundhouse-kick, big toe extended, to the inside of his right thigh, followed by two quick punches to the ribs. Ramirez, finally aware of his danger, is too dazed to counterattack. She steps in, right hand grabbing his throat, right foot knocking his right leg away, and pushes him to the floor. She then rests her heel on his throat—three taps.

Outside, in front of the mansion, she stood next to the silver Bentley, fumbling with her keys. Arms folded, Mary leaned against the gorgeous and absurd piece of machinery, her recent birthday present to Lucky. She still hadn't bothered to dress: as the queen of all she surveyed, Mary Stillwater was shamed by no one, not least because she looked half her chronological age. In a milieu where conventional beauty should have carried no weight, she was fully aware that, clothed or naked, none of her two hundred followers was in her league—except Lucky.

"Are you going to answer me?"

157

Lucky pulled open the door, thrust her suitcase into the passenger seat. She was about to get inside but then paused, brushing away tears. She didn't dare meet those bottomless grey eyes; if she did, she would fold completely.

"I forgot the question," she said.

With your weight evenly distributed, it is remarkably easy to lie on a bed of nails. What is not so easy, while lying thus, is to have a stack of roofing tiles placed on your stomach for the purpose of being split with a sledgehammer. Lucky almost said a prayer the first time she submitted to this, tightening her abdominal muscles until she felt as if her ribs would burst out of her skin. She was so disoriented afterward that she had to be helped to her feet—though in fact she hadn't been injured at all.

Third man: Yoshida. An evasive bastard. He's always on the edge of range, dancing and feinting, never standing still. Only one way to deal with him: rush in and go for the takedown. Which she gets, because Yoshida mistimes his counterpunch as she shoots in. They tumble to the floor, Yoshida grabbing her head and twisting it painfully. She breaks the hold and moves up his body, gaining the mounted position and raining blows to his face. Three taps and a broken nose.

"You hate me, don't you," said Mary with a faint sneer in her voice.
"I never said that."
"Admit it. Now that you know. It was the final straw."
"As a matter of fact it wasn't."
"Well are children a concern for you? I'm sure we could work something out."
"It has nothing to do with children, I mean I'm seventeen years old why should I care about children."
"Then what is it."
"Mary—" Lucky clenched her hands, her gaze wandering over the mansion "—what I want from you is respect. Can you understand that?"
Mary dodged the question smoothly. "What I think you want is a man."
"Well tell me something Mary: How the fuck would I know?"

The rest of the men come at her one by one. She lands many blows but takes many more. The enemy at this level is not the other fighter: the enemy is herself. Each bout is a struggle with her will, her fear of failure. The martial path is one of self-mastery, nothing more. Her arms and legs begin to ache with fatigue, and she strains to keep her breathing steady. Yet each succeeding fighter is that much fresher than she, and before long she can barely raise her hands to defend herself. After fighting the eleventh man she is bruised from head to toe and ready to collapse. But her test is not over, not yet.

The last man she fights is the *sensei* himself, a seventh *dan* black-belt with thirty years' training. Though thickly built, his hands and feet move so fluidly, so gracefully, that he seems possessed of a supernatural gift. She retreats in haste, struggling to call up the last reserves of her strength, knowing that merely to survive will be enough; but she has never felt so tired in her life. Every inch of her body is heavy with exhaustion, heavy with pain that grows worse by the second. Of course, she is entirely free to halt the proceedings at any time: she suffers this punishment by her own choice. The temptation to surrender is integral to the test, and how beautifully it sings to her at this moment . . .

She stumbles and jerks herself awake, raising her arms. Her *gi* is soaked with sweat and seems to drag her toward the ground. She can hear Mary's voice laughing in the recesses of her mind, mocking her. Not yet, she whispers. Not on your fucking life.

The master strides forward, arms at his sides, inviting combat. As the lower-ranked belt the onus is upon her to engage: hesitation is considered bad etiquette. She throws a roundhouse-kick at his ribs. He makes no effort to deflect the blow, indeed pays it no attention at all. "More power!" he yells, advancing toward her. "More power!" She plants a side-kick in his sternum; he nods, still undeterred. "*More power!*"

Summoning the last of her energy, she presses a furious attack, punching, kicking, chopping. He retreats a few paces, unperturbed, and recklessly she follows. The next moment she is fighting to regain her balance, prey to a foot-sweep. He lands a jab in her ribs, and she is knocked back several yards.

Her heart is pounding in her throat. Each hoarse breath is a struggle. Masochism? Perhaps, but she has worked toward this opportunity five times per week for the past four years. She recovers herself, tottering, and assumes a combat stance yet again.

He is coming forward, cutting off the floor. She charges.

She throws a front-kick to his groin and then shoots in, wrapping her arms around his chest, head pressed under his left armpit. She is no longer attacking: she simply hangs onto him grimly, as if to save herself from a long fall. He grapevines her leg and they fall to the floor. He hooks her other leg and positions her for a choke-hold, his left arm working under her neck. She lands a number of jabs to his ribs and stomach, but there is no strength behind them. In moments he is pressing a choke, just hard enough to block the flow of her carotid artery.

She slaps the floor, and is pleased when she doesn't lose consciousness.

Two days later she stands in the center of the room, ramrod straight, ignoring the pain that still grips her everywhere. The *sensei* stands before her. Slowly, with great solemnity, he ties the crisp new black belt around her waist. There is both ceremony and poignance in the last part of this act, in the moment when he ties the knot and, with one swift jerk, pulls it tight. He retreats a pace, stands at attention and bows to her. She reciprocates and the first chapter is finally over.

The other blackbelts approach to offer their congratulations. She reads the newfound respect in their faces, and each subsequent handshake reaffirms her admission into one of the most fabled clubs in the world; a club requiring neither the right money nor ethnicity, but merely the purest of self-determination. Of course, anybody is free to claim the title of blackbelt; but her own teacher is part of a direct lineage going back to the founders of the *goju-ryu* karate system, Kanryo Higaonna and Chojun Miyagi. Her achievement is as legitimate as they come.

When the champagne has been poured the master takes her aside.

"Remember," he says, his finger raised, "a black belt only means—"

"—that it's time to start the real training," she finishes, smiling.

"I expect you back here tomorrow to begin that training."

"So tell me," said Mary. "Tell me once and for all what on Earth you plan to do."

I will disarm you, Lucky thought. Watch this. "Mother," she said, touching Mary's cheek and looking her in the eye, "Mother, I am leaving now."

Six years after leaving California, and two following the receipt of her black belt, she is still part of the *dojo*; indeed, she has even progressed to second *dan*.

At this moment, however, she is in a different *dojo*, a *dojo* in which there are no men. It is she who presides at the head of the class, in her customary white *gi*. Before her, spread over five rows, stand twenty women dressed in sweatsuits and leotards. She is teaching them the lore that might save their lives.

She is halfway through the class, leading a kicking drill, when one of the administrative assistants beckons to her from the doorway. She points to her senior student, who takes her place and continues the drill without missing a beat.

She walks barefoot down the hall to the front office, past counseling rooms and infirmaries and a bench on which four women are seated, their faces in varying stages of disrepair. Jaws are broken, teeth missing, eyes swollen shut. Within the hour they will be fed, clothed, assigned a bed, and provided with on-site medical treatment and psychotherapy. Payment is voluntary and the scale is flexible; those without money are charged nothing.

Once in the front office she picks up a phone extension and is surprised to hear the voice of her mother.

"Lucky. It's been so long."

"Mother." Somewhat warily, she lowers herself into a chair. In the past six years she has not once spoken with Mary, let alone visited. Her letters have gone unanswered, and she has long stopped writing.

"How are you?"

"I—" she breathes deeply "—I'm fine, Mary, I'm doing OK. How are you."

"I'm dying," Mary replies evenly.

Despite herself—despite the intent of the statement (and she senses the relish in Mary's voice)—Lucky is startled. Her mother is only forty-four. "What happened."

"Ovarian cancer."

Now Lucky feels a cruel impulse to laugh: the symbolism is too rich.

". . . Are you there?"

161

"... I'm sorry, Mary. I'm here."

"Can you come?"

"Let me ask you this, Mary. What have you done to treat it."

"All the usual things. You know."

She knows all right ... This is Mary's way of claiming that she has sought a cure not by Western medicine but rather by the various herbal and metaphysical remedies for which the Retreat Center is famous: tinctures, polarity therapy, crystallography, laying on of hands, furious visualization. But Mary, while championing such treatments to her followers, has never relied on them herself. Ten years ago, when struck with mono, she ordered Lucky to call an ambulance the moment her temperature rose above 101.

"Bullshit," Lucky says. "I bet you've been through ten oncologists this week alone."

Silence, as if Mary hadn't expected that reply. Lucky waits.

"You're not very sympathetic," says her mother at last.

"You're not very inquisitive."

"... I'm sorry?"

"Well I mean the last time we spoke I was seventeen years old. Aren't you the *slightest* bit curious as to what I've been doing for the past six years?"

"You'll forgive me," Mary answers coldly, "if I'm just a little more concerned about myself right now."

"I'm working in a shelter in Manhattan. I teach women self-defense. I've received a second-degree blackbelt from the toughest karate school in New York. I'm actually doing something that matters. You'd have known this if you'd read my letters. But then you must have, or else how could you have gotten this number?"

More silence.

"I came here with fifty dollars in my pocket. I never once begged and I never used your money. So I lived in the car and starved for two days until I got hired—and you won't believe this—as a gypsy cab driver using the Bentley. It was about the only thing I was qualified for."

"Lucky I am *dying*."

"You'll also be glad to know, Mary, that I'm still a lesbian in the meantime."

A sigh. "Lucky you're not making—"

"I've even slept with five men since I got here. You know some-

162

thing, Mary, it wasn't that traumatic. It just wasn't very interesting. I gave it up out of boredom."

"Lucky *please*."

"It's nice to know that I can fuck women because I *want* to, out of preference. Not because there's nothing else available. Anyway. As to your cancer."

". . . *Thank* you."

"I may come and I may not. I'll have to think about it."

"Lucky I—I—"

"Are you trying to say you need me, Mother? For the first time in your life?"

". . . I believe I'm going to cry in a minute."

"Good. Now regarding your cancer. I'll give it some thought, Mary, but I'm not promising anything. I might show up. I might not. It might be tomorrow, next week, never. I don't know. We'll see."

There is a long pause. Finally Mary says, "You are ashamed, aren't you. You're determined to erase it all, like it never happened."

She braces herself, fighting back sudden tears. "No, Mary," she says, articulating the words with difficulty, "on the contrary, I'm not ashamed at all. But having said that—" she swallows, gritting her teeth "—this is the best news I've heard in ages. Goodbye."

She hangs up the phone.

I am cruel, she thinks. Please let me not be so cruel . . . but to whom is she praying? She cannot answer this, for she is not a Believer. If she were, she would formulate a prayer for her mother's salvation. But unlike her mother, Lucky has never worshiped the Triple Goddess of Earth, Sun, and Moon; the Maiden, Mother, and Crone. Ceridwen, she is called, and Isis and Astarte and Diana and Demeter and three-dozen other names. Whoever . . . Lucky believes in no goddess or god yet devised by the human mind, and she knows her prayers are self-mockery. Besides, her mother doesn't need prayers.

Mary Stillwater founded the Wiccan Retreat Center twenty-three years earlier in the house where she'd been raised. Her parents, both old-money scions, had been killed during a robbery when she was twenty. She was home for the summer, having just finished her sophomore year as an English major at Berkeley. She had been in the house at the time of the robbery; and like her mother, she had been gang-raped, shot, and left for dead. Unlike her mother, she had survived; and after two months in the hospital she had returned to the empty family estate that was now hers. She was unable to continue at Berkeley, and spent seven months undergoing therapy with a self-styled medicine woman who educated her in alternative healing, Native American mythology, and the Wiccan religion of ancient Europe. In the spring following the attack, Mary gave birth to a daughter.

At this time the medicine woman departed, and Mary began the ambitious project of constructing a self-contained world for women only. The attack, and the medicine woman's teachings, had caused her to revise not merely her plans for the future but indeed her whole world-view. She envisioned a sanctuary where women, especially victims like herself, could rebuild their lives without pressure from the outside world. As the years passed, the Retreat Center expanded well beyond the mansion proper. With four thousand acres at their disposal, the colonists began to raise wheat, barley, corn, and other crops. Some of the land had once supported vineyards and orchards, and these were duly restored. Surplus produce was sold to distributors, and soon the Retreat Center was a full-fledged business enterprise. Other projects followed—an arts center in the main house, workshops and retreats for curious visitors, even a feminist press.

Thus the women grew their own food, sewed their own clothes, and—as their numbers grew into the hundreds—built their own houses. Most were lesbians; men were not permitted on the grounds. Their religion was Dianic Wicca, a form of witchcraft based largely upon Mary's reinterpretations of Greek, Egyptian, and Celtic symbolism. In Mary's personal theology, the holiest bond existed between mother and daughter, among other reasons because there needn't be any restrictions. Biological concerns did not apply, since offspring were impossible. Moral strictures were subsumed by mythic imagery, in which all things female were sacred and inter-related. She rarely discussed the attack with Lucky, though she admitted that one of the rapists was Lucky's father. Since the attackers had never been caught, Lucky never learned his name. Any distress that she felt toward this violent conception was brushed aside: according to Mary, the role of fatherhood was meaningless.

By the time Lucky reached adolescence, Mary had long abandoned the fields for a newly refurbished office in the butler's pantry. She wrote several books, gave numerous interviews, hosted international conferences. As her legend blossomed in feminist and New

Age circles, so her egotism grew apace. She saw herself as the benevolent guardian of her flock, the wise and generous patron. In the first years of the colony she had deliberately lived a hard and frugal life, as if to prove her resilience to herself and the other women. As time passed, however, Mary decided that she had earned the right to spend her fortune as lavishly as she wished. There was no quarrel between separatism and fine living—was there? Nor were her extravagances limited to herself: she bought a fleet of BMWs for any of the women to borrow as needed, though most of the colonists rarely left the grounds. She paid the hospital bills of a newly arrived settler who'd suffered from breast cancer. She paid the legal fees of another woman fighting for custody of her daughter. To her followers, Mary was all-knowing and all-compassionate, and they adored her. There was never a hint of coercion from her; she ruled by the purest charisma.

Lucky often thought that Mary's impregnable facade derived from a resolution never to be vulnerable again. Even during their private moments, when Mary's defenses should have been at their lowest, she never expressed any self-doubts or questioned her convictions. Though Lucky was the most obvious reminder of her being raped, Mary's one fear was that Lucky would abandon her. Lucky represented the future, not the past; she was a symbol of hope, not anguish. Perhaps it had been the most natural thing in the world for Mary to love her the way she had, and to dread the moment when Lucky would become curious about the world outside the colony— especially because Lucky, excepting the youngest girls, was alone among the colonists in one crucial regard: she had never been more than a few miles beyond the Retreat Center. All during her mid-teens, Lucky reflected, Mary must have braced herself for the inevitable day when Lucky would decide to leave. Their relationship was Mary's only weakness, her Achilles' Heel. Lucky and the Retreat Center had been born almost simultaneously. First as a daughter, and then as a lover, she had been Mary's constant support. She knew, despite the snide dismissals, that her departure had crushed her mother. But she also knew why Mary had not previously asked her to return. With Lucky gone, Mary was consumed by a new fear: losing face among her followers.

Lucky's first sexual encounter had occurred when she was twelve; she learned of the incest taboo years later. Yet Mary, and not that taboo, had been the reason for her departure, and this unnerved

165

Lucky. Though she knew it should be otherwise, she still could not feel revulsion at the idea of her mother fucking her. She hadn't known it was *wrong*, and even in hindsight she found it difficult to impose this moral judgement on what they'd shared together. She was not a child running away from home: she was a partner separating from her spouse. Every woman in the community was a mother to her, as they were to all the young girls. She approved of this arrangement, which was common in many African and Native American tribes. She had never lacked for affection or guidance, though of course that guidance had been dispensed within a narrow ideological framework.

Hence she could not resent Mary for being an absentee mother. But in treating Lucky, after age twelve, as a lover more than a daughter, Mary created in their relationship the same dangers that faced a marriage. Lucky was too young to fully understand the transition, but there were still rules to be observed. What she had felt—what had prompted her to leave—was lover's jealousy, and the feeling of being used. The truth was that Mary, though dependent on Lucky emotionally, had grown tired of her sexually; she had taken to sleeping with her followers under a variety of half-baked pretexts. This devastated Lucky, and society's pity and condemnation of her—should she leave the colony—would not make it easier. She would be expected to hate her mother; she had been *abused*. A part of her *wanted* to feel abused, and to use this righteous anger against Mary. Try though she might, she could not.

But she had left, of course, and spent the next six years untangling the threads of the marriage. She lived at first in an Alphabet City walk-up, doing sixty hours a week in the Bentley and twenty in the *dojo*, with precious little time for new relationships. She hadn't the money for a garage, so she parked the Bentley on the street. Though broken into, it was never stolen: it was far too conspicuous a prize. When the stereo was lifted she didn't bother to have it replaced, nor did she have repaired the numerous dents that accumulated along the body. She never once thought of returning to California, though she often hoped that Mary would ask her to, if only for the sake of pride. But as Mary ignored all attempts to communicate, Lucky thought of her less and less. The lovers she took in Manhattan, male and female, were in effect diuretics—agents for passing her mother out of her body, for cleansing her of Mary forever.

In the meantime she pushed forward. After the receipt of her black belt she was hired full-time at the shelter, and she no longer drove fares. She moved into a studio only a few blocks away, just off Columbus. Her memories of the Retreat Center now had the gentlest pull of nostalgia, because they no longer included Mary: she had found a way to separate Mary from the place itself. Yet the memories did not affect the choices with which Manhattan presented her: the feminism of her childhood was inapplicable to New York City, or so she thought. Having never taken goddesses seriously *anyway*, there was no need for fairy-tales in the new life she was constructing for herself. Besides, such myths had partially been the basis for her mother's separatism, and Lucky harbored no particular animus toward men. She believed not in distancing herself from them, but rather integrating among them on equal footing. This included learning the skills to defend herself against them: to defeat her, a man would need to be similarly trained, armed, or very, very lucky.

Personal strife aside, Lucky recognized the legitimacy of Mary's achievement. At a time of great emotional pain, Mary had taken feminism beyond academic theory and political dissent and created a viable, self-sustaining world. Her followers had grown dependent not merely on the Retreat Center, but on herself as queen and protector—as indeed had Lucky—and that was not what any woman needed.

She should hate her mother, and in many ways she did. But she hated her for the wrong reasons.

There is a knock, and the door opens fractionally. "Lucky . . . ?"

"I'm sorry, come in."

A tall, elegant brunette enters the room. Her name is Megan Rosenbaum, and she is the Associate Director of the shelter and a trustee as well. She is Lucky's nominal superior, although hierarchy at the shelter has always been mere formality.

Lucky takes a deep breath. "Megan, I need to ask a favor."

# CHAPTER TWELVE

## *The Philosopher-King in Deep Shit . . .*

The three male travelers dined that evening courtesy of Truck World, a gigantic hostelry, fuel depot, and shopping mall complex just off the interstate. After dinner they walked along the main concourse, passing a motel lobby, hair salon, cinema, rodeo arena, amusement park, miniature golf course, and department store before wandering into a supermarket to supply themselves with junk food for the days ahead.

As he pushed a cart up the first aisle, Dorian remarked, "The most impressive thing about this country, the most telltale sign of its wretched excess, is the supermarket. God I love America." He reached into the nearby salad bar and shoved a fistful of cantaloupe into his mouth before proceeding to the delicatessen.

"Right, what's our pleasure?" he resumed, gazing at the neat rows of cooked flesh, as the counterman donned plastic baggies. "Why don't we get a pound of everything, plus a few of those rotisserie chickens for good measure."

"Dorian how the fuck we gonna eat all that?" asked Prophet, as the counterman trooped off to the scales.

"I expect we won't," answered the Welshman. "I just love the thrill of buying things, that's all."

They continued through the store, accumulating bread, liquor, soft drinks, pastries. Dorian led the way, tossing one item after another into the cart. Prophet scrutinized the ingredients of every package and then flung it aside with disdain.

"Look at what's in this," he said, waving a box of cupcakes. "You eat this shit you'll be glowing in the dark."

"An interesting proposition in your case," observed Dorian.

Fish, bringing up the rear, had noticed a curious change in his psyche. Since entering the supermarket he'd felt a growing sense of unreality, confronting these thousands of neatly arranged foodstuffs basking in the fluorescent glow, the strains of muzak piping bromides into further pockets of his consciousness and seeming to rinse his neural paths of every complexity, every plaque buildup of paradox and meddlesome inquiry, as if giving his brain an oil change. Everything—the boxes on the shelves, the chuckling flutes, the five-and-dime percussion—was suddenly invested with its own peculiar, inexplicable significance. Startled, he peered up and down the aisle: everywhere he looked he saw the half-hidden wink of conspiracy, the telltale gleam of bamboozlement—and he, of course, was the Fool.

"Why bother?" he asked no one in particular.

"The myth of Sisyphus," yawned Dorian, as they moved on to the **Cookies/Crackers/Coffee** aisle. "I recall Camus saying that—"

"Dorian," said Fish suddenly, "have you actually read Camus?"

Dorian glanced at him, nonplussed. "What do you mean?"

"Cause if you really have, we could talk about it."

They stopped in the middle of the aisle. Fish continued, "You see I've been trying for years to—to come to some kind of . . . understanding about whether happiness is something we can really . . . But I mean you've read him?"

"Of course," Dorian replied in his posh accent. "Not to mention the rest of the existentialist crew; you know—Dostoyevski, Nietzsche, Kafka, Sartre."

Fish shook his head. "No no, that's the mistake everybody makes, they're not all existentialists. But forget that, I mean what I'm saying is that . . . I mean there's always something tugging at you, the idea that—that maybe you should outgrow that kind of thinking, like it's trendy to just sit around and say, Life is absurd, what's the point of anything, it means nothing in the end—and it's like you feel maybe you should be getting with the program . . ."

"Polysorbate 80?" said Prophet from ten feet away, holding up Vanilla Krispz (with Cinnamon!). "The fuck kinda shit is that?"

". . . But meanwhile, you read them on a deeper level and it's like no, they were right all along."

"Well," said Dorian, "*I've* certainly never had any use for optimism. Totally unfashionable. *Naive,* for Christ sake."

Fish scowled. "Then why did you come to this country? Optimism is the cornerstone—"

"No no no, you've got it all wrong," snapped Dorian, fluttering his hands. "Optimism has nothing to do with it. This is the most cynical country on earth, and aggression is the real—"

"W-w-wait." Fish held up his hands in turn. "Are you saying you don't care about the future then?"

"Care? Why should I *care*? I mean take Camus, since we're on the subject. The thing I love about Camus is that he didn't care about *anything.*"

Fish looked as if he'd been poked in the solar plexus. "What? Well then you obviously misread him."

Dorian blinked. "I beg your pardon."

"Potassium stearate?" said Prophet from farther down the aisle. "Will it make me white just like you?"

"You haven't read Camus at all, have you," said Fish angrily.

". . . As a matter of fact I rather think I have."

"All right, then tell me: What's the central issue in Camus's work?"

". . . Well; I should think existentialism, and—"

"Suicide. And he *explicitly refutes* the legitimacy of suicide."

Dorian's mind scrambled back to his encyclopedia reading. "But I thought he crashed his car—"

"And another thing," said Fish. "If Camus didn't care about anything, then why the fuck *write?*"

Dorian smiled condescendingly to mask his embarrassment. "You've completely misunders—"

But Fish was turning away, disgusted. "Typical. I mean just when it looks like I find somebody that—that I think understands it turns out you're just like everybody else. You should be *caring* about these issues, and I spent years trying to figure out . . ." he swayed, bumping into a stack of Peppermint Fig Bunnies and displacing them from their roost ". . . But in the end it's just more fucking lies, everywhere you go. It's like how can you talk about how to live when you don't even understand why you're living in the first place?" He stalked off, his robes swirling along the waxed floor.

Prophet wandered back up the aisle, holding a container of Cheezo. "Check this shit out. You don't even have to refrigerate it."

Fish strode along the concourse of the mall, almost running, seeking only to elude the whispering chorus that followed him out of the supermarket and nipped at his heels; a whispering that he knew to be the Politburo awakening. Still partially medicated, he could recognize this advent of madness for what it was, and consider it

170

objectively for a brief time before sinking into its depths. The truckers and families that passed him—they could never understand his dilemma, the dilemma of being alive. They could not appreciate how precarious their lives were; they simply existed from day to day as if hypnotized, unaware of their tragic nature. He alone knew the secret, and to be confronted with such ignorance made him feel as if he were the last man on earth.

He emerged into the night air and breathed deeply, hearing the rumbling of trucks from the highway and then hearing laughter inside that rumbling, mocking him. He reached the Mustang, whose top was down, and threw himself in the back seat. "No," he groaned, holding his hands over his ears. "Get out of my head. Please."


"All right, a nod to health," said Dorian, gazing at the vegetable displays. He nodded to them and pushed the cart on.

"Hold on, I want some of this," said Prophet.

Dorian stopped. "The question," he said, leaning on the cart handle, "the *question* is how to get both of them into bed at once."

Prophet was wrapping up some cauliflower. "Both of who?"

"Lucky and the new girl, of course."

Prophet's head snapped up. "The fuck you talkin bout?"

Dorian began picking up bananas and squeezing them until they burst open, spewing their innards on the astroturf display shelf. "Well, I only meant to say that Lucky is going to be problem enough. The question is whether a troika can't be arranged . . ."

Prophet set aside the cauliflower. "You stay away from her," he said, approaching Dorian. "You do whatever the fuck you want with Lucky but you stay away from that girl, you understand?"

Surprised, Dorian gazed at him down the length of his nose. "Why Prophet," he sneered, "I had no idea."

"No idea what?"

"That you felt that way toward her."

Prophet's heart skipped. ". . . Who said anything about *me?*"

"You're denying that you have an interest in her?"

"Dorian come off it man, the last thing I wanna to do is mess with Ariel that's the whole *point.*"

Dorian sniggered. "And to think that I considered Fish my main competition. I thought you'd toe the party line. You know, racial solidarity and all that."

Prophet glared back up at him, his GUARD sufficiently raised

171

that he abandoned any pretense of schoolboy denial. "Yeah? Well guess what, white boy? This nigger's gonna give you all the competition your stringy-haired, coal-mining, boy-soprano, wish-you-were-English-instead-of-colonial-nonentity, pseudo-Oxonian, *tea*-drinkin, *limp*-wristed . . . *pussy*-accented, *croquet*-playin but-at-the-end-of-the-day *sheep*-fucking, one-step-up-from-the-Irish, Roman-conquered Celtic farmboy ass can handle. Dig?"

Dorian blinked, his lip quivering, unable to decide whether to face up or back down, but pausing long enough that the second happened by default. He swallowed, hating the fear that had eclipsed his anger. And wondering how the hell Prophet knew more about Britain than he himself.

Prophet smiled beneficently, patting Dorian's cheek Mafia-style. "*Good* boy."

# CHAPTER THIRTEEN

## *Perspective . . .*

Ariel slept that night in the fetal position, with Lucky huddled immediately behind her. Lucky herself slept little, considering how she might best help Ariel back to life. She might have to call the police, but what if Ariel's father had done this? Or her mother, for that matter? She wondered if she ought to examine the girl's vulva, to check for trauma there as well.

At one point Ariel placed her hand on Lucky's wrist. Lucky pressed herself even closer, holding Ariel tight as the girl twitched and shuddered from the violence of her dreams.

In her work at the shelter Lucky had been a karate instructor, not a counselor. She had seen women stagger in half-dead but she'd had little interaction with them, at least not until they were healed and chose to begin training. Most of her students, in fact, were not battered at all, but rather young professionals who wanted to learn self-defense. The intimacy of her relationship with Ariel was something new altogether, for she was providing the life-support herself. It struck her that she had never felt so rewarded in her life.

The men had returned last night with pizza, french fries, soda, and other staples of the American hearth. Awakening from her nap, Ariel had spotted the food and bore down on it immediately, all animal instinct, acting for the first time of her own initiative. She tucked in with single-minded absorption, eating four slices of pizza, a few dozen French fries, a chicken sandwich, and a hot fudge sundae. Dorian had also procured a six-pack of Nero's Ale, just in case. Lucky helped herself to a couple but was surprised when Ariel, after disposing of a large cherry soda and a vanilla milkshake, proceeded to kill the other four. Lucky half-expected the girl to pitch camp in the bathroom for the rest of the night, and was relieved when Ariel simply went back to sleep.

\*     \*     \*

The morning dawned clear and hot. They checked out of Pleasant Acres and ate breakfast at a local diner, where truckers and local rednecks gawked until their food turned cold. (Word must have gotten round the county: a few car pools arrived before long, and the natives crowded round the entrance as the hostess, with no pretense of discretion, pointed out the strangers.)

Though she said nothing, Ariel took notice of her surroundings and continued to eat. She did not seem familiar with the environs; evidently she had walked quite a distance along the interstate. She ate three fried eggs, hash browns, two pancakes, and was making inroads on a stack of French toast when Lucky, fearful for the girl's digestive system, took the plate away.

As they drove away from the diner, Lucky said, "I wonder if we should go to the police station."

Ariel, riding with her in the back seat, gripped Lucky's hand and shook her head.

"What is it?" asked Lucky.

The girl was silent, but there was naked terror in her eyes.

"You don't want to go to the police?" Lucky asked, just to be sure.

Ariel shook her head rapidly, like a child.

"A girl after my own heart," said Prophet, who was also in the back seat, and somewhat relieved that Lucky sat between them. Ariel had lingered in his thoughts all last night and for during most of breakfast. Though Dorian was no longer a threat, Prophet was too shy to speak of his affections to Lucky, especially in light of Ariel's condition. In the meantime, however, he had thought he might gain her attention—and lighten her mood—with an attempt at humor.

"Prophet shut up, this isn't funny."

He was surprised and hurt. "I never said it was funny."

"Good then shut the fuck up. We've got to figure out what we're going to do."

"Do?" said Dorian.

"About Ariel! We can't take her to California if she doesn't want to go!"

But Ariel had seized Lucky's wrist again, and her desire was plain.

"You want to go to California?" asked Lucky. "Are you sure?"

Ariel nodded, but there was nothing childlike in her manner this time. Her eyes spoke of salvation, need.

"But Ariel how old are you, I mean I don't want to be accused of . . . Wait a minute what am I saying?"

"I don't know," said Dorian. "What are you saying?"

"This girl needs me. Why should I give a fuck about the police?"

"*I* never do," said Prophet, trying again, "not unless they're shooting at me."

"Prophet," said Dorian, who, simmering with resentment from the previous evening, had been circling Prophet warily all morning and now saw his chance to strike "—have you ever been arrested in your life?"

Prophet recognized the barb for what it was, and tried grimly to play dumb. "Say what?"

"You heard me. I mean have you ever been shot at, or, or *busted*, or Christ even chased down the street?"

"Course I have!"

"When?"

". . . Lots a times!"

"Where?"

". . . Lots a places!"

"Really?" Dorian drawled the word like an English nobleman. "I say bullshit."

"Say what?"

"I *said* bullshit. Did you hear how I enunciated that? *B u l l s h i t .*"

"That does it. Stop the car so I can kick your ass."

"Hah. Am I right?"

"I said stop the car!"

"The trouble with Prophet," Dorian informed everyone else, "is that he thinks he's bigger and blacker than he really is. Oh, I'm sure he could regale us with tales of mythical shake-downs, detentions without charge, and how his best friends all got shot up by the age of three, eh homey?"

As if to check the damage to his self-image, Prophet glanced at Ariel, and for the first time made eye contact. His outrage was momentarily stalled. Those eyes: Jesus. He found himself sinking into their lacustrine depths, thinking . . . thinking that for the first time in his life he'd fallen in love.

"Don't worry, my man," continued Dorian, disrupting his reverie. "No need to boost your credibility with the likes of *us*. Remember, we're *white*. You're *black*. We hold you in awe a priori. We suffer our whole lives knowing we can never be black like you. We'll always be white, alas—dumb, stupid-looking, forever uncool. No worries eh?"

"Dorian what is with you today?" said Lucky.

"My fist is what's gonna be with him!"

"Ah, black machismo again. Isn't it curious how black people can't tolerate the *slightest* hint of insult, not even from their own kindred? I mean Christ, your fear of losing face makes the Orientals seem laissez-faire by comparison."

"Stop the car, Dorian."

"What?"

"Stop the car," Fish repeated.

Dorian blinked at him warily. "What is it?"

"Prophet wants to kick your ass."

"So?"

"I want to watch."

". . . Watch?"

"Yeah. See if *I* were black I'd beat the shit out of you right now. He deserves his chance."

"You know something Goggles?" said Prophet. "I think this could be the beginning of a *beautiful* friendship."

"I like black people," said Fish enigmatically, as though something different had been said. "Some of my best friends are black—I mean in my head, you know? I've been saved by so many black people."

"This is ludicrous," said Dorian, "but you know what?" He slowed the car. "I'm always up for a little violence. Good for the soul. It's the American way."

The interstate was divided by a thin belt of woodland. Dorian pulled into a speedtrap and stopped among the trees.

"This is surreal," said Lucky.

"Nonsense. It's a male ritual, my girl, old as the planet."

"I'll make it quick," said Prophet.

Doors opened, people clambered out—except Ariel, who remained in the back seat with a look of apprehension. Lucky took her hand. "I know this is ridiculous," she said, "but I promise it won't take long. Just sit tight for a minute."

Prophet shadowboxed, his robes fluttering. Dorian approximated a few jumping jacks and sagged against the car, winded. Fish stood off to the side, lighting a cigarette.

176

"Do you know how to fight, Dorian?" he asked.

"Well Fish it's curious. I've never fucked a woman and I've never punched a man and d'you know something? I think I've been missing out."

"Prophet?"

"Johnny, the black man is a born fighter. Ever see a boxing match between a brother and a weenie? The brother jabs, the weenie's head snaps back like a sack o shit."

"Boxing isn't real fighting," said Lucky. "As a matter of fact, from a street-fighting perspective boxing is a complete sham. For your information, Prophet, I've destroyed black men twice your size in my *dojo*. White men too, for that matter. You put any boxer in a no-rules fight against a trained *karateka* or even a good wrestler and the boxer will be out in ten seconds flat."

"Remember the bikers," said Fish.

Dorian walked into the middle of the dirt lane. "Ready when you are, Malcolm."

Prophet rushed him, inexpertly flailing. Dorian retreated, trying to fend off the attack as one might fend off bright light, his arms forming a vague, ineffectual shield. Several blows landed, and Dorian found himself with a nosebleed and a fat lip. He tried to move in and grapple, using his greater size, but Prophet hammered him relentlessly. He fell; Prophet landed atop him without missing a beat. Lucky watched, with an air of detached appraisal, and finally strode toward the melee. She plucked Prophet off, told him to retreat to a neutral corner. She then crouched over Dorian, whose face was a happy mask of blood. A front tooth had been dislodged; his left eye was swelling shut. Lucky examined the wounds, did a few quick palpations, and stood.

"You'll be all right," she said.

"*Fpleuh*," gasped Dorian. "I hate people. I hate fucking everyone."

"I'm sure they're flattered," said Lucky, turning away.

Prophet was dancing and feinting nearby. "Vengeance is mine, baby!"

"It's over," said Lucky. "Get in the car."

"You kidding? I'm just gettin warmed up."

"I said it's over."

Prophet seemed about to protest, but the look in her eyes silenced him. He shrugged, straightened his robes, and strode back to the car with elaborate, ceremonial hauteur.

Dorian sat awash in bleary disbelief, gaping at the sight of his blood. Lucky produced a tissue and knelt, wiping his face. "You're an idiot," she said. "Not to mention a bigot."

He hawked blood. "I only did it for you," he protested.

"Yeah, right," she said, ignoring his wince and applying full pressure to his tattered lip. "If you'd been my champion we'd both be up shit creek right now, wouldn't we. You can't fight worth a damn."

He guffawed weakly, with moist overtones.

"If you're trying to impress me," she continued, "you should really spare yourself the effort."

He peered at her one-eyed. "Is there no hope for us?"

"None," she answered. "I'm a lesbian, remember? The question does not apply."

Suddenly he scrambled away, backpedaling like a crab. "Fuck. Oh fuck. Jesus fucking *fuck!*"

"Dorian, what—"

"Christ!" He stood, panting, and stared at the bloody tissues. "Lucky I may be HIV-positive. I haven't been tested yet but my friends at Oxford . . ."

She felt an immediate chill but did not lose her composure. She examined her hands: there were no cuts, no abrasions, no channels through which his blood might have entered. Her pulse returned to normal. "I'll be fine," she said, standing, "but I'd better check on Prophet."

"Prophet," he whispered. "*Fuck . . .*"

She reached the car just ahead of him.

"Prophet get out, we have to see something."

"Look I'm not apologizing," he said, stepping outside. "What . . ."

Lucky examined his hands. "We need to get to a bathroom," she said. "I can't tell whether he's bleeding or not."

"Dorian what . . . Oh no . . . *Oh* no . . . Oh *shit!*"

"Prophet I'm sorry it slipped my mind—"

"Slipped your mind? Slipped your *mind*?! *Fuck* man, I oughta whup you again!"

"Shhh," Lucky intervened, "hey, *hey,* come on. Let's not get upset, OK? Dorian might not have the virus and there's no guarantee you'd get it anyway."

Prophet began to pace, holding his hands at (as it were) arm's length and flapping them violently. "This is great, just fucking great," he said, glancing skyward. "Don't know *what* the fuck I did to deserve this. I am not a bad person. I am *not* a bad person!" And rounding on Dorian: "Man you're at *risk* I mean why the *fuck* ain't you been *tested*?!"

"Because," Dorian said, "because I'm so afraid."

"That ain't right. You got a responsibility. You pick fights, you owe it to everybody to—"

"Prophet that's enough," said Lucky. "Now listen, here's what we're going to do. Fish? Can you drive?"

He'd been watching silently, with an expression she could not read. "Sort of," he said.

"Sort of," she muttered. "That's not what I need to hear, damn it." She pushed back her hair, her gaze settling on Ariel, who was watching them solemnly.

"Dorian give me the keys."

". . . What—"

"Because I don't trust any of you with my life right now. Give me the keys."

He groped in his pockets. "I think they're in the ignition."

"Good." She walked round to the other side of the car. Before getting in she said, "Oh by the way, gentlemen, you've just given a perfect example of why women should be running the world."

"What, because men fight?" snorted Prophet.

"No," replied Lucky. "Because they don't know how to."

They found a truck stop farther along the highway. Prophet and Dorian repaired to the lavatories to wash themselves. They did not speak. Fish stood behind them like a chaperon.

Finally Dorian said, "I'm sorry Prophet. About what I said."

Prophet was soaping vigorously, as if to ablate the skin from his bones.

"I mean it. I'm . . . just so frustrated, so . . . so tired." He glanced aside hopefully. "How are your hands?"

"When we get to the next town," said Prophet, not looking at him, "we're going to the nearest emergency room and you will be tested, do you understand me?"

Dorian grasped at this hint of forgiving. "Can we do that?"

"Takes five minutes," Fish chimed in. "They prick your finger, like a blood sugar test. Instant read-out."

Dorian swallowed. "Right . . . Well yes, obviously I'll do it." He looked at Prophet, who turned and left without another word.

Dorian sighed, shutting off the tap and dabbing at the various wounds on his face. "So, Fish," he said. "How's the neuro-chemistry?"

"I'm hearing sounds from a long, long way away," Fish replied. "Bells and sleighs, and a million voices laughing. I think they're getting closer."

Dorian snickered. "I can hardly wait."

The ER receptionist was not impressed by their arrival. She told them to sit down and gave no indication of when Dorian would be examined.

They clustered in the waiting room, sitting on plastic chairs. Back issues of *Witch-hunter's Digest* and *American Vivisector* lay spread on a coffee table nearby. Dorian completed a form which among other things asked his religion, to which he replied **Non-Specific**. When he came to the insurance section he conjured up a name and policy number and returned the form. The receptionist glowered and told him to keep waiting.

They waited. A gagging toddler was carried in and attended to immediately. A middle-aged man appeared out of nowhere, com-plaining of a headache; he was wheeled away in a gurney. A six-year-old was brought in raving about Geryon's tail, and bundled in a straitjacket. They waited.

A small television had been mounted in the opposite wall, near the ceiling. The channel was MTV, depicting cult hero Sesquipedalian Ithyphallus singing in the middle of a venereal disease clinic, attended by half-naked male nurses.

Next a black man named Cool Sly Ichabod, shot in a dozen places, launched into a discourse on matriphilia from the refuge of his hospital bed, attended by half-naked female nurses.

He was followed by a young woman who attested that genetic thrift in the form of small breasts had nearly driven her to suicide and how fatty tissue [**which I needed to lose anyway**] had been transplanted from her buttocks to bolster her chest measurements and self-esteem, a contention supported by the appearance of a knowing young Adonis on her doorstep and the implication of pro-creative congress just ahead.

She was then upstaged by an elderly pinstriped spokesman for

ICM, or International Cemetery Management, who informed his listeners that death need not be the great equalizer, that indeed for less than one might expect one could reserve a berth in one of fifty-eight exclusive ICM luxury cemeteries worldwide, with gravesite to be marked by replicas of the Taj Mahal or Eiffel Tower or any of thirty-two prefabricated monuments, not to mention the inclusion of a private artificial lake nearby (replete with swans) for a thirty percent surcharge. A current three-for-two family special was expiring soon, as was a limited offer to exhume deceased relatives from less prestigious tracts of earth and re-inter them in an ICM cemetery for half-price, which yielded to—

—a young man in a white lab coat who advised everyone within earshot about a brand new study confirming that lucid dreaming techniques could be used to double the average bank account in six weeks and that visualizing money was the surest way to acquire it, especially if performed in accordance with a series of six videotapes on offer for $99.95 apiece ($500 for all six), the narrator warning sadly that supplies wouldn't last.

A video came on for perennial Grammy contender Ten Inch Tails, in which an anguished middle-aged singer tore off his clothes to reveal a zodiac of bubbling white pustules on his chest and abdomen (Polaris presiding on the breastbone, the Pleiades forming a cluster near his left armpit, Sirius gone nova above his just-invisible pubis), which he then popped one by one until his torso was awash in ochre slime—

"I hate this band," said Prophet. "Turn the channel."

They flicked past the New Age Channel (a bearded Caucasian in white robes placing pebbles and cheap gems on the belly of a pancreatic cancer victim), the Military Channel (a tour of the ruins of a Central African capital, with crew-cut white host in red sports shirt kneeling beside a crater and measuring the impact radius of an American bomb), the Weight Loss Channel (overhead view of an operating table, where a balding white doctor was harvesting an unsightly hunk of flesh from a white woman's left buttock), the NRA Channel (Single Shot vs. Automatic for the Home Security Consumer), the Republican Channel (a day in the life of House Speaker Gimp Toadflax), the Money Channel (noted tax expert Wick Shipley on the deductability of household pets), the Seance Channel (a grinning bearded Caucasian assuring a distraught black woman that Reggie was remaining faithful up there) before alighting finally

181

upon the Romance Channel, chancing upon a dimly lit room in which a young blonde woman wearing a diaphanous camisole nibbled at the steely chest hairs of a white man twice her age as he spoke into a portable telephone, supplanted a moment later by—

—a nude white infant clapping her hands while a male voice-over lauded the advent of a revolutionary new diaper incapable of leaking said baby's bodily wastes, as supported by computer graphics depicting a rival diaper collapsing under the weight of digitized hypothetical feces—

"Dorian Bray?" said an elderly nurse in the doorway.

He followed her into a small room with two beds. The first was empty; the other supported the half-lidded corpse of the man who'd complained of a headache an hour earlier. His shirt had been removed; a pool of blood was congealing on his woolly chest. Staring in grim fascination, Dorian sat on the empty bed, plastic crackling beneath him. Tight-lipped, the nurse took his temperature and blood pressure and declined to inform him of the results. She then wandered off without closing the curtain that might have separated the two beds. Dorian pulled on the curtain to no reward: the track mechanism was jammed.

Ten minutes later a pudgy white technician entered the room, pushing what appeared to be a portable photocopying machine. "You the one for the EKG?" he said.

Dorian shook his head. The technician peered at the corpse and shrugged. "Whoops," he muttered, and wheeled the machine away.

Half an hour later, as Dorian watched the corpse turn white, an ancient man in ill-fitting scrubs entered the room, looking put-upon. He glanced without comment at Dorian's chart and carefully put it aside. With great reluctance, he applied a stethoscope to Dorian's chest and Dorian thought he perceived the beginnings of a sneer.

"Need an AIDS test?" said the doctor, his voice like a rusty hinge.

Dorian replied in his most condescending Oxbridge. "I thought that had been indicated."

The doctor rummaged in a nearby drawer and withdrew a small black object that resembled a calculator. He then donned two pairs of white plastic gloves and produced a fresh needle. Without preamble he jabbed this into Dorian's fingertip and squeezed a drop of blood on a thin strip of paper.

"Gay?" emitted the doctor, inserting the paper into the calculator.

"Overjoyed," Dorian replied.

The doctor placed the black object on the bed. It contained a small LED screen that declared **WAIT** ...

"If there's a plus sign you're positive," said the doctor. "A minus means negative. See the receptionist about payment." He left the room without a glance at the corpse.

Alone, Dorian clutched the little device. **WAIT** ... persisted. Unable to look, he put it down and paced back and forth, studiously ignoring the corpse, unnerved to be in such close proximity to death ... Abruptly he sauntered to the other bed, assuming what he thought to be an air of scientific inquiry, peeling back the eyelids, testing the fingers for rigidity, cataloguing the sensation of an acrotic wrist, his own pulse galloping all the while. He assured himself that *he* was not afraid of death, that he could confront death as well as the next man. This cadaver over here—what of it? Most natural thing in the world, and ... and Jesus but it felt good to be alive, and young, and not middle-aged and susceptible to heart attacks and strokes and Alzheimer's and all that other shit that made *older* people so creepy to be around, and ... He nearly jumped when the device gave a short beep, ready to pronounce his own death sentence, ready to confirm the tenancy of that micro-organism which *older* people somehow managed to avoid ... He shut his eyes, picked it up, covered the screen with his thumb, opened his eyes. He slid his thumb down, waiting for the vertical tip of a cross to be revealed— little by little, no hurry, thumb descending a fraction of an inch ... and then a flat black horizontal line presented itself, unbisected.

Thank *Christ.*

Suddenly enervated, he sat there for a minute, heart pounding not with fear but with relief. His gaze wandered over the room, settling on a dispenser of white paper cups.

He pocketed the diagnostic instrument and took one of the cups. After a quick glance at the doorway, he unzipped himself and pissed into the cup, nearly filling it.

Holding the cup, Dorian strode into the lobby. The physician, nurse, and receptionist were smoking behind the desk.

"HIV-positive," Dorian sneered. With a sweep of his arm he emptied the cup, spattering each of the natives. "And guess what, you stupid redneck fucks?" he added, as they jumped to their feet. "Now you are too."

His companions were still waiting in the lounge. "Come on!" he called, heading toward the exit.

"Dorian!" snapped Prophet as they ran across the parking lot. "Dorian what the fuck is up—"

"Relax, old son," answered Dorian as they reached the Mustang. "I was only joking. I'm as negative as your prick is long."

They stared at him uncertainly. Sighing, he pulled out the testing device and handed it to Prophet. "Come on," he said, turning toward the car. "Let's get the fuck out of here."

\*　　\*　　\*

At midnight they were driving along a two-lane road heading west.

The roof was down. Fish sat atop the back seat, almost on the trunk, arms stretched wide, crucified by the wind, head back to the sky as if receiving benediction. A billion billion words revealed themselves in the firmament like spectators witnessing their journey. Outside the radius of the headlights lay the glinting silhouette of fields stretching away into darkness.

"Has anyone checked the map lately?" asked Dorian.

"It doesn't matter, as long as we keep heading west," said Lucky.

"No it's fine, I just thought someone might be anxious to stop. Personally I could drive for a few more hours."

"Well there's no sign of a town on the horizon," said Prophet, "but hey, we could always stop now."

"Here? you mean in the open?"

Prophet shrugged. "Seems as good a place as any. We've got enough food. It could be fun."

"Councillors?" said Dorian to the back seat.

"Fine with me," said Lucky. "Ariel?"

Ariel, though still mute, was at least responding to most inquiries with simple gestures. She smiled slightly and nodded.

"Fish?"

"Take back the night," he said.

"I suppose that's an affirmative."

Dorian pulled into the scrub field bordering the road and brought the car to a stop. He killed the headlights. Only a gentle wind compromised the utter stillness and silence.

"Vastness, eh?"

"Home on the range," said Prophet. "You think we can light a fire?"

184

"It's not really cold," said Lucky.

"Yeah but what about atmosphere? We're *camping*."

"Fine," said Lucky. "But you can get the wood."

Later, as they sat around the fire, a bottle of red wine was circulated. Dorian abstained, opting for Tartarus Vodka and a box of Sugar Babies. Prophet dipped carrots and celery into a jar of peanut butter. Lucky indulged in whole-grain bread and organic nectarines. Fish husbanded a watermelon. Ariel, having finished a whole rotisserie chicken, was gnawing on a hunk of vanilla fudge.

After a time Fish wandered off amid the scrub. He looked up and up and up, spinning round and almost falling. He imagined himself leaping into flight, projecting his body among the stars, borne on the wind in pure joy. Nicely drunk, he soon collapsed and lay back, feeling his head sink through the earth. The Politburo took this opportunity to convene, stepping out of the brush as if they'd been lurking there for centuries and waiting for just such a moment. Everyone seemed to be in attendance, young and old, male and female, mammal and reptile and amphibian, and of course every combination thereof. Fish couldn't place their names in his drunken state: there were thousands upon thousands of them, an endless roiling mass that occupied his entire field of view.

"Fishy!"

"Glug glug!"

"Guess who's back you old wreck!"

A floating head alighted on his chest, a bald white head with thick glasses and no eyes and the barest slit of a mouth. Fish remembered him all too well, this titular leader of the rest.

"Grand themes tonight, eh?" said the head. "So many stars. But what do they all mean?"

"The big questions! The big questions!" tittered the chorus, with shivery ripples of laughter.

"Fickle fickle," said the head. "What's your position this evening? Does God exist or does it not?"

"I don't know," said Fish. "What do you think?"

"Ah, but that would be telling," said the head. The chorus snickered and a porcupine went shrieking into the bushes, its tail set ablaze by a fat circus clown with the ears of a bloodhound.

"We know the answer!" shrieked the chorus. "But you don't! You don't!"

"Let's put our cretin on trial," said the head. "It's long overdue.

185

All of us are victims of attempted murder. Now I'll be the judge, but we'll need an inquisitor. Who . . . ?"

"Me me me me!" several dozen piped up, clamoring forward. It was evident that they held the head in great respect. He in turn considered them gravely before selecting a three-foot hag whose refulgent hair scintillated crazily in the darkness, a sunburst of dancing particles.

"Do you swear to tell the truth, the whole truth, and everything but the truth, so help you Stelazine?" she asked.

"Maybe," said Fish.

"Not good enough! Not good enough!" jeered the chorus. A flurry of sage insects descended upon him, foot-long wasps and dragonflies and grinning bumblebees, buzzing round his face and up his nose and down his throat until he capitulated. Those in his stomach were obliged to fly out again and reassume positions with their colleagues.

They had him circled now. An army of driver ants began filing along his body.

"Right," said the head. "You may proceed."

"Question one," said the hag. "Does God exist?"

Fish considered. "Well," he said, "do you mean in the literal sense or in the purely metaph—"

"No no no no no!" she cried. "It's a simple question. It's the *only* question in the world and there's only one answer. Does it or doesn't it?"

"Yes," said Fish, feeling bullied.

A chorus of howls.

"Evidence?" cackled the hag. "Evidence?"

"I think the lad's confused," said an old Yorkshireman in tweeds.

"He's all bogged down," said the head. "You can hear the mind working through all those old chestnuts: Cartesian duality, Kant's ontological and cosmological and teleological arguments that didn't amount to anything one way or the other (hence that Nietzsche aphorism). Add Newtonian mechanics and he isn't even out of the eighteenth century! Pathetic."

"He's just being sentimental," suggested a giant grasshopper bobbing nearby, its antennae tied in a knot above its head. "You know, those old dreamy arguments that appeal to the romantic and the puritan alike. Call it fear, call it wish-fulfillment in the Freudian sense. I think the root of our failed Benedictine's problems lies in Aquinas—some of the most worthless illogic in print, if you ask me. Fire causes heat, therefore God causes goodness. What shit."

"Is that it?" asked the head. "Are you still stuck in the past Fishy Fishy?"

"Well Jesus I didn't expect the Inquisition!" snapped Fish.

"Jesus got the Inquisition," the hag pointed out, "and then his disciples got their revenge the same way. But you should know us better, Fish. We are the Inquisition, and we always will be. Anyway, back to the matter at hand. Why don't we continue with Jesus, and how Paul ran riot."

"Faaaahhh!" said the grasshopper disdainfully. "Blame Moses. Hell—blame *Abraham*."

"You can't say much for monotheism," agreed the hag. "In fact, I think it's the most overrated human development since self-consciousness. Superstition with a human face. A white man's face, if you can believe it. The pagans may have been clueless but at least they knew how to have a good time."

"Simply divine," said Tweed. "Chopping off heads, dancing naked, copulating like little bunnies . . ."

"The good old days," sighed the head.

"Women had the power," said the hag.

"Well, monotheism did give rise to modern law," suggested an ermine-clad nobleman with a spear through his left eye.

"And lawyers," sneered the head. "All right, let's move on. Now I'm not sure whether to invoke logical positivism in the next breath or—"

"No no no, forget those old fools," said the grasshopper. "Just a bunch of philosophers pretending to be scientists. I mean they were perfectly reasonable in themselves but hardly necessary, and obsolete after the advent of quantum mechanics. Start with Darwin and then make the leap to Einstein and Bohr and Heisenberg and Dirac. I think we can skip Maxwell and Dalton and Rutherford for these purposes, don't you?"

"Wait a minute," said the hag. "I thought I was doing the inquisiting."

"You just love the sound of your own voice," said the grasshopper. "And that's not a real word, by the way—"

"Balls," she sneered. "What do *you* know about quantum mechanics?"

"Peace, peace be with us," cautioned the head ("And also with us," murmured the rest of the chorus on cue).

"My point," said the grasshopper, "is that the positivists are virtually worthless in the intellectual arena. I'm simply asking to separate the wheat from the chaff."

"Duly noted," said the head.

"Can I proceed?" asked the hag. "Good. Now, when we put Copernicus and Darwin and Einstein together we nullify the Old Testament in one fell swoop—"

"Yes, yes, I agree with *that*," interjected the grasshopper, "but let's give credit where credit is due. *Aristarchus* was the first heliocentrist, two thousand years before Galileo and Kepler and good old Nicky C. came along to ruffle some feathers. Talk about getting shafted."

"That's showbiz," said the head. "Think of Boethius in his jail cell. You think either of them has sued yet?"

"Can we stick to the point?" said the hag. "I mean can we at least agree that the Old Testament is history?"

"You mean history without being history?" said a rhinoceros, its horn pierced with a diamond ring.

"All right, all right," said the head. "The Old Testament is out. What about the New Testament?"

"If those four bozos were witnesses at a trial," said the grasshopper, "they'd impeach themselves off the stand. The defendant would be executed."

"So why should we blame everything on Abraham?" said Ermine. "Isn't Paul equally guilty?"

"My feelings exactly," said the head. "History isn't a footnote to Plato and Aristotle. It's an *idiotic* footnote to Paul."

"Not to mention John," said Tweed. "Revelation, and what have you."

"Did I ever mention," said the grasshopper to the hag, "did I ever mention how I can smell your pussy clear across the glade?"

"Ha!" she barked. "So *that*'s what it comes down to, is that it?"

"It's quite an ethereal little cunt, isn't it," said Ermine.

"I sometimes wonder," said Tweed, "I sometimes wonder if we shouldn't just leave the Big Questions to others, and possibly turn our attention to the more important matter of—"

"Of fucking?" smiled the head.

"Fucking!" tittered the chorus. "He said fucking!"

188

"Well," Tweed was blushing, "I wouldn't put it *quite* so—"

"Everybody has an opinion," said the grasshopper, "just like everybody has an asshole, all of which stink."

"Well I think it's time we heard from our defendant," said the hag. "Maybe he could explain to which god he was referring."

"And why he needs comfort from outdated myths," said the head. "You really degrade yourself by behaving that way, old son. Just because most people are too simple to realize that the universe has no meaning is no excuse for you to pop tranquilizers and get all soft on us. We could have saved you from all that if only you'd let us. Why did you fight us? We're all you've got, in the end."

"Yes why, Fishy Fishy?" cooed the hag. "Is little Fishy still scared of *dy-ing?*"

"Give him some credit," said the grasshopper. "At least he hasn't twisted quantum physics into New Age bullshit. I sometimes wish that Dirac hadn't discovered that equation, and that Niels Bohr had gone into hotel management."

"The whole pop psychology conspiracy," snorted the head. "As if the keys of life are hidden in trade paperbacks."

"All right! All right!" screamed Fish. "It doesn't exist! It doesn't exist! Just leave me alone!"

"All your nightmares come true," whispered the head confidentially, in grim triumph. "Was that so hard to accept? Quit fighting us. You are nothing, you mean nothing, and you were never meant to mean anything, unless we say otherwise. Now don't disappoint me, Fish. Those drugs you took—don't you ever take them again, or I'll make you hurt everyone you love. And don't get any other silly ideas in your head, like becoming a Buddhist. Suppression never works. Nirvana is a heresy. I'll dog you every step of the way."

He rose a few feet in the air, turning to the others. "So hey!" he called. "Dinner at my place?"

*   *   *

"Is she asleep?" asked Dorian, indicating the prone form of Ariel. He'd finished one bottle of vodka and was halfway through the next.

"I think so," answered Lucky, opening another bottle of wine. "You know something, I haven't been this drunk in—in—" she screwed up her face "—there was this one time when I was like ten, on Beltane Eve, but—you know, I don't think I was *this* drunk    "

189

"Well, this calls for a celebration," said Dorian, who was drunk but not *that* drunk, and thinking, Yes, I'm going to fuck her brains out within the hour. He lurched to his feet. "Let's go for a walk."

She gave him a sloppy, knowing grin. "So you can steal me away into the night?"

"Precisely."

It took half a minute for her to stand, whereupon she fell over, spilling wine. She lay face-down on the earth, giggling.

"Come on," said Dorian, hauling her up by her armpit, and savoring even this contact with her, as if it finally proved Lucky was ordinary flesh and blood. They both swayed for a long moment and she sagged back into his embrace. He held her upright, his thumbs grazing her breasts. She took a long pull from the bottle and pushed away, still giggling.

"Look," said Prophet, tapping away at his computer. "If y'all wanna fuck around, go do it somewhere else."

"Look at him," said Dorian to Lucky in a conspiratorial voice. "He's going to be our next president."

Prophet glanced up, sighing. "Listen," he said. "I don't care if Lucky can whup Muhammad Ali. In about two seconds I'm gonna kick both your asses."

"I think we'd better leave," Dorian informed Lucky, *sotto voce.*

She primly offered her hand. "Lead me on. But don't get any ideas . . ."

"Now now, you're already jumping to conclusions. Plato said—"

"Plato had his head up his ass."

They picked their way into the darkness, walking for a time in silence, and for him the only world was that of wind and stars and earth and most of all her hand in his. Not until the campfire was a distant beacon did he speak. "What do you think of all this?"

"I think I'm going to be sick in a little while."

"No, I didn't mean *that.* I meant this whole journey. Sort of how we've all come together in this peculiar way."

". . . I think I'm going to be sick in a little while."

He threw off her hand, suddenly angry. "Damn it this is *important.* Don't you understand that—that a bunch of so-called adults could never have fallen in like this? This is a testament to the power of youth."

"Or the power of vodka."

He gave a shout of exasperation. "Bloody hell, why can't you ever take me seriously?"

She laughed so hard that she almost collapsed. "Tell me something Dorian," she gasped; "tell me what it is about you that anyone could ever take seriously."

"Because I'm a philosopher! Because—" he gesticulated vaguely "—because *I* know things that nobody else does!"

"Ah-*haaaa*," she said, raising a finger in Socratic mimesis. "And what are these things, pray tell?"

"Right," he said, missing her irony. "Take the old clichés about youth. You know, living fast, dying young, leaving a beautiful corpse."

"So we can put you on display, like Lenin?"

"Just listen to me, damn you. I'm trying to get at the idea of innocence lost, the idea of fame as the only preservative of that innocence, except clinical insanity. The idea of fame and youth as first cousins, complements to each—*what*, for christ sake?"

She was laughing again. She took another pull of wine before answering. "Dorian," she slurred, "I'm going to make a real effort to say something serious, OK? Just, just give me a minute." She paused, gathering her breath. "Right. Here it is. Dorian, I think—I think I'm going to be sick *really, really soon.*"

He stalked off into the darkness. She watched for a moment and then stumbled after him. "Oh come *on,* Dorian, I mean how can anybody this drunk have anything important to say?"

He continued walking, not looking at her. "The greatest wisdom on earth," he posited, "is related by the drunk. Only then is the truth set free."

"*Oooh*, how *profound*, I mean is that like one of those—those—fuck what do you call them . . ."

"Aphorisms."

". . . No, I meant . . . goddamn it what *do* you call them . . ."

"Christ are you stupid."

". . . Oh *really?* Well, Mister Intellectual, why don't you try this on for an afroism?"

He glanced at her. "What."

"*My* philosophy is that you should be very careful of what people try to sell you in this life, whether it's cars or culture or especially myths. Don't take their word for anything. There's always a price, and it's not just money. That's what I think." She began laughing again. "Jesus, did I just say all that?"

"What you said was trite. Here, give me some of that wine."

She held the bottle away from him. "Fuck off Dorian, this is mine. And it wasn't trite. It only sounded that way because you've bought into the whole goddamn fantasy, haven't you. And because unlike you, I don't go around beating people over the head with what I think. I can thank my mother for that—that *distinction*."

"Because she had weak opinions?"

"Because she thinks God wears a tampon and not a jockstrap. Because she thinks men are irrelevant. Because she thinks women can isolate themselves from the world and ignore everything that goes on in it. And because, having said all that, she doesn't believe in any of it. It's a front."

"Ah," said Dorian. "I see we've touched on a sore spot. Good."

But she didn't hear him: she was looking up at the sky and feeling as if she were the axis upon which the universe was spinning. "Jesus I hate her," she whispered.

"But you don't like men either."

She poured the last of the wine down her throat. "Dorian," she said slowly, as a wave of pain passed through her head, and the universe began to spin even faster, "I hate men and women equally, OK?"

After a time they came to the edge of a small lake, the stars brilliantly rendered on its surface, and began skirting the perimeter. He measured out the silence for a time before saying, "The fact that you're a lesbian—is that your choice, or your mother's?"

She started, and then realized the question had no double-meaning. "Ah Dorian, who knows. It's hard for me to talk about. It's not so much about being a lesbian that's—I mean there's more to . . . Look let's put it this way. Right now I need women. The so-called politics of lesbianism don't mean anything to me, not in the sense that 'Oh, everything I do is gay,' 'The personal is political,' all that stuff. It's more complicated, I mean I follow my instincts and . . . Look I don't *know*, all right? In twenty years I might be a devoted wife and mother of ten, I might be the biggest bull-dyke on the East Coast, I don't know whether I was born or made and I don't really give a shit I mean why does it have to be an *issue?*"

"Because I think you're stunningly gorgeous and I've got this craving you wouldn't believe."

She released his hand and stopped. His features were indistinct in the darkness, and so, theoretically, were hers. Nevertheless she felt suddenly uncomfortable and turned her back, gazing across the mere.

"Look, just hear me out," he said. "And try to overlook all this— this treacly sincerity that I'm about to spew, all right? Just bear with me." He took a breath. "The fact is, this journey is the best thing that's happened to me since I came to this country, and I'm growing used to it. It's difficult to face the fact that it'll be over in a few days. I want to extract something permanent out of it, live it forever."

There was a long silence.

"Lucky . . . ?"

"I think the trouble with you, Dorian, is that deep down you're very sentimental."

"And there's something wrong with that?"

"Maybe because it is so dangerous. Maybe because . . . because there's something mythical there too."

"Well Christ! Is there nothing you haven't deconstructed?"

"I don't believe in myths. They're all clichés."

"Yes but isn't something vital lost in the process?"

"Just the opposite. You see things much more clearly."

Behind her, she could feel, rather than see, his hands fluttering in exasperation. "Damn it," he rasped, "I am not just being sentimental I'm being *genuine*. Don't you understand what we're doing here, now, this moment, it's—Christ it's as real as it gets, I mean what else is there in life? Nothing but, but simulacra, nothing but . . . You say you're following your instincts well I'm following mine as well. You're the most beautiful gi—the most beautiful *woman* I've ever seen, how's that for a cliché? I mean has anyone ever said that to you before?"

She remained still, the stars blurring even further as she gazed into the water.

"Let me ask you something further: Have you ever loved anyone? Do you think it *possible* that you could ever love anyone, romantically that is?"

A full minute passed before she found her voice, a faint issuance in the bottom of her throat, scarcely more than a whisper, soft but unwavering as it articulated the lies that were true. "To answer your three questions: No. No. No."

Undeterred, he moved directly behind her, his hand light upon her shoulder. She started at his touch but did not shy away.

"You always speak to me as if I were a child," he said quietly. "I suppose it's appropriate, given the way I've behaved, and—and well yes there's no question that if . . . But I've meant everything I've said and . . . and bloody hell I'm going to regret this—" Suddenly she found herself jerked in a half-circle and his lips closing against hers, hungering and not in the least tentative. She stiffened; her first instinct, in accordance with her training, was to fling him halfway across the lake. Her hands had already located pressure points, were poised to manipulate him into any number of painful contortions. But if he sensed this he gave no indication, instead consolidating his advantage, his tongue drawing along her own, one hand dropping to her ass to pull her to him, her sex against his. Her muscles wavered; she felt overcome with a strange paralysis, body and mind curiously inert, and during this fleeting abulia she felt herself carried along a slow, gentle river, motionless, the current bearing her so comfortingly that she felt no inclination to resist.

Dorian pulled back, as if his courage were abruptly spent.

"You kiss very well," she said quietly.

"What? Ah well you know, Oxford and what not, the—"

"Come on."

"Sorry?"

She released his hand, stepped away, and pulled the dress over her head. She waded a few steps into the lake and turned back, smiling. "Are you coming in? or do you want to keep looking for awhile?"

His gaze lingered on the elegant breasts, then descended along the smooth white abdomen to the ghostly fleece of hair, the hint of the cleft beneath, his breath catching.

"Come on, take off your clothes. I like fucking underwater."

And she was gone, silvery in the moonlight, quickly below water and resurfacing ten yards out, a nimbus of water decorating her advent. He fumbled at shoes, socks, shirt, pants, but paused, Hollywood-like, at boxers. He trod forward hesitantly, the water warm on his calves. He could not voice his embarrassment but she did so for him.

"It's all right, Dorian. If you want to know the truth I find men with erections far more interesting to look at. But if you're uncomfortable, I'll close my eyes until you're submerged. Or you could back your way in."

He laughed. "I'm such a fool," he said, pulling them off, allowing her a brief appraisal before diving forward. Swimming out to where she waited, his feet sought bottom even as the succor of her embrace enfolded him, his skin meeting hers in a startle of electricity as they clung to each other strong as death, losing their balance and easing out beyond their depth, sinking below the surface with lips conjoined all the same, not resisting their gentle descent, her legs encircling his hips and his hand moving to hold them fast, his penis enveloped within her and his hips already thrusting instinctively against the exquisite friction. Their bodies drifted to the surface and she impelled them toward the shallows, in the same perfect concinnity, settling finally upon the shore where they sought each other with even greater urgency as the lake washed over them and then at last rendered them still.

*　　*　　*

Prophet sat with his laptop computer, checking his e-mail. There was a letter from Gyeppi advising him to cease all bomb threats for the time being, to let the riots play themselves out. He felt relieved. As much as Russell Chunk's TV appearance had titillated him, he was nevertheless unnerved that his faxes had prompted such a tangible and immediate response—the very response he'd hoped for, ironically. His place in the chain of causality felt somehow unreal: the connection between his faxes and Chunk's press conference seemed insubstantial, reminding him of a math problem solved by intuitive leaps rather than logical derivation (prompting a rebuke from the teacher, since teachers always mistrust unconventional thinking). There was something ominous about having such power that roused the beginnings of nausea in his gut.

The journey west was affecting him in other ways. Among these four white people, including a girl he loved, he sensed his militancy eroding. His separatist ideals, unlike Natare's, were not buttressed by years of hard-formed conviction; they'd been given to him like a makeover, and nothing in his immediate environment helped to replenish the foundation. In the final analysis, he didn't know how he felt toward Natare, toward Karibu, toward the riots now consuming the cities. He knew only that he was a black man, and that he

195

could not return to his earlier, colorblind life. His companions might not fully understand him—indeed, they were perhaps incapable of doing so—but he realized, for the first time, that he felt attached to them all, even Dorian. They provided a spontaneity that his life at Columbia had always lacked. With Natare, everything was predictable: every opinion was preconceived, every action part of a greater script. Once Prophet had chosen the dissident's lot, the Cause became preeminent.

He felt hollow, disillusioned, confused. Where did he go from here? Once this journey was over—what then? Was there a third path, somewhere between separatism and accommodation, that he might forge for himself? Or had he come too far now to turn back?

He had just shut off the computer when Ariel began to scream. She lay only a few feet away, close to the fire. Before setting up his laptop he had watched her sleep for a time, for she was equally beautiful in repose. She had lain on her back, an arm flung wide above her head, her face inclined toward him. There was something classical about the pose—just the way he liked—and he had to suppress the urge to draw his fingertips across her cheek.

Her reticence had not merely contributed to her air of mystery; it had also made her even more attractive to him. He knew nothing about her, but this ignorance allowed him to embellish her as he liked, as if she were merely a photograph or fictional character made flesh, a living repository for his projections. Of course many problems inhered to this scenario, where the hidden eclipsed the revealed; but as long as she remained silent, he could not still the imaginative impulse. She was too much in his thoughts, and he needed a context in which to frame her.

But now she was screaming in her sleep, curled in the fetal position, one arm raised as if to ward off an attack. Prophet hurried over and knelt beside her. He took her arm and bent down, his lips close to her ear.

"Shh, shhh, Ariel *hey*, shhh, s'all right, s'all right, shhh . . ."

She jerked awake and sat up, eyes wide, mouth agape. She looked at him without recognition, her breathing frantic.

"*Hey*," he said quietly. "It's me, remember? Only me."

She threw her arms around his neck and sagged against him, pushing him to the ground. He lay back and drew her head to his chest, brushing away her tears. She sobbed for a long time. He remained as he was, even as his right arm fell asleep. He spoke to her softly, his voice the tonic, not the words. He thought she would soon pull away; but when eventually she subsided, she surprised him by snuggling deeper into his embrace and resting a hand on his.

Lightheaded, he hardly dared move, as if doing so would disrupt the dreamlike evolution of this scene. Instead he just held her, saying presently, "I don't suppose you're ready to talk yet?"

She did speak, in a barely audible whisper. "No."

Even that one syllable startled him, and for a moment he was tempted to draw her out further. He forced himself to abandon the idea. "You want me to talk instead?"

She nodded, her head rubbing against his chest.

"S'no problem at all. Fact I got just the thing. You see those stars up there, the way they kinda form a dog? That's Canis Major, and that bright star is called Sirius. Now just over there you can see a smaller dog, Canis Minor—you see how that is? That big star there is Procyon. Now everybody knows Orion, and that's Taurus to the right, so let's see . . . That star right there is Vega, which is in Lyra, and over there is Spica in Virgo. Meanwhile we got Regulus in Leo, which of course is the lion, though you wouldn't know that to look at it. Now my personal favorites are nebulas, and if you look right there in Orion—it looks like a tiny cloud—you can see M-42, and there's another one right over there . . ."

*     *     *

She woke to a searing pain in her head and stomach, a pain so comprehensive that for a moment she hadn't a thought in her mind. She lay there for seconds, minutes, hours—it didn't matter: time had ceased to exist for her, leaving only the pain. Her head felt as if it were being drilled open like a slab of pavement. Her stomach ached with such wretched accusation that she dared not swallow, and her throat was parched in any case.

Then she became aware of a pressure against her chest. Opening her eyes, she saw a familiar tangle of blonde hair spilling over her breasts. An immediate surge of adrenaline jolted her wide awake, and for a moment she traded one pain for another.

"You," she whispered, and struck.

A crane-beak jab at Mary's left ear, the most immediate vulnerable target. As her mother recoiled with a soft cry, Lucky swung her

197

right leg over Mary's head so that Mary was kneeling between her legs, wrapped in their embrace. Mary's head was bowed, both hands pressed to her wounded ear. Lucky grabbed Mary's left wrist and pulled the arm taut, simultaneously bringing her left leg over Mary's right shoulder and around the back of her neck. As Mary was pulled down, Lucky tucked her left instep behind her right knee. Mary's neck was now trapped in the crook of Lucky's left leg, with her left cheek pressed against Lucky's right thigh. Retaining hold of Mary's wrist, Lucky contracted her legs into a triangle choke-hold and pummeled Mary's face with her free hand.

"Lucky!" her mother snarled. "Lucky stop, for Christ sake!"

"Fuck—you," Lucky gasped, sobbing. "I hate you, oh god I hate you so much . . ."

"Lucky *Jesus* it's *me*, it's only—*ahh! euhh*—"

"As if—" Lucky whispered "—as if I could ever have chosen otherwise, Mary. As if I didn't need you too." She drove her knuckles into Mary's temple.

*"Lucky for god sake you're going to kill me!!"*

The voice, something between a growl and a shriek, jerked her from her reverie. There was something wrong about that voice, something familiar but nevertheless very wrong. She extended her legs a fraction.

"Holy fuck! Is *everyone* on this trip determined to hospitalize me?"

"Dorian?" she said, staring at him vacantly.

"Well fuck it's sure as hell not Cliff Richard now will you *please* let me go . . ."

But she maintained the hold. "What were you doing?"

"I was listening to your chest, you thick-headed cunt! I thought you weren't breathing!"

Hesitantly she released him. He pushed her legs from his neck and sat back, massaging himself. In the moonlight she could see that she'd reopened some of the wounds on his face, but he ignored the blood as if to shame her.

"Um . . . what happened?" she ventured.

He glared at her. "You passed out and then you started vomiting. After *that* you started choking, and *then* you didn't make any sound at all. I thought you might be dead, for christ sake."

She sat up, her head still spinning. She looked down at her dress, saw the trails of fresh mucus. Feeling suddenly faint, she put her head in her hands, moaning. Dimly, she realized that she was not only fully clothed, but fully dry as well. So was Dorian. Which meant . . .

She struggled to her knees, whereupon she began vomiting with such force that tears streamed down her face. As she voided her guts in the long grass Dorian knelt beside her, not saying a word, resting a hand on her back. When there was nothing left she sat back, wiping at the tears. He sank down beside her.

"Do you mind telling me what that was all about?" he asked.

"I'm sorry," she whispered. "It was a dream."

He sighed. "Yes that's all well and good but—"

"I can't talk about it," she said distantly, feeling herself sag to the ground yet again, the universe careening anew. "Never. Do you understand?"

"Brilliant," Dorian muttered, as she lost consciousness. "Bloody fucking brilliant. By god I wish someone were keeping track of all this." He felt almost clear-headed, the world suddenly cold and grim but projecting no illusions of its own.

Mumbling further expletives, Dorian scooped—or at any rate wrestled—Lucky into his arms and lurched to his feet, tottering. She was almost too heavy for him, and only some vague conviction that he was for once in his life acting heroically gave him the strength to keep his grip as he shambled back toward the campfire, still cursing.

# CHAPTER FOURTEEN

## *The Case for Heresiarchy . . .*

They slept well beyond midday, and not much was said as they groped around for clothes, watches, cigarettes, the remains of food. The fire was dead, its ashes seeming to mark the passing of some otherworldly presence, like ozone in the wake of lightning. The air was hot and still, and the scrub fields lay bleakly under the burning white sky.

As they acclimated to consciousness, Prophet said, "Wait a minute. Where's Fish?"

"Off for a walk?" said Lucky.

"I haven't seen him since last night," said Dorian. "Ariel, what about you?"

The girl thought for a moment, then pointed out into the field.

"I don't think he came back," said Prophet.

"He probably passed out," said Dorian. "Prophet and I had better go and look for him."

They began searching. Prophet came upon Fish a few minutes later, sprawled in the dirt, face down, in a pose that did not look like sleeping.

"Dorian!"

He knelt as Dorian bounded over.

"Oh Christ."

"He's still warm, and yeah, there's a pulse. God *damn* he had me scared. Maybe we should turn him over."

"Gently there . . ."

When Fish was on his back they scrutinized his face. A trail of drool had petered out near a corner of his mouth. Stalactites of crusty snot descended from his nose. His breathing was labored but steady.

"You think we should wake him?" said Dorian.

"We sure as hell can't carry him, and we don't wanna stay here all day. We'll fry."

"I think you're right. Fish—" Dorian tapped his face "—Fish?"

"Think you better do it harder."

Dorian slapped with increasing force. Suddenly Fish coughed, sneezed, vomited, opened his eyes, and sat up without looking at either of them, bile running down his frock. "Tycho? *Tycho? TYCHO!!*"

"Bad dream, old son?"

"The loophole," said Fish. "The trick is finding the loophole."

Prophet sought Dorian's eyes, reading the same worry.

"Life is like a tax return," said Fish, standing. He vacillated briefly and brushed the dirt from his vestments. "Key is itemizing deductions. Depreciating over a period of years. Amortization. *Finding the goddamn loophole!*"

"Fuck," said Prophet. "This could be trouble. Yo Fish? Goggles? You reco-nize me man?"

Fish pushed him away. "No late returns though. And most certainly no refunds. Trick is finding the loophole. Creationism: write-off. Judeo-Christianity: write-off. Social Spencerism?" He held up a finger. "Non-negotiable. Subject fully to individual tax bracket. Surtax if you're black, fat, or congenitally diseased."

"Think we got a problem Dorian."

"Fucking hell. Fish? *Fish?!*" He recommenced slapping. "Fish will you acknowledge me for Christ sake?"

Fish burped in his face. "Christ died for no one's sins, got it? There are no sins. Only transactions. Loans at interest, deposits and returns."

"Prophet what was the name of that tranquilizer?"

"Uh . . . I think a woman's name, Dora, Nora, Flora . . . Thorazine that's it! no wait . . . Nell . . . Melba . . . *Stela*zine got it! Stelazine."

"Where can we steal some?"

"Well I guess any drugstore but wait, maybe there's a doctor who could see—"

"Prophet, any doctor who looks at this man is going to call the police."

"That may be true. All I'm saying's that you better be prepared to get busted."

"Well I can't see any alternative except to leave him, which is absurd. I'll tell you what, I'll do it myself. I won't ask you to get involved."

Prophet sighed. "I'm not saying I'm not up for it Dorian. I'm only saying let's not make any snap decisions, right? Let's go to the next town, check things out."

Dorian scratched his chin. "Perhaps that's best. Right. Come on Fish, we're going." He took Fish's arm and Fish threw it off.

"*Democritus!*" he hissed. "Now *there*'s a fucked-up situation. Not to mention apeiron, phlogiston—"

"Prophet can you knock him cold?"

"Not sure we should try anything like that. The man's crazy. He might be dangerous."

"Yes but we can't muck about in this heat. It must be a hundred and ten."

Prophet was looking west. "Are those mountains?"

Dorian turned, squinting. For the first time he noticed the mauve undulations running the length of the horizon. "By god, yes! It'll be cooler there. If we can just get out of this flatland . . ."

"The ghost in the machine," said Fish. "Pavlov Watson Skinner behaviorist *fucks*! Where's the goddamn loophole Prophet, where?"

"Fish? You talkin to me?"

"Christians," said Fish confidentially, "are so *crispy*. A little ketchup and presto! Now your Jew on the other hand is kind of soggy, and best served with two cups of Hindu. Muslims—forget it. Though with no risk of trichinosis—"

"Prophet find a log or something. Or there's a crowbar in the trunk."

"Be right back."

"Look at me," said Fish, arms spread. "Look at what I am! I'm a nice little package, a suitcase of atoms all spinning round and round and round. Contain me, contain me—I'm a bundle of happy molecules. It's all physics in the end, do you see? Call me Dr. Gluon."

"Right," said Dorian, as Prophet returned with the crowbar and handed it to him, "now just distract him while I go round behind . . ."

"Truth, puberty, love," said Fish. "Drugs for the Great Unwashed. Set VCRs to Stun, and send Plutarch along with a handy-cam!"

Dorian swung once, medium-hard. Though his eyes snapped shut, Fish crumpled to the ground otherwise wearing the same expression of mid-sentence discourse, his brow furrowed, mouth open wide, finger raised.

"You know something?" said Prophet. "Let's just drag the mother-fucker."

202

They each grasped an arm and hauled Fish through the scrub. When they neared the campsite Lucky and Ariel walked out to meet them.

"My god," said Lucky. "What——"

"It's the beginning of the end," said Dorian. He continued toward the road, Prophet following his lead.

They deposited Fish in the back seat of the Mustang and returned to pack up their belongings. When they were ready to travel, Lucky and Ariel flanked the catatonic Fish, while Prophet rode in the front passenger seat.

Dorian pulled onto the road, heading west toward the promise of the high country. It was already mid-afternoon. None of them spoke.

When Fish woke, half an hour later, he looked around and said, "What year is it?"

Prophet told him.

"Cusp of the millennium," said Fish. "Thousand-year reich. Should've told Chamberlain not to appease the vegetarian threat. Down went the empire."

Lucky noticed that Ariel was watching Fish with concern. "Schizophrenia," she said quietly. "We don't have his medicine."

"Prophecy for the Great Unwashed," resumed Fish. "Check your brains at the door, pin a smile on your face. Send Marduk on his merry way."

"Listen to the fucker," said Prophet.

"Higher beings," answered Fish, "have no use for such cheap devices as alliteration."

"How much longer?" said Lucky.

"Who knows," said Dorian. "There has to be a town sometime soon."

"Just call me Schlomo," said Fish. "Lord Schlomowicz, Talmudic scholar and Marquess of the Small Intestine. Perhaps therein lies the loophole; ahoy the swollen colon."

"Lucky would you do me a favor and cut a mask out of that pillowcase?"

"Mask?"

"For the robbery."

"What robbery?"

"The drugstore!" he snapped. "And I'll not hear a word against it."

"Dorian we need a doctor, not an arrest warrant."

"Only to have him put away? What about youthful solidarity?"

"He needs help! We can't help him when he's like this!"

"We could, with—what's it called Prophet?"

"Stelazine."

"Stelazine! We'll tank him into oblivion."

"I don't believe this shit," said Lucky, folding her arms. "I don't know where the *hell* you come up with these *idiotic* notions—"

"Beef jerky," said Fish. "Give Lamarck his due. What Darwin is to biology, Lamarck is to culture. But same natural selection in the end. Only the strong survive."

As the road finally ascended into the hills, they reached the outskirts of a village named Durkam, passing a series of garish bungalows and barren trailer parks. On the front lawn of one pre-fab ranch, a brown bear dangled from an oak tree, a trophy for all to admire. The bear's forelegs hung limply at her sides, as though she were standing loosely at attention.

"You think there's a doctor in this town?" said Prophet. "I'd be surprised if anyone here can *read*."

"There's got to be a hospital," said Dorian. "Even these people need doctors."

They drove into the center of town. The streets were mysteriously empty, with neither car nor pedestrian in sight. Driving along Main Street they passed deserted storefronts boasting **Crimmins' Arsenal (Every other round's on us!), Post Office/General Store, Ma's Diner, Dad's Trading Post, Sis's Hair and Manicure Palace**. At the end of the strip stood the Dorkam Baptist Church.

"Maybe everybody's in there," said Dorian. "Is it Sunday?"

"Can't even remember," said Prophet.

"There's still no sign of a hospital."

"Maybe when people get sick here they just shoot em."

"Bishop Berkeley," said Fish, who had sighted the church. "*Esse est percipi*, ho ho ho. We'll deal with your scene presently."

"Well we can't just sit here waiting," said Dorian. "I'll go in the church and see if anyone's about."

"I'll come with you," said Prophet, opening the door.

They mounted the steps toward the church, which resembled a giant white shoebox with green trim, save for the icon of Jesus's torture mounted on the roof like a lightning rod. They opened a green door and found themselves in a long narrow room. A dozen empty pews faced a lectern at the far end. The air was stale and dry, and their footsteps were absorbed without echo.

"Jesus," said Dorian. "I've never seen a church like this. Where's the altar?"

"These born-agains don't use that shit," said Prophet. "Pretty sterile if you ask me."

"And they're *Christian*?"

"Oh yeah baby. They think the Bible is literal. They think the universe is six thousand years old, I mean even the *Pope* don't think that."

"Can I help you?"

They turned. Above the door was a balcony, upon which stood an old white man in a brown suit. He held a small black Bible under his arm and his vantage point lent him an imperious bearing.

"Hello," said Dorian. "I wonder if you could direct us to a hospital."

"A hospital," said the man. "No good going to a hospital. Nobody'll *be* there."

Dorian glanced at Prophet. "Where will they be?"

"Gone to the valley," said the man. "Gone to welcome the coming of the Lord. Oh no," he said, laughing softly, "no need for hospitals. No need for anything now that His time has come."

Prophet seemed about to riposte but Dorian silenced him. "This valley," he said. "Where is it?"

"Bout fifteen miles out of town, heading west. You'll see the signs. *Everybody*'s going to be there. Are you Christians?"

"Thank you," said Dorian.

The road continued its ascent, winding through a mixed forest. When they had traveled eleven miles they came upon a long line of traffic. Dorian was obliged to slow to twenty, as he fell in behind it. "Looks like we've found the party," he said.

"I'm not sure I understand," said Lucky. "What's supposed to be happening at this valley?"

"The coming of the messiah," Prophet snorted. "Wait till they see he's black."

"I don't know what the hell it is," said Dorian. "I only know that anyone in the immediate vicinity who can write a prescription is going to be there."

Fish, meanwhile, had quietly engaged Ariel in conversation. Naturally he did all the talking. He was explaining, in great detail, his encounter of the previous evening. In order to provide context, he launched into an intimate history of the Politburo. She regarded him solemnly, as though she were genuinely listening. "But in the end it comes down to this," he said, taking her hands in his. "The purpose of life isn't about wisdom, or charity, or even simple reproduction. It's much more subtle than that. The purpose of life, above and beyond all else, is finding the loophole. So there you have it."

The procession moved slowly but steadily. Half an hour later they reached an immense glade that overlooked a steep valley—*the* valley, it seemed. The cars were pulling into the glade, which had been converted into a parking lot. Attendants clad in orange vests painted with white crosses directed traffic. Several thousand cars were already parked, and another ten minutes passed before Dorian reached a half-formed row and was guided into a space. The cars behind followed suit, like collations in a photocopier.

Signs reading **THIS WAY TO THE VALLEY**→ had been placed at regular intervals, and a steady parade of souls was following them. The travelers fell into line. Innumerable Caucasian families were clambering from their cars, the adults heaving their corpulence into the open air with a grimace, the posses of fat children looking stunned in their tank tops, clutching dolls and video games and ice cream and little youth Bibles with the same blue-eyed Jesus grinning from the covers. Trunks were opened and picnic chests hauled out, along with folding chairs, tents, canteens, air mattresses. It was advent week, and the faithful had come home to roost.

Not surprisingly, the travelers drew attention. Prophet searched in vain for a complexion other than pink, but the color spectrum was murderously narrow. He could read those glances, could see the latent hostility, the curious contempt, the enemy memory run deep. That six-letter Word lay queasily dormant in the group consciousness of this multitude, and he sensed that eruption could come at any moment. He memorized the location of the car, counting the rows as they walked. He wanted the option of leaving in a hurry.

Fish received even more scrutiny. Catholics, in evangelical parlance, have not been saved, and until then the papist is lost to the grace of the Lord. Worship of a common myth means nothing in the end: to the saved, Catholics are the Opposition, and priests are little better than Satanists. Moreover, he stank.

"This is ridiculous," said Lucky. "We need a doctor, not an exorcist."

"There have to be medical facilities," said Dorian as they tramped along the flattened grass. "Then again, they might all be faith healers."

They reached the lip of the valley. Below them spread a city of sorts, which extended a half-mile to either side and descended a few thousand feet to the fruited plain in the distance, which in turn reached eastward toward Jerusalem. Media helicopters hovered in attendance. A gentle wind had risen, and the waning sunlight bled upon the gathering as if conferring its own form of grace.

Farther down the valley, a dozen massive yellow tents had been erected, apparently for official purposes, like a town center. Family tents were clustered densely around the perimeter. A tide of white skin shifted variously as the populace roamed about, beneath a sky the color of dandelions.

Platoons of burly men in fatigue pants and powder-blue T-shirts that read **Christian Soldiers: Gunnin' For Jesus!** stood guard at the valley's edge, regarding the travelers with indulgent malice. Each carried a walkie-talkie and a Zygote Vegas-1® automatic rifle (known colloquially as the Gambler; slogan: **Take 'em to the cleaners!**), which incidentally fires nine rounds per second and takes eighty in the clip.

"Dorian," said Prophet, "I don't think I like this."

"Look we've got to get him a tranquilizer," Dorian replied, indicating Fish, who was babbling a continual stream of vague invective under his breath, something about Paul Tillich being a fraud. "Anyway this is a religious gathering. Journalists are in attendance. They can't *lynch* you, for Christ sake."

"Yeah—cause there ain't no trees."

They descended, picking their way among family encampments, where pigs were roasting on open spits and caffeine-free soda was the beverage of choice. A separate village of portable toilets had been raised, and was receiving ardent patronage as the twice-born relieved their bowels and emerged with the clear consciences of the shriven.

The atmosphere was casual; friendly bantering pervaded. A second, smaller series of official yellow tents had been pitched nearby, housing Bible study groups *(Reconciling John, Lessons from Corinthians, Creation Science Seminar)* and informal prayer gatherings. Children's swimming pools functioned as impromptu baptismal centers. Baseballs were thrown about. Free Bibles were available at designated kiosks.

By the time they reached the larger tents, the travelers were mildly surprised that they hadn't been burned at the stake or at least given a half-hearted stoning. Dorian, clad again in his black turtleneck, had the appearance of a derelict aesthete. Prophet still hadn't seen his signal for relief—another black person. Fish was asked, every two paces, whether he'd come to be cured. As for Lucky and Ariel, scarcely a man present—whether Baptist, Pentecostal, Charismatic, or just plain evangelical Christian—did not rape them with his gaze, despite conditioning worthy of Pavlov. The wives, meanwhile, adjusting thick horn-rimmed glasses and scowling beneath cheap perms, stared slack-jawed at this wanton pulchritude, this temptation set before their men.

The travelers passed food tents, water tents, hospitality tents, orientation tents, media tents. Here the Christians mingled with camera crews, print journalists, and other bloodhounds from around the country. Leaflets were in abundance: *How to Elect Christians to State Office, Analysis of Christian Lobbying Techniques, Christians and PR: A Marriage Made in Heaven.* Donation boxes were placed every ten paces.

"Seems a bit extravagant if the Second Coming doesn't happen," observed Dorian.

"Are you kidding?" said Lucky. "If it really *did* happen this would all be moot. Who would need donations then?"

A videocamera was abruptly trained on Fish, and a thickly painted woman stuck a microphone in his face. "Excuse me, father, I was wondering if you could tell me about the role of Catholics in this event."

Fish stared into the camera. "I am the last of the Kantians," he said.

The woman nodded her head vigorously, rotating her free hand to speed him up. When he said nothing more, she asked, "Is that a particular order within the Church? like the Jesuits?"

He frowned. "You realize," he said, "that by invoking the Council of Trent you're begging the que—wait a minute. Your face reminds me of Tetzel. Are you a relative of Tetzel?"

"Thank you," she said, lowering the microphone and turning away. "Fuck this, Linus," she told the cameraman. "Let's find those Jews for Jesus already."

"Any bright ideas, Dorian?" sneered Lucky.

"Well Christ where are the first-aid tents? I can't believe there's not a single case of poison ivy or something."

They pushed on a little further before coming to a halt beside the largest tent of all, which measured at least a hundred yards in length. Peering inside, they saw that rows of bleachers had been erected, as though for a circus. Camera towers had been raised, all focusing upon a stage where about twenty chairs and a lectern stood. Above the stage loomed a vast screen, as yet blank.

The tent was filling steadily. Those entering were formally dressed, a sea of bright colors in fundamentalist approximation of good taste. The men wore sports jackets, which tended toward lime green, magenta, and turquoise. The women, buoyantly coiffed, their make-up garishly abundant, wore faux-chiffon dresses of the same hues. The children were smart facsimiles of their parents: one knew immediately what they would look like in middle age.

"Jesus," said Dorian. "I've never seen anything like this. And Christ, the smell! Is it perfume?"

"Who knows what evil lurks in the hearts of Christians," said Fish.

"How're you doing, Fish?" said Dorian, turning to him. "Coherent?"

"Coherent, cognizant, cogent," Fish replied. "Let the games begin."

"It looks like they're preparing for a rally," said Lucky.

"Indeed we are, young lady," said a rolling baritone behind them. They turned to confront a middle-aged man dressed in a mustard-yellow jacket and crimson trousers. He was flushed and chunky, his watery blue eyes regarding them with faint suspicion. "Have you come to meet the Lord?" he continued.

"God the Father, God the Son, God the Pharmaceutical," said Fish.

"He needs a doctor," said Lucky as the man squinted at Fish. "Is there a medical facility around here?"

"Oh, we don't need doctors," said the man. "The pure in spirit are pure in body. What afflicts this young papist sinner?"

"He's—well he's a bit overstimulated," said Dorian. "All the excitement of, of the Second Coming, he's just bursting with apocalypse. *You* understand."

"Well now if this man is filled with the word of the Lord how can that be a bad thing?"

"Fuck the Lord," said Fish. "Let me tell you something cousin: The Lord is a fine white powder, with the chemical formula $C_{21}H_{24}F_3N_3S$."

The man stepped back a pace, considering Fish anew. "Is that the voice of Lucifer within?"

"Lucifer," said Fish, "is my shepherd. I shall not want—"

"Look he's schizophrenic OK?" said Lucky, intervening. "We need to get him to a hospital."

The man was smiling again. "Tell ya what," he said. "I think I have just the solution." He offered a hand to Dorian. "Name's J. Barnaby Thatch, and I'm keynote speaker here tonight. We got all kindsa healing planned. Why not take your friend on stage and I'll fill him with the Lord. You'll see a miracle before your eyes."

Dorian and Prophet exchanged pained glances, but unexpectedly Fish assented. "Yes," he said. "On stage."

Thatch beamed. "I knew ya'd see the light."

Fish sat in one of the chairs, blinking in the glare. Darkness had fallen outside, but racks of portable lights bathed the stage with eager scrutiny. Dozens of photographers crouched in a media pit before the stage. Beyond lay the audience, who filled the successive tiers of bleachers to capacity.

A few feet away from him, J. Barnaby Thatch was elucidating the virtues of repentance, doubled by his image on the screen above.

"Armageddon is nigh," he informed the crowd, to its tittering approval. "The time has come for every man to give a full accounting of himself before our Lord Jesus Christ. I ask you: Are you worthy? Can you stand proudly before the Lord, having accepted your sinful nature and Him as your only savior? If you cannot, I urge you to do so at once. There is still time, my friends, but that time is running out. In two days the armies of the Lord will descend from heaven and the die will be cast. Those who are not with Him will be struck into damnation. Damnation! I ask you all: Can you truly call yourself a Christian?"

He turned, indicating those seated with a broad gesture. "There are some among us who want so much to accept our Lord into their souls but just can't do it alone. I will show you the healing power of Jesus, and how every man can be saved in the end." He indicated an ancient woman. "You, my dear! What is your affliction?"

210

"Arthritis," piped the woman. "I—I can't even *stand* any more!"

"And what's your name?"

"Mabel," she said.

"Now Mabel—" Thatch placed his hand on her shoulder "—do you accept our Lord Jesus Christ as your only savior and the Son of God?"

"Oh, oh *yes*," she warbled.

"Then Mabel," boomed Thatch, "stand up and walk!"

A swell of encouragment rose from the crowd. Mabel beamed, and then her features settled into intense concentration. Trembling, she pushed against her chair, battling to propel herself upright. After a brief struggle she was erect, to the reward of thunderous applause.

Thatch had moved a few yards away. "Come to me, Mabel!" he shouted. "Show us you can walk!"

Mabel placed one foot in front of the other, wincing and tottering, her face a mask of pain. Halfway to Thatch one leg seemed to give out. She tumbled headlong into the media pit, her fuchsia dress flapping round her ears, revealing bony legs and a capacious sanitary diaper, which came loose upon impact. There was a collective gasp from the crowd: they rose to their feet, straining for a better look. A cameraman hunched over Mabel, his face dripping with urine; a moment later he stood, shaking his head.

Dead! thought Fish. Stone dead!

Declining offers of help, Thatch hauled Mabel back on stage. She slipped from his grasp and cracked her skull on the floor. Thatch stood over her, frowning pensively, as if a great weight were upon him.

"My friends," he said softly. "I hope you'll rejoice with me in the miracle that has just transpired. Our Lord could not wait for Mabel any longer. So impressed was He by her courage that He has taken her unto Him! Praise the Lord!"

The crowd, stunned into silence, began slowly, hesitantly to revive. They took up the cry as Mabel was returned to her chair, head sagging backward and mouth wide open. A female volunteer was summoned to refasten the diaper.

"For those of you watching this around the world," said Thatch, gazing into the camera, "I only wish you could feel what a special and powerful force has visited us here. God is so very, very good. He's blessing us in a thousand ways, right here in this tent. Surely no greater token of His love could manifest itself before us.

211

"Now this young man," said Thatch, turning to Fish, "is afflicted with the Devil's sickness. Oh, some of our secular humanists like to call it schizophrenia, but since the first coming of Christ it's been acknowledged that this so-called disease is nothing more than the voice of Lucifer himself, talking through the spiritually weak. This man desperately needs our help, folks, because he cannot cast that Devil out himself. Unlike our Lord and Savior, he cannot stand against this evil. Did not the Father cast Satan down from heaven? Did not the Son resist his temptations on the mountain? I believe, my friends, that no man who truly welcomes Jesus into his heart can be won by the Devil, and I will show you this now. What's your name young man?"

"Belacqua," said Fish.

"Now then Mr. Belackwuh, have you come to know the Lord?"

Suddenly the Politburo teemed in Fish's psyche, swarming all channels and flooding him with white noise. As usual, the head was at the forefront.

"Satan's puppet!" he sneered. "Do I look like Satan? Is this the face of an archangel? Is it?"

In a low, deliberate voice, Fish said, "*Shut up.*"

"You're history," said the grasshopper. "Not a psychotrope for miles around. We've got you now."

"Beg pardon?" said Thatch, leaning closer.

"Get out!" Fish screamed. "Get the fuck out of my head!"

Thatch turned to the crowd, his face gone soft and knowing. "Course," he said, "not everybody's ready to accept—"

"I do not accept!" Fish barked. "I deny!"

The hag inquired: "Did you think, in the end, that you were ever really free of us?"

"We are your soul," agreed the head. "Nothing else matters. Now why don't you tell this idiot to shut up. Come on, Fish. Does God exist?"

"No!" Fish screamed. "He doesn't exist! He never, *ever* existed! You lied! You lied to me! *Everybody fucking lied!*"

At the side of the stage Dorian and the others sprang to their feet.

"We've got to move fast," said Prophet, "and get the hell out of this nightmare."

212

Yet even before they could move two stocky Christian Soldiers had rushed on stage. Thatch stepped back, shaking his head sadly, with an expression that read, *Well folks, I tried . . .*

Fish seemed to have taken a page from the Book of Lucky. As the guards approached he kicked one in the groin and met the other with a hammer-fist to the nose. He relieved the latter of his weapon.

"Fish!" Dorian shouted. "Fish, for god sake don't!"

But Fish did not hear him. He considered the machine-gun briefly, then looked out among the crowd. They had scrambled to their feet, but most of them were now frozen in place. In the far back, some were able to leave the tent without hindrance. Those in front, however, fought the urge to begin a stampede. The bleachers would make exodus all the more difficult.

"Well done," said the head. "Though of course you realize that this act is as meaningless as any other. Everything stays the same. It amounts to nothing."

"No, no," said Fish, "there you're wrong. I have the power to effect *change*."

"That may be," said the head. "Still, don't get cocky. Whether you pull the trigger or not, keep one thing in mind: Except for us you are alone. You are alone."

"I am alone," agreed Fish. "As ever."

He raised the gun, a peaceful smile creasing his lips.

"You fools," he said to the crowd. "There never was an Eden."

The travelers crouched down as the machine-gun erupted. Only Ariel continued to watch, staring as Fish, exhilarated, rewarded the faithful with bullets. Those in the first few rows were flung back, their clothes abruptly stained with splotches of blood that might have served as Rorschach tests. He then turned to those on stage, waving them toward the exit—except J. Barnaby Thatch, who stood with arms raised in supplication, his white face now whiter. His hands and lower lip were quivering. He had the look of an addict whose habit has gone too long unslaked.

"Don't shoot," he said hoarsely. "I got a wife and three little—"

"You claim a savior will deliver you," said Fish, stepping closer, his tone oddly formal. "You may pray to him now."

Thatch glanced toward the exit and licked his lips, doubtless hoping for more Christian Soldiers. "Now you listen," he said, "I'm sure that we can come—"

"*Pray!*" yelled Fish, raising the gun to Thatch's head.

"O-O-O-OK, OK," Thatch babbled, "OK, uh, 'Our father, who art in heaven, heh-heh-hallowed bibee thy name; thy kingdom come—' "

"*There!*" Fish snapped. "That's just it. There is no kingdom come. Everywhere you turn nowadays there's a fucking lie. You lied to me about everything."

Again Thatch looked toward the exit, but no armed servants of the Lord presented themselves. The traffic was all one-way.

"You think there's a heaven?" said Fish, pressing the barrel against his throat. "You think your god will come down and save you? You all tried to make me believe that, and now I know it isn't true. You know what I say unto you, sirrah? I say beware of false prophets, for they earneth false profits."

Thatch's weak blue eyes, pleading with their gold counterparts, flicked to the gun and back again. Thick, luminous tears were forming, threatening to spill down his cheeks.

"*Listen,*" Fish whispered, increasing the pressure. "Do you hear horsemen? I hear *nothing.* I hear the silence of deep space, pure silence. I hear your prayers dying in an anechoic chamber. If you have a savior it is I, for I bring you truth—truth of the Void and the dreamless sleep; truth of the silence without end. My friend, I hereby consign you to that silence."

Amen.

Leaving Thatch's corpse, he strode to each of the television cameras in turn and fired into their lenses. "A day more fair or foul I have not seen," he remarked, "but now it's time for some privacy, goddamn it." When all of the cameras had been destroyed he turned, and gazed up at the screen that no longer bore his image. "Twilight of the idols," he proclaimed, "or, How one philosophizes with an assault rifle." He released the last of the clip into the cables that supported the screen, which jerked loose from its moorings and fell to earth. Fish grinned as it descended upon him, casting the gun aside, arms raised perpendicular to the floor and lips puckering for a kiss, a kiss to meet the glass monster that bore him to the ground, shattering into crystalline oblivion, the shards nailing his arms and legs to the stage, and he still smiling.

The congregants were massing at the exits. The Christian Soldiers, arriving all too late, were confronted with the tides of exiting faithful and dozens of bodies slumped in the bleachers, their trigger fingers rendered useless as they realized their quarry was dead.

"Like I said before, let's get the fuck out of here," said Prophet.

"What about—"

"We're fair game, Lucky. Those boys'll be looking for an excuse to shoot something or other."

And so they ran, tearing a hole in the canvas where stray bullets had partially rent the fabric. The tent city was brightly lit, in part from the helicopters reconvening overhead. Holding hands, the travelers pushed through the crowd as a brigade of reporters swarmed the other way. The chaos worked to their advantage. The Christian Soldiers, unsure themselves of what had happened, simply converged on the main tent. Sobbing families comforted one another while journalists barked questions among them. The travelers alone had a clear purpose, but the oncoming swell broke upon them and they floundered against the great press of bodies.

They had reached the outskirts of the main village when they felt the first drops of rain. The slopes were lit only by battery-powered lamps and a few stray campfires, which were quickly extinguished as the rain grew into a downpour. The travelers fought their way up while the curious scrambled their way down. Evidently word had spread, via walkie-talkie, to all corners of the valley; the weather was deterring no one. The travelers clung to each other, stumbling in the mud, blinking away rain. When asked what had happened below, they did not answer.

More helicopters arrived, some flying very low. Tents were uprooted and scattered across the hillside, and families became tangled in the fabric. Ashes, clothes, and Bibles were all borne in the sirocco, and within moments the valley was strewn with debris. Women and children screamed as men in pajamas staggered to their feet and were flung back down. The rain accumulated quickly and many possessions became flotsam as the hillside began to flood. Searchlights were beamed down upon the spectacle, and not merely for the cameras: the helicopters, suddenly at risk, were seeking to make emergency landings. As they descended the twice-born scrambled away, babies clutched in their mothers' arms, but the women could not find purchase on the slick ground and slid down the slope in beleaguered parades.

The travelers shut their eyes against the rain and ashes, clinging together as they crawled upward, pressed flat to the ground. Lucky positioned herself behind Ariel to prevent her from being swept away. Prophet's fez lay crushed upon his head like a flattened paper cup. Dorian found himself marveling that any of it was actually happening.

Another half-hour passed before they reached the escarpment. A company of state and county police cars had already arrived, their blinking red lights seeming to jeer at the travelers as they passed. And still the rain came down.

"Where the fuck's the car?" Dorian shouted.

Prophet looked around and spotted a row of cars that seemed familiar. "This way!" he called, starting forward.

The glade was empty of people. They moved easily now, still holding hands. Prophet led them a few hundred feet, counting off the rows, and finally turned down a flooded avenue. They arrived at the Mustang moments later.

"Thank god we put the top up," said Dorian.

"Do you think there'll be roadblocks?" asked Lucky.

"Probably," said Dorian. "We'll need to get rid of our gun."

"Like hell," said Prophet. "I don't trust these cops for shit."

"Prophet if they find that gun we'll never leave this state again," said Lucky, opening the trunk. "I refuse to have it with us."

Dorian took the Kalashnikov and slid it under a station wagon nearby. When he returned the others were already inside.

They sped west higher into the mountains, passing dozens of police cars heading in the opposite direction. It seemed as though every officer in the state had been conscripted for emergency duty.

"What time is it?" said Prophet.

Dorian checked his watch. "8:55."

"We should drive for at least a few hours," said Prophet. "If we come across an interstate, get the hell on it."

There was silence as they came to grips with themselves. They were all soaked through, but the rain had washed away the mud. Even their shoes were relatively clean.

"It's not as though *we* did anything," said Dorian after a time.

"We abandoned him," said Ariel.

There was another silence. They all turned to her.

"We abandoned him," she repeated dispassionately, her voice a strangely mature contralto.

216

"I know we did," said Prophet. "But we had to, Ariel. We'd have been dead meat."

Ariel considered this for a moment. "It's all right," she said at last. "He's safe now. He's with God."

"That would be an irony," said Dorian.

"He didn't mean it," she continued, as though not hearing him. "God will understand."

"Wherever he is he's free," said Lucky. "What an awful disease."

"He's with us now too," said Ariel. "He's here. He didn't mean to hurt anyone."


It was nearly midnight, as they headed west along an interstate, when they saw the neon sanctuary of a motel.

"I'll go in by myself," said Lucky, as they pulled into the parking lot. "I'll pretend I'm traveling alone and get one room, so we can keep together."

Five minutes later they were in a small unit with two double beds. Lucky drew the curtains and Prophet clicked on the television, revealing a black-and-white image of marching skinheads.

"What the fuck is CNN here?" he said, reading the template on the cable box. "32 all right let's see what's up."

Channel 32 welcomed them with an interior shot of a shopping mall whose concourses were strewn with indeterminate debris and filling rapidly with black smoke, in front of which a squinting white man in suit and tie confided that he was Shane Major reporting for CNN.

He was supplanted by a pallid anchorwoman with spiked white-blonde hair and a haunted expression, heralding the return to the breaking story in Colorado **where as many as fifty worshipers at—**

"Yo check it out here it is!"

"Christ," whispered Dorian, as the anchorwoman, warning that the scenes which followed were very graphic and perhaps not appropriate for children, was upstaged by an aerial night-time shot of those familiar yellow tents, harshly illuminated in the helicopter's floodlight, in turn yielding to a medium shot of J. Barnaby Thatch asking Fish if he'd come to know the Lord.

"Oh my god," said Lucky. "I don't know if I can watch this."

"*Shh!*" snapped Dorian, as Fish jammed the barrel of his rifle into the throat of J. Barnaby Thatch and was rewarded by a sudden cataract as he pulled the trigger and Thatch collapsed. And then

217

Fish was looking out at them, quoting Shakespeare, and raising the rifle to shoot the camera.

**Earlier in the evening,** said a female voiceover, **the man now identified as Michael Fishbein of Scarsdale, New York granted CNN an exclusive interview in which I asked him about the role of the Catholic Church in the event, given the Church's well-known dispute of the timing of Christ's second coming.**

**I am the last of the Kantians,** said Fish to the camera, deadpan.

**Spokesmen at the Vatican were unavailable for comment, but the Kantians are not believed to be one of the more prominent orders within the Church. Meanwhile** [a shot of pelting rain, hunched men in yellow slickers, stretchers bearing bodies whose vital signs were not immediately apparent] **authorities have confirmed twenty-six dead and thirty wounded, ten of them critically. Six children are among the dead and twelve among the wounded, and the toll is expected to rise.**

A familiar Caucasian woman in a hooded black coat squinted at her viewers as rain dribbled in her face, which was streaked with running mascara.

**One of the many questions being asked tonight concerns the identities of the priest's four companions, described as a short black man in traditional African robes, a blond man with a German accent, and two white women, all of whom are believed to be in their early twenties—**

"German! Do I sound like a bloody *German*?"

**—have begun a state-wide manhunt for the accomplices, who are believed to have escaped from the valley shortly following the massacre.**

"*Accomplices?!*"

"Shut up Dorian listen."

**—whose sponsors are determined to continue what they call a vigil for the return of Jesus Christ, despite the exodus of as many as half the congregants already. Meanwhile, those who insist on staying are bracing against the heavy rains that have flooded the hillsides, causing pandemonium and hampering the efforts—**

"Do you think we're safe here?" asked Lucky.

"For now," said Prophet, "unless someone happened to get us on tape before or during that rally."

"I think it's just a matter of time," said Dorian. "Remember that woman at the Pleasant Acres? She knows us all. And you saw the way those families looked at us today in the car park. Someone's bound to remember."

"Well where does that leave us?" said Lucky. "Should we shave our heads? Buy costumes? Give ourselves up?"

"But Christ we didn't *do* anything!"

"I don't like it," said Prophet. "What happened tonight is different, I mean I agree we didn't do anything wrong. What's worrying me is New York. Fish stole that money, and those cops saw us drive away."

"Stole *what* money?" said Lucky.

"There again," said Dorian, "we weren't the ones breaking the law. We didn't know shit from salmon until we were out of the City."

"Maybe. All I'm saying is if they can nail our asses on *something*, you better believe they'll try. But now Lucky and Ariel, that's different. Maybe the best—shit turn that up Dorian."

Channel 32 was advertising none other than New York City Police Commissioner Russell Chunk standing at a news conference, clad in a tuxedo, his face blackened with dirt, saying that the explosion had occurred near the stage.

**Do you think this is a copycat crime?**

**Well obviously we're not going to rule that out. What I can tell you is that we're taking the matter of African Fist! very seriously now. A joint investigation with the FBI and BATF is already in progress.**

"Oh my fucking god," said Prophet.

"What is it?" said Lucky.

**—don't flatter myself to *that* degree. I was invited to the opera only this afternoon, so I don't see how anyone could have—**

"Prophet are you all right?"

"Prophet," said Dorian, "is this what I think it is?"

"No," he was whispering. "No way. Ain't fucking possible."

**—immediately ran to the front to start helping people. The first ten rows and the orchestra got the worst of it, but to my knowledge no one on stage was killed.**

"Look you guys," said Lucky, "would you mind telling us what's going on? I mean Prophet you're turning white!"

"Didn't you say it was untraceable?"

Prophet glanced at Dorian. "In theory."

—as much as I do at this point. The figure I have is sixty-one dead, a hundred and twenty-two wounded. Beyond that I wouldn't care to speculate—

"Prophet I'm ordering you to speak to me."

—course I saw it! I was looking at the stage like everybody else.

"They couldn't have," said Prophet to himself. "They wouldn't do that to me, no way . . ."

—hit the floor. I got up about ten seconds later.

Sighing, Dorian explained about the press releases.

"Unbelievable," Lucky said finally. "Though I have to say you've got balls, Prophet. My mother could take a page from your book. Feminist terrorism in cyberspace, I mean think of the possibilities."

"As for Fish," Dorian continued wearily, "you remember that first night, after the biker incident, how you asked about the gun?" He explained that as well.

"So we're fugitives three times over," she said, laughing in disbelief. "The money, the bomb threats, and the Second Coming. Somebody should write a book about us."

—at the Pierre Hotel and Metropolitan Museum of Art has been tightened—

"Can't watch this shit," Prophet murmured. "Can't watch." He clicked to a different channel, just in time to hear **This suburban family drama contains adult language, nudity, graphic violence, and explicit sexual content. Viewer discretion is advised.**

"Don't touch a thing," said Dorian, as the camera panned along a leafy residential street featuring wide lawns and mini-mansions, over which the words **Cul-de-sac '84** appeared.

"Excellent," said Dorian. "I've heard about this show. It's the first soap opera with real sex, that's why they have to show it at 12:30."

"Dorian," said Lucky, "we've just seen a friend of ours kill dozens of people, including himself. We're running from the law. How the *hell* can you be thinking about sex right now?"

"I'm only living in the moment," he replied, as the camera encroached upon the heaving buttocks of a middle-aged blond man, beneath whom a brunette was splayed.

"You are *such* a little shit, you know that?" She punched one of the nerve points on his shoulder, eliciting a shriek, and turned away in disgust. "Prophet come over here, are you OK? Come here."

As they huddled on the other bed Dorian leaned forward, his penis awakening.

*Christ.* **He's coming!**

**Unh?**

**He's back!**

He raised his head. **What?**

**Pollo's back! Pull out, quick!**

**Pull** *out*? **I'm about to come, for god sake!**

**Get the fuck out, Kevin! Oh Jesus, the door—**

He found himself evicted, and then pushed to one side. *Pollo?*

**Get under the bed! Here—**he was laden with crumpled trousers, a black sock, boxer shorts. **Hurry!**

**Well Christ! I thought he didn't come home until—**

**Here, here's your shirt—**

**Mary?** issued from downstairs.

**This is great, dammit, just great. I—**

**Fuck, your shoes. Here—**they were thrust at him where he sat bedside, phallus wilting. **Now move!**

He squirmed underneath, face up. Heavy footsteps approached, floorboards creaking beneath their weight. **Mary?**

**I—I'm in here!**

From under the bed he saw white Reeboks in the doorway. **Honey?**

**I—hi.**

**Hey baby. The fuck you doin up here?**

**I was just, I—**

**Feelin OK? You sick?**

**No I, I was just taking a nap I fell asleep—**

He saw a foot raised, and lowered again unshod.

**Think I'll have a quick one then, before dinner.**

**Oh Pollo, I don't think—**

**Aah, come on.** Denims fell among feet now bare, which struggled free and approached the bed. **See, look at it. Can't leave it like this, ahn?**

**Wait—**

**What the fuck.**

**Pollo, I—**

**Since when you takin naps without your clothes? Ahn?**

**I was just—**

**Waitin for me, you sneaky little whore.** The mattress sagged abruptly, pinning him to the floor beneath. **Howya doin?**

I, fine. Fine, I—

**The fuck's that smell?**

. . . Excuse me?

Snorting; **You smell that?**

Snorting; **I, I don't know what you—**

Snorting; **I *know* that smell . . . aah, never mind. Commere.**

Saliva was exchanging. The mattress shifted variously. Under the bed, breathing for him proved difficult.

**M'mm.**

**Wait, you need to—*ah!*—**

**Damn, you're all squishy.** The mattress swelled like an amoeba reconsidering its position, to the lament of a rusty spring.

**Ouch . . .**

**Hahn?**

**You, you're squeezing too hard . . .**

**Whoops.**

The tempo increased. He bit his lip, listening.

*Ah yeah . . . Ah yeah . . . Oof . . .*

**Nnn . . .**

*Pfff . . . pffffff . . .*

**Uhn. Uhn.**

*Haaaaaaa . . . whoooo . . . guhhh! . . .*

**Uhnnn.**

*Aaaaaahhhh . . .*

The motion ceased. Crushed even further, his lips worked impotently over clenched teeth, miming m/th/f/k.

**. . . Pollo? . . . *Pollo?***

A snore rent the air.

**Pollo, damn it!**

A second snore, deeper and less nasal.

**Jesus . . .**

He wriggled his way toward freedom, gripping his clothes. Once emerged he sat up, confronted by stacked bodies. He stood with difficulty, gazed down at the hirsute expanse of a man's back and the fuliginous cleft of his buttocks.

**Kevin . . .**

His eyes flicked toward her own, peering over the crest of a meaty shoulder. A hand waved him toward the door.

**Marry me, for Christ sake,** he whispered, clutching his clothes to his breast like a threatened mother.

Her eyes widened imploringly, swiveling toward the door and back.

He grimaced and then goosestepped out the door and into the hallway, where, almost bent double, he crept toward the staircase. Once descended he stopped to dress. Boxer shorts, socks, trousers, wingtips, shirt, necktie, and pinstriped jacket were donned in turn. He then walked through the front door into Halloween.

Dusk threatened. Jack-o-lanterns leered from across the street, refulgent in the thick air. He looked up, saw mauve and lavender clouds against a crimson sky. He strode across the lawn to the white colonial next door, fumbling for keys.

Inside, the foyer—indeed, the whole first floor—rewarded him with darkness. He crossed the front hall and mounted the stairs, turning right toward a closed door under which light seeped. He opened the door, began to enter the room, was greeted with **Take off your *clothes*, damn it!**, whereupon he withdrew and shut the door. He undressed in grim silence, jacket, tie, shirt, shoes, pants, socks, boxers, tossing them aside like food gone rotten until once again he opened the door and stepped within, shutting the door carefully behind him.

The hum of an air purifier greeted him, punctuated by the rustling of sheet-wrap that hung from all walls and covered the floor. He fixed his gaze upon the bed that was the room's only furnishing, upon the fair woman with sunken cheeks and spectral eyes who studied him blearily from its refuge.

**How many times have I *told* you, for god sake.**

**I'm sorry.**

**You're late.**

**I'm sorry.**

**I'm hungry.**

He sighed. **What'll it be then, tonight?**

**Carrots.**

**. . . Just carrots?**

**Boiled. In spring water.**

He moved toward the bed, sat near the foot. She extracted a skeletal arm from beneath the covers to wipe the perspiration from her forehead.

**How was today?**

223

How do you *think*.

He stared through the sheet-wrap and the window it covered, as a fresh wind rose to rustle the branches immediately without. I wish you'd go to the hospital.

What good would it do.

You're sick, Elise. Very sick.

Look will you fuck off I am not sick!

Well what are you then! Two fucking months in this bedroom, not a *molecule* enters that—

You know damn well what's going on! She sat up in bed, the blankets falling to reveal skin stretched taut against a lattice of bones, shriveled breasts hanging limp. (Now *that's* make-up, thought Dorian.) Why don't you ever believe me? It's like you think—

It's not normal is what I think! "Universal Reactor." Who the fuck ever heard of a Universal Reactor? You *can't* be allergic to everything, for god sake! *No* one is allergic to *everything!*

She'd gathered breath to reply but was forestalled when he stood abruptly, pacing the room. God only knows what you weigh now. You won't eat anything, you can't read a book because the ink makes you sneeze, you can't wash because soap gives you a rash I mean Christ! I can't wear my clothes in here because cotton gives you hives!

It *does*, I mean you've *seen*—

I've seen *shit*. It's psychosomatic, Elise. You've got an allergic personality, is what the trouble is. I must've borrowed fifty books from the school, there's a whole fucking *library* downstairs that proves it's all in your head! His fists were quivering, clenched white. God knows why this happened, I mean three months ago everything was fine and then this, this *guru* freak comes—

Everything was *not* fine, they told me I couldn't have children and don't you *dare* insult Saheed—

Saheed, for Christ sake. The guy's whiter than I am, and he's adopting some ridiculous Indian name like he's just found every answer in the world—

Well at least he listens to me!

Yeah, he listens all right. You think he's helping your neurosis I got news for you Elise, he's *feeding* your neurosis! He tells you you're allergic to everything, you believe him so he can come around three times a week and cure it all away with this white light crap—

224

Kevin—

Hundred bucks a shot, what are you getting for your hundred bucks a shot? Opening your chakras, I mean just *what the fuck* is a chakra? He's on to something, I'll tell you, suburban housewives sitting around with nothing to do, this guy walks in like the second coming no *wonder* he drives a goddamn Mercedes, why are you giving me this.

It needs emptying.

Can't even walk next door to the bathroom, the dust might kill you. He took the container and walked to the window where he parted the sheet-wrap and began turning the handle until the window swiveled out. He flung the contents into the gathering twilight, and stood staring for a moment at the cul-de-sac, at the houses lit against the night.

Don't push me, Kevin.

Dorian clicked off the television. The others had fallen asleep, all three of them in the same bed. He was still nursing a near-lethal erection from the earlier sex scene; only the advent of Ms. Anorexia had saved him from shooting off. While the going was still good he staggered to the bathroom, as the others slept on.

# CHAPTER FIFTEEN

## *Y-Chromosomes Revisited; or,*
## *The Need for a Stronger Pornocracy . . .*

Gerard has brought the coffee, which we sip in companionable silence. I've found one of Lank's anoraks to keep him warm, not to mention a Russian bearskin-hat (fake, of course). We should be panhandling together in Gorky Park.

I come now to the Incident.
Pull up a chair. It's pretty intense.

\*     \*     \*

Man in the singular is problem enough; mankind in the plural is even worse. To wit: I was hired this previous May for a bachelor party. I'd done three of them in the past, and had emerged each time feeling like a used condom myself. But the money was always too good to refuse, and I never learned my lesson.

. For this particular occasion I wore a black cocktail dress, as instructed. Actually it was more like a camisole, given its scanty length: I could hardly sit down without baring all. There were the usual black stockings with garter, black underwear, and black stiletto heels to round it all off.

One thing was different: the groom's cohorts had requested a blonde, so I'd spent the afternoon in a salon. For the sake of authenticity, I had my eyebrows and pubic hair done as well, and bought some blue non-prescription contact lenses. Fortunately my skin was still relatively pale from the winter: I didn't look precisely Nordic, but I could pass for a Slav just back from Antigua.

As I surveyed myself in the mirror, exquisitely painted, I thought, How *nice* I look . . . Even the dress appeared stylish, and not tasteless as I'd feared. I could have been going on a date.

Then I thought: Why *aren't* I going on a date? What about the simple pleasures in life, like quiet dinners, strolls along the pier,

226

snuggling in the back seat of a cab to dispel the winter chill? Companionship would be enough; I wouldn't hold out for love. An easy companionship, with plenty of warmth, affection, and intimacy. Ah yes . . . it would be enough.

But no: I wasn't preparing for a date because I hadn't been asked. In fact I hadn't been asked in years, which wasn't surprising. The only men I met were the men I fucked for money; and despite what you see in the movies, it's no way to begin a relationship.

Looking at my lips, newly coated in a blaze of scarlet, I couldn't help noticing how forlorn they seemed. Those lips were feeling cheated right about then, because they deserved something better. They were meticulously prepared, but not for the real thing. Whoring wasn't the real thing, and my lips resented the deception. In all my sessions they had not once been kissed.

I sometimes wonder, of a cold dark evening, how much time I have left to save myself. I wonder if the last of my youth has slipped through my fingertips, unnoticed. I wonder if everything I do is a mere approximation of youth, a strained sense of recapture. Then I remember that I never had a youth to lose.

Yet it is still possible, I think, to sit beneath a tree in summer's cauldron and forget my body, and my past, and to feel what I have otherwise not felt in years—*at ease*; and to have access to a space, if only psychological, where I am safe and sheltered. Where the world is kept at bay. Where the mantle of cynicism, jadedness, and resentment is haltingly cast away. Where I can forgive myself.

But I am afraid of this space. I am afraid of its seductiveness and false hope. I am afraid of its impermanence. And with each passing year it becomes harder to find.

I wonder if I can ever let down my guard again. I'm inclined to think not.


I hopped a cab to the Atheneum, the premier health club of the Upper West Side. Located at Broadway and 75th, it commanded the patronage of the Riverside/West End crowd, not to mention interlopers from Central Park West and the leafy cross-streets inbetween. It must have cost a fortune to rent for the evening, and it was an odd venue in any case for a bachelor party. What would it be tonight? Nude aerobics class? Treadmill striptease? Oral squash?

I arrived at nine-thirty. The door was unlocked and unguarded, so I let myself inside. The lobby was vacant, the building eerily

227

silent. I wandered toward the interior, looking for the party.

Nothing in upscale New York is merely functional. Had I been in the market for a health club, I would have preferred a dank Brooklyn gym full of third-rank boxers and stale sweat—something *authentic*. Luxury health clubs are designed to make exercising pretty, and not just therapeutic, as if the rarefied atmosphere could prevent one's perspiration from accruing beyond a manageable sheen. As if plush carpets, ten-dollar cranberry juice, and gold-plated dumbbells lent class to breaking a sweat.

The Atheneum, to no surprise, was modeled around Greek motifs. A vast atrium spread beyond the lobby, with seven fountains frothing in what seemed like self-congratulation. Doric columns supported the ceiling; fresh flowers were everywhere. It was more like a hotel.

I crept through the half-lit rooms. The silence was incongruous; the dormant machinery seemed forsaken and without purpose. Not that I was unimpressed: the Atheneum had allowed nearly every sporting whim to be fulfilled artificially. There were the usual arrays of weight machines, stair-climbers, treadmills, bicycles. There were Skimasters and Sledmasters and Boatmasters and Batmasters. There was a fifty-foot wall for would-be rock climbers. There were Sisyphean pools in which one swam in place against a motorized current. There were tennis courts, squash courts, racquetball courts. There were four dance studios. There was in-house dry cleaning, shoe-shining, hairdressing, and manicuring, to judge from the signs; not to mention plenty of masseurs and masseuses and chiropractors— no appointment necessary. There was a health food store with macrobiotic snack bar, its refrigerators glowing like alien probes. There were paramedic stations and MRI facilities and radiologists and nurse practitioners; there were plastic surgeons. There were mud baths and electrolysis booths and sensory deprivation tanks. There were ultrasound therapists and sports psychologists, who I gathered roamed back and forth to be summoned at the athlete's whim. Cellular phones and remote fax machines had been placed in every corner. Commodities trading could be conducted electronically from most exercise stations. I envisioned the patrons, dwarfed by the immensity of the place, laboring at the machines with grim industry as their portfolios collapsed. I imagined latter-day Herculeses sweating next to tubby executives, florid and gasping. Curious that such activity was so stationary, a flux of continuous motion that went nowhere. Rather like life.

I found the party moments later. The club boasted an actual swimming pool, Olympically proportioned, and here the doomed bachelor was spending the last of his freedom. In the moment before they noticed me, I had the chance to observe some thirty Caucasian males in knee-length swimsuits splashing about the pool. Some scampered along the edge, taunting their comrades within; others leaped from the diving boards, executing haphazard cannon balls. They were unusually well-built, and most sported crew-cuts. The average age seemed about twenty-four.

A bartender had been hired. He was set up near the deep end and practicing a very busy trade. Another uniformed caterer stood at a table nearby, which offered cold-cuts and junk food.

At last one of the revelers, emerging from the pool, saw me standing in the doorway. He let out a whoop and clapped his hands. "Ayy boys!" he shouted, looking me up and down. "Looks like we got ourselves some live cunt!"

His cry was taken up by the others. I stepped into the room and smiled, and started to ask where I might leave my purse. I didn't finish the sentence.

Two of the men had closed in. One grabbed my arms, the other my legs. Before I had the chance to protest, or scream, I was heaved into the shallow end of the pool and the feeding frenzy began.

My shoes and purse had already been lost, I couldn't tell where. The water soaked through my nice clothes immediately, and the dress became deadweight. As I surfaced, choking and blinking, the first of the revelers was upon me, grabbing my shoulders and forcing me underwater. I opened my eyes. Leering goggled faces were converging from every angle. I tried to kick them away, but someone grabbed my leg and turned me upside down. Disoriented, I felt water rush up my nostrils, searing my nasal cavity.

By now survival instinct had kicked in. I thrashed and twisted, breaking the surface, whereupon I was grabbed by a dozen hands and fogged with moonshine breath. I couldn't itemize every hand, but two had laid claim to my breasts and someone was shoving rough, scaly fingers down my throat—tangy, distinctly *masculine* fingers. Some were probing my nether regions, while others tried to remove my dress. Too many hands were pulling in too many directions; they compromised by simply peeling the dress away like old skin. The rest of my apparel was easy, barely an afterthought.

Under normal circumstances, the sensation of water enveloping one's bare loins is to be savored: there are few experiences more natural, more Edenic. This time it was different. When my sex had been duly exposed, and water flooded my vulva, I felt like a patient being prepared for a shot. The loss of my underwear was the equivalent of alcohol being rubbed on the targeted skin, leaving the same squirmy tingling, the same anticipatory recoil. I was imagining the pain before it began. I didn't have long to wait.

I heard a cry— *"GO BILLYEEEE . . ."*—and felt the familiar stab. Somewhere along the way I had been pushed back against a wall. Now I was forced partially out of the water as Billy locked his hands on the backs of my thighs and pulled my legs wide, the better to facilitate his thrusting. I looked at him. He was gazing half at me, half over me, teeth bared, eyes squinting, each fusilade accompanied by an exertive, manly grunt. I had the feeling there was something I should be doing—screaming my head off would have been a start—but I found myself gripped by a curious paralysis. I've read that some rape victims dissociate themselves from the experience, hovering out of body until it is safe to return. I didn't quite make it that far. In fact, although I seemed incapable of action, every nerve in my body felt strangely alive, tuned to a feverish pitch. I was all too aware of my ransacked cunt; my subconscious was not letting me escape, not on your life.

Where was my power now. When I needed it.

Billy, having staggered away, was superseded by Troy. Troy was a big mother, hefty and hairy. Unlike Billy, who had stood back and left his dick to the task, Troy smothered me. He crushed my torso, his skin clammy against mine, my arms breaking out in gooseflesh, his hundred-proof breath scorching my face . . . all accompanied by a soundtrack which, if memory serves, went something like this: "Aw yeah baby, m'mm-h'mm . . . that's right honey, *ooh yeah* . . . you got it sister, I'm givin it to you, come to daddy baby . . . this is it, baby, this is where it's at . . . here it comes . . . here it comes . . . *Eeeuuhhhh! Eeuuhhhh! That's right baby, whew-haa!*"

Next came Chad, whose mercifully brief assault can be approximated as follows: "Shh-hah-shh-hah-shh-hah-*shh-hah-shh-hah-shh-hah-SHH-HAH-SHH-HAH-SHH-HAH—SSSSHHHHHHHH—HOOOOOOOOOO!*"

From my perspective we existed in a separate space-time. The real world was in stasis, in suspended animation, awaiting the termination of this incident. The only time was rape-time, which I experienced moment to moment in a barrage of perceptions. I was incapable of thought; I was simply receiving sensory data in a continuous yet discrete flow. I could not muster the semblance of an emotion. The only reactions I experienced were at the physiological level. For example, I noticed that I was crying, but I certainly hadn't willed that. *That* decision must have been made by someone else.

Bruce and Wade and Gavin . . . I found myself facing the wall: someone had a taste for sodomy. So did the next, and the next. Meanwhile, Ron and George and Dan and Bill and Al queued up for oral relief; but let's not forget Lyndon and Ricky and Gerry and Jimmy and lurking aft . . . not to mention Pat and Ollie and Pat II. Each man was buoyed by vociferous encouragement, like: "*Attaboy Lyndon . . . Check him out, my man is a fucking animal . . . My boy is not to be denied!*" Or: "*You slip it there Ollie . . . Man you are a fucking force of nature! You ain't fucking human!* (aside: *A fucking law unto himself, Jesus.*)" Or: "*You just lube that baby good Cal, that's it man, you slick that mother good . . .*"

And I in the middle of it all, inanimate. Chronicling. Cataloguing. Recording.

Everything blurred together . . . The dick in my mouth was Everydick. The dick in my ass was Everydick Jr. To attribute ownership to the countless hands and fingers would have served no purpose. The hands were always there. The fingers were always there. Only I had an identity, I at the center of this maelstrom. And I was fast losing that, losing—my ego? My attachments? Was this the road to enlightenment, to spontaneous being?

How detached I am. I still cannot feel a thing.

When I was young the orphans were often taken to the beach. I was a water-spirit back then, a naiad; and I cannot think why, over the years, I have become estranged from water, estranged from the dark, liberating sea, my cold mother . . . What was I thinking when I took up residence in this inhuman City, this indifferent and murdering City, so far from the pure and sacred and holy? Often it kills swiftly and without warning; but it also kills by strangulation, by slow poison, by exhaustion, the tireless predator always lurking a pace behind, omnipresent, waiting for the first misstep, the stumble, the fatigue, ever ready to make that killing leap; or sometimes hovering, like a vulture, content to remain aloof until the victim is

231

dead of its own initiative, and then swooping in to feed, feed, feed . . .

But water: water, my eternal love . . . How is it that we are reacquainted in this way? Could you do nothing to help me? Could you not rise up and sweep them all away, suck them down into your depths, the roll of your tide covering them, and so devour them as they have devoured me, and leave no trace of their passing?

Occasionally, at the beach, I would be caught by an incoming wave and flung limp and bedraggled on the shoreline. In those brief moments I had the feeling of involuntary surrender, conscious that my fate was in all-powerful hands. And so it was in the swimming pool. This was another tsunami upon which I was borne along helpless, at the mercy of the elements. *A force of nature . . .*

Involuntary surrender: Was *that* what was prolonging this ordeal? My inability to protest, to resist, to scream that one-syllable word that my enlightened brethren are supposedly conditioned to heed? In the revelers' currency of language, did that word have any value? I didn't know—I hadn't tried it. I hadn't tried it because I think, at root, that I had given up the whole struggle long ago—the struggle to write, to publish, to create any meaning in my life beyond the rigors of mere survival; beyond draining the lifeforce of those I fucked. (Witness my comeuppance.) I did not resist because the City had defeated me. I did not resist because it would not have made any difference—not to me. Not any more. Because I was finally lost to myself.

In the meantime, I think the two caterers had stripped down and were getting a piece of the action. A piece of me.

But suddenly, yet again, my body chose to behave of its own volition, without bothering to consult my mind. My body seemed to have recognized that my mind was on holiday, that my mind had other plans. Sensing mortal threat, it chose to react in self-preservation, that most blessed of instincts. I don't recall who was fore and who was aft—maybe Lance and Pierce, or Whitey and Jay—but from my standpoint it didn't really matter.

Five inches of evolutionary malpractice were mining my rectum, but it was the four inches in my mouth that gripped my attention, where semen had already accrued like phlegm and my tonsils had been bludgeoned to a pulp. There were hands in my hair, abrasive against my scalp. There was a ubiquity of heaving flesh, a continual cyclone of fermented breath. Yet all my attention became riveted upon that reproductive conduit in my mouth, that clitoris gone awry which an idiot Viennese would have me envy. I'd come a long way, baby. I bit down with the force of the almighty.

It wasn't quick, or easy. I shook my head violently once or twice, like a lioness hastening the kill. At last the whole four inches came away in my mouth.

Matt or Mark or Luke or John, or whoever the hell was kneeling before me, gave a long, loud, scream. I lifted my head and spat, adding some blood for good measure. So wide was his mouth, and so true my aim, that I wasn't surprised in the least when the missile vanished in that maw and followed a swift course into his trachea.

His eyes, previously squeezed shut, flew open in bewilderment. He began to gurgle. His hands flew to his throat. He jumped to his feet and staggered along the poolside, spluttering uncouthly, his phallic stump pissing blood, as if to fertilize or consecrate the water. A few colleagues rushed to his aid, pounding his back. He collapsed on his knees, still gripping his throat. The last I saw, his face was turning that familiar shade of blue . . .

I remember thinking that I wouldn't survive a minute. There were still plenty of them to block my retreat, and I didn't even try to escape. Instead I bent my fury upon causing as much injury as possible to these men before I died. I began with an Amazon scream, or some facsimile thereof. So high was its pitch, so penetrating its timbre, that as it caromed between the walls even I shivered reflexively. For a moment, each man was silent, immobile. Then they came at me.

What's-his-name was still plugging up my rear. Blindly I swung my elbows in the approximate direction of his head, twisting my midriff to add torque. My left elbow seemed to connect with his temple, for suddenly my rectum filled with water and I felt him sag away.

Unlike my heroine Lucky, I am no martial artist, but I made use of what weapons I had. My fingernails were rather long, and my next assailant got one in each eye. A third gripped me in a bear-hug; I in turn wrung his scrotum.

As more of them rushed in, I dived beneath the surface. Feeling that liberation of old, I swam into the deep end, right along the very bottom. I outdistanced the nearest pursuers, but I had no idea where to go next. The pool was illuminated by a series of green lamps, which were magnified to hideous proportions underwater: they seemed to leap at me like headlights to a rabbit. Looking up, I spotted the murky, wavering blur of a ladder. I pushed off the bottom and shot toward it.

Oh, but it was close. I clambered up that ladder and hauled myself out of the water. The exit was perhaps forty feet away, and no one stood in between. They were still in the water, now paddling toward the side in a frenzied rush, plumes flying everywhere.

I ran.

The door came ever closer; I was going to make it. An image flickered briefly in my psyche, of emerging onto the sidewalk dripping and naked and never so glad to see my urban neighbors. I was oblivious to the screams behind me, and my hand was already reaching for the handle . . .

. . . when I slipped on the wet floor, falling heavily onto my left side. Only a quick movement of my arm allowed my shoulder to absorb the fall, instead of my head. Surprisingly, there didn't seem to be much damage, and my adrenaline masked the pain. I scrambled to my feet and actually touched the door handle before an arm clamped round my stomach and I was heaved away.

They came at me with hands and feet. They came at me with belts and broken bottles, multiple impacts at machine-gun speed, the pain setting off like firecrackers all over my body, *bang bang bang bang bang.*

I opened my mouth to scream.

A length of towel was shoved down my throat, tasting of detergent.

Then, mercifully, I did shut off for a while.

\* \* \*

I lay there for a very long time, in a state of pure acethenesia. It wasn't quite sleep, for my eyes were wide open. Yet as best as I can recall, there was not a single thought in my head. I was numb, hyponoiac. I lay on my right side, my cheek pressed to the wet floor, staring. Perhaps it was sensory overload; perhaps I was in shock. Everything was quiet. Only the smell of chlorine broached my senses, from a pool now perfectly still.

Sometime later—it must have been a couple of hours—I climbed to my feet, swaying uncertainly. The improvised bar and table of half-eaten food lay abandoned. Rivulets of blood ran along the floor, among fragments of broken glass. I was bleeding in countless places, but I didn't notice my wounds. I had no idea where I was, indeed no idea of my own name.

I didn't actually look for my purse. It happened to be lying near the door, and so entered my field of vision. I picked it up and clutched it to my breast, as though withholding it from a mugger. It felt like something newfound, rather than something that already belonged to me. Still, I felt oddly proprietary. If someone had tried to take away that purse, I would have guarded it like a mother her young.

There was no sign of the revelers. I wandered through the health club yet again, unsure of my bearings, staring without reaction at the sleek equipment, blinking stupidly in the dim fluorescent light. I wandered past the red glare of a digital clock, which read 12:21.

I proceeded as if mesmerized, though to what end I had no idea. I was like a computer programed to random patterns. There was no fixed hypnotic suggestion: I was following to the whim of the current variable.

I suppose another hour had passed when I finally chanced upon the exit. I descended the six marble steps and gazed through the glass door at Broadway, which was still haunted at this hour by shambling vagrants and affluent club-hoppers, the latter passing in a babble of voices that quickly receded, such collegial souls, all of them no doubt having some purpose greater than my own.

I opened the door and stepped outside. A passing entourage of well-dressed, middle-aged Caucasians stared at me, dumbstruck. The two men seemed drawn to my nakedness, though also repelled by my wounds. Maybe they were looking around or through the blood and extracting what pleasure they could. One of the women frowned, and seemed about to step toward me; the other's features screwed up into an expression of resentful loathing, of *put-upon* loathing. *(Did I really have to see this? I mean did I* really *need this to happen, at this time of night?)*

I shuffled toward them as a tentative alien might approach indigenes on a new world. I don't know what I sought from them, except perhaps the most basic of human contact.

Had I the possession of my faculties—had I been able to initiate a normal conversation, something along the lines of "Um could you please help me I've just been raped and had the shit kicked out of me," I have every confidence that my fellow New Yorkers would have responded with swift and genuine charity. But no doubt they saw the emptiness of my stare, the air of disease that every sick animal carries, causing everyone to shun it; nor did the blood help. Fresh from the opera, a late dinner, a later round of drinks, they just wanted to get home. Collectively they backed away, the men forming a rearguard as if to protect their wives. I extended my hands, my face inquisitive, like an early hominid transported in time, dazzled by the wonder of the modern world—the kind of behavior that wins bad actors an Oscar®. They retreated more quickly than I advanced, and lost me at a corner.

I do not remember much more of that night. I remember walking for what seemed like an eternity. I remember the impassive looks from vagrants, their eyes perhaps a little wider than usual as they regarded what even to them was something of a novelty. I was grateful for my wounds. Without my wounds, any of the various youth brigades I encountered would have seen my nudity as an impetus to hop aboard. At one point I passed a group of black teens loitering on a street corner and smoking marijuana. My passage elicited the following commentary:

"Yo check this shit out."

"Ai baby, the fuck happen witchoo?"

"God *damn* thassome serious damage."

"Ai bitch whyin't you look at me when I talkin to you."

"Think I like those titties."

"The fuck you talkin bout nigger can't *see* no titties."

"Say it, that blood look rusty and shit."

"Ai where you goin baby?"

"Man leave her alone, prolly *infected* or somefin."

"I'm up man, I be like *Git-cho* bloody shit out my face."

"Say it man, that shit attract flies and shit."

"She be swarming wit de shit."

And on I walked.

I awoke on 84th Street between Columbus and Central Park West. At some point I had simply curled in the fetal position next to a flight of stairs, which led to the front door of a brownstone. It must still have been early, not long after dawn. A pony-tailed young white woman, resplendent in a blue designer tracksuit, was peering at me with considerable alarm.

"Oh my *god*," she said, kneeling down. She shook her head,

236

apparently unable to find words, and keeping a reasonable distance. After a quick appraisal she stood.

"I'll be *right* back," she said, edging away. "Just stay *right* there, OK? *Right* back . . ."

No danger: I wasn't going anywhere. I had no inclination to move. I was dimly aware of pain everywhere in my body. Every square inch of my skin seemed to smart with anger: I was a landscape of epidermal protest. I closed my eyes, reasoning that once asleep I would not feel the pain.

But the Good Samaritan returned a moment later in a shiny red Jaguar convertible. Leaving the car idling, she walked over to me and knelt again, covering me with a soft white blanket. I noticed the rubber gloves on her hands. "I'm going to take you to the hospital, OK?" she said. "We'll get in my car and drive right over."

I blinked at her. Speech seemed like a forgotten power, something I had unlearned in the past few hours. My eyes traveled to the Jaguar.

"Come on," she said, grasping my arm. "We'll go straight across the park."

I let her drag me to my feet, triggering exquisite agony. I was still clutching my purse, and so could not hold the blanket in place. My savior bundled me as best she could and tucked me in the front seat. She moved round to her side, got in, and pressed a button that raised the top.

"I'm Rebecca," she said as the car glided through the park, passing a few armed joggers. When I didn't reply in kind she glanced at me sidelong. "Were you raped too? besides beaten, I mean?"

I wanted to say yes, but I still felt dissociated from everything around me. My senses took in all the data and stored it away, but I was incapable of mustering output. Rebecca, bless her soul, seemed to understand. She kept up a monologue as she drove, commenting about danger in the streets and the vulnerability of women.

"It's never going to get better," she said, as we reached Fifth Avenue and the leafy silence of the Upper East Side. "It's like everybody's been saying crime is down but it still keeps getting worse? A woman I went to school with was raped last week. Not in Central Park. Not at two in the morning. Nope; get this: she was raped on the *6 train at lunchtime.* Can you believe it? I mean go figure."

We were moving past tidy brownstones, crossing Park Avenue.

"That's why I'm packing," continued Rebecca. "After that

happened to Liz last week I went out and bought a gun. It's nine-millimeter or something, I forget the name, maybe like Signal or Sigmund? The model's a few years old but I liked it better than this other one they had, some Lady Zymox or something. It was really light and everything, made specially for women, but——" she sighed "——I don't know, it looked *too* small? The guy told me it could stop a three-hundred-pound man dead in his tracks, but somehow I wasn't convinced? I decided that if I was really going to buy a gun I'd go the whole nine yards. The Signifier or whatever, I mean it is pretty big but it's got some serious kick. That's what my instructor calls it? kick? I had my first lesson Monday and he told me that even some total cokehead wouldn't have a chance, like even with the adrenaline it kills them anyway?"

Ah, chirpy Rebecca, and her litany of the liberated rich girl . . . Her words didn't make much of an impression, but I found the sound of her voice soothing.

"Here we are," said Rebecca, pulling into the emergency entrance of some hospital or other. "Oh, and I almost forgot. I brought you a dress in the back seat. It's an old one I used to wear at college. I think it'll fit you."

She stood by me for the next hour as I confronted a battery of forms. She searched through my wallet, but I carried no form of ID. I didn't own a car and I certainly had no credit cards. In the end I had no information to provide, nor the volition to provide it: I didn't so much as raise a pen. The receptionist—an unsmiling Asian woman who did not seem worried about my condition—must have concluded that I was crazy. Eventually she took back the forms and told us to wait.

When at last I was summoned for treatment, Rebecca stood and took her leave. "Good luck," she said, resting a hand on my arm. "If there's anything else I can do to help, here's my number." She handed me a business card, which I clutched as I was led inside.

The emergency room contained six beds, five of them surrounded by curtains. Judging by the screams, each contained someone in even worse shape than I. I waited for a long time, listening to the brusque dialogue of trauma teams as they labored over would-be corpses. Emergency rooms have a curious feature, don't they: nobody expects to be there, except the personnel. We've all got other plans, and then suddenly God leaps from the woodwork, laughing at our expense. And make no mistake: if he exists, which he doesn't, he's not gazing down during these moments with compassion, puckering his lips in sympathy. No way: he's standing there in the corner, outside the swell of activity, watching some fat arteriosclerotic sedentarian or hapless junkie or shit-for-brains teen-ager who should have known better than to raise a water pistol at a policeman—he's watching them spitting up the blood, convulsing like marionettes. He's pointing his finger at them, as if to make perfectly clear the object of his derision. Forget any pretense of discretion: he's throwing his head back and he is fuh-kin *howling* at the pathetic sight of your sorry ass bleeding all over that clean white bed. He's rolling in the aisles, baby. He's having the time of his life, and why the fuck not? Wouldn't *you* be?

*I do not want to grow old.*
*I do not want to die.*
*I hate everyone.*

When my fellow travelers' fates had been resolved one way or another, I was finally given some attention. My doctor was a woman, thank god: I don't think I needed another man's hands on my body, not just then. I don't remember her name, but she was relatively young, probably a resident. She had auburn hair, blue eyes, and what struck me as a kindly Irish face, round with soft lines. As she dressed the wounds with some vile-smelling liquid, which stung like hell, she hazarded the usual concerned inquiry. I think she suspected a vengeful spouse or lover. Then she examined my wrecked cunt, and her beatific expression became stony. My whole genitalia must have been in tatters: she studied them for a good five minutes, with the occasional tender palpation. It didn't take her long to stop asking *Does this hurt?* Gently she turned me over, and had a look in there as well. All this ruled out spousal abuse or date rape, unless I was a polyandrist.

She glanced at my chart, which probably read "Jane Doe." I gathered that someone should have already taken my temperature and blood pressure, which they hadn't. She mumbled a few expletives and stuck a digital thermometer in my mouth. She then shackled my bicep with a blood-pressure band. She probably thought I was in shock, and she might have been right—I didn't ask.

The iodine or antiseptic or whatever the hell it was gave my entire body the feeling of sunburn. As though intuiting my pain she dug an IV trench in my forearm and hooked up some morphine. I lay

239

back in a blissful stupor, barely alive and knowing that I wasn't missing much.

Before falling asleep I heard my doctor arguing with a male voice. They were wrangling about my medical insurance, or lack thereof. The male voice, patient and condescending, was explaining hospital policy. My Celtic patron launched into a strident reply. She was the last thing I heard as I drifted into the netherlands, where even my pain could not follow.

*   *   *

I was lying on my back in the dark. You will note, my dear Sam (did you have to stop waiting? I miss you), that I had no company. I had gone worstward (ho!), and this was my endgame. I had suffered the pricks and the kicks, though which was worse I cannot say. I was not surprised by any of it. My punishment was condign; it was in my whoroscope. That's how it was.

*   *   *

I slept for the better part of six days, a period marking the first of many black holes in my past that memory cannot reclaim. I know that I was fed through the IV, that I was wrapped almost head to toe in gauze, that I never got out of bed, that a team of nurses disposed of my bodily wastes, and that I didn't say a word to anyone. Every now and then I'd wake to find some whitecoat or other poring over my chart, asking the nurse on duty, *Has she said anything yet? No? Believe it or not we still don't know who she is.* And on one occasion, that ultimate accolade: *Well, she certainly is a survivor . . .*

On the seventh day my bandages were removed, and my body aired itself out. I woke that night to the same darkness and the silence of the ward. I remember that I got out of bed and found walking very difficult. I tottered about the room, turned on a light, and noticed that my purse at least had been preserved. There was even quite a bit of money inside. Cornell Bodleian usually paid me in cash, and the money must have been from a previous assignment. Having no bank account, I usually stuffed it under my mattress.

The next thing I remember is shambling down the hospital corridor, with its gleaming plethoric off-whites. I was no longer wearing a hospital gown, but rather the blue cotton dress that Rebecca had given me. I had no shoes. The floor had recently been mopped and felt clammy against the soles of my feet. The purse was strapped over my shoulder.

I wandered right by the nurses' station in the middle of the ward. There were two of them on duty, quietly talking. They were facing away from me, so they didn't notice my silent passage. This was a stroke of providence: the thought of concealing myself never crossed my mind.

I walked into an elevator that happened to be lurking on my floor, its doors open. I pressed every button, and spent what must have been half an hour visiting each floor. On the sixth floor, going down, a black male nurse stepped inside, a stethoscope slung around his neck. He pressed the button for the first floor, and was somewhat surprised that we would be looking in upon 5, 4, 3, and 2 in the meantime. He appraised me for a long moment, and seemed about to say something, but then changed his mind. He settled back against the wall, watching stoically as each floor passed. I have no idea what he was thinking, but clearly he didn't want to get involved.

I was virtually sleepwalking. Without conscious choice, I roamed the corridors of the hospital until I found the main exit and moved outside. It must have been fairly early, perhaps around midnight, for the streets were well populated. I headed west, passing through walk-up land, crossing the busy avenues one by one. The air was hot and humid, and within minutes I was sweating.

Ah, how this City demands vigilance. The ground rules for navigating Manhattan are few and simple, but nevertheless vital. We are told to walk briskly, confidently, eyes forward, chin high, as if the weight of our resolve will be absorbed by everyone else, permitting us wide berth. Would-be muggers will mark our passage with a philosophical shrug, noting the fixity of our purpose, and move on to more timorous prey.

All of which, of course, is complete bullshit. It should be perfectly obvious that muggers (and killers) choose their victims by other criteria: Size. Attire. *Gender.*

The fact is, most women don't cut a very impressive figure on the street   not white women, at any rate, who feign menace even worse than they feign orgasms. There's something incongruous about Caucasian women in a place like Manhattan. Their whole relationship to the City is one of blind trust. In the dark gloom of the cross-streets, or even in the promenades of the avenues, they (we?) are always ready, if not prepared, for an assault. It's a matter of odds, and white women play them the same way: day is preferable to night, Midtown to Harlem, women to men, whites to non-whites, anyone to blacks, cabs to subways. The mere act of stepping outside is like a spin of the roulette wheel. At some point, sooner or later, your number will come up.

And what then? Confronted by a snarling, gun-wielding assailant, what's a girl to do? Well, she gives him everything, of course—anything he wants. The roulette wheel spins yet again, to determine whether he will fire the gun anyway.

The point is this: women are always targets. Unless she is carrying an Uzi, or is a martial arts expert, your average female pedestrian is the universal mark. Her firmness of stride means nothing to the man who can knock her down with one blow. And maybe it's healthy that way, at least if she's white. Maybe it's a reminder, as Gyeppi Natare might say, that she lives in a Darwinistic milieu and cannot insulate herself forever.

Yet I discovered a possible solution. The next-best thing to armament is not the appearance of strength, but rather the appearance of madness. One week ago, I had walked naked for hours without incident, my blood the main deterrent. Tonight that deterrent was insanity. I charted a wavering course across town, occasionally mingling with crowds, occasionally walking long stretches alone. My gait was unsteady, and I'm sure my expression was suitably vacant, if not downright hollow. There is something about madness that repels humans in the same way as AIDS. As for criminals, it is the one thing they don't understand. Guns are clear-cut: you have one or you don't, and act accordingly. Madness, however, is a variable. You might earn a few jeers or even a shove. If they sense you're merely on drugs, you haven't got a chance. But with genuine madness comes unpredictability, which is the criminal's Achilles' heel.

Then again, maybe I'm full of shit. Maybe I was just goddamned lucky.

I traced a circumforaneous route around Midtown, backtracking now and then. I remember divagating west along Central Park South, past the Plaza and St. Moritz and Essex House and other tourist fortifications. Eventually I found myself in Times Square.

There is probably no other place in the Western world where a person can feel so thoroughly disenfranchised from Nature—not even central New Jersey. I stood there bemused, motionless in the flood-tide of people, awed by the frenzy of activity and the manifold sensory assault. No one paid much attention to me: there were more profitable attractions every step of the way, both indoors and out.

Actually Times Square is very much a part of Nature. There's an irony at work here; for despite the concrete and steel, despite the postmodern exoskeleton, the substance of Times Square—indeed the Prime Mover—is biochemistry. Civilization, presented here with such glittering muscle, is shown up by its own narcissism for the sham it is—a rickety, paper-thin carapace, a moldering escutcheon beneath which the essential human impetuses teem in fine fettle, and nowhere else with such variety.

There I stood, out of my depth. Humans, in the way they mark time, have regressed to sharing a characteristic with most other species: they are nocturnal. Never mind work: we eat and fuck at night, and that's what matters. This was merely a different sort of wilderness, and the predators had emerged from their warrens to feed.

I stumbled into the Port Authority Bus Terminal at 42nd and Eighth. Despite the late hour, the building was well populated with midnight travelers and aboriginal vagrants. As I wandered along the concourse something clicked in my dormant brain: I was able to understand the concept of buses, of buses going places. At that moment the spirit of departure hit me. I became aware of a need to flee this City, this outpost in deep space from which the buses could deliver me to other, more familiar planets. I went to the nearest ticket desk—Greyhound—and opened my purse.

I actually made an effort to speak to the middle-aged black man behind the counter. My lips formed syllables, my hands gestured vaguely. He naturally assumed that I was foreign or deaf, or both, and made an exaggerated but poignant attempt to communicate in sign language.

"You want to buy—" he rubbed thumb against fingertips "—buy—a—ticket?"

When I nodded, he smiled and said, "Where—" he shrugged his shoulders "—where—are—you—going?" He mimicked the sound of an engine, as children do with toy cars.

The question flustered me. Where indeed . . . ? I wanted to speak very badly, and even managed an exploratory grunt. I compensated by fluttering my hands.

He frowned, swaying rhythmically, as if to better divine my intentions. The poor guy was really trying . . . At length he grimaced and shook his head, wearing an expression of pained regret. Then he snapped his fingers.

"I know!" he said. "I'll tell you—sorry—I'll—*tell you*—which *buses*—are leaving now. Are you going to *Arcadia? Are-cay-dee-uh?*"

It was my turn to look bewildered. Did such a place exist?

"What about Elysium? *Eh-lee-see-um?*"

I was pretty sure I knew where Elysium was, but thought it well beyond my budget.

"Valhalla? *Val-holluh,* Valhalla?! Yeah?!" for I was nodding my head, smiling. I'd read my Snorri Sturluson, damn it. Suddenly I was filled with hope: I'd raise a few jars with Odin and company, breathe a bit of Nordic air, clear my head . . . Valhalla it was.

The ticket was eighty-nine dollars. I shoved a moist clump of fifties across the counter. He smiled to himself and pushed most of them back. He gave me change and handed me a ticket.

"The bus leaves from Gate 192," he said. "*1-9-2* at—" he held out his left arm, pointed to his watch "—*three-thirty-four.*"

A kindly policeman escorted me to the gate, where a few other travelers were being harassed by panhandling noctivagants. I was just in time.

As I boarded the bus and handed over my ticket, I realized that I was still holding my money. I took the nearest seat and opened my purse. Inside I noticed, among the various coins and cosmetic implements, the coiled links of a necklace, which I extracted. The necklace had been given to me by a teacher many years ago, when I was about six, on one of our seashore holidays. Wandering through a gift shop, we had come across a rotating display of such necklaces, each bearing a female name. My own was not particularly common, but my teacher found one anyway. God, how I felt special. To a child, the appearance of her name marks a powerful sense of recognition, as though the powers that be have singled her out with approval, confirming her existence. Swollen with pride, I wanted to skip as she fastened the necklace in place.

Light years from the sea, from the warmth of summers long past, the 3:34 bus to Valhalla rumbled through the bowels of the Port Authority Bus Terminal and emerged into a different darkness. Slowly, I put the necklace on.

244

# CHAPTER SIXTEEN

## *The Amber Waves of Flames . . .*

They drove south along roads not traveled, where the barren sweep of the desert spread toward horizons without promise, toward the purgatory of a sky burning ivory in the midday glare. Nothing moved in this outland, not car nor jackal nor hare, not even the silhouette of an eagle from the eastern mountains to challenge the heat and emptiness. The Mustang did not have air-conditioning, and even with the top down the travelers were covered in sweat. Before leaving the village Lucky had gone into a convenience store while Dorian filled the gas tank. She had emerged with seven bottles of spring water, in which the travelers now sought relief. They did not know which state they were in: this was a self-contained yet limitless country, a land of infinite ramifications.

"We can't run forever," said Lucky.

"Spoken like a true fugitive," replied Dorian.

"Look, it's like I meant to say last night," said Prophet. "You and Ariel haven't done anything. We can let you off anytime."

"Out here you mean?" said Lucky. "Anyway, even if we did find a town we'd get picked up immediately. They want all of us."

"Maybe we should come clean," said Dorian. "The truth is on our side. If we get rid of the money and the computer there's not much evidence against us. Prophet can certainly deny everything about those threats. What do you think?"

"It might be our best hope," said Lucky.

Prophet sighed. "Give me some time to think about it. I've got some real important files in that computer, some personal shit it's taken me months to write. I don't have the disks to back it up."

They drove on, not a town or car in sight. The water was quickly consumed, and by evening they had also run out of food. The landscape passed without change: the mountains to their left neither approached nor receded, and still the road stretched empty before them until finally, at dusk, they passed a hand-painted wooden sign that read **MUDDY GAP 30**.

245

"A town, thank god," said Dorian. "Are we agreed then?"

"Maybe," said Prophet. "If we can find a good place to ditch everything, let's do it. We can't do it out here, not without a shovel."

"What kind of stuff do you have in there?" asked Lucky.

"Journal, essays, a few programs I designed. Not to mention my saved games. I'll have to start all over again from scratch."

The twilight deepened. A lavender cloudscape rippled across the sky, refracting the waning sun into soft, bloodstained relief on the desert floor. The heat eased its grip slightly, and even this hardened landscape seemed to sigh in relief, as if a lull had been reached in some battle of wills.


"There's a crossroads up ahead," said Dorian twenty minutes later. "Some buildings as well. This must be it."

As they approached the intersection, however, they were greeted only by a series of abandoned houses and an enormous barn with the words **MUDDY GAP** painted white on the slanting roof. A single, larger building, constructed of ferro-concrete, stood apart from the rest. At the corner lay the remains of a gas station, the rusted pumps several decades out of fashion. Dorian stopped the car. "Some fucking town," he said.

"How much gas do we have?" asked Lucky.

"About an eighth of a tank. We won't last another thirty miles."

There was a squawk from the trunk, causing them to jump.

"A rat?" said Lucky, looking from Prophet to Dorian.

A second squawk.

"I think it's my fax-modem," said Prophet.

They stepped from the car and Dorian opened the trunk. Prophet withdrew his computer and activated the screen, everyone crowding to read:

**TO: Kenley O'Hare**
**FROM: Dana Saddle**
**RE: Interview**

**It has come to my attention that you are one of Michael Fishbein's friends currently on the lam.**

**Have you been waiting for the right opportunity to tell your side of the story? Does the deck seemed stacked against you? Are you thirsting for that chance to let yourself be heard?**

As you are no doubt aware, *Fix* is America's leading television news magazine with over two years' experience. If you and/or any of Mr. Fishbein's other friends are willing to grant an exclusive interview to Fix, we will be happy to pay each of you the sum of $50,000. I can be reached at the following mobile phone number: (800) 383-5968.

You may have every confidence in us. Should you agree to an interview we would not divulge the location to police. We will also cover your expenses. I urge you to take advantage of this rare opportunity.

"How the *fuck* did they get this number?" snapped Prophet.

"Is that your real name?" asked Lucky. "Even I didn't know that. How did she?"

"It hardly matters," said Dorian. "Anyway, what's that noise?"

A continuous drone had impregnated the silence; a deep, rhythmic chanting that seemed to originate within the largest of the buildings, the one detached from its neighbors. It was shaped like a cube, each side measuring perhaps two hundred feet. As they stood, listening, the drone changed pitch. An orchestra burst into song, the drums and cymbals providing a jaunty beat. The droning voices gave way to spirited arias and choruses, the voices all male, the words indistinct.

"The fuck?" said Prophet.

"Come on," said Dorian, starting toward the building. "We need gas. Maybe these people can help us."

As they rounded the corner of the building, looking for a door, they came suddenly upon several dozen police cars parked in neat formation. "Think we better leave," said Prophet, edging away.

"Wait a minute, listen," said Lucky, raising her hand. "It—doesn't it sound like a Broadway show?"

"*Cops' Night Out*," snorted Prophet. "Remember Russell Chunk?"

"Well, I'm for going inside," said Dorian. "There's an entrance just over there."

"Dorian hold up man what the fuck. What's inside that's gonna help us?"

"Perhaps nothing, but I have to admit I'm curious. Besides," he said, walking toward the front steps that led to the entrance, "if we're fucked we're fucked. Why prolong the inevitable?"

The exterior of the building had looked Art Deco, but the theater itself was a frescoed neo-Renaissance monstrosity whose ceiling had been modeled on that of the Sistine Chapel. Only a few seats in the front row were occupied. The travelers remained in the shadows.

A fire had been raised in the middle of the stage. Gamboling around this fire, hands linked, were some three dozen naked policemen. Actually they weren't quite naked: each man wore a wide-brimmed hat and a gun-belt. Pinned to his left nipple was a gold or silver badge, depending upon his rank. They were dancing in a clockwise two-step gallop.

A symphony orchestra resided in the pit, the musicians policemen all, though dressed in full uniform. They were playing triplet patterns like those of Beethoven's Ninth, second movement, but the progressions were not nearly so intricate. The key was A-minor; the melody varied between only two notes, A and E, a triplet allotted for each one. Back and forth, back and forth, *A-A-A-E-E-E-A-A-A-E-E-E,* the dancers bouncing along in their ring, a few nude onlookers clapping encouragement, until the men gave voice in a wash of lusty baritones:

*Po-leeeeeeeeeeeeeeee-sman!*
*Po-leeeeeeeeeeeeeeee-sman!*

A new performer emerged from the wings, dressed in a flowing black cape. He carried an antique flintlock rifle, which seemed to embody totemic significance. He issued a command and the orchestra and dancers stopped, standing at attention. He then passed the rifle among the dancers, each of whom reverently kissed both barrel and trigger before handing it to the next man. When the gun had completed its journey the caped man kissed it in turn. He then lifted it toward the ceiling, eyes gazing toward heaven, lips working through an invocation that the travelers could not discern. Moving with great deliberation, as if acknowledging that every gesture was choreographed, he aimed the gun into the fire and pulled the trigger. In brisk unison, each surrounding officer withdrew his own standard issue, pointed it toward the fire, and proceeded to empty his clip in a brief but deafening volley.

Still in synch, the men holstered their guns and again stood at attention, right arms locked in salute. The strings took up with a flourish, a single tremolo A that built in a gradual crescendo, the faintest buzz from the snare drum heckling its accompaniment, until finally, at the apex of tension, the men shouted *Heuh!!*

Following this declaration, all was momentarily still. Then a soft, keening piano broached the silence and yet another performer emerged from the wings, naked but for gun-belt and hat; a man with a farouche yet sensitive face, eyes simmering at some mythical wrongdoing, reedy tenor ascending in a petulant lament:

*Oh thee whom they could never understaaaaand!*
*Oh thou who wert ashamed to hold my haaaand!*
*Oh-how I felt so bolllllll-stered,*
*When I gazed upon thy holllll-ster,*
*How thy bullets tapered so trimmm-ly;*
*How thy buttocks sashayed so primmm-ly!*

*My Baretta-man, ohhh Baretta man,*
*Neither Glock nor Colt for theeeeeee!*
*My Baretta-man, ohhh Baretta-man,*
*Fifteen bullets in the clip for theeee.*

*Death was cruel to thee my chevalll-yer;*
*In thy coffin thou looked ten pounds heaaa-vyer.*
*The mortician smeared your mascarrrr-a,*
*And the dress of my dear Aunt Sarrrr-a*
*Rode up above thy derrrr-ier,*
*Revealing a displaced terrrr-ier.*
*But I shan't be the least bit charrr-ier,*
*In fact I am all the merrr-ierrrrrrrrrrr . . .*
*(whew!)*

*Oh Baretta-man, choice Baretta-man,*
*The apple of my eyyyyyye!*
*Oh Baretta-man, sweet Bar—*


"Um," said Lucky as the travelers withdrew, "shouldn't they be arresting us or something?"

"One thing's for sure," said Prophet. "I ain't asking these boys for gas."

"We'd better get the fuck out of here," Dorian agreed. "We'll just have to hope the Mustang holds up until the next town."

"Something tells me," said Prophet, as they returned to the car, "something tells me these people don't have much to do around here, know what I'm sayin?"

Prophet had left the computer on the trunk. As he was about to put it away he saw that a new message occupied the screen.

TO: Kenley O'Hare & Co.
FROM: Dana Saddle
RE: That Interview

**Perhaps you didn't get my first fax. Perhaps you were unhappy with our offer. What would you say if we increased the ante to $100,000 each?**
**Oh, and by the way—we know where you are.**
**Remember, that number is (800) 383-5968.**

"They know where we are, like hell they know where we are."

"Maybe we should agree to it," said Dorian. "It's a lot of money and a lot of limelight and we can clear our names in the meantime."

"Don't even think about it," answered Lucky. "I've seen that show of hers, I think last week they interviewed a man who shot his wife for impersonating a warthog, something about Spousal Anti-Zoanthropical Syndrome. They paid him seventy-five grand and someone's making a movie of the whole thing. He's even writing his autobiography."

"Well what are we going to do then?"

"Keep driving. What else?"

They turned at the intersection and proceeded west under a canopy of stars, the moon rising over the mountains to cast its own eldritch light on them, as if beckoning them toward some ghostly sanctuary. They had scarcely gone ten miles when Dorian noticed a bright light approaching from their rear, though not along the ground.

"What the hell is it?" he said. "A plane?"

"Could be a UFO," said Prophet. "How'd that be for an escape."

"We'd be famous enough for ten lifetimes. Fingers crossed."

"It's not a UFO," said Lucky, craning her head back, "and I don't think it's a plane. I could be wrong but it looks like a helicopter."

"Christ, the police," said Dorian. "And nowhere to hide, damn it."

At length they could hear the ominous swell of the rotor, could indeed feel its resonance in their bones like some premonition of epilepsy. The helicopter was flying very low, at perhaps a hundred feet, and narrowing the distance rapidly. As it drew abreast it slowed, matching their speed. A blinding light was cast down on them.

"*Fuck!!*" Dorian pumped the brakes, bringing the car to a gradual halt in the middle of the road. The helicopter banked into a shuddering descent, landing fifty yards ahead.

"That's not the police," said Lucky. "That's from a TV station."

"They're blocking the goddamn road," said Prophet.

When the airfoils had stopped the door opened and three figures emerged, two male and one female. One of the men held a video camera, the other a portable light. The woman was a thirtyish brunette in a white Goering business suit, its double-breasted military cut the latest rage among businesswomen (**Goering: Ready to war**). "Mr. O'Hare?" she called, eyes searching among the travelers.

Prophet did not reply. The first technician raised the camera to his shoulder; the second turned on his light and trained it on the car. The woman stopped a few feet away.

"Kenley?" she said, looking at Prophet.

"What."

"I'm Dana Saddle from—"

"What the fuck are you doing here."

"We traced the signal from your remote fax," she said, smiling. "It's amazing, isn't it, how far—"

"What do you want," snapped Lucky.

Saddle glanced at Lucky and Ariel, then made a brief appraisal of Dorian.

"You're all Michael's friends, right?"

"I asked you a question."

Saddle looked at her again, as if to gauge how much trouble she would be. "As I said in my fax, we're prepared to offer—"

"Forget it."

"—will you let me finish, we'll increase the—"

"I said forget it."

Saddle folded her arms. "Let me give you a piece of advice. I don't know where you think you can run, but the police are looking for you in every town within five hundred miles of here."

"We had nothing to do with the shooting," said Dorian. "He was a sick man, a schizophrenic. We had no idea he would snap like that."

"Maybe," she said. "But they also know that Kenley sent those faxes about the bomb. He'll be looking at Murder One."

251

"How do you know that?" asked Prophet.

"We're tapped into all the networks," she replied. "We knew as soon as anyone, we just traced you a little faster. For all I know they'll be here any minute. This may be your last chance to tell your side of things."

"How much did you say?" said Dorian, now sitting atop the seat.

"One-fifty each. I'd think it over very carefully."

Dorian glanced at his companions. "I vote we take it."

"What!" barked Lucky. "How the *hell* . . . ?"

But he was already stepping from the car. They watched him approach Dana Saddle, who offered her hand. He accepted it and looked back at them.

"Come on," he said. "We're going to be famous."

Prophet opened his car door. "Dorian—"

"Save it, old boy. We're part of the crime story of the decade and we're innocent in the bargain. Don't be a fool and spoil the fun."

"I've got the contracts in the helicopter," said Dana Saddle. "In the meantime—" she turned to the cameraman "—tell the studio we'll be ready to go live in two minutes."

"Ah, the satellite age," said Dorian, lacing his fingers together and cracking his knuckles. "Ms. Saddle, I wonder if you haven't got a mirror I might bo—"

"Dorian," said Lucky, from somewhere behind him.

He turned. "Yes?"

She was standing a few feet away, arms folded. "Can we talk about this for a second? alone?"

Dorian winked at Saddle. "Won't be a moment."

They walked three dozen paces up the road, passing the Mustang, the moonlight leering down on them. When she turned to face him, and he saw the expression on her face, he felt a thrill of panic and immediately cowered, raising his arms to protect himself.

"You *shit*," Lucky rasped. "I don't know what the *fuck* is with you, Dorian, but if you go through with this so help me god I will never speak to you again."

Embarrassed—for she hadn't so much as lifted a finger—he straightened to his full height, with a look of pained exasperation. "Lucky there's absolutely nothing wrong with—"

"It's totally *fucked* is what's wrong with it, I mean how the *hell* can you even *think* about this when our *friend*—" she waved toward Prophet, who was now standing with Ariel next to the car "—is

252

about to be charged with aggravated murder? I mean never *mind* the idea of friendship or loyalty, it's not like you'd give a fuck anyway would you, but—but hasn't it *occurred* to you that you might be *jeopardizing* his *defense*?!"

Only the darkness allowed him to hold her gaze, though for a moment her grey eyes seemed eerily refulgent as the moon caught them sideways. Nor could she see the burning in his cheeks, which gave him further courage to meet her head-on, for once. "You listen to me, you self-righteous bitch," he grated. "This whole fucking journey I've been listening to you whinge on with nothing but disapproval for everything I've done. Well tell me something, Lucky: Why the fuck should I care whether you speak to me or not? The *fact* is that I am innocent of any wrongdoing and yet *here* I am in the middle of *god* knows where running *day* and night from everyone and their lesbian parakeet and I am *fucking sick* of it, d'you understand? I've been waiting half my life for this moment, half my bloody life! Everything is happening here, right now, this moment, and yet here you are—" he drew in breath, fumbling for words, shaking his head as if to clear it "—always so bloody superior, aren't you, always cluck-cluck-clucking about every godawful thing I mean answer this for me, for Christ sake, just do me a favor and answer this one bloody question: Do you have *any* idea at all, *any* inkling whatsoever, how *big* this is?"

In the long silence that followed he braced himself for her response, for the venom that surely must be imminent. He was therefore startled when a tear escaped her eye and forged its way down her cheek. She looked away, biting her lip, but even in the darkness he could see her jaw quivering. He stepped closer, resting his hands on her shoulders and thinking, I've done it, I've finally actually done it. I've won.

"In less than five minutes," he said gently, "the whole country will be watching us here. This moment is ours. It will never come again. Everybody wants something that only we can provide, and it's going to change our lives forever."

She met his gaze, her eyes still damp, and her vulnerability so exhilarated him that he almost crowed in gratitude to the night sky.

"So this is what it comes down to," she said quietly.

A callous reply sprang to his lips; he checked it just in time. He bent his knees slightly, imploring her with his gaze, kneading her shoulders to emphasize his words. "Lucky this is *huge*. It's bigger than all of us, and we couldn't fight it if we tried. It's always like that with these things. You either use it or let it use you."

She pulled off his hands and glanced down the road. Thirty yards away, Dana Saddle caught her eye and beckoned impatiently.

"I've got to go," said Dorian, brushing past her. "If you have any sense you'll come with me."

She watched his retreat and took a deep breath, which she held until the tears no longer threatened; then, slowly, she permitted the air to escape her pursed lips in a long glissando of resignation. Painfully, she followed him.

"Are we live?" he asked as he rejoined Dana Saddle, who stood bathed in light and shimmering like an angel in the darkness. She held a cordless microphone and wore a cordless earpiece. The cameraman, now sporting headphones, waited a few feet away. The technician adjusted the light to include Dorian in its radiance.

"Sixty seconds," she informed him. "Cherice Liverpool is doing the lead-in already in the studio. Now we don't have a monitor here, so you're going to have to watch me for your cues. I'll be asking you a few questions about how you met Michael Fishbein, what happened at the rally, and how you managed to dodge the police afterwards. You're going to have a hundred million people watch-ing—" she held up a hand, listening to her earphone "—OK thirty seconds, now I want you to look at me and not the camera, and when you speak—wait, come here a minute—" she frowned, placing the microphone between her legs, and grabbed his chin in one hand and rubbed his cheek with the other "—it's some kind of smudgy stuff, I've spread it out a little because it looked stupid all in one place, but now it's more like you were near an explosion, like you had an adventure or something—"

"Get ready," said the cameraman.

"All right, here we go." She retrieved her microphone and turned to face the camera, her hand on Dorian's bicep pulling him closer.

"*And*, five, four, three, two . . ."

Trembling in anticipation, Dorian sucked in his cheeks.

"Cherice, I'm standing with one of the most wanted men in America—"

The airfoils suddenly growled to life, and Saddle's voice was immediately squelched. The helicopter lights came on as a blast of wind enveloped the news crew and their subject.

Dorian stared beyond the cameraman, his mouth opening in cinematic disbelief. He jerked his head toward the car, then back to the helicopter.

"No," Dorian breathed, starting toward the craft. "*No!!*" He broke into a run.

He heard Saddle call after him, and increased his pace.

"Lucky!" he shouted. "Lucky, for god sake wait! Please wait!"

He was twenty-five feet away as it began to lift. He lunged at the runner, for all the world like Saigon 1975. His hands gained purchase and he found himself rising, his feet dangling as they had once done in more frivolous times, outside a bathroom window. He peered up into the craft, saw Lucky gazing down at him without expression.

"*Lucky!*"

His fingers slipped and lost their hold. He plummeted a short distance and hit the ground flat on his ass. Stunned by the impact, he could only stare as the helicopter receded into the depths of the firmament and the news crew ran up beside him, following his gaze.

"The fuck," said the cameraman, panting.

"Well, there goes our satellite link," observed Saddle, also huffing her lungs out. She paused, catching her breath, and then looked down at him. "We can still tape an interview, you know."

He did not reply. He watched the helicopter as it vanished in the west, watched until its lights had utterly disappeared and silence reasserted itself.

He staggered to his feet and brushed himself off. Raggedly, without looking at her, he said, "Like hell."

"Mr. Bray you *agreed*—"

"That was then, old girl." He began shuffling toward the Mustang.

"I don't believe this," she declared petulantly. "I just absolutely refuse to believe it."

When no adequate response was delivered she skittered after him, her heels clopping on the pavement. "Two hundred and fifty thousand," she said, drawing abreast.

He snickered. "You'll have to do a lot better than that, Dana. After all, I'm your ride out of here." He glanced at her. "In the meantime, you'd better pray that my gas gauge is wrong."

\*　　\*　　\*

255

Lucky pulled open the sliding door and climbed inside, followed by Prophet and Ariel, who were dragging the luggage. A fat red-headed pilot was slumped in his seat, dozing blissfully. Lucky grabbed his hair and jerked him awake.

"Wha?" he cried, blinking. "What the—"

"Fly us out of here," she said. "Now."

He stared at her, then looked outside for the crew. "What happened to—"

"My friend here," she said breathlessly, indicating Prophet, who immediately collapsed on the floor. "His appendix is bursting, he needs it out right away."

He winced as Prophet, bent double, began to scream. "Yeah but—" he glanced outside again, raising his voice above Prophet's agony "—I mean what're they—"

"My friend has a car," Lucky answered. "He'll drive them to the next town but we *really* have to leave now, it's an emergency—"

"All right, all right." He waved her away. "Sit down."

She strapped herself in as the rotor shuddered into motion, while Prophet remained groaning on the floor with Ariel kneeling beside him. Looking up the road, Lucky noticed figures running toward the craft, and her heart-rate trebled. Jesus, she thought, and waited for the pilot to spot them also, or for Dorian—now discernible as the frontrunner—to come pounding on the door.

But the pilot was intent upon the controls, and in moments they were ascending into blackness. Lucky watched as Dorian caught the runner. Their eyes met briefly. She had the urge to slide open the door and stomp at his hands—or perhaps drag him inside, she couldn't be sure—but he was already slipping back to earth. She put her hand upon the glass, as if to steady herself, and watched him shrink into oblivion as inexplicable tears gathered in her throat.

She glanced at the pilot. He was frowning at her and grinning at the same time, one of those grins that asks the question, *You're shitting me, right?* "Whoa-whoa-whoa, wait a minute wait a minute wait a minute now, hold on here," he said. "Aren't you all fugitives?"

She kept her voice steady, helped by the drone of the rotor. "Are you fucking kidding?"

He was shaking his head, the grin now fatalistic. "I'm the stupid-est sum-bitch alive, aren't I," he posited. "Just I never seen a convict as pretty as you. Now I guess I should be scared, but I'm not, and you know why?" He winked sagaciously. "Cause if you kill me, none of you people can fly this thing, can you. So I figure I'm safe."

Feeling helpless, Lucky glanced at Prophet.

"Fuck," he said, sitting up. "Guess *that* didn't work, know what I'm sayin?"

Lucky put her hand on the pilot's arm, waited until their eyes met. "I've never been convicted of anything," she said. "And I promise you my friends here would never hurt anyone, OK? This whole thing is a misunderstanding."

"Partially, at any rate," muttered Prophet, strapping Ariel into the back seat.

"Well," answered the pilot, "that may be true, and it may not be true. All I know is there's no way I'm gonna be caught aiding and abetting." The craft swept into a broad turn.

"Please," Lucky groaned.

"No can do, little lady," he replied. "And like I said, you wanna keep your hands off me. Without me, you're nowhere."

"Know somethin?" said Prophet, now strapped in himself. "At first I thought you was a dumb motherfucker and a pushover too."

"Yeah?" said the pilot, sniggering. "Whaddaya think now?"

"Now I think you're just a dumb motherfucker."

For a moment Lucky felt paralyzed, and could only watch as the pilot returned them to Dana Saddle and Dorian Bray—or headed to the nearest police station, wherever the hell it might be. The strain of the past few days—the frenetic pace, the heady confluence of emotions, above all the crescendoing unreality—overcame her like clinical shock, blood vessels opening wide and everything gone cold. For the first time in her life she knew real, unmitigated despair.

But Prophet's remark galvanized her thoughts. There is no escape from this, she thought. We are the dead.

*The dead* ... She was struck by the salience of this metaphor, the words having revealed themselves without apparent reason. We are the dead, she thought sadly, knowing how trite it sounded, how clichéd—and how true. Never mind that she could not utter these words aloud, that no one would feel their import, that they would carry no weight of irrefutable, dearly gained wisdom. They rejuvenated her, and for that reason alone they sufficed.

257

We are the dead, she thought. And why not? Better to reign in Hell than to serve in Heaven.

Methodically she unfastened her seatbelt and stood. She stepped behind the pilot, yanked his head back, slipped her right arm under his chin, and pushed his head back down, tightening her muscles. "I don't care if I die," she whispered into his ear. "My friends don't care if they die either. The question is, do *you* care if *you* die?"

He twisted in her grasp, clawing at her arm with one hand while holding the stick with the other. He could not struggle very effectively, for he was strapped in. She maintained her grip, constricting her muscles an extra notch, and his breathing became stertorous.

"This is a carotid choke," she informed him. "If I want, I can put you to sleep within three seconds. That's not enough time for you to resist, and I'd still beat the shit out of you anyway. Are you getting this?"

"All right, all right!" he gasped. "Jesus!"

"Good," she said, without easing her hold. "Now I want you to turn around and fly west again—as far west as you can. And by the way, I know where the compass is, so don't fuck around."

The helicopter began to turn.

"Now," she said, when they had straightened out. "I'm going to sit down again. I want you to do everything I say, or I'll make goddamn sure we don't come down alive. Are we clear on this?"

But she was choking him too hard: try though he did, he couldn't reply. She released him and resumed her seat as he reacquainted himself with breathing. She was afraid to look back at the others.

\*　　\*　　\*

"All right," said Dana Saddle from the passenger seat. "Half a million."

"I love this country," answered Dorian, glancing in the rear-view mirror. "You lads all right back there?"

"Holy shit," said Dana Saddle, before either of the technicians could reply.

His gaze returned to the road, to the forest of blinking red lights suddenly visible in the distance. His whole body went hollow, and he felt so weak that he couldn't keep the accelerator down. His hands were shaking on the wheel as the car glided to a stop.

258

"Looks like a roadblock," said Saddle, folding her arms. "They're not coming any closer."

"I feel lightheaded," he said.

"The question," she mused, "is whether we'll have time for a short interview before they start moving. That would be a hell of an angle, wouldn't it."

Dorian gripped the wheel, waiting for the dizziness to pass. "Can we turn around? outrun them?"

"I don't think you want to try that, sweetie," she said, opening the car door. "All right, let's start right here, I want to get the whole thing on tape—before, during, and after the arrest."

The technicians clambered out.

"Let's hope they don't shoot us," Saddle continued, kneeling in front of the headlights with a compact mirror. "Now Dorian, we'll start with a few basic questions and then walk on down the road. We'll keep up a running conversation, like how does it feel to be finally arrested, where your friends might be, stuff like that. Shit, I've lost my eyeliner."

A lone siren pierced the night.

"They're coming toward us," said the cameraman.

She stood, looking down the road. "Damn them!" she muttered. "We're going to lose the whole . . ." She glanced at Dorian, who was gazing at the approaching lights as if transfixed by their splendor; as if an alien ship were about to land, revealing unimagined wonders.

"Right," Saddle resumed. "You know what, let's just tape the arrest. That'll still be an exclusive, and maybe keep us from getting shot, and best of all we won't be paying him a dime. Get back a few paces; we'll leave him to them."

\*      \*      \*

"Is that a city down there?" asked Lucky, two hours later.

"Yeah," said the pilot. "It's hard to tell cause of the blackout—you know, from the riots."

"Where did you fly in from? I mean back there, when you were chasing us?"

"We were covering the rally. Matter of fact Dana was in the back of that audience when your friend shot everything up. Why the hell'd he do that, anyway?"

"Schizophrenia. It wasn't his fault."

259

He glanced at her contemptuously. "You mean cause of insanity?"

"Yep."

He snorted. "I don't buy that for a minute."

"Then you should shut up about things you don't understand."

A sudden wind buffeted the craft, and their luggage went flying.

"Shit," said the pilot.

The wind increased. The helicopter bobbed like a cork at sea.

"Look," said the pilot, "it's gonna be real dangerous if we stay up. We're running into some kinda front and it's not gonna get better anytime soon."

"What city is that?"

"Hell if I know."

"Well don't you have instruments or maps, or, or *something*?"

Another gust jolted the helicopter, which bucked violently.

"Come on," said the pilot, suddenly nervous. "I got a wife and kids, I promise I won't—"

"Shut up and take us down."

The pilot nodded gratefully. "Where . . . ?"

"Anywhere."

The darkened city rose to meet them, looking like the matrix of a circuit board.

"Not sure if the National Guard is there or not," said the pilot. "So many other places they gotta be too."

A spark flew off the wall of the helicopter, accompanied by a thud.

"What was that?"

"Oh shit," said the pilot. "We're being shot at."

"Put us down on that building then, right there."

"Not sure if—*goddamn it* they hit us again!"

"Is this glass bulletproof?"

"I don't wanna find out."

"All right forget it, just put us down on the street. And watch those power lines." For the first time she turned to the others, to whom she had given no choice regarding their destination. She looked at them anxiously, feeling the violence within her evaporate, as if she were coming to her senses after a long fever. She expected Prophet to chastise her, to demand explanations. But he only returned her gaze with a kind of childlike wonder she hadn't seen in anyone for years. She was about to speak when she noticed that he was holding Ariel's hand. He followed her gaze and smiled.

"It's all right, Lucky," he said quietly. "I'll look after her from now on."

Confused, she read the emotions in his face, and was startled by the candor of their declaration. He was in love with her. She glanced at Ariel, who impulsively threw her arms around Prophet's neck, pulling him against her. Lucky suppressed a flare of resentment that was partially sexual in nature, but primarily maternal. She had always been proprietary toward the girl, and now she felt like a parent giving her child away. She blinked away tears, and found herself smiling too.

"You take good care of her," she said, as if she were on TV.

The helicopter was settling in the middle of an urban boulevard. Hotels and casinos lined either side of the street, all of them mere darkened husks, their lower windows shattered. There was no traffic; the city appeared deserted.

"What are we going to do about him," said Prophet, as they unbuckled their seatbelts.

Lucky glanced at the pilot. "You'd better radio for help. Your friends back there might need it."

"You mean we're letting him go?"

"What else are we going to do Prophet, take him hostage?"

"Oh sweet Jesus," said the pilot.

She looked up. A few hundred yards away, at the edge of her vision, the ground seemed to shift and reform like the crest of a dune in a strong wind. She heard the clamor of distant voices, and soon could discern hundreds, perhaps thousands of figures advancing along the boulevard in a slow run. A gust of wind jolted the craft, stirring up dust and tiny shards of glass, which snickered against the windscreen as if mocking their predicament.

"Great mother," she whispered. "Get us the hell out of here."

"Can't," said the pilot. "It's gonna be as dangerous up there as it is down here."

Lucky slid the door open and jumped out. "Come on," she said to Prophet and Ariel. "Never mind the luggage."

"Well what the hell about me?" snapped the pilot as the others climbed out.

"That's not for me to say," she answered. She shut the door and ran toward the sidewalk, the others following. Shells of burned-out cars cluttered the street; the pavement was covered with broken glass. The entrance to each hotel was open to the night air, doors and windows seemingly blasted out of their moorings. Farther up the street, the mob was now less than an eighth of a mile away. The travelers could hear voices raised in jubilation and anger. Then the brief clattering of automatic gunfire.

"Let's fucking hide," said Prophet.

They headed for the nearest hotel. A young black man was slumped near the entrance, charting their approach with wide, glassy eyes. He held a gun in his right hand.

"Check out my nigga man he think it's Halloween!" he said, raising the gun. "Say it nigga, you gonna come haunt my house?"

The travelers stopped, Lucky thrusting the others behind her. She found herself staring down the barrel of a long black revolver, and for a brief moment she froze. The gun wavered, rising and falling, back and forth, weaving crude infinity signs in the air.

"Y'all got any Nuke?" he said, referring to the hallucinogen known officially as Radioactive.

The mob was a hundred and fifty yards away, the swell of voices filling the street with white noise.

"Comin to get you," said the gunman, laughing sluggishly.

"Prophet talk to him," said Lucky.

"The fuck you want me to say?"

"My friend here—" Lucky indicated Prophet "—he's, he's a black nationalist, he's an important leader in the struggle!"

"Wha?"

"Listen man," said Prophet, casting a venomous glance at Lucky, "I'm tight with Kweisi Natare and—"

"*Who?*"

"Kweisi Natare, he's the—"

"Ain't hearda no crazy-ass barley," said the gunman, rubbing snot from his nose.

"Fair enough," said Prophet, pulling Ariel toward the doorway. "See ya round."

There was no more time. Heedless of the gun, they turned and fled inside the hotel.

\*     \*     \*

What here, then, of the dreams of women, and the dreams of men? What here of the soul, that most curious of human inventions?

Every year, in tax-deductible conferences across America, writers and academics gather to ask of themselves, "Whither the novel?" Alas: they misdirect their inquiry. The business of every serious novelist, we are told, is to apprehend the universal; but what is universal among us, except for our bodies and their functions? Only one thing: the soul. Now the body grows less mysterious by the day, or so medical science informs us. The question, therefore, is not "Whither the novel?", but rather—*cognoscenti* take note—"Whither the soul?" In the tradition of mayors, governors, and presidents, who each year deliver to their constituents a prognosis for their city, state, and nation respectively, so every novelist reports, through her fiction, on the state of the soul. And not merely the individual soul: by implication, every serious novelist describes the so-called universal soul. Not all of us can deliver a State of the Union address—we know better than to fuck around with politics—but all of us can interpret the state of the soul. Though Science has wrested the soul from theology and psychology, it will never displace fiction as the literature of the soul. The novelist, the poet, the dramatist—the soul is their inviolate domain.

Here's a question for you—and yes, it will be on the exam: The first cousin of the neurophysiologist is a) the psychiatrist; b) the evolutionist; or c) the Buddhist.

*     *     *

Imagine a world without sound, except for the sound of Thought; a world where all sound is therefore subjective, acousmal, generated only from within: the soundtrack of dreams; the soundtrack of nightmares. You want to share this noise but can't: we each have our own private demons to contend with, never mind yours. This is the sound of your own head screaming.

Our travelers now find themselves in just such a world. Let's check it out.

They are in a lobby of generous dimensions, many-storied and not a wee bit sepulchral, both in mood and content. Light is supplied by emergency generators, flaring in isolated pools that leave most of the room in darkness. There is no breath of wind in here; all is still.

In the center stands a fountain, now silent. Bodies lie motionless in the water amid the spare change, amid wishes. Other bodies are scattered about the floor as if casually disarranged, mere pawns in a set piece, art made flesh. The nearest are three elderly women, expensively dressed, inelegantly sprawled, faces ghostly white in the rictus of disbelief that death unlooked-for leaves in its wake. Art made flesh indeed: for how else to explain the swept-back hair, meticulously dyed; or the strings of pearls, or the nails and lips glossed as if to match the blood; or even the shoes, now shorn of utility? There must be an Artist at work here, a set designer: the scene is a composition. To deny the Artist his due is to suggest that these mannequin creatures, these *objets d'art*, have been engaged not in Life but in something altogether different—a grand contortion, perhaps, in which case why the hell bother at all? Because you don't expect Death, not dressed like this. You don't expect, once awakened of a morning, especially at this age, having been spared yet again, for the evening to turn out like sanguinary *this*. You don't expect your blood to be discoloring the carefully waxed floor, while a different wax awaits you at the undertaker's. What here of the soul? Well, there it is—there to be mopped up, absorbed, diluted, rinsed away, these pieces of you, your DNA, your information. The soul has not fled for greener pastures. The soul is sticking around, in every sense of the term. If it existed. Which it doesn't. Hence the Artist. Therefore it does. Confused? Good.

Ah, these women, these golden-agers . . . don't pity them, for they are in good company. At one end of the lobby—and do mind the blood, you might slip there—we find a young man and a young woman at rest, attired in Vegas bellhop chic, among crocodile suit-cases. Death caught you presentable, my lovelies, toting the vanities of your superiors. That's worth a few brownie points where you'll be going; we'll be sure to put in a good word.

The travelers move as one, clinging to each other, propping them-selves up, because let's face it—you don't want to deal with this stuff alone, though of course you have no choice. They proceed toward the interior, coming upon what might be viewed as a chil-dren's playroom. Look at the toys: card tables, roulette wheels, slot machines, endless colored chips. The air is stale and discarded, and the heat has sunk into every pore and crevice. If you look among the bodies, you might find yourself inventing ways in which to classify them: Male and Female. Old and Young. Patron and Employee. But what's really curious is the six or seven black corpses scattered among the rest, young men in street clothes, as if the mailroom staff had been issued guest passes, not to mention pistols—for pistols there are, in their rigid outstretched hands. Much of the light emanates from the slot machines, which have been linked to the generators, so that no guest might pass a typhoon unamused. Pensioners and addicts sag against the machines, their brains spattered across the glass like birdshit. Everything smells sweetly of death, and loss.

So—this cast has forfeited their flesh, that others may live. What others? Rats, for instance—and they are having the time of their lives. These are rats overcome with their good fortune. They cannot believe, this sultry evening, the surfeit of Nature's bounty. They gaze about the room and they do not know where to begin. A few steps here, a few steps there, inquisitively sniffing—well all right, this one looks as good as any. Soon the word gets round, as it always does in these situations. There are more rats here than in a Bronx schoolhouse. Friends, cousins, in-laws, journeymen—they're tucking in with gusto. It's like a family reunion.

Not that they're alone: it wouldn't be a party without the flies, clouds upon clouds of them, a trifle batshit from the heat and doubly wired given the circumstances. These flies just can't sit still: no sooner do they alight on one corpse than they're skipping to the next, buzzing with delirium. And all this to say nothing of the centipedes, but don't worry: there's plenty to go around.

You've all lost the sweepstakes, friends—you came, you rolled, you expired. God does not play dice with the universe? Bullshit, genius—you wanna bet? And to think how wise you were in other matters, before Niels and Erwin and Paul and Werner did you the same way you did Isaac and James. Answer this one, mate: If God does not play dice with the universe, why should the dead look so unresolved?

God does not play dice with the universe . . . because although there is chaos beneath the order, there is still order beneath that chaos? Everyone knows by now—everyone with access to a decent education, that is—that the butterfly's meanderings in Fukien contribute to the hurricane in Fort Lauderdale. The casino is no different: the same order bankrolls the random. Math is sovereign here, as everywhere, because money is nothing without math. Equations form the basis of conduct. Indeed, equations are God in disguise, and that's their weakness: they don't work when it really counts. They always break down in the end, just as all laws collapse at the Big Bang or Big Crunch, leaving the rest of us adrift. Yes, God does play dice with the universe, but it would be miserly of us to spoil his fun.

So let's collect ourselves, and figure out where the hell we are.

The travelers have fled the casino and stand now in a ballroom. The bodies here are all male, dark of hair and fair of skin, and dressed in white bell-bottoms inlaid with gold studs. They lie face down, hands linked, in concentric circles around a dais in the middle of the room, on which sits an enormous crystal punch bowl containing the dregs of some red liquid. The smell of death here is subverted by something even stronger—something acrid, bitter, emetic. The travelers cannot name it, but they gag all the same.

I can't take this shit, Prophet gasps.

It's coming from the punch, Lucky says hoarsely. Let's get the fuck out of here.

They turn to leave, discovering another man slumped near the doorway. He wears an open-collared shirt and large white-rimmed sunglasses, plus the same studded bell-bottoms. The initials KCN have been drawn across his belly.

You remember, issues thickly from his throat.

Remember? says Prophet.

Santayana, he answers.

His death is trite, anti-climactic, perhaps the greatest non-event of the day. As for our travelers, we'll address them presently.

*　　*　　*

There is a problem with all this, in case you haven't noticed. That problem is me. All this time I've been pretending to write a best-seller, but in the end I am writing about myself. I have become tangled up in my own story: it's all about me. Those first-person tales of whoring—true enough in themselves, but still a mere smoke-screen for my own Nabokovian intent, the hidden agenda I warned you about earlier. Oh, I began quite well: a group of strangers, one carrying a gun, and their quick escape from New York. But I am leaking onto these pages now, and you know this. I am *bleeding* onto these pages, and losing all sense of self-possession. We've almost reached the moment where I can no longer remain invisible.

266

This world of interior sound is my world, the sound of my own nightmare. You witness everything through my eyes. I must acknowledge myself, and become the First Person for good.

But not yet. I still haven't been reborn.

\* \* \*

The travelers find themselves, at last, on the floor of a convention center that adjoins the hotel. There are more bodies here than they have yet seen, and the blood has congealed into thick, syrupy pools. Display stalls have been erected across the length and breadth of the floor, each with a company logo prominently advertised—Smith & Wesson, Zygote, Filigree, Python. There seems to have been no power failure here: the whole arena is bathed in fluorescent light from the ceiling fifty feet above, lending the corpses an additional pallor.

A small stage has been constructed at one end of the hall, faced by rows of folding chairs. More bodies are sprawled in and under the chairs, and yet another is draped over the lectern as if exhausted.

The travelers cannot contain themselves any longer. It is remarkable, all things considered, that they have held themselves in check for so long. As one they kneel and vomit on the nearest corpse, again and again and again, until there is nothing left.

\* \* \*

"I hate to say it," Lucky said, "but I think we're safer here than anywhere else, at least for now. It looks like—like they've already been here, you know? Maybe they won't be back. Plus the flies aren't as bad."

"The one question," said Prophet, "is where the *fuck* is the National Guard?"

"You heard the pilot," said Lucky wearily. She was sitting against a Zygote display counter that had been smashed open and emptied, presumably of firearms. She now found it strangely easy to ignore the corpses at her feet, as if they were mere furniture. "They have to be everywhere. They obviously haven't gotten here yet."

"If they ever do," said Prophet, "I'll never be so glad to see a policeman in my life."

267

"It's weird, isn't it," Lucky agreed. "First we try to avoid the law, now we can't even find it. The local cops must have run like hell, and who can blame them."

"Well, there'll be nothing for you two to worry about," said Prophet. "You didn't know about the faxes, you didn't know about Fish stealing that money. You'll be fine."

"Prophet, I wish you would quit saying things like that, I mean where does it leave you?"

"I'll confess."

"What if—" she swallowed, not looking at him "—what if Dorian's confessed for you already?"

Prophet snorted. "If he has, maybe the police will come for us after all. With us here, it ain't just any other city."

Lucky sighed, tilting back her head. Her gaze swept across the room, over the predominantly male, predominantly white corpses. They were men of all ages, dressed variously in jeans, fatigues, and khakis; T-shirts, sport shirts, and blazers. Given their coloring and rigidity, they had obviously been dead for many hours. As in the casino, there were a few black corpses among the rest, mostly teen-agers in T-shirts and baseball caps. Everyone, black or white, seemed to have met death by gunfire, though there were no weapons immediately visible, only thousands upon thousands of shell casings that littered the floor as if tossed there like confetti during a parade, or rice after a wedding.

Her gaze fell at last upon Ariel, who was huddled against Prophet and trembling uncontrollably. The girl had not spoken since the night of the rally, and though she seemed to respond to Prophet's ministrations, Lucky sensed that she had withdrawn once again into her private world. It was a wonder that she hadn't gone to pieces completely—a state to which Lucky herself was in dangerous proximity. Despite her calm facade, she had the feeling that she was sliding into an emotional void. Only sheer exhaustion and sensory overkill allowed her to note this regression with detached consideration. The journey was dismantling every girder she had constructed these past six years, every levy she had raised against the loneliness of her adult life. Though she was numb—though she could sit amid these thousands of corpses without revulsion—she knew that she had hours at most before her defenses eroded and despair flooded the breach. Not that it would matter: they would never escape this city alive.

She wondered how Prophet was holding up, but was afraid to ask.

"I'm sorry about what I said back there, in the street," she said, looking at him. "I didn't mean to treat you like some barometer for your race."

Prophet shrugged. "I was your only frame of reference, I guess. But in the future, remember something: I don't treat you like the universal lesbian, and I am not the universal nigger."

She nodded. "Touché. It won't happen again."

"Anyway, I learned something back there too," he went on, sniggering unexpectedly. "I learned that Kweisi Natare's vision of black nationalism hasn't exactly spread to the masses, know what I'm sayin?"

She laughed. "I know all about that, Prophet. Believe me." She leaned back, closing her eyes. The hall was enormous, and they could hear nothing of the chaos that must certainly have been raging outside. But moments later, from the hotel corridor through which they'd come, she heard the sound of marching feet. She opened her eyes, glanced at Prophet. "Soldiers?"

He listened. Presently they could hear voices accompanying the footsteps—voices singing in unison.

"If they are," he said, "they're all women."

The song was a military chant. Each sentence was proclaimed by a single female voice and then seconded by the rest:

> *I don't know but-it could be right:*
> *That Latin girls can fuck all night.*
> *And-I don't know but-it could be true:*
> *That Swedish pussy tastes like glue.*
>
> *Now-I don't know but-it could be so:*
> *That Inuit girls can go-go-go.*
> *And-I don't know but-it could be thus:*
> *That Chinese cunt is full of pus.*

Two dozen women marched into the hall, arms linked, in six lines of four. Each stood at least five-ten and wore an aquamarine tutu covered with glittering sequins; black fish-net stockings; black stiletto heels; and a silver Trojan-style helmet sporting an insouciant magenta plume. Most were white, and looked between twenty and

269

forty. They stopped short as they confronted the corpses, and there was a moment of silence.

Then one of them giggled, setting off the rest. They burst out laughing and fell to the floor, kicking up their legs and rolling through puddles of blood.

"Ha-*haaaaa!*" shrieked one. "An NRA convention!"

The travelers stood, alarmed. The women also clambered to their feet and fanned out among the stalls like children on a treasure hunt. Three of them approached the Zygote display, picking their way among the bodies, and the smell of perfume met that of death head-on.

"Looks like civilians, eh Fontainella?" said the hindmost, a middle-aged blonde, in a smoker's rasp. "Oh and watch it Kandy, you're getting blood on your shoes."

"Poor things," said Fontainella, an olive-skinned woman of roughly the same age. She stumbled as she reached them, her breasts grazing Prophet's forehead as she recovered her balance. "Whoops! Say Kandy, this one's kinda cute. How old are you kid?"

"You aimin to nurse him?" said Kandy, a young redhead, in a midwest farm-girl twang. Her heel caught the edge of a dead man's teeth and she too lost her balance, reaching toward Lucky for help. Lucky took her hand but could not support her weight, and fell onto the corpse with Kandy atop her. She fought to disentangle herself, her cheek pressed against the man's denim groin while Kandy's sequined breast smothered her mouth. When Kandy proved too heavy, Lucky's teeth closed on her nipple.

"Whew-whewww!" Kandy exclaimed, rolling to the floor. "Y'all're fresh now, yew know that?"

Lucky stood, panting, feeling herself slip another yard into the abyss. Her earlier dispassion was already gone, dissolved by the immediacy of this encounter. "Jesus," she gasped. "Who are you people?!"

"*Haa!*" Thus spake Fontainella, in a reasonable approximation of a trumpet-blast. "We're the Clits, honey, otherwise known as the Cunningly Lingual International Troubadour Showgirls. Coming to a boudoir or windowsill near you." She glanced around the hall approvingly. "Look at this place. It's like too coincidental to be true, an NRA convention right when the riots break out, and suddenly the homeboys got firepower on demand! *Haaa!!*"

"As if there wasn't like enough irony in the world already," noted

Kandy, appraising Lucky from head to toe. Lucky knew that type of gaze, and slipped another yard down despite, or perhaps because of, the reflexive tingling in her loins. She swallowed, looking for Prophet and Ariel. The girl seemed oblivious to everything, and clung quivering to Prophet as she stared into space. Prophet held her like a boa, as if to squeeze the anxiety from her body.

The other showgirls, meanwhile, had struck gold and were considering their spoils.

"Filigree Home Bazooka!" screamed a giant brunette, heaving said armament onto her shoulder. "Heads up, ladies!" She discharged the weapon; a shell went fizzing into the ceiling. The congregation ducked, covering their heads, as plaster rained briefly upon them.

"Jesus, Tammi!" somebody yelled. "Watch where you point that thing!"

"Look what I found!" called a blonde Amazon, holding up the body that had been decorating the lectern. "It's that spokesman guy I seen on TV, Pee Wee Calais!"

"See if his prick matches his name!" suggested a colleague.

"Know somethin?" queried another. "Let's take the measure of *all* these boys. I got this idea that the bigger the gun, the tinier the cock."

Fontainella looked on in amusement as her friends began stripping the corpses. Lucky swayed on her feet, suddenly faint, and felt herself falling. She barely noticed when Kandy rushed forward to save her, easing her to the floor. She cradled Lucky's head in her lap, stroking her forehead, and Lucky relaxed into her grip as the festivities continued.

"Pee Wee it is!" shrieked the woman from the stage.

"Holy shit, look at this one! He could garrote a hippopotamus!"

"This one ain't too bad either. Look, I've tied him in a knot!"

"It's like sex in reverse! Everything else is hard but the cock is soft!"

"Look at the color of that thing. Periwinkle Penis strikes again!"

"Lucky—" she heard Prophet's voice as if from a great distance "—think maybe we'd better leave."

The floor shook with another explosion, followed by laughter; but Kandy held Lucky still, her hands soft and warm and soothing.

"Lucky are you all right?"

"Think she fainted," said Fontainella. "By the way, I meant to ask you. You must feel really proud about everything that's happening."

271

"Happening where?"

"All across America, kid."

"I can't believe they missed all these! Anybody need ammo?"

"—of course it *is* equal opportunity looting, oh *look* at those two, how *cute*—"

"Python Do-It-Yourself Home Mortar Kit! This calls for a new song and dance!"

Prophet was saying, "—taking advantage of her I mean just because she's a lesbian—"

Lucky saw Kandy look up. "No way!"

"—move them out of the way there ooooh, now *that*'s a prick with no future—"

"—doesn't look like one of those stuck-up intellectual types, you know, those tight-assed professors who wouldn't know tongue from tallywacker if it—"

Kandy looked down again. "Yew sly devil yew," she said, smiling.

"—bet this one carried a Howitzer to compensate—"

"—these rich white girls who think they got the prescription for—"

"—need more room to stretch, Freddie—"

She wasn't slipping any more. She was sinking.

"—time for that theoretical crap," continued Fontainella, "it's like get with the real world—"

*Bang!*

"Watch it you Slavic slut!!"

"—of respect for Sappho, yeah, but what we're about's more like—"

"—they really don't bleed when they're like that, do they—"

"—Sappho in the raw, Sappho in a *fin-de-siècle* kind of—"

"—disappointed with the quality of cock on display—"

"—got your asexual types, you got your academic types, and you got people like us—"

Kandy was drawing her fingers along Lucky's cheek, still smiling.

"—fact is, honey, we are not overburdened with subtleties here—"

"—a pulse over there I'll be the first to stomp on his balls—"

Her first memory: Mary sitting with her at a piano, holding her index finger over the keys, guiding her through a melody she had long forgotten. Mary holding her close. "Mother," Lucky whispered to the face above her.

272

"—Agamemnon Suburban Defense Shield!—"

"—in-your-face approach, for real authentic living, and fuck this victim shit—"

"—that submarine cannon assembly, or maybe that anti-aircraft battery—"

Prophet was saying, "—about any of that OK, the point is y'all are out of control—"

In the meadows of summers past they walked through dandelion fields, mother and daughter, hand in hand. "Mother. Please hold me." She sighed, closing her eyes.

"—is losing it too in case you hadn't noticed—"

"—of something to the tune of *In the Mood,* and maybe we could do it in an American honky-tonk kinda French—"

"—me stop you. Kandy, what's up there?"

"Oh Fontainella, can we *please* take her with us?"

"Lucky come on." Prophet was kneeling beside her, pulling her upright. Lucky opened her eyes, just in time to see seven or eight showgirls in night-vision goggles jiving on the stage:

> *Hey-hey veneeeeez, ici!*
> *Hey-hey veneeeeez, ici!*
>
> *Dites-dites pourquoi? PARCE-QUE!*
> *Oh-dites pourquoi? PARCE-QUE!*
>
> *Je vous demandais*
> *Que vous me commandez!*
>
> *À cause de votre vagin,*
> *À cause des vos très grandes seins,*
> *Et parce-que vous êtes ma reine;*
> *Oh! Venez dans mon jardin!*
>
> *Je vous demandais*
> *Que vous me commandez!*
>
> *Oh! Assiez-vous sur ces lèvres*
> *Et je ne serai jamais pauvre,*
> *Parce que je vous lécherai,*
> *Encore, et encore!*

*Donc venez, donc venez,*
*ici ici ici ci ciiiii—"*

Yet another explosion, and this one the mother of them all. The wall behind the stage disintegrated, disrupting the showgirls' tune and hurling them ignominiously onto the folding chairs, the corpses absorbing the worst of the impact. The travelers were knocked back as well, and for a moment their vision was obscured as dust filled the air.

"Prophet!" yelled Lucky, her eyes tearing. "Prophet, where—"

But she saw only Kandy, or rather smelled the peppermint on her breath: "Don't you worry, lover. I'm gon take care a yew forever."

"Help me," Lucky moaned, caught in her embrace. "God please what is happening, please help me—"

The blast had opened a corridor to the street, and figures were scampering over the rubble and into the arena. A fresh wind stirred up further dust, but for a brief moment Lucky glimpsed the darkness of the night sky, felt the touch of desert air. She pushed away from Kandy, stumbling toward the street, transfixed by the possibility of meeting death outdoors, on her own terms.

"Lucky, now wait a minute where yew go-win—"

Eyes burning, she pushed forward until she was among the newcomers, most of them scrawny white skinheads in fatigue pants and black t-shirts and covered with tattoos. One of them whooped as he saw Lucky and skittered down the rubble toward her, fumbling with his belt. She stopped and turned to face him, waiting until he was almost upon her and then moving inside his guard to drive her right fist into his Adam's apple. She felt the bones snap all the way in the back of his neck and knew, as he sagged to the ground, that he would not live.

"Prophet!" she screamed. "Ariel!"

"Neo-fucking-Nazis! I love it!" exclaimed Fontainella. "Take a look around, boys! You're a little late for the convention!"

Lucky clawed her way through the rubble as the battle was joined, the skinheads ambushed by the showgirls and coming off worst, judging by the screams. There was an exchange of gunfire and another explosion, and she almost slipped to the bottom of the pile. "Prophet," she whispered. "Prophet help me, please . . ." Her elbows and knees were scratched, her dress had torn along the right flank, and she had never felt so alone in her life as she scrambled higher

274

amid the debris. Nobody remained to her—not Prophet, not Ariel, not even Kandy, her flirtatious minister. She had forsaken Kandy just as she had forsaken her mother.

She reached the summit and climbed to her feet. Below her, on the other side of the rubble, the mob was running along the street in the direction from which they'd first come. She looked among the faces, saw men and women, blacks and whites, Indians and Latinos, children and adults. Some carried bats, others revolvers; some carried videocameras, stereo amps or guitars. Theirs was not the distracted, piecemeal advance of looters on the make: they looked as if they were running for their lives.

She heard a rumbling in the distance and looked down the street. She was surprised to see the helicopter standing precisely where it had landed, only a hundred yards away. She began to slide down the debris, drawn to the craft not because she expected to escape in it but because it was her only link with the world she'd abandoned.

As usual, she was moving against the grain: she inched her way down the street, caroming off rioters, glass crunching beneath her shoes, particles of dust blown like nails against her face. The mob was screaming around her, and though she paid little attention to their words, she understood that the National Guard was now in the vicinity. She ducked her head, forging a path through the oncoming tide, pairs of feet crossing her line of vision and vanishing just as quickly. The rumbling noise grew louder and she looked up, seeing a Guard convoy farther down the street. She stopped, the mob parting to either side as if she were a rock in midstream. The helicopter was still fifty yards away and the convoy was approaching fast.

"Lucky!"

She turned, saw Prophet and Ariel coming up behind her. Tears sprang to her eyes, tears that owed nothing to the wind and dust. Suddenly she felt lucid again, if uneasily so. Prophet had a strained, resolute look as he supported Ariel, who appeared barely able to stand.

"We followed you!" Prophet shouted as the mob continued to flow past them. "We need to get out of the street!"

She was about to reply when she heard another noise behind her. The helicopter's airfoils had stirred into action. A young black man jumped inside and slid the door closed. For a moment she simply stared. "Who . . . ?"

The convoy was much closer. Two armored cars and a tank were rumbling along the street, filling the canyon with a wall of mechanized sound. A smattering of gunfire marked their advance. The helicopter began its ascent, buckling in the wind, its teen-age black occupants grinning down at the travelers and waving goodbye. The convoy halted and soldiers poured out, circling beneath the craft. One of the men approached the travelers, clutching his helmet to his head.

"Who the hell's in there?" he yelled.

But the three of them were staring upward, watching as the helicopter—now two hundred feet high—banked sharply, like a fish caught in a swell, unable to regain equilibrium as it drifted into a hotel, airfoils shattering the glass, the craft still advancing until its main body impacted in a flurry of sparks, and then keeling on its side as it began its sudden descent, plummeting to earth, the soldier pulling Ariel and Prophet to the ground, Lucky following suit as glass rained over them and the helicopter broke upon the opposite sidewalk, the ground shuddering terribly, a plume of flames rising like an exclamation point as the travelers were blanketed with currents of scalding air, the pressure driving their faces into the thankless, unyielding pavement.

And then there were voices, a clamor of pitiless voices.

They had scarcely climbed to their feet when they heard approaching sirens. The soldiers had moved toward the wreck and were watching it burn; the rioters pulled farther away. Ariel sagged against Prophet; being six inches taller, it was she who appeared to support him, despite the violence of her tremors. Lucky, though uninjured, was covered with a layer of grime.

The man who had helped them—a lieutenant—spoke to them sidelong as he stared at the flames. "What the hell were you people doing here, anyway?"

But no one could reply, for the sirens were now upon them. Tires shrieked against the pavement; doors sprung open to a clatter of footsteps. Prophet watched the approaching mass, the cops and paramedics and reporters, the lights and cameras and pistols, drawing Ariel tight against him as they were enveloped and knocked to the ground. He positioned himself over her back, trying with every square inch of his body to cover her, wincing at the variegated screams from every direction, at the sudden glare of the floodlights. He pressed his lips against her ear and whispered, "I'm with you, baby, I won't let none of them hurt you." She was still shivering; if he hadn't known better, he'd have thought she was suffering a seizure.

A hand closed upon the nape of his robe and pulled. He maintained his embrace, fastened to Ariel like a crab. Other hands joined in, but they could not pry him free.

A woman yelled, "Kenley, can you tell us if the shootings at the rally were related to the bomb attack in any way?"

"Let her go, you son of a bitch!" barked a male voice in his ear, as though in reply. It seemed that a thousand hands were pulling at his head, shoulders, arms and legs, but he did not relinquish his hold. As long as he clung to Ariel they would both be safe. It was the only truth remaining to him.

Suddenly the hands pulled in concert, and he was raised bodily to his feet, Ariel still in his arms. A fist struck his left ear; his hands were pried loose, finger by finger. He was lifted in a bear-hug and hauled backward. He pushed off the ground and kicked at the uniforms surrounding him. Flash bulbs went off like applause.

"Ariel!" he shouted, still kicking. "*Ariel!*"

But he could no longer see her: she had vanished in the tide of bodies. "Ariel!" he cried again, knowing it was hopeless. She was lost to him now. She was lost to him forever.

"We won't see each other again," said Prophet to Lucky, as they were thrown side by side over the hood of a police car, arms pinned behind their backs, cameras leering at them from a variety of angles.

Their heads were pressed flat against the metal; it was as if they had their ears to the ground, listening for portents of enemies. She stared at him grimly. "I'm not saying goodbyc to anybody."

"I'm sorry we didn't get to know each other better," he continued as the handcuffs were applied.

"Prophet *please.*"

"If you see Ariel again, tell her that I love her."

"Prophet," she whispered, her face glistening.

"Think maybe I love you too, if you know what I mean."

They heard the lieutenant's voice. "Sergeant what the hell is going on?"

"What's going on is we got the other three. Tell your men to get these assholcs away."

"The other three who?"

"Who the hell do you think? We're sitting here on national television making the arrest of the goddamn century and you're telling me you don't recognize the suspects?"

"Officer could you move, you're blocking my shot of the woman's head."

"Think you just lost a promotion, Lieutenant."

"Lucky could you tell me how many other white people are involved with African Fist!?"

"Sergeant these people might be injured from the explosion!"

"Like fuck they are. Now tell your men to keep these idiots back so we can get the hell out of here."

"We always get fucked in the end," said Prophet as he was pulled to his feet.

Before Lucky could reply they had been separated, and he was lost in a swirl of uniforms.

*     *     *

Prophet sat in a windowless grey room with a metal table in the center. Upon arriving at the station he'd been treated by a bored medic and then deposited in this room without further comment. He hadn't even been fingerprinted.

He did not worry about the charges against him. Innocent of the bombing itself, he intended to confess his involvement with Gyeppi in the hope of a light sentence. With no previous criminal record, he might well get off with probation. Issuing bomb threats was hardly a trifling offense, yet he couldn't imagine any reasonable judge sending him to prison. He was a high school valedictorian and Ivy League star; this flirtation with radicalism had been an honest mistake. He'd fallen in with the wrong crowd; he'd been naive and idealistic. But most important, he'd learned his lesson. With any luck, he would be back at Columbia in September.

As for black separatism: fuck it. Natare had used him, pure and simple. Had Prophet known the bombing would actually take place, he'd never have signed on as the messenger. Gyeppi knew this. And with no knowledge of the plan itself, Prophet would have no evidence with which Natare might be incriminated. If they ever met again, Natare would say it had all been a test of his loyalty, and

278

that the rite of initiation was complete. He would also remind Prophet that the faxes had been presumed untraceable.

Prophet smiled grimly. In all likelihood, Gyeppi and his father were running damage control already. His arrest had probably surprised them as much as anyone.

That is, anyone except Kenley O'Hare Sr.

He felt tears of shame welling in his chest, and took a deep breath. Please, sir, he thought, actually folding his hands in prayer. Please forgive me. I'll never betray you again, I promise. I'll be good. *I promise* . . .

He shuddered, and bent his thoughts toward Ariel—another depressing subject, but not without hope. That he loved her was beyond any doubt. He was drawn to her in the manner of any first love, without forethought or conscious intent. Even her circumstances were immaterial. Yes, he knew little about her past. Yes, she was probably insane. But her beauty and innocence, indeed her simple presence, suffused him with a yearning that could be defined in no others words. He was in love with her—end of story. He wanted her naked in his arms, wanted to kiss all memory of pain from every inch of her body.

He wanted to believe it was possible: after their evening under the stars, he'd wanted to believe that anything between them was possible. But another voice had already established residence in his head, jibing away from the sidelines. In part, it was the voice of Gyeppi Natare: *You fool. You muthafuckin crazy five-foot nigger fool. You can't never go back, man, can't never cross that line again* . . .

*RIGHT vs WRONG* . . .
*RIGHT vs WRONG* . . .
*Choose, muthafucka, choose* . . .
*Shit: You* got *no choice, man* . . .

The door opened and three white men entered the room, each wearing a black suit and carrying a briefcase which he set upon the table without a glance in Prophet's direction.

The first was tall and blond, and somewhere near thirty. There was confidence and competence in the set of his broad shoulders, in the press of his suit, in the brisk and precise manner he snapped open his briefcase and drew up a chair. His mouth was wide and his lips thick and red, as if they'd been glossed, and he seemed to be wearing eye-liner. He gave Prophet a wet, lewd smile.

279

The second man appeared roughly ten years older. He was of medium height and going to fat, his gut sagging over his belt like a toddler scooped unwillingly into its father's arms and straining to be put down. With the exception of a brown moustache, his head was entirely bald. In contrast with the first man, he had a listless, almost lugubrious air: there was a droop to his jaw and his eyes were lidded with fatigue.

The third man seemed out of place. He looked very old—at least eighty, Prophet guessed—and he walked slowly, with a cane. Though balding, a tangle of white hair protruded from the sides of his head in long, unkempt wisps. His angular face tapered into a ragged goatee, and his long white moustache was a century out of fashion. Slowly, grimacing, he lowered himself into the middle chair, helped on either side by his colleagues.

The other men then sat down. The second—now on Prophet's right—withdrew a small tape recorder from his briefcase and placed it on the table, pressing one of the buttons. "Mr. O'Hare," he said in a grumbling baritone, "I'm Special Agent Casey, and my colleagues are Special Agent Buchanan—" he nodded to the blond man, who winked "—and Commander in Chief Samson." The old man glared at Prophet balefully, his blue eyes watery and unblinking. "I am hereby informing you that this conversation is being recorded. I am also informing you that anything you say may be used against you in a court of law. Similarly, your failure to respond to a given question may also be used against you."

"What about my right to remain silent?" asked Prophet, surprised.

Samson gave a wintry smile. "Not any more. Or haven't you heard of the New Deal?" His voice was as worn as his physique, an asthmatic whine that grated on Prophet's nerves like fingernails across a chalkboard.

"FDR," said Prophet, shrugging.

The smile elongated. "Wrong decade, my friend. I'm talking about the one passed three hours ago."

"Things are out of control," said Casey, before Prophet could reply. He spoke wearily, conversationally, as if they were coffee-house philosophers slumped over a nightcap. "They had to act quickly, keep it from getting worse."

"That's putting it mildly," said Samson, his smile receding, his upper lip curling almost to his nose, as if he'd just caught Prophet masturbating. "The fact is, Mr. O'Hare, we're at a unique juncture

280

in this nation's history. The nature of our role in the world during the next century will be determined in the coming weeks and months, at a time when we have more criminals than civilians. As such, it gives me great pleasure to be sitting across this table from you. You are the epitome of what's gone wrong in this country, and we're going to talk about that for a while. By the time of the dawn's early light, we shall have a taken a brief journey through history. And you, my friend—you will have confessed to everything."

Prophet was nonplussed. He'd expected direct questioning, not a sociological lecture. Samson continued to stare at him, his lip quivering, as if he saw the opportunity to close a long-fought vendetta. Prophet looked down, suddenly afraid. He'd meant to cooperate but dared not say a word. The old man frightened him.

"Mr. O'Hare," said Casey, "the charges brought against you are making terrorist threats, conspiracy to commit murder, and aggravated murder. We have an order for your extradition to face these charges in New York City, and you'll be on a plane later today. Until then I am informing you that counsel is unavailable; however, your cooperation with us in the meantime might benefit you in the long run. I am constrained to remind you that silence can be interpreted as an admission of guilt."

Unnerved, Prophet stood and walked away, arms folded, making every effort to keep his gait steady. "I ain't sayin shit."

"I believe, Mr. O'Hare," wheezed Samson, "that the correct way to articulate that would be 'I refuse to say anything.' And *that*, incidentally, is but one of the many subjects we'll be considering during the course of the night. For example, your dossier indicates that you've been at Columbia. With grammar like that you must have been Joe Quota from the beginning."

Prophet spun around. "I was the valedictorian of my high school!"

Samson shrugged. "By whose standards?"

"I don't fucking believe this," said Prophet, indignation getting the best of his fear. "We're at the end of the 1990s and listen to you assholes."

"Be assured, Mr. O'Hare, that I am just as surprised as you," replied Samson. "The republic is more than two hundred years old, and its children cannot even speak its language. The key is standards, Mr. O'Hare—nothing more, nothing less. It has become fashionable to exempt black children from standards, with the result that we now live in a bilingual society. Make that trilingual—I forgot to include the Hispanics. It's like the goddamned Tower of Babel."

Prophet slowly sat down, no longer intimidated by that gaze. His own eyes were projecting sheer, unremitting malevolence. "That's a redundancy, Mr. Samson."

Samson's eyes narrowed, and Prophet could see him working through the statement. Buchanan continued to leer at him, his lips pursed. Then Casey intervened without the slightest reference to the exchange, as if he'd been programmed to fill silences.

"Mr. O'Hare, have you anything to say regarding these charges against you?"

Samson suddenly nodded, and flashed his cold little smile. "Touché, Mr. O'Hare. I underestimated you. But I haven't finished my discourse yet, and you'd do well to listen.

"Consider. For the whole of this nation's history, there have been two recurring problems—Indians and blacks. Now I'm not here to argue about the Indians. They were displaced by simple migratory patterns common to every species on the planet. Besides, they've pretty much faded into the woodwork. There aren't enough of them to cause any trouble, and they're so goddamn drunk half the time it'd be child's play to put them down.

"But the blacks—they're a different story. Unlike the Indians, blacks are propagating like flies. I've seen black girls with five children by the time they're eighteen, every one of them by a different father. Where does this leave us, Mr. O'Hare? It leaves our country with a whole subspecies that can't find its niche. We stand at the edge of the twenty-first century, and the Race Problem is more unresolved than ever."

"Yes," said Prophet. "It certainly is." He glanced toward the door, half-expecting the entrance of some third party to explain this evolving farce. Only the vague conviction that it was all a joke deterred him from leaping across the table. Of course, even as a joke it was beneath contempt. He might have to attack Samson anyway, out of simple pride, but there was still something creepy about the guy that forestalled him, maybe the sense that Samson might crumble into dust from the slightest impact.

Samson stood and began to pace: at any rate he hobbled back and forth, leaning heavily on his cane. "Now the question becomes," he said, waving a finger, "the *question* becomes, What is the root of this failure? Black people claim that whites continue to deny them opportunity, but let's be realistic. For the past thirty years we've had affirmative action and quota mandates to the point of violating the Constitution. Black children are admitted into Ivy League schools with half the GPAs of whites. Black workers are hired with half the experience, if any at all. As for the poor, they all receive welfare, Medicaid, and food stamps. How can this be interpreted as a lack of opportunity?

"The question is even more pertinent when considering other immigrant groups. How is it, Mr. O'Hare, that I have watched so many Oriental kids step off a boat speaking not a word of English who wind up at Harvard four years later? Why is it that generations of dirt-poor Irish, Jews, and Italians have now ascended into the upper middle-class and even higher? Why not the blacks? Can you answer that?"

Prophet wanted to stand as well, to confront the asshole face to face; but he was trembling so violently that his knees couldn't support him. Samson was pushing his buttons, pushing all the buttons that every black man carries. Despite his association with Natare, he suddenly realized that he had never suffered from racism in his life, and that this was his baptism of fire. This was what it felt like. The candor of Samson's hatred left Prophet shaken, made him feel as if he were confronting an opposition so monolithic, so ubiquitous, that any words of resistance would—what was the expression Fish had used with Thatch?—would die in an anechoic chamber. Without resonance. Without trace. And judged on a historical scale this was *nothing*. This wasn't even a goddamned flesh wound. "I'm not getting into it with you, got it?" he said thickly. "You bring me your supervisor right the fuck now."

"So you have no answer."

"I never said that. I am not going to *dignify* your question with an answer."

"I guess I'll have to supply the answer for you," continued Samson ruefully. "The answer, Mr. O'Hare, is quite simple. Blacks are incompatible with Western acculturation."

Prophet gripped opposite edges of the table, arms splayed wide. He was unable to prevent the tear from escaping his left eye, and he shuddered as it descended lazily along his cheek, in no hurry. "I hate you," he whispered. "I hate you all, you racist scarecrow motherfuckers. You fuck yourself, man. Every one of you just *fuck* yourselves."

Samson faced Prophet, leaning on the back of his chair. Buchanan's tongue was tracing his lower lip. Casey appeared to be sleeping. "Don't get me wrong, Kenley. There have been anomalies. Biological fluctuations. But the fact is, one black genius out of a hundred doesn't offset the problem of the other ninety-nine. The data prove it. We may have all come from Africa, but we didn't all stay there. Consider the truly great civilizations. Greece. Rome. Britain. China. Now look at modern Africa today. Nearly every sub-Saharan country is Third World except the one created by whites—South Africa.

"So you know what I think? *I* think what it comes down to is this." Samson leaned across the table, his face approaching to within inches. Prophet didn't blink. His fists were clenched, and he was waiting for precisely the right to moment to divest Samson of his nose. "I love this country, Kenley. I love everything it stands for. And I am not going to stand around while a bunch of colored riffraff lay siege to our cities. The fact is, blacks have been nothing but a liability to this country. Jefferson and Washington didn't know what to do with them, and two hundred years later neither do we. But we're finally getting a chance to do something about it."

Prophet stayed his attack. In spite of himself, he wanted to hear what Samson would say next. He hoped Samson would declare the advent of a racial war: he wanted it to be official.

"Regarding these charges," said Casey wearily, distracting him. "We have knowledge of two bomb threats faxed to various media agencies and law enforcement organizations. Do you deny sending those faxes?"

"Go fuck yourself," Prophet repeated. He was speaking to Casey but his eyes remained on Samson, whose smile had recurred like a goddamn sunrise.

"Now you might be thinking," said Samson, "that people like me are dismayed by all this chaos in the streets. On the contrary, Mr. O'Hare, I welcome it gratefully. You see for years the criminal classes have hidden inside the loopholes of our legal system, and the police have been powerless to act. Well, not any more. You might be thinking that the revolution has started, but I think not. From my standpoint we finally have a green light to do what's been needed for decades."

"We also know," sighed Casey, "that you were roommates with Gyeppi Natare. Now here's where you can help yourself, Kenley.

284

We always knew you were working under the umbrella of a larger organization, and this connection explains everything. Give us names, dates, places."

"As we speak," said Samson, "National Guardsmen are patrolling the cities of America, and they've been authorized to shoot to kill. Now some people didn't think this could happen Kenley. Not here, they protest; not in America. El Salvador, Nicaragua, China, Russia, Bosnia—but no, *never* in the USA, except in science fiction novels. But that's the problem we've had here, Kenley—only the smartest among us read science fiction, because everybody else cares only about the present. What people like me have known for years is that the average citizen looks out at the world with a bad case of tunnel vision. They haven't learned the lessons of history. They haven't learned the lessons from all the wars that've been waged this past decade. They didn't learn from L.A. in 1992 and they didn't learn from Oklahoma. But I'm not one of those people, Kenley. I look around and I'm not surprised in the least. I've been waiting for this moment all along. I saw it coming. It couldn't be going better. We've got so many suspects coming through the precincts that the troops aren't bothering to arrest people any more. The firemen are staying home. For every Beverly Hills that's gone up in flames, at least three ghettos have done the same, because your people can't resist destroying everything in their paths, even their own houses. And Beverly Hills isn't going to happen again, Kenley. Your people did some nasty work in the suburbs a few days ago, but that's been stopped. We've got tanks in every street and those soldiers are itching to pull their triggers. In the meantime, you have Compton burning down and no one raising a hand to stop it. Our logic is simple: when everything has settled down, you people won't have any neighborhoods to return to. After that, refugee camps. It gives us the excuse we've needed for ages to make Marcus Garvey's dream come true."

"We've suspected for years that Kweisi's hands are dirty," said Casey. "So far we haven't come up with anything that'll stick. Now I can virtually guarantee you, Mr. O'Hare, that the US attorney in New York will be seeking the death penalty. On the other hand, if you can provide us with enough information to bring charges against Natare, you might be looking at something more like ten or fifteen years."

"If I were you," said Samson, "I'd consider Mr. Casey's words very carefully. And perhaps I can help you in your decision by outlining the provisions of the New Deal. I'm referring to temporary emergency powers. Suspension of the Bill of Rights until things are brought under control. You think that couldn't happen either? Ha: the public *demanded* it."

Prophet sat back in his chair, smiling. A sudden thought had struck him, and he felt oddly calm.

"The basic premise of the New Deal," said Samson, "is one of simple expediency. Since the troubles began law enforcement has made fifty thousand arrests in the big cities alone. The jails are standing room only, the courts are logjammed, the hospitals can't keep up. Right to demonstrate peacefully? Forget it. Right to a trial by jury? Forget it. You'll be tried by a judge, pure and simple. We can detain you without charge indefinitely. We can search and seize anything we want, warrant irregardless, and we can make you testify against yourself. Forget the Fifth Amendment. Congressmen on both sides of the aisle have had their phones ringing off the hook telling them to chuck it. The only one they don't want touched is the Second. Hell, the stores are selling out."

Prophet nodded. "What about lawyers?"

"Come now," said Samson. "There'll always be lawyers."

"Where's mine?"

"You'll get one in New York. As Mr. Casey said, counsel is unavailable at this time. They're all busy with other cases."

"What about any other charges? You know, with the helicopter?"

"The DA here is overlooking them," answered Casey. "Certain cases take precedent before others, and the bombing is the most serious allegation. That's why you're going back to New York."

"What about my friends?"

"I can't really say," said Casey. "Probably assault and hijacking, but I couldn't be sure."

"You consider one more thing, Mr. O'Hare," said Samson, pointing a skeletal finger at him. "You consider a conversation that Gyeppi Natare had with our New York bureau only yesterday. He denied any involvement with either the faxes or the bombing, and claimed that he was never your friend in the first place."

Prophet smirked. "I expected nothing less. He's a very smart man."

"It hurts, doesn't it," said Samson.

286

"On the contrary," said Prophet. "Tough times demand tough talk. They demand tough hearts."

Samson looked puzzled, but Casey intervened. "That's why we need your help. We have no physical evidence to tie anyone to the actual bombings, but we figure Karibu must be involved. The fact is, Kenley, the US Attorney is going to press Murder One even if he can't implicate Natare. In the end he'll just go free and you'll be sentenced to die."

"Keep this in mind too," said Samson. "With the New Deal, trials move along much more quickly. You'll be brought to trial ASAP, and a death sentence could be carried out within months. You're entitled to one appeal to the Supreme Court and that's it. So if you're thinking of keeping quiet in the name of racial solidarity you should reconsider. Your friends at Karibu have sold you down the river. Now you tell us what you know about Natare and his father and we'll try to get you out in ten years. We'll say you never knew the threats were real, OK? We'll get the conspiracy and the Murder One out of the way."

At last Prophet was able to stand. He looked from Casey to Buchanan to Samson, upon whom he allowed his eyes to settle. "A few minutes ago, Mr. Samson—and as you see, I too can be formal and anal retentive in that peculiar way you white people have—a few minutes ago, I wanted to kill you with every bone in my body. I wanted to peel off your white skin and piss all over it. But you know somethin? I'm over it now. Iss cool. I'm fine."

He began to pace, mimicking Samson's delivery. "Consider this, Mr. Samson. Consider that I shall not divulge one iota of information to either yourself or Mr. Casey, or indeed to any of your brethren at the good FBI. Consider my fond importunity that the US Attorney feast upon his own excrement. Consider my assertion that neither Gyeppi Natare nor his father sanctioned the bombing with which I am being charged, and were entirely ignorant of my faxes, just as they claim. And consider, for the sake of historical clarification, that the precursor to Western civilization was ancient Egypt, where blacks were just as populous as Semites.

"Consider as well, friend Samson, my gratitude for the airing of your opinions. For you have stated nothing more than the collective innermost thoughts of white people everywhere. I derive a curious strength from such imprecations, and do you know why? Because that which does not kill me makes me stronger, and surely it explains

287

why African Americans are stronger than any other people in the world. Our culture is *vibrant*, my pale friends, so vibrant that it is beyond your limited capacities to appreciate. And perhaps if we cease praying to the god you've wished upon us, to the white man of your dreams, our prayers will finally be answered. We built this country, my friends. We can destroy it just as well.

"In conclusion, gentlemen, consider this last. Consider that as regards the so-called Race Problem, I submit that black people are finally about to solve that problem for you, in their own way, since you white folks have been hopelessly inadequate. I submit that you *stupid weenie cocksuckers* better use every soldier you can find, cause you know somethin muthafuckas? We gonna burn your scarecrow cities down, man, you got that?! We gonna *burn your cities down*."

\*　　\*　　\*

"I don't understand what you're so upset about," said another special agent in the interrogation room next door, which had a small, barred window. "It's obvious the girl's out of her friggin head. We're not *charging* her with anything."

Lucky brushed away tears. "Why can't I at least see her then? I haven't seen her since we came here."

"Nothing I can do about that," he said briskly. He wore a full three-piece suit and his dark hair was immaculately combed. A few papers were spread before him and a coffee mug sat to one side. "She's being evaluated right now. They'll try and find out who the parents are, maybe transfer her to an institution."

"But that's just it, have you seen her? What if her parents did all that?"

"We'll make the appropriate inquiries. I really wouldn't worry about her."

She took a deep breath. "Look, I don't think I'm getting through to you. This girl needs me. She's probably terrified with all these strangers coming and going, I mean it's like with a puppy—sometimes they need to hear a familiar voice, to tell them everything's all right."

"You're not allowed contact with any of the other detainees."

"You said she isn't being charged!"

"Look those are my instructions, OK? Give it a rest."

288

She stood and turned away, sobbing quietly. The agent shuffled through his papers, sipping coffee, and then abruptly looked up.

"Look could you get over it? You're distracting me."

"Fuck you," she whispered, leaning her forehead against the wall.

"I mean I realize you've been here all night but there's no room in the cells. We still don't know where we're going to put you. We got forty suspects waiting in a personnel carrier outside because we're short on space."

"Can't I just see her for a few minutes?"

The agent sighed. "What *is* it with you? You've only known her for three or four days but it's like you're in love with her."

She faced him again. "What's that supposed to mean."

"It means you're acting like a friggin dyke, and it doesn't suit you. You're way too attractive for that."

The coffee soaked his face a millisecond before she leaped across the table, fists pounding his jaw, her weight knocking the chair backward and bearing him to the ground. He landed on his side, spitting out teeth. She pushed him face-down and mounted his back, pressing him flat against the stone floor, her legs grapevined through his own, her right arm under his chin, her left hand forcing his head down, aggravating the pressure against his throat.

"I *do* love her, *dickhead*," she hissed into his ear, "and I *am* a friggin dyke, you got it?" She gripped the top of his head and drove her first and third fingers into his eyes, pressing the balls.

"Heh—help," he gasped. "*Eeehh—euhhh—*"

"I want two things. First I want you to understand that I can break every bone in your body more easily than I can break a sweat. Are we clear on this?" Her fingers dug harder.

"*Yehh—yehh—*"

"Good. The second thing I want is five minutes alone with her. I don't see why that's so fucking unreasonable."

"*Icchh—euchhh—*"

"They can't hear you outside. I could knock your balls out through your teeth and no one would know. I could rip your dick out and stuff it down your throat. You say something like that to me again and I'll kill you. Are you getting this?"

"*Yeeee—yeee—*"

"Good."

She released him and moved clear, ready for his counterattack. He was potentially dangerous now, with his pride so irrevocably wounded. He struggled slowly to his feet, his suit in disarray. His hair, amply sprayed, had been pushed against the grain; his head looked lopsided. He was bleeding generously from his lips. Three of his front teeth had been evicted.

He regarded her for a long moment like some terrible jack-o-lantern, features thick with loathing and humiliation, eyes betraying his desire to reach within his jacket and extract the gun she knew must lie beneath. She met those eyes without yielding, watching the pupils, waiting for the impulse to declare itself. She had already killed one man in self-defense; she was quite prepared to kill another in outrage. Perhaps he recognized her ability and willingness to do this, for abruptly he relaxed and strode to the door.

"Open up here!" he yelled.

When the door opened he brushed past the guard immediately without, his voice reverberating along the hallway. "Get the DA here now. I want her fucking out of here."

The guard glanced inside. "You pack one hell of a punch," he said. "What it's worth I never trust these Fed bastards either."

\*      \*      \*

Two hundred miles away, Dorian sat in a similar interrogation room with another agent, an Asian man who was chain-smoking and wearing sunglasses, despite the darkness outside. Following his arrest—duly chronicled by Dana Saddle and her crew—Dorian had been whisked to the nearest town, one untouched by the riots ("No niggers here," said one of the deputies, grinning). He'd been driven along silent, empty streets to the municipal complex, where a few National Guardsmen had been stationed but nothing much was happening.

"It's cut and dry at this point," said the agent to Dorian. "The Guard'll take you to the airport and you'll be on a plane to New York before noon."

"Why New York? Do I have to face charges there?"

The agent shook his head, expelling smoke. "Deportation. We've got enough trouble prosecuting Americans at this point. We send the foreign nationals home and don't let em back in. You'll be in London by tomorrow morning."

"I can never return to the US?"

The agent shrugged. "Give it a few years," he said, lighting a new cigarette with the old one and stubbing it out. He squinted, blowing smoke through his nose. "Talk to an immigration lawyer. You never know."

"So I won't be going to jail?"

"Not in this country. Besides, I don't think they could make anything stick. From what I can see it doesn't look as if you *did* anything."

"What about my friends?"

"Heard they got caught in Vegas. The hacker kid is in shit so deep he couldn't fly his way out of it. I don't know about the women."

"I suppose I won't be able to see them."

"Fraid not. I'm waiting on the US Attorney right now so we can get you on that plane east. Space is at a premium, in case you haven't heard. In a few hours they'll be sending us prisoners that they can't fit anywhere else."

"But the woman, the brunette." He sighed, fighting back tears. "Ah Christ, forget it."

"I'm sorry, Mr. Bray. You want me to give her a message?"

Dorian thought for a long time, arranging words in various combinations, none of which sounded right. "No," he said finally. "No, I think she knows already."

\*     \*     \*

The District Attorney, a white albino, clearly had not slept in days. Pouches hung beneath his bird-bright eyes like old burlap. His clothes looked as if he'd just done a triathlon in them. She waited, not caring what happened to her.

"I'm sorry," the DA said, yawning so deeply that he seemed disoriented upon exhaling. He blinked, frowning, as if noticing his surroundings for the first time. "Excuse me. Anyway, he was out of line saying those things."

Lucky shrugged.

"At any rate . . . I've been doing a little thinking about this case."

She looked up. He was standing against the wall, collar open, tie loosened, sleeves rolled up to his elbows.

"I don't know what the hell's going on out there," he said, gesturing through the window. "Maybe it's been a long time coming— who knows. The point is, my office is like a major artery and the

291

cholesterol's sky-high. We're already in cardiac arrest, and I just don't have time for everyone we pick up. Sometimes you gotta take a few chances. I'm letting you go."

For the first time that day she felt the beginnings of a smile. Her eyes widened a little too eagerly, and he raised a finger in admonition.

"*But* . . . now you just listen to me for a second. Under normal circumstances I might try and put you away for a few months. I can't do that now, so I gotta make a decision. From the facts now available, I'm betting that you're not a threat to society. You'd better prove me right."

"What about Ariel?"

The opaque eyes looked away. "I'm sorry to have to say this."

"She's being hospitalized?"

". . . I'm afraid she's dead."

She waited for him to look at her again, but he did not. "No," she whispered.

He shook his head, eyes focused on the ground. "Strange case. We got no ID on her, no one reporting her missing. So with the hospitals booked solid, and the police psychologist telling me she's not suicidal, I think what the hell. I was going to release her into your care. But then she starts having an epileptic fit again, like when she was arrested. The guard called for an ambulance but it took an hour for one to get here. In the meantime she just got worse, like she was being electrocuted. If things were different we might do an autopsy and get to the bottom of it, but right now it's out of the question." He sighed. "Unfortunately we can only release the body to a relative or legal guardian, but if you'd like to see her before you go I can arrange it."

She managed a small nod. Only the shock prevented her from collapsing in tears, from screaming her execration at anything, everything around her.

"One more thing. Your name's in the computer now. You get anything worse than a speeding ticket and we'll make room for you somewhere, understand?"

\*    \*    \*

She was beautiful in death as well as life, her face both innocent and knowing, as if she'd had some insight upon her end that still

292

lingered in her soft features. She had been fitted into the drawer of a human filing cabinet, and was covered only by a blue sheet. Lucky rested a hand on that cold forehead, remembering how warm it had been only a few days and a few lifetimes earlier.

A fat white man in scrubs stood nearby, watching Lucky as if expecting some revelation. She neither moved nor spoke, and presently he stirred.

"She was in pretty bad shape," he said.

Lucky wanted to look at that scarred body once more, but she refused to remove the sheet in his presence, regardless of what he had already seen.

"You uh—you got any idea who did it?"

"Oh love," she whispered.

"Awful pretty, that's for sure. I figure it musta been her old man, bangin her day and night."

Drawing back the sheet a few inches, she saw that Ariel was still wearing her necklace. She removed it with trembling hands and fastened it around her own neck.

"Really too bad, what it comes down to. No one to claim the body, so they'll be sending it to the med school. Gross anatomy. Assuming it reopens."

Smoothing back the hair, Lucky bent down until her lips met Ariel's, where they rested for a long moment. A vestige of warmth and softness remained.

The man said, "You uh—you knew her pretty well, I guess."

Lucky ran her finger along her cheek until the tip was wet with her tears. She then drew this finger along the inside of Ariel's lips. Lastly she kissed each of the closed eyes and pulled the sheet over the girl's head.

\*　　\*　　\*

I found myself at the entrance to a tunnel of light, floating in stasis. Behind me there was only darkness.

Though overwhelmingly bright, the light seemed oddly diluted, as if refracted through a blurry lens. I tried heading for it but I could not move.

The light was suddenly bisected by a thin black line, which advanced toward me like a long, stiff rope. It had been bent into the shape of a hook, and in moments I was duly snared. The rope began to retract, jerking me into motion, and I was slowly pulled toward the light.

The tunnel gradually ascended, and the brightness intensified until I was bathed in a white halo. As I was drawn upward, I saw that the light was being filtered through what appeared to be a clear rippling sheet. And then it struck me: I was underwater.

Still I was pulled up, until finally I breached the surface of the water and was elevated farther into the light.

When the motion stopped I blinked, and found myself confronting a fat, swarthy giant with a greasy moustache. He must have been twenty times my size, and it was he who held the rope. His cap bore the legend **Flushbusters**, and the name tag sewn into his white overalls read **DEMIURGE**.

He considered me for a moment, frowning. Then, in a voice loud enough to rattle my bones, he said, *NOW THIS SURE DON'T BELONG HERE.* He tossed me back into the water. As I surfaced, gasping, he reached for a silver handle above me and pushed. The water began to funnel, forming a whirlpool, and I was swung ignominiously round until abruptly I was sucked feet first into the tunnel again, borne fast into the darkness.

I awoke flat on my back, freezing. Still reeling from my experience in the tunnel, and numb from the cold, I began stirring by only the tiniest degrees. In doing so I realized I was naked. I opened one eye.

A man was standing above me; a white man about thirty with thinning brown hair and wire-rimmed glasses. One hand was fastened on my breast and the other was fumbling at the waistband of his scrubs.

Despite my neo-natal daze, I realized what was happening at once. I had been through it so many times before that even the slightest preamble had the mark of familiarity. Having said that, my instinct was to scream, but at the last moment I held myself still. I closed my eye, listening as he peeled off the scrubs and then hoisted himself aboard. As he lay down I opened my eyes, enfolded him with my legs, and stuck my tongue down his throat.

He jerked away and fell off me, hitting the floor with a pleasant crunch. I sat up, peering over the edge of the metal slab on which I'd been lying. Bottomless, he was scrambling backward along the floor, and screaming to . . . well, to raise the dead, goddamn it. And so I rose, swinging my legs round and easing myself to the floor, feeling my limbs ignite with renewed circulation. The man crouched against the far wall, his legs rather inelegantly spread. His testes had retracted, giving his scrotum the appearance of a golf ball.

Slowly I advanced upon this wide-eyed, quivering wreck, gazing down with benevolent condescension, like a teacher approaching a truant child. "I don't recall giving you permission to fuck me," I said, stopping a few feet away.

"Jesus!" he gasped. "You're supposed to be dead!"

"That would seem at variance with my current disposition."

"For god sake," he continued, swallowing heavily. "You scared the fucking shit outta me."

I looked around. On one of the tables nearby lay a naked young man whose skin was partially cut away, like old fabric.

"Is that a scalpel on the table there?"

". . . Yeah. So?"

"And that corpse? Has it been autopsied?"

". . . Yeah . . . So?"

"Looks like a botched job. Even I can tell you've put the liver back all wrong."

He was climbing slowly to his feet. "Nobody cares."

I picked up the scalpel, considering it gravely. "You mean you don't tell the relatives. You just sew it all back up and dress the guy in his Sunday best."

"My god you scared the shit outta me."

"I didn't realize scalpels were so sharp. I guess they have to be, don't they."

"I mean sweet Jesus, you know?"

"Would you like to fuck me now?"

"I mean I can explain everything, all right? Just let me find my pants."

"Come here a minute."

"What . . . ?"

"It's not nice to fuck people when they haven't given you permission. Right?"

"Look I said I could explain, I mean it's not like I thought you'd *care*. You probably think I'm a pervert or something."

"You know it just occurred to me."

"What?"

295

"Well, if this were some bestselling novel I'd kill you with this scalpel, wouldn't I."

He laughed. "You'd probably cut off my balls."

"And if it were real life I'd sell my story afterward, right?"

He swayed a bit, like a Hasid at prayer, as he considered the question. "Yeah. I don't see why not."

I sighed and moved closer. "You know something? I don't either."

# CHAPTER SEVENTEEN

## *Pomp and Circumstance . . .*

They were waiting for him just beyond Customs, a dense thicket of microphones and camera lenses and a sudden whitewash of shrill voices, *Doriandoriandoriandoriandorian??!!* Within seconds he was engulfed. He tried to push his way forward, a lens bouncing off his forehead, the sheathed phallus of a microphone poking down his throat, the human noose constricting further and further and further until finally he gave it up and simply fainted.

He awoke in a room without windows or color, a room with a grey floor and white walls and a small white infirmary cot on which he now lay. A uniformed policeman was sitting beside him.

"Had trouble with that lot, did you sir?"

Dorian propped himself on his elbows, blinking. The white walls seemed to oscillate in the fluorescent light, dancing crazily. He experienced a sudden nausea. "How—how long have I been asleep?"

"Twenty minutes now."

"Christ." He sagged back, rubbing his eyes, and then glanced at the policeman—a young man with red hair and blue eyes and a permanent half-smile. "Am I still at Heathrow?"

"That you are sir. Ordinarily we use this room for strip searches."

". . . Was I?"

"I don't believe so, sir."

"Thank god."

"There's a car wai-in soon as you're ready. Couple lads from Special Branch as well."

"Where are they taking me?"

"Reckon that's up to you sir."

"So they're not arre . . . Really then I think Paddington would be most helpful, thank you."

"Perhaps Wales would suit you better?"

"Wales? Isn't that a bit extravagant on your part?"

"Don't reckon Paddington's the safest place righ about now sir."

"They're waiting there too?"

"Reckon they're just about everywhere sir. Seen the papers?"

"No. No, I mean obviously I've—"

"Quite famous now Mr. Bray. Seems they all want your story."

"Yes it's funny isn't it, I mean one moment you're ... Wait a minute you don't—you don't think they'll follow me to Gwynedd, do you?"

"I couldn't say, sir."

"Brilliant. Just bloody fucking brilliant."

"Oh I don't know sir. Reckon there's a bit a money in it, don't you?"

A slight rain was falling as they headed west, the hills and fields spread before them in the diffuse morning light, the sky weighing upon the land like a terrible grey blanket, that sky which covers all England as if to chloroform her into some gentle endless sleep.

And he did sleep, intermittently, while the two officers quietly conversed in the front seat, everything from Arsenal and Liverpool to the upcoming trial of the Peckham Twelve, those infamous National Partymen allegedly responsible for the bombing of a West Indian nightclub in Tottenham, killing 43 and injuring 112; not to mention the upcoming trial of one Neville Scone, the former Opposition Leader from Ipswich who had fired a nine-millimeter bullet through the Prime Minister's left eye during Question Time last February.

It was early afternoon when he woke, and he knew immediately that he had passed from England to Wales—something about the rounder shape of the hills, the more compact curvature of the hedge-rows, the deeper shades of green. As the car eased into the bowels of the country, into the hinterlands, these hills stretched into mountains, and became once again the mythopoeic dreamscapes of his childhood. They seemed to welcome him like Odysseus, patient to the last. He felt as if he'd betrayed this land in some fundamental way, as if others had accroached its rightful pre-eminence in his heart and his allegiance had been cheaply bought. The notion was bizarre, but he felt the need to apologize to this country, this small corner of the earth.

A few hours later they pulled into Abergynolwyn. The stone village lay quiet in the rain, cradled in the surrounding mountains, their spires cloaked in the sempiternal mists. The sky here was as fine as gauze, weightless and infinite, seemingly woven into the same fabric as the open air beneath: it was hard to tell where one ended and the other began.

"I'll get out here, if you don't mind," said Dorian.

The driver looked back at him. "Thought you lived on a farm."

"It's quite all right, I can walk."

The driver shrugged. The other man got out of the car and opened the back door. Dorian stepped out, his only possession a knapsack he'd bought in New York. Everything else had been confiscated by the police and never returned, including his notebook.

"You're going to get wet," said the man, a bit scornfully.

"I know. Thank you very much."

He began walking along the side street that led to the Dysinni Valley, passing a terrace of grey-brown houses before the road veered up into the hills, leaving the village behind. He was soaked within moments, but the rain too was as familiar as the landscape, and he didn't mind in the least.

A short time later he rounded a bend in the road and then the valley was laid before him like his private kingdom, an emerald jewel of some almighty, each field a different green, the scattered farmhouses nestled in the bosom of these steep hills like a mother's young. Sheep stood at the roadside, mouths gyrating, regarding him with wary disinterest. He checked their markings: they were his family's stock, and he remembered suddenly that he was on his father's land. He extended his hand among them but they shied away, eyeing him critically. He laughed self-consciously and continued walking, glancing up at the brooding bulk of Cader Idris, the immortal summit suddenly visible through a break in the fog.

"You wait," Dorian said to the mountain. "You wait, old son."

Nothing had changed here, of course, as it hadn't in a few hundred years. The silence itself was beguiling, disorienting. He had stepped into another century.

His century? He did not know, not yet. But for the first time since leaving America he relaxed, in this place as intimate as a lover's body, as forgiving as any friend, where he knew he could find life and sanctuary and solace; the place whose moods, secrets, and hidden corners were free of evil as nothing else could be in this world, not for him. Never should this valley change. Never should the world claim it, dilute its singular purity.

He heard a car approaching behind him. A moment later it pulled abreast to his right, a white saloon whose make he didn't recognize. The electric window was already sliding down. He thought it might be someone he knew, and stopped to peer inside.

"Mr. Bray?" He confronted a young woman's face—a not very pretty face, hard and calculating and rather unevenly planed. He glanced down at the passenger seat, at the crumpled disarray of an ordnance survey map.

"Mr. Bray my name is Phillipa Jove from the *Quasar*. Can I speak with you for a moment?"

"Phillipa," he said, straightening, blinking away rain, "I've had rather a long day—"

"Won't take a minute." She had opened her door and stepped out and was rounding the front of the car. She was little more than five feet tall. Her stiff auburn hair was rich with chemicals, an acanthaceous canopy upon which the rain found no purchase and slid off as if she were waterproof.

She offered a tiny hand, which he accepted briefly. "This is where you live?" she asked, gazing across the valley.

"Yes."

"You grew up here?"

"That's correct."

"I'm not surprised you left," she said, shivering slightly. "Bit creepy, don't you think?"

"For some."

"These hills—" she was frowning, gesturing at them "—something odd about them in all this mist, like someone's watching you and you can't see them."

"Perhaps."

"Well as I said, I'm not surprised you left. I know I'd be bored out of my head. There's not much to do around here, is there."

He shrugged, resetting his knapsack.

"Let me get to the point, Mr. Bray. It seems I'm the first one here but I don't expect I'll be the last. It's only a matter of time before everyone else finds the place. I just got lucky. The last I heard a bunch of them were lost near Tywyn."

She paused as though expecting a reply. He remained silent.

"I'm sure you don't want them bothering you," she resumed. "And you can nip everything in the bud right now. The *Quasar* is prepared to offer you exclusive rights for your story."

"Offer *me* rights?"

"Yes, we're proposing a joint multimedia deal with Tandem Louse Publishing and Haute Line Cinema. We're all part of Foremost Entertainment, as I'm sure you know, so everything's in the family. You'd have first serialization in the *Quasar*, hardcover publication with Tandem, and film development at Haute Line beginning immediately."

"Really."

"Yes, in fact I just received a fax half an hour ago confirming our terms, right there in the back seat. Apparently Sid Edelweiss himself wants to meet you."

"Does he."

"It seems he likes your face. He wants to set you up with acting lessons immediately so you can play yourself in the movie. We'd have the best one of the lot then."

"How much."

"Right. Foremost envisions—oh, do get him away—" for a ewe had wandered up the road and stopped a few feet away, staring at her impassively.

"She won't hurt you, Phillipa."

"Anyway, payment would be scheduled as follows: a hundred thousand pounds upon signing, a hundred upon hardcover publication, a hundred on paperback publication, a hundred at the finish of principal photography, and a hundred upon broadcast of the movie in the States. That's half a million pounds in all."

"Not interested." He began to walk away.

"Wait a minute *please* Mr. Bray . . . !"

He stopped, turned.

"You *have* had other offers, haven't you. Can I ask from whom? *White Dwarf? Red Supergiant? Black Hole?* We'll top the highest by ten percent."

"Look, I'm just not—"

"It's Nigel Burden isn't it. You know, the Vixen Network? Larker-Follies publishing?"

"Ms. Jove I only want . . ." He stared as another car pulled up behind hers, a young blond man jumping outside even before the vehicle had stopped moving.

"Oh *shit*," grated Phillipa Jove. "Mr. Bray I've been authorized to increase the offer by a factor of two, that's a total of one mi—"

"Ah! Phillipa!" said the young man, beaming. "I thought you were leading me astray. You said Aberystwyth to throw me off, didn't you, instead of Abergynolwyn. Good thing I stopped for petrol and double-checked." He offered Dorian a hand. "Mr. Bray I'm Simon Pock-Cresskill from *Supernova*, how are you this after—"

"Simon *bugger* off I was here first—"

"Oh, no need to fight," said Simon genially. "I'm sure everything'll be settled in due course. Is there an offer on the table?"

"Top a million," sneered Jove.

"Baby food," pronounced Simon Pock-Cresskill. "How does two point five sound, Mr. Bray? We'll get a deal memo signed immediately and I'll fax it to—"

"Don't decide anything yet Mr. Bray," said Jove, producing a mobile telephone and jabbing at the buttons. "I've got Sid Edelweiss's *private* line, oh bloody hell who's that."

"Ah," said Simon, craning his head. "Looks like Giles Tallow from *Dark Matter*. No matter, as it were. We'll match anything he mi—"

"Someone having a party?" exclaimed the newcomer, a short, fat brunet. "Still space at the table?" He looked around the valley. "Gob, it's lovely innit? Oh I'd mind where you're stepping Phillipa, there's sheep turds all along there. Mr. Bray I presume? Giles Tallow from *Dark Matter*, and without further ado I'd like to offer two million pounds for exclusive—"

"Save your breath," said Pock-Cresskill. "Two point five is the current bid."

"Yes well I strongly suggest you interrupt him Ms. Sobel, my god these New York secratrees and their hideous accents—"

"We'll do three," said Tallow, leaning against Jove's car. "Gobs, what a view."

"Three one," said Pock-Cresskill, settling beside him.

"Two. Feature film guaranteed."

"Three. Mr. Bray to get above-title billing."

"Four. Five percent of one hundred percent of net profits on film plus screenwriter's credit."

". . . Fuck wait here, don't move a *muscle* Mr. Bray I just need to check with . . ."

"Look who's coming now," said Tallow, glancing down the road. "If it isn't Squirmy St. Andrews himself, and in a chauffered Daimler to boot."

A balding Caucasian wearing a pinstriped suit and horn-rimmed glasses emerged from the limousine, his hand outstretched. "Mr.

Bray don't say a word to anybody until we've spoken, I can get at least five for this no question, now if somebody's representing you already that's not a problem, I'll show you right off the bat how we can bleed these—Mr. Bray? Mr. Bray where are—"

"Sid thank *god* I reached you, it's five-thirty here I'm in the middle of nowhere but I've got our man, hold on what's the offer now? Giles? Christ where is he just, just hold on a minute Sid Dorian? *DORIAN??*"

# CHAPTER EIGHTEEN

## *The Return of Odyssea; or, The Advantages of Formal Karate Instruction . . .*

Two days after her release, Lucky began her walk up the driveway to the Retreat Center, the cab hissing away on the wet street behind her. A steady rain was falling, and the woods and fields where she'd once played seemed to luxuriate in its touch. She inhaled deeply, drawing the fragrance of her surroundings into every fiber. The mnemonic immediacy of each scent—pine, oak, barley—drew her with startling celerity into the past. They were conduits to memories long dormant, memories now revived with exhilarating strength.

She followed the long driveway through the village, passing log cabins and dormitories and even a few tents. Ahead of her, the grain fields and vineyards spread west toward the dark bulk of the mountains. The deserted ambience of the village made her uneasy: it was unusual to see nobody outside, despite the rain. Shivering, she tried to sink her feet a little deeper into the ground, as if to absorb some hidden essence that would make everything seem right again; but she found none.

She crested a small hill and caught her first glimpse of the mansion, still two hundred yards away. It was a turn-of-the-century English Gothic manor, its castellated towers in stark relief against the slate grey sky. It seemed to sag in the rain, its gables drooping with ivy, its windows tenebrous and stoic. She felt nauseated at the sight, and was almost ready to leave forever when figures began emerging from the front entrance, one after the other, forming a line that advanced along the driveway in her direction. For several minutes they kept coming, hundreds upon hundreds of them, white women of various ages, all dressed in the forest-green kimonos that over the years had become the Retreat Center's ceremonial uniform. Lucky squinted, trying to pick out faces she might recognize.

At the head of the procession, four women were carrying a stretcher between themselves, each holding a rung. A white figure lay on the stretcher, perfectly still. Lucky knew immediately who she was, and her vision began to blur.

"Mother," she whispered.

The procession continued toward her. She stood at the side of the road, her tears falling silently. She had escaped the cacophony of burning cities only to be greeted with the eerie silence of her mother's funeral. Without Prophet or Ariel—without Fish or Dorian—she felt as if she had no context in which to place the dream-like unraveling of this event. And she would never see any of them again.

The foremost women had noticed her, and she saw the surprise and joy on their faces. They stopped a few feet away, bringing the line to a halt, and one of them, Autumn—plump, greying, owlish—stepped over to meet her.

"Lucky," she said, with a curious awe in her voice. "How did you know . . . ?"

"I spoke with her," Lucky answered as they embraced. "I'm sorry I couldn't get here any sooner but I—I was kind of delayed . . ."

Autumn drew back without releasing her, holding Lucky at arm's length and studying her with an expression of adoring wonder. "You've got the gift, haven't you," said Autumn, shaking her head. "Just like she did."

Lucky frowned and glanced among the women. She saw the same reverence in their faces, the same quiet veneration.

Then Autumn was hugging her again. "Now everything'll be like it was. You've come back—just like Mary said you would."

Great mother, thought Lucky, turning slightly, so that the others wouldn't see the anger and confusion in her face. "I didn't realize Mary was so far advanced," she said, evading the implications of that last statement.

Autumn finally disengaged. "Well we always knew she was unique, of course, but after this I'd say she's—oh she was *such* a highly evolved being, so gifted . . ."

Lucky grimaced. "I meant the ca—" She stopped, struck by a sudden thought. "Was she in pain?"

"No, she just kind of drifted away in the night. It was almost like she'd planned it, though of course—well obviously she *didn't*, but now it's all starting to make sense."

Lucky groaned. Mistaking this for grief, Autumn touched her arm, but Lucky shook her off. Choosing her words carefully, she said,

"But what—wait a minute explain exactly when it happened."

"We think about two in the morning. She was—I mean this morning when Jade went to check on her, she was pretty white."

A day too late, thought Lucky, wiping her eyes. She wanted to look down at her mother's body but couldn't, not in front of the others. She kept her back turned, and asked, "How was she the past few weeks? Had she—had she been out to the doctor?"

"Oh, I don't think she'd seen a doctor in twenty years," replied Autumn proudly, missing Lucky's wince. "But you know that of course. She did say something about the flu recently, or maybe it was mono . . . I think that was it, mono, she'd been running a fever for awhile and lost a little weight, you'd have to ask Jade but . . . Well none of us was worried, I mean everybody gets mono at some point. I still can't believe it, but you coming home, oh Lucky it's the best thing that could have happened."

Turning, Lucky glanced at her, then stared at the rest—four or five hundred of them, all gazing back at her with such empathy and love that she felt weak. She began to laugh as she looked at them, gasping hysterically until she was crying, until she was kneeling upon the ground and beating it with her forehead, screaming. Hands reached out to touch her, to comfort her, but she was oblivious to them all. She prostrated herself on that driveway before her mother's corpse, her palms and forehead dripping blood, and beat herself unconscious.

*   *   *

She lay in the Center's hospice for three days, leaving her bed only to use the bathroom. She passed the hours sipping valerian tea, which soothed her nerves, and picking at the food that was brought to her. She thought about everything and nothing. For a time she would drift into the groves of memory, reliving old celebrations or quiet spring mornings swimming in the river north of the house. Then she would stare into space for hours at a stretch, her mind blank. Quite often she thought about the previous week, unable to make sense of it and not trying much in any case. But she thought very little about her mother. It was as if those particular memories had been locked inside a vault to which she no longer had the key.

Mary's funeral had continued following Lucky's collapse. The women were not able to embalm her corpse, and she had been buried in Lucky's absence. Insofar as she thought about it, Lucky didn't mind. She would soon reunite with her mother anyway, in private.

*　　*　　*

"I always loved this house," said the blonde woman in the black Goering business suit, as she seated herself in front of the desk that had been Mary's. Lucky, dressed in a green kimono, was seated behind the desk in her mother's chair. She permitted herself a wan smile.

"Ms. Stillwater, my name is Heather Hornet, and I'm the executrix of your mother's estate. My firm has been representing the Center for six years now. What I'd like to do is walk you through the particulars of the will and go over every asset this place has. Now I know this must be a very sad time for you so I'll try to be brief, but I generally find it best to see to these things as soon as possible, especially with a portfolio of this size. Now I understand you'll be taking over the directorship of the Center, which makes perfect sense with your being Mary's sole heiress."

"That hasn't actually been decided yet."

"Oh really? My impression from Ms. Autumn was that the Center couldn't survive without you."

"I think she was just flattering me."

"Now as you can see here, the Retreat Center's non-profit status is being audited by the IRS, and there's going to be a hearing in the next few months to sort that out. In the meantime, your mother's personal net worth, in round numbers, is forty-one million dollars. That includes the house and four thousand acres of land, plus stocks, bonds, cars, jewelry, and art. It's all broken down individually on pages two through eleven, perhaps you'd like a moment to review them."

"What I'd like, Ms. Hornet," said Lucky, "is a mother."

"... Well I can imagine, and you know something? I couldn't *believe* it when I heard she died, I thought my *god*—" she thumped her breast, her eyes widening "—she's only forty or something, and she *looks* twenty-five! You must be just devastated."

"Ms. Hornet," said Lucky, "is there something I have to sign? Or what?"

"Pages twelve through fourteen, they've all been marked with an X. You know something, I read two of your mother's books this past year and I couldn't agree with her more. That's one of the great things about Lung Carbuncle being an all-female firm, I guess that's why Mary used us. I wasn't much of a feminist in college but I had this law professor you wouldn't *believe,* I mean she politicized me overnight. You look around, and for all this women's lib stuff we still have men running practically every corporation and government in the world. It's like your mother said, men are completely worthless and they have no other function except to plant the seed. Beyond that, they're nothing! Why else do we have politics and Wall Street and six gazillion wars? Because men have nothing to do!"

"Ms. Hornet," said Lucky, signing where indicated, "my mother was a remarkable woman in many ways, but when it came to men she was full of shit. If it weren't for men you and I would be living in a straw hut and fishing for our breakfast. Assuming, of course, that we'd have somehow been born in the first place."

Heather Hornet looked surprised. "Is that why . . . I mean you've been away for awhile, haven't you?"

"Several years."

". . . So you disagreed with her ideas?"

"I never really agreed or disagreed."

"But you must . . . I mean did you get married, or—I'm sorry, I'm being nosy. I'm in the middle of a divorce myself, it's been a nightmare these past few months." She looked around the office. "It's funny, you know. I was actually thinking of spending some time here. I've always been fascinated by the place."

"Really."

"And these women here, I was talking to a few of them earlier. They practically worship the ground you walk on."

"Yes, I know," said Lucky, smiling coldly. "It's surreal. They haven't got the faintest idea who I am. It's funny how history repeats itself, over, and over, and over, and over—"

"Well, Ms. Stillwater," said Heather Hornet, gathering the papers, "I'll let you go now. I know there must be a lot of important matters you have to attend to, don't let me keep you." She stood, offered a hand. "You have a good day."

*     *     *

That night, in the bed she once shared with her mother, Lucky read the note Mary had left for her with Heather Hornet.

308

Darling Lucky,

I hope you won't have to read this letter, because if you do, it means that I died without a last chance to speak to you.

As you will have learned by now, none of the women knew about my cancer. It was diagnosed six months ago, and at the time I was told it was inoperable. It's been frightening how quickly it's gotten worse, and it's been an enormous effort keeping it from the others. I've pretended to have mono, which seemed about the only way I could explain how weak I've become these past few weeks.

As you also will have learned, I have left my entire estate to you. Despite your leaving six years ago I never had any intention of doing otherwise. I realize that you will be tempted to refuse it, which I beg you not to do. Regardless of what has happened between us, the women here need you. No one else can do it. I always believed that you would some day return, and that we would be together again for many more years. The estate is financially healthy, despite some trouble with the government, but I worry that it may go downhill quickly. Again, I beg you to do this. Not for me, but for the others.

I hope, also, that you will be able to forgive me. I know that I hurt you very badly. All I ever wanted was for you to come back. I love you more than I love anyone in this world. I am very, very scared—scared in a way I've never been except for the night I was raped. I desperately wish I could let the others know, but I don't dare. For I am also ashamed of what this illness has done to me, ashamed at the way my body is wasting away. I fear even you would hate the sight of it.

One thing only kept me going after I was raped, Lucky, and that was you. For Goddess' sake come home.

Mary

\*     \*     \*

309

The rain was warm, so she walked naked up the hillside to the oak grove that contained the cemetery.

The oaks were massive and ancient, and formed a protective ring around the thirty-odd graves that lay before her in the darkness. All were marked by a simple headstone, which, in addition to the decedent's name and dates, bore the design of a pentacle or ankh or crescent moon, and occasionally a line of verse. Mary's grave was on a hill at the highest point of the cemetery, but her gravestone—finished only that morning, five days after the service proper—was indistinguishable from the rest.

She had not brought a shovel, but it didn't matter. In the darkness and rain she knelt at her mother's grave and began clawing at the wet earth. The Goddess felt rich and soothing in her fingers; she rubbed the soil over her body, even as the rain washed it away. She worked for hours, the rain falling softly on the trees, and she felt exhilarated to be small and naked in Nature's caress. Despite the task before her, she felt as if she were already healing.

A few feet down she uncovered something white—a hand. Carefully she began removing the dirt around her mother's body, liberating an arm, both legs, the torso, the other arm, and lastly the head until Mary lay naked beneath the sky, free.

Mary's grey-brown corpse had already begun to decay, and stank accordingly, but Lucky crouched in the grave and pulled her mother against her breast. "God damn you," she whispered. "God *damn* you for doing this to me. You think you get away with this, like a thief in the night, right when I need you most? You don't get any of it, do you. You never did."

She gave in to the tears, rocking back and forth, her mother's cheek cold against her breast. "Do you know what I came through to be with you?" She laughed bitterly. "That's all right—the others don't either. Typical of all of you, not a television or newspaper in the whole bloody—the whole *fucking* house. I should leave all of you here to fend for yourselves. And I can't, god damn you. I *can't*."

She cried for a long time, still holding her mother fast. Eventually she eased her mother back into position, and huddled over her until the tears abated. For a moment she thought of sinking even further into that grave. She would cover Mary and herself with earth, and give herself forever to the Goddess, to the cold arms of the Mother. She lay on Mary's body, feeling the rain on her back, the wet soil against her legs and feet. She felt herself being carried toward sleep, a sleep from which she never wanted to awaken. She couldn't recall having ever felt so at peace in her life.

But then she began to shiver. The rain came down harder, driving against her face with angry insistence. Slowly she raised herself until she was kneeling. She began pushing the dirt back, starting near Mary's feet. The work went much more quickly this time, and ten minutes later only Mary's head remained exposed.

"I want you to remember something," she said, as she prepared to sweep a pile of soil over her mother's face. "I want you to remember that I'm not doing this for you. I'm not doing it for the other women. I'm doing it for me. And maybe for the girls who can still be saved. You haven't heard the last of me. This doesn't let you off the hook."

# CHAPTER NINETEEN

## *Our Penal System: An Exegesis;*
## *or, Bottoms Up! . . .*

Eight-thirty: it is almost time to go.

I am now huddled in front of the television, watching CNN, where the barest glimpse of a black man's face can be perceived within the hood of a red parka. Behind him stand perhaps a hundred cucullate figures in similar dress, all carrying placards. A microphone has been introduced into the maw.

—typical example of the white man's justice, issues from the depths of the hood.

You deny then, Mr. Natare, that Karibu has any connection to an organization called African Fist!?

As I've said repeatedly, Karibu is not a paramilitary organization and I've never heard of anyone calling themselves African Fist!

So you believe Mr. O'Hare is innocent?

Mr. O'Hare has confessed to making those threats; that's a matter of record. But threats and actions are two different things. The evidence that this man committed aggravated murder is non-existent. The fact that he hasn't implicated Karibu doesn't mean that he was the one responsible. What we're saying is that plenty of people knew about the contents of those faxes in advance of the bombing, and any one of them could have carried it out. The FBI has been trying to bring us down for years and we're calling for a full investigation to determine whether law enforcement itself wasn't responsible for this crime and whether they aren't trying to frame the law-abiding citizens of Karibu as part of a government conspiracy. As for Kenley O'Hare, we all know that other criminals, mostly white, have been excused for more serious offenses to save jail space. Can you tell me why eighty percent of the people executed this past month have been black? Can you explain why black defendants are still four times as likely to get the death penalty as white men convicted of the

312

same crimes? We're hours away from the year 2000 and we're still fighting the same old (*beep*) as our ancestors at the beginning of this century.

Congress has voted to reinstate the Bill of Rights at 12:01 tomorrow morning. What do you think of that?

Well it doesn't do Kenley O'Hare much good now does it?

I click off the television. It is time to go.

I merely have to shed my blankets and I am ready.

*     *     *

You are undoubtedly wondering about some things. True?

Let me anticipate some of your questions.

First: Rest assured that I had a different Valhalla in mind when I left the Port Authority.

Second: Whether I did or did not murder the necrophiliac pathologist is immaterial. It honestly doesn't matter, and that in itself is the whole bloody point.

Third: My rapists—Navy boys, incidentally—had their day in court. To wit: they pressed charges against me. I was fined ten thousand dollars for deadly assault (i.e., biting off a dick) and given thirty days in jail, suspended sentence.

Fourth: I'm not sure whether Prophet will recognize me tonight; your guess is as good as mine. I've recast my hair in its original hue and discarded the blue contact lenses. All in all, my feeling is that he probably will not.

Fifth: I can't answer that yet.

*     *     *

It is so cold outside that I don't *feel* cold: the very air seems numb as well as numbing. I have the impression that my body might succumb to this cold without my knowledge, without any pain or warning. One moment I'll be carrying on as usual; the next I'll be growing icicles in my lungs.

The streets are so still, so silent, that I feel as if I have walked into a painting. Manhattan is never this quiet: it is not supposed to be like this at all. There is no motion anywhere. I have the world to myself.

I start to grope for any measure of familiarity, anything to assure me that the City has not been deserted. There are lights in apartment windows but no silhouettes within. The shops are all closed. I cannot even hear the distant engine of a car.

I begin walking down Broadway. A procession of happy green traffic lights leads into the distance, presiding over the empty street as though conducting an invisible orchestra. I've walked about three blocks when I hear a car approaching from the rear. I turn. To do so I must swing my entire body around, my arms protruding like a snowman's. A lone cab is gliding down Broadway.

I hail the cab, simultaneously wondering whether I should go through with this. I am half-expecting the driver to be a Charon figure, an escort to the Stygian deep. The cab stops. After a moment's hesitation I open the door and climb in.

The driver, in fact, is a cheerful Nigerian who has never seen winter. He's not even looking for fares this evening; he is simply outdoors to marvel at the cold.

"But of course I cannot leave a lady stranded," he adds, wagging a finger for emphasis. "Now where you going tonight?"

"To the Island."

He looks at me, surprised. "You?"

"Me."

"This is a bad thing," he says, easing down Broadway. "A terrible thing to shoot an innocent man."

This Island, by the way, is not Riker's, which is in the East River and known colloquially as the Rock. The Island is moored in the Hudson, not far from the Statue of Liberty—a nice thematic counterpoint. It marks a new era in prison design, for the Island is, quite literally, a floating fortress, a self-contained world that navigates up and down the Hudson on a seemingly capricious itinerary, so that its prisoners—having no idea where they are most of the time—will have greater difficulty escaping.

A ferry is running to the Island for the dozens, possibly hundreds of journalists who will be present to witness the event. Icebreakers have spent the last week cutting dark, narrow channels in the waters around Manhattan, allowing a small amount of naval traffic in the region. Even so, the docks are largely empty.

Two Federal Marshals search each of the passengers, while a third asks for official identification and checks the names on the guest list. I've been mailed my own press badge for the occasion, which is in fact the only ID I've ever had, aside from my necklace. Despite

314

the cold they are grim and thorough, especially with me. They know what the journalists do not—that I alone have been granted an interview with the condemned, that I alone could be his means of escape.

We sit in an empty cell, on either side of a table, watched only by a surveillance camera. Through a small window behind him I can see pinpoints of light in the distance—not stars but the City that lives and breathes like an organism itself. I even spot the moving headlights of a car, no more than a flickering on the West Side Drive. Perhaps it is my cab returning uptown, my driver in his separate world so far from this one.

Oh, Prophet, my love . . . His prison greys hang despondently upon his gaunt frame. He is not wearing glasses and his head has been recently shaved. His face is drawn and oddly colorless: there is a chalkiness to his complexion, an almost milky pallor. His eyes are sunken and weary, but even thus reduced there is dignity in those features, a very handsome dignity.

"Bad hair day?" I ask—a brilliant opener, in hindsight.

"Bad *body* day," he replies. "I'm getting rid of it in a couple hours."

He considers me carefully, as if to gain the measure of this woman with whom he has corresponded these past few months, this woman who convinced him to reveal his secrets because she needed them more than he; because they will save her life even as they forfeit his. By contrast, I have not been forthcoming with my own biographical particulars. Prophet knows only that I'm a failed novelist and that I've been raped. He still remains ignorant that I, Venus Wicked, am the same as his beloved Ariel.

No: he didn't recognize me. He does seem to regard me a bit oddly, as if subconsciously perceiving the resemblance, but he has not made the great leap forward. The crux of my problem is this: Will it be crueller to tell him, or not?

I am uncertain. Right now I can only improvise.

"Why me?" I ask him. "You could have sold this story for millions."

"I don't need millions where I'm going. Besides, I knew I could trust you."

I feel another pang of regret. How often, these past months, have

315

I cared so little for him. How often have I considered nothing but my own survival and redemption. Remember, at the beginning, how I spoke of my selfishness? my need to use him? In this I am crueller still. It is yet another inadequate response to the love he so willingly shared with me. Oh Prophet dearest, please forgive me . . . I am unworthy of you in every way.

I must tell him everything. I must . . .

. . . but I cannot. Yet.

Instead I ask, "Why the firing squad?" (The State of New York was pleased to offer him several means of sanctioned homicide.)

"Look at the alternatives," he replies. "Electric chair? Worthless. I'm not convinced it would work the first time. Lethal injection? Reminds me of that old saying: Don't take it lying down. Gas chamber? Forget it. I'd try to hold my breath and where the hell would *that* get me?"

". . . Which only leaves the firing squad."

"Reliable sources," he says with a faint smile, "have assured me that death is instantaneous. That one bullet supposedly *clobbers* you into oblivion."

"What if they had gallows?"

"Funny you should mention that. One of the guards showed me an MRI scan of some guy that'd been hanged in Washington. You know the first word that leaped to mind? *Giraffe.*"

"All right then. Hemlock."

He smiles again. "Don't flatter me."

He tells me that he hasn't eaten properly since his incarceration; and while they've offered him anything for his last meal, he's chosen to fast entirely. "Intestines," he explains. "Think of all that food being digested right up until—" he throws out a hand "—just kinda stewing there pointlessly . . ."

For a man soon to be executed he is surprisingly calm and well-mannered. I comment upon this.

"You can't change it," he says. "The more you think about it, the more it'll bother you."

"Yes but how do you . . . *feel?*"

"Stillborn," he replies. "As if time has stopped. Like living . . . metaphysically." He shrugs. "I suppose this is what death must be like, only less."

I've led him down a morbid road; I quickly change the subject. "Have you heard from the others lately? They've all been very helpful to me."

"Yeah?"

"I've done phone interviews with Dorian and Lucky and they've sent me a lot of great material in the mail. Even Fish's parents were willing. I owe everyone so much, though of course I owe you most of all."

"Aaaaa." He shrugs dismissively. "Anyway, Dorian sends his regards. He wanted to come but they won't let him back in the country. As for Lucky, I told her to stay home. I would have felt . . . I don't know, self-conscious or something if she were watching. Like I was suffering the ultimate humiliation. Ariel might be different, but of course she's dead."

". . . And your parents? How are they handling this?"

"Not very well at all." He smiles wanly. "They've visited every day and I can read my father's thoughts perfectly: I Told You So. But he never says anything, never says, Well Kenley, you should've stuck with physics. He's just so scared. They both are. But I can see his point, you know. I look back at everything and think what a fool I was."

"About nationalism, you mean?"

"About so many things. I got caught up in the whole idea of a race war, and look what happened. Sure, we had a few months of rioting, but now we're back where we started. Neither side won anything. Everything's the same as it ever was, except just a little bit worse. Pretty soon it'll all happen again and it'll be *much* worse, especially if Karibu gets involved."

"It's remarkable how you've stayed loyal to them."

"I had no choice. There wasn't any reasonable alternative to that kind of racism. Now Kweisi and his crew are out there picketing, but what the hell does it mean in the end? They've still denied their involvement, and my being a martyr's not going to change anything, least of all the fact that I'll be dead." He sighed, gazing at the ceiling. "I feel like I've aged about twenty years in the past six months. I feel like I don't even recognize who I was back then. It's all so cut and dry when you've got a cause, all so crystal clear, but you know something? Give me a computer any day. Give me a telescope. I used to look at the stars every night, especially in winter, and it was the closest thing there was to real magic, out there in the

317

cold and the snow and the sky so brilliant. It taught me a lot about perspective, though I couldn't have put it into words back then. Things like race, they don't mean jack-shit at that moment. You know what I want to tell Natare and Samson? You know what I want to tell *anybody* these days who thinks they know a goddamn thing? Look at the stars. Look at the fucking stars and tremble." He pauses. "That was another great thing about Ariel. She never said a word but I know she understood all that."

There is a long silence. I reach across the table and take his shackled hands in mine, his hands so warm and soft. The same hands that held me under those stars, that soothed away the madness in my dreams. "Prophet, there's so much I want to say. I feel like I know you better than I've known anyone. And for god sake I envy you more than you can possibly imagine, in so many ways, because . . . because it's like you've had the chance to live authentically, if only for a little while, instead of—of crawling through this pale facsimile with all its boredom and terror like I've done for so long now."

"Yeah but you know something Venus?" he answers quietly, tightening his grip. "I'd take the boredom all over again if it meant getting out of this place. If it meant bringing back Ariel."

I must confess to him, goddamn it I must . . .

But I have waited too long.

The door to the holding cell opens, the warders step in, and Prophet Kenley O'Hare stands to be led away. I stand as well, groping for words that I cannot find. As always. I feel as if I have killed him more than any bullet.

He is the only man who has ever loved me, and I have denied him.

"Thank you," is all I can say, touching his arm. "Thank you so much for everything."

"Ah, Venus," he says, sighing. "It's actually helped me to write it all down. I felt like there was so much I wanted to talk about, and that I couldn't just die without saying it. The fact is, I'm counting on you to write the definitive version of this story, tell what really happened. I've seen the instant paperbacks and they're not worth shit, especially because I'm guilty in all of them! You just tell the truth and I'll be happy."

I've been wondering, through the course of the interview, whether

I shouldn't give up the book entirely. How could I stand to profit from it? How could I live with myself? And even if this book was simply a means to getting published, what then? Having so comprehensively failed as a writer in the past, where the hell did I expect my *next* story to come from?

But now everything is clear. I will publish this book, though not for myself. I will publish it because I owe him nothing less; because my hypocrisy and cowardice deserve to be exposed, if there is to be any justice in his death.

Then something else strikes me: by allowing me to publish this story, Prophet is revealing Natare's true role in the bomb threats. It is a reversal of his decision to take the rap on Karibu's behalf— and yet he's still going to die in the meantime, when he might be exonerated.

Surely he knows this . . . ?

I open my mouth to call his name but I am interrupted.

As he is led outside there is a commotion in the hallway. A large black man is pushing his way forward, his advance hampered, rather unsuccesfully, by four or five guards. They are trying to wrestle him to the ground, but they cannot contain him.

"Kenley!" he yells. "Kenley!"

Prophet stares toward the melee. "Sir!" he breathes, straining forward against his captors.

The face of Kenley Sr. shimmers with tears. His deep, rich voice fills the corridor with anguish. "*Kenley!*"

"The fuck is he doing here!" yells one of Prophet's warders. "Get him the fuck out!"

An alarm sounds, adding its own insistent cacophony. The corridor is a mass of struggling bodies.

"I'll kill ya. I'll kill all y'all!" cries Kenley Sr., throwing off one guard while another jumps on his back, struggling to bring him down. "Takin my boy away, Kenley! Kenley . . ."

Several more guards have arrived, the alarm still shrieking imprecations, Kenley Sr. collapsing beneath an avalanche of bodies, and struggling violently all the same. "I'll kill y'all," he repeats, although this time it is more a prolonged groan, colored by grief. "I'll kill y'all, that's my boy right there oh Kenley, Kenley my boy-hoy-hoy . . ."

"Sleep that muthafucka now!" barks the warder, as another guard approaches carrying a syringe.

*"Dad! Daaad!"*
*"Kenley! Kenley tha my boy Keh—Keh—Kuhh . . ."*

*   *   *

I am on a balcony overlooking the field, so still and cold and empty. Everyone else is in the lounge nearby, content to stay warm and watch the proceedings through a long plexiglas window. There are dozens of them, full of nervous laughter, champagne in hand, to herald the millennium that isn't, here in this ultimate of theaters.

I will remain outside here, alone. I want to feel this cold in every bone, in the farthest recess of my soul. This ice that covers the earth—this is who I am. Beyond the field, half a mile away, the City towers over us all, so permanent and implacable, a glittering monster. How it mocks us. A fresh wind rises, chilling me almost to unconsciousness, but I will not move. I will stand and watch here until dawn breaks over this worst city in the world, and every one of those lights is extinguished.

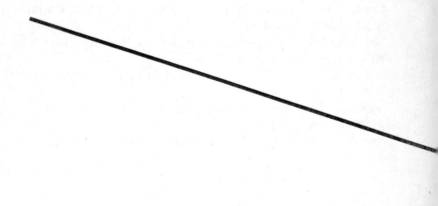